Lethal Control

ALSO BY
KATE SCANNELL

NONFICTION
Death of the Good Doctor—
Lessons from the Heart of the AIDS Epidemic

FICTION
Flood Stage—
A Novel

Immortal Wounds—
A Doctor Nora Kelly Mystery

ESSAYS AND COLUMNS
www.katescannellmd.com

Lethal Control
A Doctor Nora Kelly Mystery

KATE SCANNELL

First Edition, 2021. Word Haven Media

Cover and interior design by Maureen Forys

Library of Congress Cataloging-in-Publication Data available upon request

ISBN: 978-1-7325714-6-4 (print)
ISBN: 978-1-7325714-5-7 (epub)

For Diane

*And in loving memory of
Andrée Abecassis*

The more hidden the venom,
the more dangerous it is.

MARGUERITE DE VALOIS

It is not light that is needed, but fire;
it is not the gentle shower, but thunder.
We need the storm, the whirlwind, and the earthquake.

FREDERICK DOUGLASS

ACKNOWLEDGMENTS

I AM GRATEFUL TO FRIENDS and fellow healthcare workers who, through myriad acts of kinship and encouragement, accompanied me while writing this book during the first year of the Covid pandemic. Thank you for the sustaining talks, walks, and companionable silences. You know who you are.

I thank Diane Buczek, who, yet again, bravely served as my stalwart first reader. And for their good-hearted close and repeated readings of this book, I am indebted to Susan Riter, Michelle Paymar, Ruth Palmer, and Véronique Martinaud. I also thank dear friends who critiqued earlier drafts: Leslie Lopato and Jean Kaufman. And for her keen editing, I am grateful to Adrienne Armstrong. Any mistakes in this book are entirely my own.

CONTENTS

PRELUDE

Tuesday, November 20, 2018

I laughed when Yusra told me my skin was turning blue. But she kept saying it. I began to worry something terrible was happening to her eyes.

But it turns out, my daughter was right. It was my eyes failing to see.

The change was so slow. In the beginning, I assumed my skin was darkening from the hours I spent in the garden. My vegetables keep food on the table for Yusra and me. And, really, I had no time to waste on monitoring my appearance.

But now I regret not acting on Yusra's concerns before I got so sick. She needs me. I am all she has, and she must see me strong. Not like this. Not blue. Not dying.

Part One

Fire

WEDNESDAY, NOVEMBER 21

ER Doctors' Workstation

Oakland City Hospital

FINALLY, RAIN HAD ARRIVED, delivering an antidote to the lethal megafires destroying homes and communities up north near Paradise. It would help to quell those raging wildfires and reduce Oakland's smoky downstream air. It would rinse soot and ash off the city's houses, cars, and streets. People would breathe more freely, and fewer poor souls in respiratory distress would be crowding the ER. For this, Dr. Nora Kelly felt grateful.

And what relief to anticipate an end to her cabin fever. Forced by hazardous air quality to remain indoors for days, she even found herself longing for her old exercise routine. She could appreciate, in retrospect only, how her daily jog around the lake had helped to bolster her spirits while also fending off the stubborn five pounds that insistently clung to her abdomen. This morning, weighing in at 150 on the bathroom scale, she looked into the mirror at the hazel-eyed, chestnut-haired woman who stared back with a hopeful expression.

Dr. Aditya Singh, midway through his second year of ER residency, smiled at his mentor and said: "Dr. Kelly, this rain gives good reason to celebrate Thanksgiving tomorrow, yes? Let us just pray it causes no mudslides or further misery for the fire victims."

Nodding halfheartedly, Nora struggled internally to extinguish grim associations of major holidays with her friend Lydia's murder. All week, she'd been distracted by memories of her final visit to Lydia's office days after her death—still adorned for Valentine's Day, alive with decorations blanketing its walls. And last year's Thanksgiving, her first without Lydia, had been as festive as a DMV appointment.

"How will you celebrate tomorrow?" Aditya asked.

Nora braced herself, suddenly aware how she'd been marking holidays in terms of time passed since loved ones had died. Tomorrow's Thanksgiving would mark the second since Lydia's murder, and the fourth since her daughter and husband drowned. "Well, I'm having Thanksgiving dinner at Carrie Chamber's—"

"Excuse me, *please.*"

The blunt intrusion startled Aditya. But Nora instantly recognized the voice and turned to greet Dr. Carl Kluft, who stood looming in the doorway, his coal-black hair grazing the casing. Though she'd known him since residency more than thirty years ago, she could still be surprised by his large build and the fact he'd chosen obstetrics and gynecology as his specialty. "Hello, Carl," she said. "What brings you here?"

"There's a blue woman in room seven," he replied, his thick brows knotting.

How endearing, Nora thought. *Nobody tries harder than Carl to elicit a patient's emotional state.* Still, lately, she worried that his obsessive attempts to compensate for his social impairments may be taking a toll on him. Hoping to ease his apparent distress, she offered: "But it's not uncommon for people to feel depressed around major holidays."

Carl looked at her, concerned. "Perhaps you didn't hear me."

"But what she claims is true," Aditya said. "Also, we have been having such depressing weather. And, of course, such terrible smoke and ash from the wildfires."

Here we go again, Carl thought. *Doctors confused by their own confounding metaphors.* He brusquely responded, "I'm telling you that the patient in room seven is the *color* blue."

Aditya flinched. "Cyanotic? But I heard no call for a Code Blue!"

Attempting to project patience, Carl adopted a measured tone: "You're midway through ER residency, Aditya. Before that, you completed three years of internal medicine training. Surely, you know one doesn't call a Code Blue when a patient's skin is blue. Or a Code Red for someone with third-degree burns—"

"Hey, Carl," Nora interrupted, familiar with this rodeo. "Let's go see your blue patient."

ER Exam Room

Head nurse Sarah June Ferguson figured it was worth a try. She soaked a 4×4 in alcohol and scrubbed the blue patient's skin. But the discoloration didn't rub off.

"I already tried that," said nurse Lizbeth Tanner, pleased to see her mentor reenact her clinical instinct. "But I think that blue is *inside* her skin, Fergie. Like your tattoos."

Fergie stared apprehensively at their blue patient and tried to rouse her again, loudly repeating, "Ms. Habani?"

Lizbeth said, "She's been barely responsive since they brought her in a few minutes ago. And so weak and short of breath when I roomed her. I didn't know what was wrong, but I knew it must be something terrible. So, when Dr. Kluft passed in the hallway, I just yanked him in. He ordered some tests and said he was going to summon Dr. Kelly."

"Did you get any history from her? Meds? Prior illness?"

"She could barely speak. But she did spell out her name for me. And she asked about her six-year-old daughter named Yusra. Then she passed out."

"Where's the daughter?"

Lizbeth shrugged. "One of our ER clerks found Ms. Habani alone under the camellias by the front walkway. He just picked her up and carried her inside."

"Well, did she have a purse? Cell? You checked her pockets?"

"I followed protocol for a due diligence search," Lizbeth said, handing over the patient's personal-effects bag. "But as you see, there wasn't much to search."

Fergie donned exam gloves and withdrew the items from the bag. A black cotton sweater. A maroon scarf. Faded jeans, frayed at the ankles. Trouser socks, black. Green tennis shoes caked with mud. "I don't get it," she said. "How'd she end up here alone, under the camellias? And why no ID?"

"Yeah," said Lizbeth, grimacing. "And, well, why is she *blue*?"

Old Stadium Site

West Oakland

Yusra Habani knew what she was supposed to do. Although the Nice Lady who was about to take her away had never been overtly cruel, still, Yusra had learned that "Nice People" were capable of doing strange and hurtful things—often and unpredictably, according to her mother. Trying not to cry—another lesson mastered—she internally recited her mother's steadfast warning: *Never trust anyone in this country, even the nice smiling ones. And never give them any information about yourself or us.*

Yusra watched the Nice Lady rifle through the abandoned camper that she and her mother had reclaimed as their home. The Nice Lady wore dark purple lipstick and was tall; she had to bow her head to walk through the hall and doorway. She kept searching . . . the kitchenette cupboard, the storage boxes under the sleeping cot, the plastic grocery bags containing their worldly possessions. She shook the canned foods, listening for something. *What is the Nice Lady looking for?*

Finally, the Nice Lady sat down on the workbench that Yusra's mother had repurposed for a dining table. She locked eyes with Yusra and said: "Your mama *must* have a secret place where she hides her valuables. And I mean her important papers that we gotta find *now*."

Yusra shook her head.

"Honey," the Nice Lady said, without discernible sweetness. "How 'bout a special box maybe? Or . . . I dunno . . . a cookie jar?"

A jar for cookies?

"Don't stare at me like you don't understand, Yusra! And you had enough time to gather your mama's valuables while I was taking her where she needed to be."

Tightening her grasp on her rumpled doll, Yusra looked away.

"Oh, hell," said the Nice Lady, her frown forming a sad purple crescent. "You also had enough time to collect your own stuff. Is that old doll the only thing you're fixing to take with you?"

Yusra nodded.

The Nice Lady pinched her lips. "You know, if you *really* wanna help your mama, you gotta tell me where she hides her special things. If she … *when* she gets better, she's gonna need her ID. She could get into a helluva lot of trouble if she doesn't have them. She could end up going to jail. Do you even know what jail is?"

"Yes," said Yusra, biting her lip.

The Nice Lady's naturally ruddy face turned purple, almost matching her lipstick color. "It's not like on TV, Yusra! It's a helluva lot worse. And people inside jail are real mean and spiteful."

But Yusra knew that. Jail had been her first home in the United States. And she hadn't yet decided whether it was any worse than living here with her mother, in this tumbledown camper, in this scary dark lot behind the old stadium.

ER Hallway

Oakland City Hospital

Nora followed Carl toward room seven, her rust-colored Keens squeaking along the hallway. He advised, "You should sprinkle baby powder in your shoes."

"You're right," she said, though knowing full well she wasn't going to take his advice. She regarded her squeaky shoes as essential dress accessories at work, possessing the power to distract her during the haunting silences that remained in the wake of so many colleagues' deaths. They were the shoes she'd stood in throughout the awful aftermath of Lydia's murder. The shoes she'd worn during a colleague's violent attacks. In these shoes, she could withstand any hell. They were perfect for work.

Squeaking down the hallway, she began to speculate about Carl's blue patient. Because the potential causes for blue skin discoloration were diverse, the differential diagnosis was engagingly broad. She recalled the last time she'd seen a blue person: someone on a TV talk show years ago, who'd turned *permanently* blue after ingesting colloidal silver in hopes of curing his sinusitis. And before that, perhaps a decade earlier, she'd seen a patient with blue skin caused by hydroxychloroquine—

"Dr. Kelly?" said Aditya, interrupting her ruminations.

"Sorry," she said. "I was lost in thought."

"Of course," he said. "You were probably thinking through the differential diagnosis of blue skin. And saying to yourself, as you always say to us: 'Yet another example of patient care that requires more than a software program or algorithm.'"

Nora looked appreciatively at him. Although she'd been mentoring him for four and a half years—through his residency in internal medicine and this subsequent one in the ER—she was still amazed by his unfailing ability to make her smile. And though he looked so different than she—male, a foot taller, mustached, brown-skinned, and at least a quarter-century younger—she often felt as if she were looking into a mirror whenever she saw him.

The Nice Lady's Car

Oakland

Before getting into the Nice Lady's black station wagon, Yusra picked some lavender from her mother's garden. She placed it inside the Rite Aid bag containing the clothes the Nice Lady had chosen for her. She gazed at the winter crops she had helped her mother to plant—the beets, broccoli, cauliflower, fava beans—wondering who would care for them now. Then she looked longingly across the crumbled asphalt lot, to the orange tent where her friend Luis lived with his uncle. She wished the tent had a window through which she could see him now. She wished she could say goodbye to him; to anyone, really.

"Get in the car," the Nice Lady barked after locking the camper door and pocketing its only key. "It's raining, case you hadn't noticed."

Yusra fastened the seat belt around herself and her doll, feeling increasingly unsafe as the station wagon drove away. "Are you taking me to my mom?" she asked.

"No."

"But how can she get back in our home if she doesn't have a key when she comes back?"

"Oh, so, you want I should leave the door unlocked? You want robbers to get inside? Worse, you want immigration to come here tracking—?" The Nice Lady's mouth pulled down in a bitter sneer. "Never mind."

"Please take me back home. I want to wait for my mom."

The Nice Lady chided, "'Back home'? You got no idea what you're talking about." When they approached the stadium's gate, she threw a coat over Yusra and instructed her to crouch down. A minute later, she announced "coast clear" and told Yusra to "sit up straight now."

But immediately after turning onto the Nimitz Freeway, they encountered horrific holiday traffic. The car slowed to a cheerless crawl and the Nice Lady seethed: "So many damn people on the same damn road! And of all the days the good lord could've chosen to *finally* give us rain." After pounding her fist on the steering wheel, she said, "I give up! We're turning back." Then, inching toward the nearest exit ramp, she glanced at Yusra and repeated, "You got no idea."

But Yusra knew exactly what "back home" meant. Home was wherever her mother happened to be, whether in an old camper, a detention camp, a jail cell, or a border cage. If anyone here "got no idea" about that, it was the Nice Lady.

Besides, Yusra secretly knew that "back home" factually meant Yemen. Averting her gaze from the Nice Lady, she recalled last year when her mother confided that information in her, insisting it be kept secret to protect them from the dangerous people who could hurt them or force them to return if that information was revealed. At the time, drawing on her own experiences, Yusra had asked: "Like the soldiers and the jail people?" Her mother had pretended not to cry and said, "You have known too much unkindness in this world for a child who has only lived five years in it. Still, you must understand how the world works, for your safety and mine. You must remember that you can never tell a person's evil or goodness by the uniform or clothes they wear. And some very bad people have very nice smiles. Promise that you will never tell anyone about our real home." After Yusra nodded, her mother hugged her and said, "And please, do not worry so much. We will be safe together. Besides, most people here don't even know that our country exists. They could never find it on a map."

Recalling that conversation now, Yusra finally derived some comfort in her mother's words. Because wherever the Nice Lady was taking her, it wasn't going to be Yemen.

ER Exam Room

Oakland City Hospital

News of the blue woman had traveled fast among the hospital staff. While Fergie and Lizbeth drew blood samples for the tests Carl had ordered, rubbernecking staff crowded around the patient's bedside. "Give us some room here," Fergie kept warning.

Still, curious clerks, doctors, and nurses arrived. An intern pulled out his cellphone and jockeyed for an optimal position from which to photograph the patient.

"What the hell?" Fergie objected. "You can't do that!"

"Come on," he argued. "I won't identify her! It's just for my Facebook page."

Freakin' unbelievable, Fergie thought. *As if that's justification!* She shot back, "Well, picture this. Me reporting you to admin and then posting a Facebook photo of you being fired."

"She's right," another doctor chimed in. "You can't photograph a patient without their consent."

He snickered, "Well, she *can't* give consent. And some anonymous photo isn't going to harm her." He snapped his picture and left.

Fergie clenched her fists around the glass vials of blood she'd collected. After taking a deep breath, she told Lizbeth, "Your choice: running these samples to the lab, or trying your luck with crowd control here."

Lizbeth didn't hesitate, although her heart began to race. Standing up to powerful others in service of patients' needs was a skill she intended to master. So, after clearing her throat of fear, she firmly proclaimed above the din: "Everyone, leave *now.*"

~ ~ ~

Yes, leave, all of you! I can hear everything you say. You people who are supposed to be healers talk as if I do not exist! But every time you gasp at me, I am frightened even more. Please stop talking, everyone! I am still here! And where is my Yusra?

~ ~ ~

To Lizbeth's great relief, people began shuffling out of the room, even the six-foot-tall ortho chief who'd seemed affronted by her boldness. And after everyone left, she let out the breath she'd been holding deep within her chest.

Cafeteria

Oakland City Hospital

After delivering Ms. Habani's blood samples to the lab, Fergie dropped by the cafeteria to grab an orange juice, still fuming about the arrogant intern-photographer. *What a freakin' moron! Treating that patient as an object for his entertainment. No respect for patient privacy! And "anonymous"? How delusional. How many nanoseconds does he think it'd take to track down a hospitalized blue woman through his Facebook page—*

"Oh, *you* again," someone said, interrupting her internal dialogue.

Fergie cringed. Although a year had passed since she last stepped into this cafeteria, she immediately remembered the caustic tone and the worker to whom it belonged. She smiled stiffly, placed her juice on the counter, and replied, "Yeah, hi."

"Good to see you finally," said the worker. "Might I interest you in today's *specials*?"

"No, thanks," said Fergie, recalling her last fraught visit here. She held out a dollar to pay.

"Hold on," said the worker, pointing a finger at her. "I remember you being very interested in *special* stuff."

Fergie groaned. "Come on. I haven't been here in forever."

"But you're memorable. What can I say?"

"Look. I got to get back to the ER—"

"I could ask our chef to prepare you something *off-menu,* as they say?"

"Please?"

"Hear me out. We also started serving fancy pastries since you been here. They're imported from San Francisco, and they're called crow-sahntz—pardon my French."

Fergie defiantly returned the worker's deadpan expression, but the woman just stared defiantly back. After tortured moments of neither one backing down, Fergie privately conceded that she'd met her match at the stare-down. She asked, "You enjoying this?"

"More than you know."

Fergie plunked down her dollar, held a hand up in surrender, and walked away.

"Come back soon," the worker called out. "And ask for Marla! That's me!"

Old Stadium Site

West Oakland

Luis heard the familiar sputtery sound of the station wagon that belonged to the Nice Lady who occasionally brought him bread and peanut butter. But it wasn't slowing down, and by the time he peered out of his tent, he saw her car heading toward the stadium exit.

"You're letting in too much cold," Uncle Tomas complained.

After collecting a palmful of rain, Luis dutifully closed the tent flap. He then opened his hand to his uncle and said, "Look."

Uncle Tomas smiled feebly. "Yes, rain," he said. "It's been a long time. It will help with all the fires. Did you remember to . . .?"

"Yes. I put all our pots outside."

"Good boy," Tomas said, turning over inside his sleeping bag, his eyes closing. "Now go wash up. And take the soap."

"I will. But maybe you can come with me?"

"No, Luis. You're old enough now. You don't need my protection. But remember, look out for rats. And that strange boy with red hair."

"Maybe you'd feel better if you took a shower, too?"

"Stop worrying about me. I'm fine. Go."

Luis stared at his uncle, who was most definitely *not* fine. And all the pretending otherwise only worried him more by leaving everything unsaid to his imagination, where anxiety increasingly reigned. Worse, he was running out of ideas about how to make his uncle feel better. Maybe, he thought, by taking his first shower alone and demonstrating independence, he could disburden his uncle a little. So, he grabbed their soap bar, his clean underwear and tee, and the garbage bag he'd fashioned into raingear. Then he dashed out of their tent, peering over his shoulder along the way, looking out for rats and the red-haired boy.

ER Exam Room

Oakland City Hospital

Lizbeth stood in the doorway as the doctors approached the exam room. She greeted them: "Hello again, Dr. Kluft. Dr. Kelly. Aditya."

When Aditya's face flushed with her mention of only his first name, Carl said: "It appears that you and Lizbeth are attracted to one another." Aditya glanced uncertainly at Lizbeth. Carl asked, "Am I wrong? I've been working on exploration of the emotional content and contextual meaning of human exchanges."

"Ah, no," said Aditya, "you are correct." Then Carl and Aditya smiled at one another and entered the exam room.

Nora was already at the patient's bedside, beginning her exam by observation: *The woman is so blue against the bright white sheets. Blue cheeks, blue forehead, blue neck. The blue of the slate tiles on my kitchen walls. The blue of an airless sky. The color of something decidedly wrong.*

"Her name is Daleen Habani," Lizbeth offered. "She's unresponsive. Her heart rate is unstable, and her pulse ox is low."

"And the tests I ordered?" asked Carl.

"Fergie ran them to the lab herself. And radiology is on its way."

"Then my work here is done," Carl replied, taking leave.

But Nora heard nothing of those exchanges. Everything external had silenced—conversations, the beeping oximeter, the rush of oxygen through plastic tubes, the infusion pump's whirring. She had entered the inner sanctuary she'd cultivated over decades of contemplating the body's mysteries. All she heard now were her thoughts assembling, taking orbit around her core love of medicine. From initial observation alone, telling diagnostic connections were forming between her experience, knowledge, and instinct. *This patient's contour, in relief under the blanket, suggests a thin woman, about five feet tall. The blue discoloration is most prominent over her lips and inside her opened mouth. Her cropped black hair looks pathologically thinned, and exposed scalp patches are brown. Her hollowed temples suggest significant weight loss. Three coarse scars run parallel across her left mandible. This is a woman in acute crisis, but also chronically ill with the telltale signs of premature aging; adjusting for them, she's probably in her mid-thirties.*

She continued observing, scanning the patient's personal effects that Fergie had laid out on the bedside stand. She saw a maroon scarf matted with black hair, suggesting it'd been worn as a head cover. The sweater and jeans were faded and unmatched. The green tennis shoes were caked with mud, but emitted a lavender scent.

Now she proceeded to her hands-on exam. She lifted the blanket and felt the patient's right hand. *It's warm, and its radial pulse is strong; so, given her normal blood pressure, the blood flow through her larger arteries isn't obstructed to account for the discoloration.* Next, she pressed on the woman's dark blue fingernails; and when she released the pressure, their capillary refill was quick. *So,* she concluded, *small-vessel blood flow is also adequate.* Then she gently pinched and lifted a skinfold on the back of the patient's hand to assess turgor; when she released the fold, it swiftly flattened back in place. All these findings made it clear: *This patient's blue skin isn't due to inadequate blood flow or pressure or volume. It's a problem with the blood itself.*

She then lowered the blanket to examine the patient's heart and lungs. As she expected, they sounded normal through the stethoscope. Then she palpated the abdomen, finding no abnormality, but noting spidery striations across the abdominal wall: *Evidence of prior pregnancy.*

After stepping back from the bedside, Nora stood still, waiting for her clinical findings to gravitate toward a diagnosis. In times like this, when diagnostic clarity could claim a small private victory over the body's mysterious eruptions, it felt blissful.

Indeed, soon she was confident of her diagnosis. She pleasurably took in a deep breath while transitioning back to externalities. Then she turned to her resident and said, "Come here, Aditya." She was inviting him to discover the decisive physical finding that would confirm the diagnosis with dramatic didactic impact.

Throughout years under Nora's mentorship, Aditya had regularly watched her pull a diagnosis "out of a hat" after skillful bedside questioning and examination of patients. Her elegant reveals were always sure-handed, without drama or bravado. But he remained troubled that he so rarely could match her. He said, "I recognize that tone of your voice. You are going to reveal what the patient has."

"No," she said, "*you* are." Then she lifted the blanket to expose the woman's left arm.

Aditya froze, fearful about disappointing Nora. Finally, he said, "I see a forearm with two bandages." He turned to Lizbeth and said, "Bandages over the IV site and also where you drew blood, yes?"

Lizbeth nodded.

Nora said, "Look again." After he only frowned, she asked: "What's the color of the patient's fresh blood, seeping through the bandages and spotting the bedsheet?"

It was glaringly obvious now, but an "obvious" Nora had to point out for him. And how embarrassing to also falter in front of Lizbeth. He grimaced and said, "Her blood is brown, like chocolate."

"And, so?"

"So, she has methemoglobinemia. That is why her skin is blue."

"Bingo!" said Nora, beaming. "I'll leave you to obtain an arterial blood gas to confirm our diagnosis and establish a baseline level of methemoglobin. Meanwhile, I'll place a stat order for the antidote."

After she left, Lizbeth handed a blood-gas kit to Aditya and said: "Dr. Kelly was incredible to watch! And I'm so relieved that Ms. Habani has a diagnosis now, especially one we can treat. But what's the antidote Dr. Kelly is ordering?"

"Methylene blue," Aditya flatly replied. Then, while prepping Ms. Habani's skin for the blood gas test, he said: "Someday, I will surprise Nora by making a diagnosis like that." He stuck the needle into the radial artery and watched the chocolate blood flow into the glass syringe. "In fact, I'm going to diagnose the underlying *cause* for this patient's methemoglobinemia."

Old Stadium Site

West Oakland

Luis ran through the rain, heading for the private clearing behind the giant junk pile where he regularly bathed. Oily brown puddles had materialized irregularly across the potholed parking lot that he masterfully crossed. Several times, he checked to verify he wasn't being followed by the nosey red-haired boy who always loitered by the stadium's entrance gate.

When he reached the clearing, he rested against the junk pile and caught his breath. Then, as his uncle had taught him, he peered above the wall of discarded plastic and metal, scanning for rats and snarly dogs. Seeing none, he undressed and soaped his body while khaki-colored groundwater seeped from the junk pile and encircled his feet. He lathered his hair and let the pelting rain rinse it clean. After donning his clean tee and underwear, he washed the ones he'd been wearing.

But when he set out to return to his tent, he saw the red-haired boy approaching and calling out, "Hey, kid!"

Oceans of adrenaline surged through Luis' small body; his heart hammered inside his chest. And he ran toward his tent, faster than he'd ever run in his life.

Inn-N-Out Motel

Near the MacArthur Maze, West Oakland

Yusra couldn't understand why the Nice Lady would bring her to this smelly motel room. Or why she would lie to the gruff man in the big office by claiming to be her mother. And when she mounted the courage to ask, the Nice Lady only answered, "Cuz."

The Nice Lady flopped down onto one of the twin beds and clicked on the TV's remote. Then she removed from her backpack the food she'd intended for the drive she'd been forced to abandon. Handing over a greasy paper bag, she told Yusra to "eat up."

Yusra opened the bag and found a cold hamburger wrapped in wax paper. She put aside the ketchup packets, planning to use them to make soup with her mother. She dared to ask again, "Where's my mom?"

"Look," said the Nice Lady, her gray eyes narrowing. "If you're *trying* to irritate me by repeating that same damn question, you *are* succeeding. Now, quiet! I wanna hear the news. In fact, go take a shower."

"I want my mom."

"I've told you every which way to shut up about that!"

Yusra trembled.

"Oh, hell," the Nice Lady grumbled. "I don't want to scare you. But you're testing my usual good nature! Just no more asking about your mama! That's the rule. Understand?"

Yusra put down her burger and headed for the shower, wondering why her mother had always insisted on referring to this mean woman as the "Nice Lady." Yes, she occasionally provided them with bread and peanut butter, and once with eggs and milk. Still, in between her sporadic kind acts, she seemed so very not-nice.

ER Doctors' Workstation

Oakland City Hospital

Fergie popped into the doctors' workstation and asked, "Lunch?"

"Sounds great," Nora replied. "Want to try the newish sandwich place on Franklin?"

"It's closed."

"But they got great reviews!"

"Yeah, but they couldn't maintain enough staff. Minimum-wage workers can't afford our local rents." She scoffed. "Neither could I."

Nora frowned. "Every day in the papers, I read about local businesses folding because of that."

"You *still* get news from 'the papers'?"

"Well, I enjoy having my hands on the news, especially when I read about politics. Then, when I get furious, I can crush it or rip it to pieces!"

"Therapeutic reading," said Fergie, nodding agreeably. "And lots of opportunity for that now. Still, all the trees and the carbon footprint that newspapers require?"

Aditya appeared. "Excuse me, Dr. Kelly. But the blood gas confirmed your diagnosis of methemoglobinemia." He shook his head, incredulous. "And we spent hundreds of dollars for all the other tests to diagnose what you had diagnosed clinically."

"Still," said Nora, "now we can jump to the next differential diagnosis: establishing the underlying *cause* for her methemoglobinemia. Perhaps she—"

"I know," Aditya urgently replied.

"Okay," Nora said, raising her brow.

He cringed, aware of having revealed his insecurity. "I also wanted you to know that pharmacy delivered the methylene blue you ordered. Lizbeth is about to administer it."

"Great," said Nora. "Did you—?"

"Yes," he cut her off again. "I checked the patient's G6PD, and it is normal, so we can safely proceed with treatment."

Nora and Fergie exchanged knowing looks. "Well," said Nora, saluting Aditya. "Sounds like you've got everything under control, and it's time for me to take my lunch break."

Old Stadium Site

West Oakland

Upon his panic-fueled return to the tent, Luis found his uncle motionless on the ground. "Uncle Tomas!" he cried out, shaking him. Then the red-haired boy who'd followed him appeared; rain-soaked and breath-less, he asked: "What's going on?"

"Get out!" Luis shouted, grabbing the kitchen knife. "Leave us alone!"

"Hey, little shithead, put the knife down!" he shouted back. And easily overpowering Luis, he wrested the knife away.

"Don't kill us!" Luis begged.

The red-haired boy scoffed. "What the hell's wrong with you, kid? I'm not gonna—"

Luis shook his uncle's limp body and cried.

The red-haired boy shoved Luis aside, and after checking Tomas for breathing and a pulse, said: "Fuck. Your uncle needs to get to a hospital."

"Is he dying?" Luis sobbed.

The red-haired boy pulled out his cell and placed a call. Luis over-heard him say: "This is Red. The guy in the orange tent needs an ambulance. . . . You got to take care of this. It's your fault. . . . No, it's got to be *now*. The guy's barely alive. . . . I don't give a fuck. Call the damn ambulance."

Luis began to shiver, from the cold and rain, the chilling fear. He stared fretfully at the person who'd just self-identified as "Red"—so tall and skinny, so very white and freckled. In the current light, his hair took on the color of carrots.

"Listen, kid," said Red. "Someone's coming to take your uncle to the hospital. Understand?"

Luis threw himself over his uncle's body and moaned.

"Fuck," Red grumbled, taking stock of this new misery, wondering how to handle the boy. Then he surveyed the tent for what could be salvaged, deciding on the kitchen knife, a blanket, a soap bar, two coffee mugs, boxes of saltines and cereal. He released a sigh and told Luis, "Get your stuff together."

Luis dried his eyes. "To go with my uncle to the hospital?"

"No," Red said, "you're coming with me." Then he grabbed a garbage bag and tossed the coffee mugs in, but they fell out through holes in its bottom.

"That's my raincoat," Luis said, pointing to the bag. "And I'm staying here with my uncle!"

C-Suite Conference Room

Dr. Fred Williams, chief of Oakland City Hospital's medical staff, sat at the head of the long conference table, beaming. His coppery eyes glistened, and his shiny black scalp glowed under the ceiling lights, casting a halo on him. He felt blessed, scanning the expressions of his hospital board members, all mirroring his satisfaction. In moments like this, he gave thanks to his mother, who'd supported his quest to become a doctor by sacrificing dreams of her own.

Remarkably, the fiscal year was closing on a high note: Oakland City Hospital would be losing the least amount of money it had lost in a decade! After the board stopped applauding the announcement, Fred began to wind the meeting down: "On that cheery note, we'll end our final meeting for 2018, given the upcoming holiday recess. But first, looking ahead to an even brighter year in 2019 . . ." He stood up, opened the door, and ushered in a tall, willowy blonde. "I'm delighted to introduce Ms. Samantha Greeley, who will be joining the board in January. As everyone knows, I've been courting her and the Greeley Family Foundation for years."

The board clapped, Fred beamed even brighter, Samantha smiled receptively. One member—Larry Larbor, the CEO of Larbor Microbrewery—said: "Fred, I'm just sounding a word of caution." He winked at Samantha and continued, "You got to be careful about the words you choose in these 'Me Too' times. You could get in trouble these days, 'courting' women in the workplace."

A few members smiled, if rather uncomfortably. The women, including Samantha, exchanged jaded expressions. Fred said, somewhat defensively, "That's not what I meant."

Larbor persisted: "Your 'courting' could lead to an actual court *date*."

"All right now," said Fred, trying to redirect the discussion and reclaim its prior cheer. "I think you're drinking a few too many of your company's products."

Samantha broke in: "May I have a word?"

"Please," said Fred, shooting Larbor a vexed look.

After establishing brisk eye contact with everyone at the table, she said: "I look forward to our future collaboration. For generations, my family has been actively engaged in the economic, civic, and political life of the East Bay. And Greeley Enterprises, through its philanthropic Family Foundation, has long supported this public hospital, which provides a vital safety net for the entire community. Now, for me, it becomes a *personal* pleasure to serve this hospital as a board member."

Fred initiated another round of applause, after which Samantha said: "Our business mission at Greeley Enterprises has always embraced values of community service and social justice. And in that context, I'm pleased to announce that we're on schedule to finalize a major real estate transaction next week that should benefit the patients and hospital staff by—"

"Really?" exclaimed Larbor. "The stadium deal is *finally* closing? We've been reading about that for years! It's been vacant for . . . what? A decade? A bit of an eyesore, really. It'd be great to see it redeveloped."

Samantha rolled her eyes ever so slightly. "As I was about to say, we've had many potential buyers over time who've been interested in commercial development of our stadium property. But our moral compass kept pointing us to the same conclusion: that our land should be repurposed with the goal of alleviating our dire housing crisis in the East Bay." Fixing a censorial gaze on Larbor, she continued: "It was a long and complicated process to obtain every requisite stamp of approval from city and county regulators, but we persisted. And it took years to find the right buyer whose values aligned with ours." She returned her attention to the board at large. "I wanted to make the happy announcement here, in time for the holidays. Greeley Enterprises will be finalizing the sale of the old stadium complex to Highmark Construction next Friday."

Fred privately claimed some of the board members' reprised adulation. Having spent inordinate time and political capital to steer the land's development toward low-cost housing, he believed he deserved some credit. On a more personal level, he hoped the news would disabuse certain friends and family members of claims that he'd lost touch with the poor and minority communities his hospital served. Now, as a major advocate for this housing development, he could point to a redeeming counterclaim.

Samantha concluded, "Our deal with Highmark stipulates the inclusion of affordable and low-cost units in their massive condo development.

And because the property is close to the hospital, we expect that will benefit many of its minimum-wage workers and their families."

"Indeed," said Fred. "It's been impossible to maintain a stable workforce when employees can't afford to live within driving distance of the hospital." He almost added, *And reducing staff turnover will also help the hospital's bottom line.*

Inn-N-Out Motel

Near the MacArthur Maze

"I swear," the Nice Lady said. "You so much as move outta that bed, I'm gonna whip you."

Yusra froze.

"And I'll know if you do," she cautioned. "'Cuz I put tracer dust on the carpet. So, don't go thinking you can trick me." She threw on her raincoat and grabbed her car keys. "Now, you got a TV. You got food. You even got a bathroom. You got everything a person could need. Agreed?"

Yusra nodded; she knew she must.

At the door, the Nice Lady warned, "And don't you answer this door. I don't care who comes knocking. I don't care if it's George Clooney himself."

George Clooney?

Rigby's Diner

Uptown Oakland

Fergie nudged the tofu platter toward Nora and said, "C'mon. It's good for your bones."

"Just what I need," Nora said. "Tofu bones."

Fergie leaned back in her chair and ran her muscular hands over her clean-shaven head, revealing more of the copious blue tattoos encircling her arms. "Suit yourself," she said.

After signaling their server for take-home boxes, Nora asked, "How's Winston?"

"My husband's wrestling with his sanity," Fergie said. "He finds it challenging to write in Carl's house. Don't get me wrong. We're both grateful to him for providing us a place to live. But it's hard living with someone else, and—"

Nora looked quizzically at Fergie, but a moment later understood her abrupt silence: Carl was approaching.

"Hello," he said, sitting down as the server arrived with the boxes.

"Oh, a new tablemate," she said to Carl. "I'll grab you a menu."

"Wait," he said. "Has the menu changed since February 18, 2017?"

The server cocked her head. "Don't think so. Not in the last four years I've been working here."

"Then I'll have platter twenty-nine, please."

"Right," she said, taking leave, glancing curiously back at him.

Nora said, "Your photographic memory, Carl. It never ceases to amaze."

Fergie had tensed up with Carl's mention of the February date, praying it wasn't going to trigger Nora's traumatic memories surrounding it. Hoping to create interference, she blurted out: "So, Carl, when's the last time you saw a blue patient?"

"This morning," he answered. "In the ER. You were there."

"I meant *before* that," she said.

"I occasionally deliver newborns with the blue baby syndrome. My last was forty-four days ago. His cyanosis was caused by a congenital heart defect: tetralogy of Fallot."

Fergie struggled to sustain the conversation while anxiously tracking Nora's increasing withdrawal. *Damn,* she thought. *Nora's probably remembering that date now. It was crazy-times-ten to come here today!* Still, the choice of this restaurant had been Nora's, and Fergie had worried at the time that any attempt to dissuade her might've unwittingly created a trigger itself.

But Carl didn't hesitate to address Nora's withdrawal. He said, "I see you've become silent, and your body language conveys detachment. That communicates disengagement from our conversation."

Prodded out from withdrawal by his comments, Nora refocused on Carl as if emerging from fog. "Sorry," she said. "I suddenly remembered that we were at this restaurant before. That awful February, of so many deaths . . ."

"Nora," Fergie tenderly suggested, "let's not go there again."

"But we *are* there now, Fergie," Carl said, his eyes questioning her. "We're *at* the restaurant."

His intensely earnest response jarred Nora, redirecting her from another free-fall into post-traumatic panic. She stared affectionately into Carl's doe-eyes, reminded of the shelter she'd found while looking at him like this, on that awful night while police arrested the killer who'd nearly taken her life.

ER Exam Room

Oakland City Hospital

Lizbeth and Aditya watched the methylene blue drip from the medication bag and flow through plastic tubing into Daleen Habani's vein.

"It seems counterintuitive," said Lizbeth, "to inject something blue to get rid of the blue in her body."

Aditya matter-of-factly replied, "Methylene blue converts the methemoglobin inside her red blood cells to normal hemoglobin. That will enable her red cells to carry oxygen more effectively."

Looking concernedly at him, she asked, "What's wrong?"

"Nothing."

"Look, if you're still bent about not making the diagnosis . . ."

"It is not that. If Nora had not been here, this patient's diagnosis and treatment would have been delayed. Or missed. She could have died. I should have—"

"Look!" she said, pointing to their patient, whose blue eyelids fluttered now. Then her mouth twitched, and her heart rate began slowing toward normal on the cardiac monitor.

"She is reanimating," he said.

"And now she's moving her legs," said Lizbeth. "I'm so happy. A real miracle!"

Her unguarded joy pierced his defenses. Still, he thought: *This patient's life and all this happiness might have been lost had I been in charge.*

Old Stadium Site

West Oakland

Again, Luis yelled, "Let me out!"

Red stood outside his white crew cab truck, mottled by wildfire ash, and struggled to remain patient. But the boy's incessant demand was grating on his last nerve. Besides, it was raining, and this godawful lot smelled of human decay. *And where the fuck is that ambulance?*

"I want to be with my uncle!" Luis cried, pounding the dashboard.

Red glowered at him through the windshield. "Stop that! No one but me can hear you!"

Luis slumped into the passenger seat, sobbing.

"Kids," Red muttered. *I'm never going to have one of those. Such pains in the neck. So useless and annoying. And so fucking needy.* He conceded now that his parents had been right to come to the same conclusions. *Proving,* he thought, *there's a first time for everything.* Still, they'd been wrong about everything else. *Wrong about me not surviving. Wrong about me starving to death, dying of AIDS, ending up in juvie, becoming an addict.*

He scanned the devastated landscape he now considered home. The soiled tents. Abandoned cars. Stuffed shopping carts. The junkyard dogs too hungry to fight. And he was surprised to experience something new: genuine gratitude for his parents' thudding lack of faith in him. For had he not been determined to defy their damning expectations, he couldn't imagine having been otherwise motivated to survive this so-called life.

This time, when the passenger door opened, he didn't try to block Luis' escape. Instead, he resignedly watched the boy run toward his tent, thinking: *Little shithead will have to learn for himself.* Still, he called out: "Come back, kid! You don't want to go there!"

But that's precisely where Luis wanted to go. He wanted to be with Uncle Tomas. Especially now, with soot and ash swarming in the sky, with everybody living inside tents or boxes or old cars, with always having to look over your shoulder for lurking threats. With everything being so fragile, so close to ending.

ER Exam Room

Oakland City Hospital

"But I know you understand *some* English," said Lizbeth, looking curiously at Daleen Habani. "Earlier, you answered when I asked your name. And you said you had a six-year-old daughter named Yusra."

Daleen looked away. *Who are these people demanding information from me? What have they done with my Yusra? Why does my head hurt? Why do I feel confused?*

Aditya said, "Please talk to us. Let us help you."

You want to help me? Then bring my daughter to me! And stop asking dangerous questions.

"Okay," Lizbeth relented. "Just try to relax. We'll admit you to a room as soon as one becomes available. But that could take a while because the hospital's full. In the meantime, is there anyone you'd like us to call?"

Who do I know who even owns a phone?

Aditya said, "I'm sorry you are not comfortable speaking with us, Ms. Habani." He pulled up his coat sleeve and placed his bare forearm alongside hers. "When you came into our ER, you were blue. Now, look! You are close to brown again, like me."

I remember now. I was blue. Yusra kept telling me that.

"Well," he said, giving up. "I'm just happy you are improving. And some nice people from social services will be coming by to talk with you—"

"No Nice People!" Daleen insisted as Nora simultaneously walked in.

Surprised, Nora said, "I'm not sure how to take that."

Lizbeth said, "She wasn't referring to you, Dr. Kelly. She was referring to 'nice people' from social services."

Aditya winked at Daleen and said, "The prospect of their visit seems to have helped you recover your ability to speak."

Nora stole a moment to register Daleen's alertness, normalizing skin color, healthy output of green urine in the Foley bag, and improved vitals on the monitors. She additionally registered Daleen's ostensible fear—so common among ER patients, many of whom distrusted doctors and the healthcare system, or feared being reported to immigration. And as she'd learned throughout her career, the majority of patients coming here had lives broken in places medicine couldn't reach; you usually had to step back to give them the space they needed to engage on their own terms. So she smiled at Daleen and said, "I hope we can speak soon. Whenever you're ready, okay?"

But when she turned away, Aditya whispered to Daleen: "That was Dr. Kelly, who saved your life."

Suddenly, it came back to Daleen: she recognized Nora's voice, and her body remembered the sureness of the doctor's examining hands that had moved so confidently and purposefully along her arms and wrists and fingers and nails. *Yes, that is the doctor who intervened and pulled me back into life.* Mustering all her strength, Daleen called out, "Dr. Kelly!"

Ocambo Law Firm

Lakeshore District, Oakland

Peering out his office window, Quentin Ocambo took in the lakeside view he'd cherished since 1989. Despite relentless construction and gentrification of the neighborhood, stalwart Walden Pond Books and the Grand Lake Theatre still stood at the shimmering northeast corner of Lake Merritt. *Defiant survivors, like me.*

He caught his reflection in the window: *Not bad for a man my age.* Still tall and unbent, with a full head of silver hair, he could pass for fifty. He straightened his blue silk tie and matching pocket square, deciding to wear them tomorrow to Samantha's Thanksgiving banquet. *Where, for the seventh year in a row, I'll be the oldest person again.* He rued the fact that her father Bert was no longer alive to host the traditional Greeley Thanksgiving. Since Samantha had taken over as the family scion in 2011, the annual banquet felt unwelcoming and inelegant. What was once a stately gathering of financial titans around the table had become, in her hands, a manic "event" attended by tech and media "celebrities" who merely fed off one another.

And how assaultive to his eyes, having to witness Samantha at the head of the table. *So wrong, so ironic.* She couldn't be less informed or more disinterested in Greeley businesses and polity. She was form without substance, gravy without turkey. And forget about Bert's traditional after-dinner retreat to the library for spirited discussions about the future of Greeley Enterprises. Forget about drinking the special single-malt during all-night brainstorming over new acquisitions, offshore investments, shareholder returns, real estate deals.

Quentin stared at the desk photograph of himself and Bert, taken on the day he was hired, straight out of law school in 1989, to work for Greeley Enterprises. No one could've predicted the phenomenal success their nascent partnership would become. *And I couldn't have predicted how tiresome it would become to work here without you. Tiresome, and still hard to accept you leaving Samantha in control of everything, after all that we risked.*

In a sour mood now, Quentin returned to his paperwork on the impending stadium sale. Such a lucrative deal: $300 million for the 170-acre property with its rundown stadium complex and its crumbling parking and storage structures. Bert would've been impressed by the fraught coming-to-fruition of this particular sell-off in ways that Samantha could not, would not, fathom.

But looking at the paperwork, he lost interest immediately, imagining Samantha blithely scrawling her signature all over the contracts next week. She had *no idea*—and never *once* conveyed even a polite pretense of wanting to know—of the significance of this stadium property to him and her father. She had *no idea* how they bent their backs, twisted law, and compromised their morals to steer this and other Greeley holdings into profitable waters. She had *no idea* what risks *they* undertook. Her rote signing-over of the stadium property to Highmark Construction felt farcical, inauthentic, *wrong*.

He put down the paperwork, popped an antacid, and took a moment to reminisce about the stadium's storied history. He recalled Bert telling of his lifelong dream to build a sports complex in Oakland. And how in 1950 he acquired the ideal site upon marriage to Winifred, who, as sole heir to the Alpers family fortune, owned the Regal Chemical Company. Within a year, Bert tore that factory down and built the main sports coliseum. Its expansion proceeded over time, sports teams came and went, big bands performed; a great deal of money was made.

Quentin recalled the thrill of being pulled into Bert's dream when he was hired in 1989 to oversee the stadium's renovation. And when he brought that renovation to completion in '91 to glowing public and architectural acclaim, he not only earned Bert's trust; he also proved his business savvy by selling off parcels of peripheral land at *twenty times* base to neutralize the construction costs.

And that's how our partnership began and developed, Bert. So, knowing the stadium is selling off to Highmark Construction next week, I'm experiencing . . . what? Nostalgia? Hurt, perhaps? Anger, most definitely.

But of all the businesses and real estate I've overseen for you, the stadium was special; it was ours. How could you just leave it to Samantha? She cares nothing about it, beyond its selling price.

He stared again at Bert's photo and said, "So, you leave *her* the stadium. But you leave *me* alone with its secrets. Old friend, that's just not right."

Old Stadium Site

West Oakland

It was too late. By the time Luis arrived, two men were hoisting his uncle into an ambulance.

Luis hid behind a discarded refrigerator and peered out, reviewing the drill he'd rehearsed with his uncle a million times: *Hide, and do NOT follow if they come to take me away.*

But Uncle Tomas looked so alone and vulnerable on the gurney. And they'd strapped him in, like an animal.

Then the ambulance doors closed. One of the men said, "This place is scary, man."

The other said, "Copy that. I'm just glad I got my vaccinations!"

Vaccinations? Luis had no idea what that meant. But if it was something that made this place less scary and also cost money, he knew he hadn't "got" them.

While watching the ambulance drive away, Luis struggled to keep his promise to stay behind and hidden. But in the wake of its departure, another sound emerged that he recognized as the Nice Lady's station wagon. He ran after it, her, his hope for bread.

Monarch Terrace Apartments

Downtown Oakland

Patty Dobrovski stared at apartment #308, debating whether to knock.

But I gotta, she told herself. Because everything was going sideways to hell, she was way over her head, and she could think of no one else to talk to. She was going to lose her mind if she didn't make contact with another human being, no matter how superficial.

She knocked. The door opened to the limit of its interior chain guard. Someone from within said, "Well, what the . . .? That you, Patty?"

"Hi, Gianni," she said, glimpsing a slice of his leathery face and one chestnut-colored eye around which radiated many fine creases. So many pockmarks and stubbles, but, still, that alluring crooked grin.

He unlocked the door and ushered her into the living room. Which also appeared to be the dining room. And bedroom. And storage room. "Sorry things are messy," he said. "I wasn't expecting company."

"Well, I would've called if I had your number."

"How'd you know to find me?"

She smiled nervously. "Remember the first time we met?" But he merely shrugged, leaving her to feel embarrassed. "Anyway," she shouldered on, "you showed me the map you drew of your worksite that day, and I kept it since. I thought it was pretty, to tell you the truth. Colored pencils and all. But on the other side was your name and this address. Look." She withdrew the drawing from her purse.

Gianni instantly recognized his drawing: a map plotting out a work order for gutter drain installations and asphalt repairs at the stadium. He said, "Now I remember. You'd just taken over management of the homeless camp there." He also recalled showing her the drawing in hopes of seducing her with his artistic sensibility. *And, wow, it took a while, but my strategy finally worked, because she's here now. But what the fuck? How could I have been so careless?* He'd drawn the map on the backside of an official Moretti Landscaping invoice reserved for his legitimate, above-the-table business. But his under-the-table jobs for select clients, like the enigmatic boss who supplied him with the stadium work, had to remain untraceable and undocumented. "Well," he said, "mind if I take this back for my tax records?"

Patty looked crossly at him, humiliated by his dismissive response, especially after she'd complimented his drawing skills. She argued, "But it's already near a year old."

"Yeah, see, I'm a visual guy. When my boss at the stadium calls and tells me what to do, I sketch it out. Like my dad always did when he ran the business. Course, he didn't speak much English. Anyhow, our sketches are our business records."

"Just who is this boss of yours? I never seen you working with anyone at the stadium."

"Truth is, I never met him. He's got a funny English accent, and we always talk business on burner phones." He pulled his out from a pocket and said, "See?"

"Your way of business sounds shady," she said, feeling argumentative. "And if that's how you keep your business records, why aren't there any money figures on that map?"

Gianni felt backed into a corner. *If I make her any more upset or suspicious, she might go yapping about my "shady" way of business to people. She seems ornery enough.* But if his boss heard that their shadow arrangement had been exposed—a conceivable notion, given that Patty ran the non-profit supporting the encampment—he'd lose his stadium gigs. "Truth is," he said, appealing for understanding, "I get paid in cash, and the money gets dropped off in a postbox on Franklin. There's no dollar figures or signatures written down anywhere because we don't want to leave a paper trail. But, see, this English guy who calls on the burner pays way more than I can make through my regular business. I can't afford to lose the stadium gig. We just don't want Mr. Tax Man coming to visit."

Patty suppressed a laugh. She was definitely understanding of—and, herself, dependent upon—the shadow cash economy. But though accepting of Gianni's "way of business," still, she was smarting from the sting of humiliation. Needing to retaliate, she said: "You can have your stupid drawing. Don't know why I even kept it, come to look at it again."

"Now, don't be mean like that," he said, giving her a hurt look. "I just can't risk evidence of my stadium jobs being out in the world. It's a condition of my employment."

Patty felt relief, witnessing how upset he'd become, realizing she could affect him. "So," she said, looking around the apartment, "this address on your invoice—it's also where you live?"

It was his turn to feel humiliated, but finances were tight. Sheepishly, he replied, "Well, I guess I'm gonna ask you to keep another secret. But please don't tell anyone, because this building isn't zoned for commercial use."

"Don't worry about me," she said. Then, unable to stop herself, she needled him with: "Least, not for now."

They smiled uncertainly at one another. He said, "Stay a minute," and proceeded to clear space on the couch. "How about a beer or water, Patty?"

Sitting down, maneuvering to avoid a mysterious red stain on the taupe upholstery, she thought it safer to choose a bottled or canned beverage. "A beer if you got one to spare."

He winked and headed to another room. Meanwhile, she looked around his "office" and was struck by how un-officey it appeared. No desk. No computer or printer. No file cabinets, office chairs, landline.

Still, bags of planting and potting soil were stacked high against the walls.

Gianni reappeared with two beers and a question: "So, tell me, Patty. What *really* brings you here tonight?"

"I was in the neighborhood," she said, pulling her can tab and taken by surprise when froth instantly gushed out and onto her.

"Sorry," he said, offering her paper napkins that seemed to be in small piles everywhere in the room.

She daubed the beer on her shirt and scowled. Then she sighed, adopted a confessional tone, and said: "I wasn't just 'in the neighborhood.'"

He took a swig of beer. "Waiting."

Looking somewhat forlorn, she said, "I just been feeling lonely a while. And, well, you see how long I held onto your address." She guardedly took a sip of beer. "So much bad shit started happening near a year ago. And then, all of a sudden, *everything* went sideways to hell for me. Now I got nothing and no one to turn to, and you're the only person been half-decent to me."

He tried to sound convincing when he replied, "Nah. That's hard to imagine."

She shook her head. "The few times we ran into each other at the stadium? You were always nice enough. And to other people, too."

"I sound like a saint," he laughed. "No one's accused me of *that* before!"

Pointing to his soil stockpiles, she said: "Like when you help that woman and her little girl grow vegetables in that hellhole. If you hadn't given them all that good soil . . ."

"Truth is, I can't take *all* the credit. My boss pays for it—though he don't know that. I just make sure I have a little extra dirt and time when I go to the stadium." Gianni laughed and said, "Guess that's secret number three, Patty! But that woman and her kid—they remind me of my folks, coming from Italy, trying to grow food for the table."

"Still, that's nice what you do."

"Wait up now. What about your boyfriend? Isn't he nice to you, too?"

She nearly gasped, and reflexively placed her hand over her necklace key. *He can't know about that.*

Looking concernedly at her, troubled by her silence, he asked: "Are you saying the guy with the crazy red hair isn't nice to you?"

Her tension suddenly released. "Him? His name's Red, and he's not my boyfriend."

Gianni's expression conveyed doubt. "Well, whenever I've seen you together, you look, shall we say, 'intense.' And 'Red' never speaks to *me*. Just passes me through the gate. I thought maybe he was a jealous type."

Patty rolled her eyes. "'Intense'? Yeah, maybe. But trust me, it's not *romantic* intense."

"Oh? Then . . . what? You drug dealing with him? Or—"

"Please! No love, no sex, no drugs. *Period.*"

"Wait up now. Calm down."

"Sorry," she said, getting up to leave. "It was stupid to come here. And an intrusion on you. I don't know what I was thinking."

But he threw his arms around her and kissed her so long and forcefully that she almost fainted. When they disengaged, she gulped for air. He said, "There's more where that came from." Before she could marshal any response of her own, he removed his shirt and kissed her again.

ER Exam Room

Oakland City Hospital

"Tomas Ruiz. Forty-ish-year-old male, found down twenty minutes ago. No history. Vitals unstable, systolic skirting 80. Was in torsades."

"Thanks," Fergie replied to the two EMTs, who helped to transfer Tomas' limp body to the bed. Lizbeth hung IV fluids and connected the cardiac monitor while Aditya began the examination.

"Any witnesses?" asked Fergie.

The EMTs shook their heads. The shorter one said, "He was alone, inside a tent. In a backlot behind the old sports stadium."

"Homeless?" asked Aditya.

"Well, I don't think anyone goes camping *there*."

"How'd you get his name?" asked Fergie.

"Some woman who wouldn't identify herself called 911. Said it was a life-and-death situation."

"Thank god someone called," said Lizbeth, inserting a nasal cannula.

The taller EMT nodded. "The oddest thing, too. That backlot was filthy, and it smelled like everything was moldy or rotting. But when we went inside this guy's tent, it was clean as a whistle. And it smelled good, like a restaurant. Italian. Maybe Chinese."

Aditya placed his stethoscope over Tomas' heart and, now near the mouth, he smelled it, too: an aroma reminding him of his mother's kitchen. *Yes . . . her chicken tikka masala . . . her daal . . . the stovetop garlic naan that she secretly makes with store-bought pizza dough.*

"Well, whatever," said the shorter EMT, taking leave with his partner. "It's stirring up my appetite. Should we grab a bite somewhere?"

Fergie began a standard blood draw and asked Aditya, "What tests do you want besides the routine panel and tox screen?"

"A test to identify that aroma," he replied.

"Funny," she said. "Hurry, while I'm still drawing blood."

"Blood cultures, please," he said. Then, fearful of missing something, he hedged: "And draw an extra red-top to put aside." *I'm going to figure this out before Nora gets involved.*

Suddenly, Tomas opened his eyes. He looked directly into the blinding overhead lights and wondered if he'd died. But then he heard a woman addressing him in English, and he figured he was still in the old world. He took several deep breaths, trying to pin down his fugitive thoughts: *I'm lying on a mattress. There's a soft pillow under my head. This place is not cold or damp. Luis isn't pestering me with questions.* His attempted vocalization proved raspy: "Where am I?"

"In Oakland City Hospital," said Lizbeth.

"I'm so . . . thirsty," he said. "Can I have water, please?"

"Sorry," said Aditya. "It is not safe to drink until you are more conscious. Besides, we need your stomach empty so we can take special X-rays."

"Still," said Lizbeth, "we can moisten your mouth with swabs. And the IV fluids you're getting will help soon."

On her way out with the blood samples, Fergie said, "I'll run these to the lab and grab those swabs on the way back." Lizbeth smiled, pleased that Fergie was comfortable leaving her alone with such a critically ill patient.

Meanwhile, Aditya was examining Tomas' lower extremities, searching for physical clues to the mystery of his cryptic condition. But he observed no rashes, ticks, swelling, bruises, old surgical scars, rodent or insect bites. He palpated the feet and ankles: the soles felt scaly, but there was no pitting edema, and the posterior tibial pulses were symmetric, though weak. But when he rolled his pinwheel across the feet, Tomas didn't flinch, and his legs didn't withdraw from the normally painful stimulus. When the reflex hammer tapped against Tomas' Achilles and patellar tendons, there was no reaction. Aditya shot Lizbeth a concerned, knowing look.

Aware that the findings indicated a neurologic problem, Lizbeth asked: "Mr. Ruiz, do you feel *anything* when the doctor rolls his pinwheel over your feet?"

Tomas struggled to prop himself up in order to see. He watched the doctor roll a spiky pizza-cutter across his feet and legs. His eyes widened. "I see that thing pressing into me. But I don't feel it."

"Can you wiggle your toes?" asked Aditya.

"Of course. Wait . . ." Tomas was stunned, discovering his feet couldn't follow his intentions. And how odd that they could feel numb and painful at the same time. A panicked expression overtook his face.

"Let us stay calm," Aditya said, as much to himself as to Tomas. "We will figure out why you have a sensorimotor neuropathy."

"A what?" asked Tomas.

"He means, a problem with the nerves that control movement and feeling in your legs," said Lizbeth.

"But why?"

Aditya replied, "Many potential causes exist. And many are treatable, so we must stay hopeful."

When Tomas began to hyperventilate, Lizbeth tried to comfort him. She held his hand and said, "I'm going to breathe with you, okay? Nice and slow, together." She modeled controlled deep breathing, but Tomas didn't follow. In fact, his hyperventilation accelerated and he started gasping for air. Lizbeth wondered whether Aditya's incessant and disquieting inquiries might be aggravating their patient's anxiety: *Do you have diabetes? Cancer? Heart disease? Do you drink alcohol? Take drugs? Smoke? Have you lost weight, had fevers, chills, shortness of breath, chest pain, confusion . . . ?* The kitchen sink, really. "Aditya," she said, "please be quiet and let our patient breathe."

I'm doing it again, Aditya thought. *Missing what is in front of me because I'm so intent on being correct.* "Of course," he said, "and I will breathe with you."

But even their team modeling failed to inspire Tomas. His respiratory rate peaked, its pattern became irregular. His eyes closed, and his body went limp again.

"We must intubate!" Aditya said. "Set up a tray, please."

Lizbeth was already in motion before Aditya voiced his order. She'd pressed the code button, ripped open the intubation kit, and began arranging its contents on the table: laryngoscope, blades, stylet, ET tubes, Magill forceps, tape. Then, while she repositioned Tomas' head for the intubation, up close she identified what Aditya and the EMTs had smelled: an aroma of garlic that wafted from his mouth. Still, she said nothing, not wanting to distract Aditya while he intubated.

Aditya deftly inserted the laryngoscope and visualized Tomas' vocal cords, threading the endotracheal tube between them. Then he inflated the balloon to anchor the tube inside the trachea and exclaimed, "Just in time."

After waving away colleagues who'd responded to the Code Blue summons, Lizbeth said: "It happened so fast, Aditya! He suddenly stopped breathing. Why?"

"I do not know," he replied, calibrating the ventilator, hoping for his own adrenaline-fueled heart to slow down. But when he turned to face her, the answer had come and he let out a sigh. "I feel like a fool."

"Honestly?" she said, with unguarded exasperation.

Decided that he'd already exceeded his daily quota of embarrassment, he hesitated to admit his failure. But he'd suddenly realized that Tomas' hyperventilation wasn't of psychiatric origin. Rather, it had occurred because his diaphragm muscle had gone flaccid—something he should've considered in a patient with ascending motor weakness who began to hyperventilate.

"What?" she said, like an ultimatum.

He said in a confessional tone, "Our patient was hyperventilating because he physically *had* to, not because he was anxious or scared. His diaphragm muscle was failing, so his lungs could not move air in and out."

During recent weeks, Lizbeth had been tiring over Aditya's relentless self-flagellation in an unrealistic pursuit of doctorly perfection. It was proving heartbreaking, too, having to constantly witness his inability to celebrate the great good he routinely provided to his patients. Now watching him type clinical information into the electronic health record, she wondered if he would always be like this, constantly undermining his own happiness—and the possibility of theirs. Would she always have to bolster him and prop his ego? And why was it so critical for him to surpass Dr. Kelly's expertise? *It would be exhausting to live forever with a man like this.*

He looked up from the computer to find her staring at him. "What are you thinking, Lizbeth?"

She debated whether to reveal her misgivings about their relationship; not in this particular moment, but soon. Scrambling for some alternative reply, she recalled her observation of Tomas' fingernails and said: "Do you remember my 'nail file'?"

He shook his head. "Should I? Is it remarkable?"

"My nail *file.* You know. That folder I keep with pictures and medical articles about nail pathology?"

"Ah, yes. Your extensive *medical* file on nails *and* hair."

"Well, for whatever reasons, those topics interest me."

"Please! I was not being critical. Everyone in medicine has unique interests. You know about my files on parasites, especially schistosomiasis. Besides, at least your special collection is not as gross as mine." He paused, sensing she was holding back. "Oh, wait. Are you trying to say . . . did you detect something on our patient's nails?"

Lizbeth heard the self-doubt rush back into his voice. Clearly, she'd reactivated his insecurity. But she decided to take a risk this time. Rather than assuaging him, she stepped boldly into the possibility of a new dynamic between them. *If we're going to have an honest relationship, I need to be visible, too—even if that intimidates him.* She said, "Yes. I detected Mees lines on his fingernails."

Aditya returned to the bedside and saw that now: the thin white lines traversing Tomas' fingernails. "You are right. Classic Mees lines. They can signal almost any systemic illness, but often it is poisoning or infection."

Lizbeth steeled herself to continue: "And about his breath. If you sort out dental hygiene influences, you're left smelling garlic."

Aditya looked away momentarily while his deep insecurity placed its familiar stranglehold on him. Would he ever achieve the professional mastery of Nora or his grandfather? Then, suddenly, he realized: *My god, how terrible to see how difficult it is for Lizbeth to tell me what she found. What am I doing that makes her afraid?* But when he turned back to her, he saw her staring expectantly at him, her expression without any discernible judgment. Something shifted internally, creating new space in his self-punishing mind. He smiled and said, "I'm very impressed, Lizbeth Tanner."

"Honestly?" she said, her face relaxing.

He nodded. "And, I'm so sorry. I know I can be self-absorbed. But it is remarkable what we can see when we look together."

She was heartened to hear him say "we" without hesitation. "And what do 'we' see, Dr. Singh?"

"Unfortunately, we see arsenic poisoning. Our patient's garlic breath. His Mees lines. His thirst. The torsades and neuropathy and respiratory failure. His scaly soles. It is most likely Mr. Ruiz suffers from arsenic toxicity."

Psychiatry Office

Glenview District, Oakland

"You mustn't be so fearful. And I return in a few weeks."

"Actually," Nora replied, "in six weeks and a day."

Her psychiatrist, Dr. Solène Barteau, said, "You are very precise. As if you had counted."

Nora blushed. "Well, the *last* time you took an extended vacation . . ."

Dr. Barteau nodded. "Yes. February 2017. Still, you survived and moved on, no?"

"No" is correct, Nora thought.

Dr. Barteau continued, "I'm confident you'll be fine while I'm away. You also have my colleague's number if you wish to talk with somebody. Your alprazolam has refills. *Vous comprenez?*"

"But I think I'm beginning to experience your imminent leave as another trigger for a panic attack. It feels as threatening as anything more directly linked with Lydia's murder."

Glancing at the clock, Dr. Barteau said, "Again, I'm sorry for that. But we have only three minutes left, and I need you to listen carefully. *Oui?* You must remember while I'm gone—"

"To France again?"

Unflinchingly, Dr. Barteau said, "If we had more time, I would explore *why* you ask. I would not answer that question, but together we would explore your need to know."

Nora expected that response. She wished she could drop by Lydia's tonight with a bottle of merlot and review this psychotherapy session with "Frenchie." She wished she could sit on Lydia's couch and sing together *Que Será, Será*—the most healing type of couch therapy she'd ever experienced.

"But," Dr. Barteau continued, "as I started to say, there are things you *must* keep in mind during my absence. First: you've been severely traumatized. Your family drowned four years ago; two years later, your best friend was killed, and her killer stalked you."

Nora gasped. Hearing all the trauma so starkly laid out threatened to erase the "post" from her post-traumatic stress disorder.

"Secondly: you've steadily improved. *Oui,* of course, an occasional step backwards; but always followed by a longer one forward. You've been able to return to work . . .

But only if I wear my squeaky shoes.

. . . "renew your friendship with Jacques . . .

It's "Jack."

. . . "and survive several major holidays without Lydia or your family."

Thanks to the California wine industry.

"So, Nora, you must see those successes as evidence of your strength and capacity to conquer fear."

"Why do I feel like you're about to award me a merit badge for effort?"

"I don't know what you mean by that," said Dr. Barteau, rechecking the time. "But we must end now."

Walking to the door, Nora said, "Well, have a nice vacation in . . . wherever."

"Wait," said Dr. Barteau. "A final matter. If you do identify triggers for your PTSD while I'm gone, you must remember that they've never destroyed you. No fatal bullets have been discharged. So, if you feel that you're in the crosshairs again and a trigger is pulled, you must remind yourself that the gun isn't actually loaded."

Old Stadium Site

West Oakland

The kid's return was taking too long. "The little shithead," Red muttered to no one in particular. "Well, fuck. Let him figure things out for himself. That didn't hurt me any."

He reached through the window to retrieve the saucepan he'd placed on the hood of his truck. After transferring its rainwater to his water bottle, he zipped up his black leather jacket, reclined the seat, and lay back. And, as was often the case when he closed his eyes before sleep, he saw it happen all over again, as vividly as his original witness of it two months ago: He's standing in a supermarket, deciding what to buy with the few dollars in his pocket, when his parents appear in the aisle. It'd been nearly three years since they'd kicked him out of their home. Their eyes meet his with willed oblivion. Then they blithely pass by with their food-laden cart.

Red was awakened some time later by thumping on his truck. Reflexively, he grabbed his knife and looked out the window, only to see little shithead, shivering and drenched. He grabbed a blanket, got out of the truck, and told Luis to dry himself off. Then, after ushering Luis into the passenger seat, he halfheartedly warned, "Don't be getting my truck all wet."

Luis' teeth were chattering, his face was shiny and swollen. Red handed over a dry sweatshirt and told him to put it on. "And quit sniveling, okay?"

Luis' struggle to hold back tears proved short-lived; moments after putting on the sweatshirt, he dropped into sleep.

Inn-N-Out Motel

Near the MacArthur Maze

Someone knocked on the door. Yusra gasped. Who was coming for her now?

Another knock.

She instinctively considered hiding under the bed, but then remembered the tracer dust on the carpet and the Nice Lady's threat.

"Open up!" someone shouted.

She didn't recognize the voice with the TV still blaring. *But even if it's George Clooney . . .*

"Yusra, open the door!"

It was the Nice Lady! But fearing she was being tested, Yusra replied: "You told me not to." She remembered the security guard who lured her mother out of their detention cell with a bag of chips, only to punish her for stepping out.

Pound, pound, pound!

"Don't hurt me!" Yusra cried.

Silence. More silence. Finally, the Nice Lady said, "I lost my key. Let me in. I'm not gonna hurt you."

Yusra knew she had no good option. Punishment would follow, regardless of what she decided. So, hoping at least for the scary pounding to stop, she unlocked the door. She looked up at the Nice Lady, who stared warily back.

Nora's Home

Montclair District, Oakland

Nora uncorked the merlot and put her feet up on the coffee table. Bix, her tuxedo cat, joined her on the couch.

"Wow," she said, surprised by his voluntary company. "Even if I don't have treats for you?"

He crawled onto her lap and purred while she sipped wine and stared out through the bay view doors opening to her upper deck. Car taillights crawled along the Bay Bridge toward San Francisco, dimmed by the ash-strewn sky. She considered checking the current air quality and status of the wildfires up north, but decided against the predictably depressing reports. Instead, she relaxed into the couch and reviewed her work day; what a full but interesting one it'd been. Enlivening days like today made it difficult to envision early retirement, though she'd been considering that prospect nightly the last two years.

Now her mind alighted on Daleen Habani. *What a mysterious woman, and with such a rare and troubling disorder. Most patients lie to you, but Daleen seemed more secretive than deceptive. And she chose silence over dishonesty when questioned about her family or home.*

And what a relief it'd been—initially, at least—when Daleen summoned her back to the room to talk. *But the price I had to pay for that!* Still, there seemed to be no other way to obtain the information she needed to decipher Daleen's illness. The bargain they struck allowed her to ask Daleen, and expect answers to, any clinical question. That had allowed Nora to review lists of medications and chemical exposures that could cause methemoglobinemia; Daleen denied any known exposure to them. And then the family history: Daleen knew of no family members with inheritable blood disorders, although she knew almost nothing about her scattered and threadbare family. Given the clinical information she could obtain and considering Daleen's age, Nora determined that the methemoglobinemia was an "acquired" condition. *But acquired how, from what, and where?*

And what about her daughter Yusra? Why is Daleen so fiercely secretive about her, even pretending not to understand the social workers? Why would any mother refuse help from authorities to secure her child's safety? If I had a daughter . . .

When I had a daughter . . .

Nora looked at portraits of family and friends on the fireplace mantle: her daughter and husband, parents and grandparents, Lydia—all dead. Then, eyeing the photo of her gang-of-six residency mates, she whispered: "And just four of us left standing."

When Bix reflexively darted away, Nora decided to shift as well, and began sorting through plans for tomorrow. But the increasingly troubling bargain she'd struck with Daleen was weighing on her mind. Still, she resolved to keep her end of the deal: in the morning, she'd stop by the hospital to obtain Daleen's instructions about locating Yusra at the old stadium; then, she'd drive to the stadium to make contact with Yusra on her mother's behalf. But, per Nora's insistence, it was mutually agreed that they would notify the police and social services if Nora didn't find Yusra in the safe circumstances that Daleen guaranteed.

After setting Bix up for the night with his usual treats, Nora headed for bed. Flopping onto the mattress, she realized how ambivalent she'd been feeling about the outcome of tomorrow's search for Yusra. *Of course, I want to reassure Yusra about her mother's safety—and vice versa. But could the life of a six-year-old girl living under child protective services be any worse than living in a homeless camp?* And the old stadium, after years of closure and neglect, had to be uninhabitable. In fact, a month ago, she'd heard it described as such by another patient who'd lived there—a migrant Nigerian fieldworker named Abeo, who died from organophosphate toxicity. She remembered attributing his death to pesticide exposures in the fields where he'd forcibly labored, and even filed a report with the health department—which had yet to elicit a response. After making a mental note to follow up with them after the holiday weekend, she resumed thinking about tomorrow. Besides her stadium visit, she needed to pick up appetizers for Carrie's Thanksgiving dinner. That was her customary assignment for any group meal, owing to her notorious culinary ineptitude. And, thankfully, she was ahead in planning: she'd already checked the internet for stores conducting business on the holiday, and the stalwart Emeryville Target would open tomorrow at five P.M. *This year,* she thought, *I might forgo the pretense of arranging the hors d'oeuvres on my serving platters. Does anyone ever fall for them being homemade anyway?*

Carl's Home

Piedmont

Fergie checked on her two veggie lasagnas, hoping to finish in Carl's kitchen before he came home. His obsessive attention to her habits and whereabouts had been wearing her down. Still, for the millionth time, she reminded herself of his great generosity in allowing Winston and her to live gratis in his guest suite. Had he not offered to share his home, they'd have been forced to move somewhere affordable beyond the Bay Area. And it was hard to imagine leaving her job at Oakland City's ER. Hard to imagine not joining friends tomorrow at Carrie's Thanksgiving—

"Hey!" Winston belted out from the doorway.

She jolted and said, "You jerk! You scared me on purpose again!"

"Well, happy to see you, too," he said, wrapping his arms around her.

She shoved him away. "Not funny! I could've dropped the lasagna or burned myself."

"Doubt that. Because I was observing you through the door and studiously plotting a safe moment." He pulled her close and kissed her until she laughed.

"You're still a jerk," she said, returning her attention to the oven.

He sniffed and said, "The lasagna smells great."

"Good. Because I was pressed for time and made two: one for dinner tonight, one for Thanksgiving tomorrow. But in this oven, it's taking longer than I expected. And I'm so tired. I was hoping to finish before Carl—"

"Hello! I'm home!" Carl announced, loud enough to ensure they'd hear, in keeping with their informal cohabitation agreement.

Winston whispered, "Just finish baking. I'll keep the conversation alive."

Carl appeared, put down his briefcase, and surveyed his bustling kitchen—quite unlike the empty stage it usually was. He languorously inhaled the complex aromas, wondering when was the last time his kitchen had smelled of something other than cleaning products. He said, "Neither Cheryl nor I cooked. But we owned all this expensive cookware. She loved buying things."

"Oh?" said Winston. "You always ate out?"

"Not *always*," he said. "Some dinners were take-out or delivery. We purchased lunch at work. Breakfasts just didn't occur."

Winston and Fergie exchanged guilt-ridden looks. Then Fergie offered, "Well, would you like to share dinner with us tonight?"

"Yes," said Carl. "And it will establish a new record for us, Fergie."

"Sorry?" she said, withdrawing lasagna pans from the oven.

"Because today we will have shared *two* meals. That'd be a first for us."

"Well," said Winston, setting the table, "it appears to be a record-setting day. Because it's also our first threesome dinner here in the main kitchen."

Carl watched Fergie and Winston transform his kitchen into an *actual* dining venue. It felt gratifying and disorienting at once. Plates, glasses, and silverware were removed from their designated storage locations. A rich aroma of garlic, oregano, tomatoes, and cheese replaced the standard vinegar-and-pine-scented air. The oven's heat had dissipated the usual coolness of this room. And, though he could barely tolerate it, he watched dirty bowls and utensils being stacked in the sink.

Noticing Carl's tense preoccupation, Fergie said: "Sorry, Carl. I should've asked permission to use your kitchen. I just needed a bigger oven for two lasagnas, and I figured I'd finish before you got home."

"No permission is required," he said. "We made a cohabitation agreement concerning schedules that allow each other privacy in this house. But you're welcome to use this kitchen any time. Your guest-suite kitchenette is only forty-two square feet, which must be limiting occasionally."

After they all sat for dinner, Carl asked Fergie: "What happened with the blue patient this morning?"

Winston's eyes widened to accommodate his astonishment. He was used to overhearing them discuss, in a humdrum sort of way, odd and extraordinary medical conditions. Shocking diseases, ghastly accidents, harrowing births . . . cited like items on a shopping list. And, having been educated about Carl's aversion to metaphors, this time he matter-of-factly said: "A *blue* person?"

"Yeah," said Fergie, ingesting a forkful of lasagna. "She has methemoglobinemia. Something that makes your skin look blue."

"Is it permanent?" asked Winston, clearly alarmed.

"No," Carl answered.

Winston privately marveled at their seeming nonchalance: *Shouldn't this merit more robust discussion?* He said, with incredulity, "I can't imagine what it would take to amaze you two. But, as a layman at the table, it sounds mind-blowing what you've witnessed."

Fergie and Carl looked at one another, shrugged, and continued eating. Winston thrummed his fingers on the table and, finally, asked: "Okay. Why would a person turn blue?"

Carl set down his glass, adjusting its precise central placement on its coaster. "A person could turn blue through various mechanisms, so the differential diagnosis is broad. Some causes are hereditary, while others are acquired during life. We've established that our patient's discoloration is due to methemoglobinemia; and, having expressed that condition for the first time during her adulthood, she's undoubtedly acquired the problem. An adult acquires methemoglobinemia usually by ingestion or exposure to a drug or toxic substance that exceeds the enzymatic capacity of normal hemoglobin to reduce—"

"Excuse me," Fergie interrupted, watching Winston's head spin. "But Nora read lists of the usual suspects to Daleen, who said she wasn't aware of any contact with them."

"Huh," said Winston. "Could the exposure be occupational? What kind of work does she do?"

"I heard she grows vegetables. Maybe she sells at the farmers' markets downtown?"

"She'd have to own a good-sized plot to live off that. Where does she live?"

"All I know, is somewhere near the old stadium. But you could ask Nora at dinner tomorrow, because in the morning she's driving to the patient's home."

"That makes sense," said Carl. "Nora is a consummate diagnostician. I remember her driving to a pet store in Fremont in 2002, to investigate whether its parrots were the infectious source for her patient's psittacosis. In 2010, she collected food samples from an Emeryville restaurant to test for salmonella because of three sickened patients who'd eaten there."

"I'm impressed," said Winston. "She'd make an excellent investigative reporter."

Fergie said, "I don't think her stadium visit is in keeping with that tradition." She covered the second lasagna with foil, handed it to Winston, and said, "Put this in our fridge for tomorrow."

"Why?" asked Winston.

Carl said, "Because you should always refrigerate lasagna—any perishable consumable—for food safety concerns."

Winston said, "Sorry. I meant: then why would Nora be driving to the patient's home if not to investigate her patient's meth . . . methema . . . her illness?"

"Because," Fergie said, "when I asked Nora how she got our patient to talk, she said she had to make some 'deal' with her. She wanted to tell me about it, but she'd also promised Daleen to keep it confidential."

"Intriguing," said Winston.

"I suppose," said Fergie, rinsing glasses in the sink. "But the entire time I was in the ER with the patient, the only thing she'd ask about was her daughter. Ergo, I'm guessing the deal involves Nora contacting the daughter in exchange for the clinical information she was able to get."

"That's brilliant," said Winston.

"I disagree," said Carl. "Nora shouldn't get involved like that. She could be endangering herself. If the patient has been afraid to reveal her child's precise whereabouts, it may be for reasons of an abusive or violent domestic situation—one that Nora would be walking into, alone. And for all we know, that child could be ill, like her mother, and Nora has no clinical or legal authority to initiate the child's care. It also speaks poorly of the doctor-patient relationship when you must *bargain* with a patient for clinical information."

"I meant," said Winston, "it was a brilliant deduction on Fergie's part."

"Only if it proves correct," said Carl. "It's premature to assume that now." He watched fretfully as Winston cleared the table. Then, recalling how Nora had kept him company at his wife's deathbed, he announced, "I'm going to accompany Nora tomorrow."

"You're going to the stadium?" asked Fergie.

"Yes," said Carl, moving edgily toward the sink. "And I'd like to finish cleaning up."

"You sure?" she said, secretly wishing to be relieved of the task.

Carl couldn't fathom why Fergie would remain uncertain after his clearly stated declaration. Besides, everything had to be cleaned in a specific order.

Sensing his internal struggle, Fergie succinctly offered, "Thanks." She followed Winston to the stairwell leading to their guest suite. As soon as the door closed, Carl began regrouping the dirty dishes on the countertop. Then he stole back to the table to clear the crumbs that Winston had missed. With those pressing tensions resolved, he returned to the sink, held the soap in his left hand and the sponge in his right. Finally, proper order would be restored.

~ ~ ~

Part Two

Thunder

THURSDAY, NOVEMBER 22

*They claim this Mother of ours, the earth, for their own
and fence their neighbors away;
they deface her with their buildings and their refuse.*

SITTING BULL

Morning

NORA WAS AWAKENED by her cell's ringing. She fumbled for her reading glasses. *Carl? Calling me at seven-fucking-o'-clock! And on a holiday!* She answered, "Carl?"

"Yes," he replied. "Didn't your phone identify me?"

"Yeah, but . . . why are you calling?"

"Because during dinner last night, Fergie said you made a deal with a patient. She suggested it might entail you driving to the stadium this morning to establish contact with the patient's daughter. Is that correct?"

Nora stalled. "I don't remember telling Fergie that."

"That's not what I asked."

She sighed.

He said, "Your silence, in context of the confidentiality you reportedly promised your patient, conveys the answer. I'll pick you up in thirty minutes, then drive you to the hospital and stadium. Goodbye."

"No!" she said. But all she heard was the dial tone.

~ ~ ~

Luis awoke with the sun in his eyes and the strange red-haired boy sleeping beside him in the front seat of the truck. Trying to remain quiet, he pushed off his blanket and reached for the door handle. But when he thought through his escape, he realized he had no safer place to be. Uncle Tomas had been carted away in an ambulance. No one was home at Yusra's. The sooty air was still hard to breathe. Even the Nice Lady passed him by twice yesterday.

He looked appraisingly at Red and wondered how a person could be so bright white. Did he shine in the dark? He'd watch for that tonight.

~ ~ ~

Winston roused Fergie with a kiss. "Happy Thanksgiving," he said, exaggerating his usual baritone.

Fergie groaned. Still, she privately acknowledged her good fortune in having such a sexy and affectionate husband. She tousled his thick black hair, and traced a finger around his chiseled cheeks. "Why are you waking me so early?"

"Because," he laughed, "*I'm* up." He pressed his body against hers to make his point.

"Ugh," she said. "Let me sleep."

"C'mon, Fergs. I need something to remind me that I'm alive if I'm going to spend all evening with your work buddies."

"But you like most of them."

"That's not it. It's . . . well, it gives me the creeps, seeing Carrie. She looks exactly like Lydia."

"Because they were identical twins, genius! And, wow! Finally, someone scares *you*?"

"With her living in Lydia's house . . ." He adopted a menacing tone: "Whenever we visit, I feel Carrie channeling Lydia. Their voices are the same . . ."

"What's *really* creepy is you trying to scare me again!"

"Carrie dresses in Lydia's clothes . . ."

"That's it!" shouted Fergie, smacking Winston with a pillow.

"Bring it on," he laughed. "Great foreplay!"

~ ~ ~

Yusra rolled over in bed and stared down at the carpet, wondering whether it was actually covered with tracer dust. Then she glanced at the Nice Lady, who was still sleeping in the clothes she'd worn last night. She pressed her hands against her mouth, stifling a cry.

But: "Oh, hell," the Nice Lady muttered. "I hear your sniveling."

Yusra hid under the covers.

"Just what I need," said the Nice Lady. "Well, happy Thanksgiving to *me*!" She walked to the TV and turned on the Macy's parade. "Watch this," she said, yanking off Yusra's covers. "And try to be a little appreciative. Try to get in some holiday kinda spirit!" She shuffled to the bathroom and slammed the door.

Yusra glanced at the TV and saw an enormous bloated rat, bigger than any she'd seen before. It floated eerily above tall buildings, in the sky above gawking crowds. Now she pressed her hand against her mouth, trying not to scream.

~ ~ ~

"It's our first Thanksgiving as a couple," said Lizbeth.

Aditya readjusted settings on Tomas Ruiz' ventilator and said, "The first of many."

She smiled. "I just wish the holiday weekend wasn't delaying Mr. Ruiz' test results. It doesn't seem right. Patients can't coordinate getting sick around holiday schedules."

"Agreed. But we are doing all we can. At least we got his hair and fingernail samples delivered to the specialty lab before it closed yesterday. That puts us ahead in the queue of any holiday backlog. And we will receive results of his urine screen today."

"But you said spot urine tests weren't reliable for arsenic poisoning."

"Still, they are useful to tell us about *any* arsenic exposure within the last several days. But of course, we are most interested in evidence of chronic exposure. And because nails and hair store arsenic over time, they give us the better answer."

"Well," said Lizbeth, "just in case, I've initiated standard nursing decontamination protocols and sent Mr. Ruiz' clothes to biohazards management. Have you decided about starting treatment presumptively?"

He shook his head. "I called the poison control center; they were iffy about us starting chelation therapy with DMSA." Then, after brief deliberation, he smiled at her and added, "But I will consult with Nora. First, we must admit Mr. Ruiz to a monitored bed."

Lizbeth nodded appreciatively, then looked worryingly at Mr. Ruiz and said: "I wish we knew more about him. And all the while we wait for confirmation of his diagnosis, other people could be exposed if something has been poisoning him."

"Some*thing*," said Aditya, grimacing. "Or, some*one*."

~ ~ ~

Daleen checked the time: 8:10 A.M. If Dr. Nora Kelly was going to keep her promise, she should be here soon.

A nurse walked in. He said, "Good morning, and happy Thanksgiving."

She nodded.

He said, "I'm going to take your vitals now. Your breakfast should be up any minute. But we're always short-staffed on holidays." He checked her IV site. "And the social worker's at the nursing station, so she'll be here soon." He stepped back and studied her. "You're mighty quiet, sweetheart. What language do you speak?"

Daleen sized him up. His practiced niceness and pristine blue uniform. His ostensible obliviousness to her dire circumstances. His chipper Thanksgiving greeting. *They are all blissfully unaware,* she thought. *And they must designate a day to remind themselves to be thankful for all they have. So American.*

Old Stadium Site

West Oakland

The creak of the passenger door opening awakened Red. He asked Luis, "Where you going this time?"

"I have to pee," said Luis.

"Well, go then. Don't do nothing like that in my truck."

But Luis hesitated. It was cold and rainy outside, and a long trek through mud and puddles to his usual private spot for personal business.

Red sighed and tossed a CVS bag to Luis. Pointing to a nearby metal shed, he said: "There's a drain-ditch behind that shed. Flushes everything away when it's raining."

Luis held the bag above his head and ran out, once losing footing on the slimy ground. He found the drain-ditch gurgling with rainwater, and happily relieved his bladder in it. He watched his urine flow downstream toward a storm drain, wondering if it would ultimately join the ocean.

Loud rat-a-tat-tats sounded from within the metal shed, so he peered curiously into it. Through a shattered window barricaded with iron bars, he saw raindrops tapping against rusted storage drums, one leaking fluid with a beautiful oily sheen. How strange, he thought, to see rain falling inside a building. Stranger, still, to look up and see sky through the roof.

This shed could be fixed up, he optimistically supposed. *It could make a nice house for me and my uncle.* Yes, a tarp—perhaps, even, their orange tent—could be tacked up for a roof. He could clean out all the garbage inside and repurpose the metal drums for tables. He'd need to cut the padlock off the door, but Red probably knew some guy who could do that. Perhaps he could begin the work now, and surprise his uncle when he returned from the hospital, whenever that might be.

Luis reached through the window bars to catch drops of rain from his future home. Then he ran back to the white truck. And though he found Red pounding furiously on the dashboard, he opened the door and went inside.

9th Floor Hallway

Oakland City Hospital

Nora steadied herself against the wall, breaking a fall-in-progress.

"Sorry!" said the woman rushing out of Daleen's room.

Viewing her crossly, Nora said, "You can't go running around here! Hospital corridors aren't racetracks."

"Forgive me. Are you okay?"

"Yes," said Nora, collecting herself, trying not to sound so shrill.

"You look familiar," said the woman.

"I'm an ER doctor here. And you?"

"Of course," she replied, rolling her eyes. "If I'm going to knock over *someone* today, it'd have to be a doctor."

Nora's brows arched, and the woman said: "I didn't mean it's worse to knock over a *doctor* than . . . gosh . . . another human being. It's just more . . . more *something*." She groaned. "Look, if you want to report me, my name's Lola, and I'm the 9th floor social worker."

"I don't want to report you. I just want you to be careful."

"You're right. I'm *literally* running today. I was assigned holiday coverage for *two* floors."

"Well, so . . . you probably just spoke with my patient, Daleen Habani?"

She rolled her eyes again. "I wouldn't say 'spoke with.' More like, 'spoke to,' because she wouldn't tell me anything. But I've been doing this work a long time, and it's my opinion she's not talking because she's afraid. Afraid of what, I don't know. But her behavior's typical of someone who's been traumatized. Like someone with PTSD."

Nora looked away momentarily, trying to conceal any visible flash of self-identification with the diagnosis. And after they parted ways, she steeled herself and entered Daleen's room.

~ ~ ~

Meanwhile, having just driven Nora to the hospital, Carl waited in the ER for her return after visiting Daleen. But the wait was proving more unsettling by the minute. He found himself in the unusual position of wrestling with a categorically irrational impulse as he stood, for the first time since his wife Cheryl's death, in the exact spot where he'd argued with her the night before she was murdered. His dread expanded exponentially with each passing second.

But it makes no sense to feel anxious just standing here! Cheryl is gone, her murderer was imprisoned 648 days ago, and I'm in no danger. And what's even worse than the anxiety is knowing I'm being irrational—

Someone screamed. A primal scream, a male voice, down the hallway. Carl froze. But then another scream followed, clearly from Lizbeth, and he ran reflexively toward her.

Inn-N-Out Motel

Near the MacArthur Maze

When Yusra heard the Nice Lady's shower running, she decided to take her chance. She put her doll and leftover hamburger into her Rite Aid bag of personal belongings. She stuck the ketchup packets inside her anklets. Then she stole out of bed, planning to be long gone by the time the Nice Lady finished showering. The tracer dust on the carpet would merely confirm her obvious escape.

But when she tiptoed past the TV with its ongoing parade coverage, an enormous inflated snake popped up and slithered across the screen. She involuntarily gasped and dashed for the door.

Monarch Terrace Apartments

Downtown

Gianni decided to forgo a shower. Though he'd done the deed with Patty last night, the transaction had been tidy and efficient—*Just the way I like it. Besides, no way around it, I'm gonna get down and dirty at work this afternoon.*

He gathered the empty beer cans from the living room—one rimmed with the bruised half-moon left by Patty's purple lipstick—and reflected on his good fortune in not having had to put out for a dinner or drinks with her. Then he scanned the room to make sure nothing had been stolen. Though Patty seemed like a nice gal, he'd interacted with her only a handful of times—all briefly, until last night. And though regretting she'd become privy to his "way of business" at the stadium, he had to accept fault for leaving the invoice with her in the first place. *Hope I can trust you, Patty.*

Now downing coffee, he reviewed the map he'd plotted for today's stadium job. After estimating the cubic feet of soil it would require—*And a little extra for the quiet lady's garden*—he dragged the requisite number of bags to the doorway. All the while, he found himself wondering whether Patty had a good time last night. Then he slung the first bag over his shoulder and headed out the door.

Guest Suite, Carl's Home

Piedmont

Fergie watched Winston typing at the desk, struggling, she knew, to meet his deadline for the newspaper. It amazed her that, after so many years, she remained so curious about him. And desirous, too. Studying his statuesque profile and graceful flurrying fingers, she wondered at his effortless beauty. "Win," she called from bed, "come back for an encore."

"Can't," he said, without looking up. "This piece is due tomorrow. I won't have time to work on it tonight since we're going to Carrie's dinner."

"Surely, you can spare one paragraph for the time of your life."

He watched her remove her bifocals and fetchingly bare her tattooed chest and arms. "Fergs, you're killing me! But you're also killing my column in the process."

"What are you working on *instead* of me?" she asked.

But he returned his focus to his laptop. "On yet *another* low-income housing project that was scuttled for luxe condo development."

Fergie sank back against the headboard, frustrated. She had to remind herself about the importance of his advocacy for unsheltered people in the community. Since becoming the ER head nurse, she no longer had time to volunteer. *The least I can do is support his work.*

Hoping to mitigate her disappointment, he carried his laptop to the bed and sat beside her. "Let's at least stay close."

She agreeably nodded, and he resumed his typing. But whenever he glanced up from this new position, he saw through the bay window a jaw-dropping, gazillion-dollar view of the East Bay Hills and San Francisco skyline. It distressed him every time. *How can I sit here, writing about the plight of homeless and poor people?* He felt like a phony. That he'd morphed into somebody else after moving from life lived "on the edge" to Carl's mansion. In truth, he'd become *comfortable,* with a free roof over his head, steady employment with the *Oakland Register,* and Fergie's increased salary as head nurse. The sense of righteous anger that had driven him to write about social and economic injustice had been tamed; perhaps, even, delegitimized. His felt urgency about writing had shifted from its internal wellspring, toward externalities like jobs and deadlines.

Noticing his pensive expression, Fergie asked, "What's wrong?"

He looked intensely at her while also looking intensely inward. Finally, he shrugged, put down his laptop, and said, "Excellent question."

Then he grabbed his Warriors jacket and promised to return after a short but necessary walk.

9th Floor Ward Room

Oakland City Hospital

"I'm glad you're feeling better," said Nora.

Daleen replied, "Thank you. When can I go home?"

"Well, I'm not the doctor who determines that. Once you leave the ER and are admitted to the hospital, I'm no longer in charge of your care."

Daleen couldn't understand the sense of rotating doctors while a patient was ill. Still, she said, "I understand. And, have you kept your promise?"

"I've told no one. But, to be honest, I've been feeling uncomfortable with our agreement."

"But we know *they* will take my daughter from me if *they* get involved!"

Nora paused before responding: "But that could happen anyway, right? Remember our agreement? If I don't find Yusra safe, I'm obligated to contact the police and social services."

With firm conviction, Daleen said, "You will find my Yusra. She is very smart and resourceful. She knows how to survive on her own." She handed Nora a sheet of paper and said, "This is where we live. At this X, behind the stadium, in the D-lot."

Nora studied the drawing. "Anything more specific?"

"We have no addresses or street signs," Daleen replied with a hint of rebuke. "But our camper is easy to find. It is beige with a black stripe."

Nora's gut knotted. "Might anyone be there with your daughter?"

"She will be alone. If she is not there when you arrive, she will be visiting her friend Luis, who lives in the nearby orange tent."

"So," said Nora, "we haven't spoken explicitly about this, but I'm wondering if you're living there in a homeless camp?"

"We *have* a home!" snapped Daleen. "My Yusra *has* a home there with *me*. And no social worker can—"

"Sorry. I didn't mean—"

"We have each other and our community!"

"Again, sorry. I'm just trying to prepare for what I'm walking into."

"And I'm telling you. You will be walking into my *home*, and into my *community* of friends and neighbors. They are good people."

"Of course. But will members of your community have a problem with me visiting? I'm a stranger, and I'll be at your camper. And if I find Yusra, how will she know to trust me?"

"I am prepared," said Daleen, handing over a scarf-wrapped bundle. "Yusra will recognize this and trust you. And you can show it to the red-haired boy at the gate if you need to."

"I see," said Nora, recognizing the maroon scarf as Daleen's.

"And you must reassure Yusra I will see her very soon."

"I will," said Nora, though feeling pressured to deliver an unduly optimistic message. "Oh, by the way, I need to stop for groceries, so I could pick up a few things for Yusra."

"I can take care of my own daughter."

"Of course," said Nora, turning away.

"Wait!" Daleen called out, acutely aware of how hardened she'd become since forced to flee her homeland. *But soft people don't survive what Yusra and I must.* "I understand today is a special holiday in America. And I want to say thank you for doing me this favor."

ER Exam Room

Oakland City Hospital

When Carl rushed into the exam room, he found Lizbeth struggling to restrain a patient. She pleaded, "Help! He's trying to pull out his ET tube!" Aditya was writhing on the floor.

Carl swiftly analyzed the scene. (A): An agitated patient was about to injure himself by yanking out his breathing tube. (B): Lizbeth was likely to be hurt if she continued wrestling with him. And (C): Aditya was already injured, likely during a scuffle with the patient. It was obvious what must be done: he yelled "Stop!" so loudly that it succeeded in grabbing everyone's attention. Then, in one seamless efficient move, he grabbed a syringe, deflated the anchoring balloon, and withdrew the patient's ET tube.

The patient fell back into bed, coughing spasmodically while also attempting to apologize. Aditya stood up with Carl's assistance and said, shamefacedly, "This is my fault. I should have extubated Mr. Ruiz earlier, when he started getting agitated. But I was rushing around, and I thought I had more time." He pressed a hand over his abdomen and doubled over.

"You're injured," said Lizbeth.

"I will be fine," he replied. "Just . . . a little sore, here where he kicked me."

"Over your spleen," Carl noted. "Did you pass out?"

"I'm not sure. It happened so fast. For some reason . . . wow . . . now my left shoulder really hurts."

Carl said, "The pain in your shoulder likely reflects a positive Kehr's sign."

"What's that?" asked Lizbeth.

"An indication of splenic injury involving rupture, when pain radiates to the shoulder," said Carl.

"That cannot be," said Aditya. "We are too busy. We have only a skeleton holiday crew."

"Aditya!" said Lizbeth. "Please listen to Dr. Kluft."

Aditya's eyelids fluttered and he slumped to the floor.

Saint Frances Cabrini Church

East Oakland

Samantha Greeley told her chauffeur, "I won't be more than fifteen minutes." Then, as a family representative had done on Thanksgiving for generations, she entered Saint Frances Cabrini Church and headed to its dining hall. But . . .

How rude! No church officials here to greet me? No photographers, no reporters? And these volunteers look like they've nowhere else to be on Thanksgiving. She instructed someone stacking biscuits to notify her when the priest "finally arrived," and that she'd wait inside the church "five minutes, *max.*"

Samantha took a pew in the empty nave and used the downtime to phone her boyfriend Marty with her final decision: that, against his wishes, she was not going to fire his father Quentin as her primary legal counsel. Of course, that would upset Marty. But she had no good cause to fire Quentin, who'd served her family so well and so profitably for nearly three decades. The bad blood between Marty and Quentin wasn't her problem. Yes, Quentin was ancient; but she'd seen no evidence to support Marty's contention that he'd been losing his marbles. No, not given Quentin's ongoing successes with Greeley business matters, including the imminent sale of that albatross stadium property. And though his services were inordinately expensive, he'd flawlessly provided the one thing she most desired: personal and psychic distance from the internal operations of Greeley Enterprises.

Still, Marty was a hothead. She knew that about him the moment they met in Quentin's law office when she happened to walk in while he was cursing-out a young boy who'd delivered pizza "cold as fuck." But his heatedness also aroused her, as did his thick-muscled torso and bad-boy swagger. The fact of him missing a left ear oddly intrigued her.

Expecting Marty's anger, she nonetheless called to inform him of her decision to maintain his father's services. He replied, "Sam, you got to reconsider."

"Not really," she said, reminding herself, and him, who was the boss. "Besides, it's Thanksgiving, and he's coming for dinner, as he's done for centuries. You're cruel to suggest I'd fire him today."

"I can't tolerate it much longer," said Marty. "He keeps getting in my way. And you got to tell him about us. Hell, I should be with you at dinner tonight—not him."

"I'm not going to choose between you and your father." And before he could launch another rebuttal, she cut him off with: "I must go; the reporters have arrived." But of course, they hadn't.

She looked at the statue of Saint Frances Cabrini that loomed near the altar. It appeared to be eyeing her judgmentally. "Don't look at me like that," she said, getting up and walking out.

Old Stadium Site

West Oakland

Red stopped banging his fist on the dashboard when Luis entered the truck. Still, Luis fretted: *What did I do?* Maybe, he thought, Red realized he didn't want to share the drainage ditch behind the shed after all; everyone in the camp was fiercely possessive of some small private claim on this property. Or maybe Uncle Tomas was right to warn him against Red, who just might be going ballistic on him now. The tension was unbearable, and Luis blurted out, "I'm sorry!"

Red looked puzzled. "For what, you little shithead?"

"I don't know," Luis said, fighting back tears. "But I'm sorry if I did something bad."

"Wow," said Red, looking blankly through the windshield at the entry gate. *This kid is so fuckin' damaged. Like me, at his age, except for him being nice. He'll never make it alone out here.* "Think about it," he finally said. "Why would I be mad at you? Unless you did something I don't know about. Did you?"

Luis shook his head. "Not that I know about either."

Red smiled. "That's funny. And pretty sad."

Not understanding Red's response, Luis asked, "Then why are you mad?"

"It's got nothing to do with you. Thing is, the battery in my phone is dead. So now I got to drive to Betty's or somewhere to charge it."

Luis had eaten once at Betty's, and his memory of a quarter-pounder kickstarted his appetite. He said, "I went there one time."

"Betty's? It's my favorite place."

"Mine, too," said Luis, beaming.

Lake Merritt

Oakland

Winston Wang loved to feel cool rain on his face, and to hear rain-drops ping off his leather jacket. He loved the rain's unique enliv-ening scent, one he could never precisely describe. Walking around Lake Merritt now, he could better sense himself in the world. On a day like today when Mother Nature was proving unpredictable, he could feel the unpredictability of his own nature resonating with the heavens.

He loved this lake, so large and improbably located in the center of a city. A harmonious blend of city and country, of mundane yet transcendent beauty, it offered an occasion for his mind to wander wherever it needed to.

Today, he was trying to re-center. He'd become unbalanced after living in Carl's mansion for twenty-one months—tiptoeing around Carl's schedule, losing self-direction and solitude. And just having to worry about disturbing Carl whenever he and Fergie made love . . .

He'd lost a quiet sure sense of himself. The old authentic voice that arose from his heart and mind to inspire his writing had become nearly inaudible. *Who am I now? Who am I to be writing about homelessness and poverty, living in a mansion?*

The hounds of self-loathing and self-doubt gathered at his heels now. Enacting an instinct to escape them, he impulsively ran. But no matter how fast and furiously he ran around the lake, they followed close, up Lakeshore, past the amphitheater and boat house, then along Harrison and the Cathedral of Light . . .

He stopped abruptly at the pergola at the lake's north end. Dozens of people in pup-tents and sleeping bags were gathered there, seeking shelter from the rain.

MacArthur Maze Area

Oakland-Emeryville Border

So many railroad tracks to cross, Yusra thought, making her way through the scrapyard near the motel. The Nice Lady was probably out of the shower now, but Yusra doubted she'd come to this junky place searching for her.

She stood on a track and, scanning it in both directions, wondered how to tell its end from its beginning. She wondered whether this particular track channeled the loud trains that regularly passed near the camp where she lived. Some of them were so long, she wondered if one could reach her real home in Yemen.

She removed the itchy ketchup packets from her anklets and added them to her Rite Aid bag. Then she continued walking toward a chainlink fence topped with spiraled barbed wire. Because it looked exactly like the fencing surrounding her camp, she expected it would likewise offer a breach or two through which she could pass.

Indeed, after following the fenceline a short while, she found a passable opening and snuck through it. She found herself in a garbage-strewn enclave beneath a highway overpass. It contained old mattresses and sofas. Refrigerators without doors. Plastic pipes and jugs. Crates, cloth, and carts. The place felt very familiar. *But why is no one living here?*

After checking the cushions for insects and used syringes, she sat down on a damp blue sofa and contemplated her next move. But try as she might, she couldn't figure out the direction back to her camper, and she had no idea where her mother might be. *But the Nice Lady knows the answers. Because she took my mom somewhere, and she took me from our home. And she lied about being my mom to the man at the motel. She is no "Nice Lady" at all.*

Yusra remembered her mother's warning about strangers who could take them away. And she'd learned about "kidnapping" and "human trafficking" from discussions she overheard in detention centers and jails. At least she'd escaped the Not-Nice Lady's clutches; her mother would be happy to hear that. *But how will she ever find out?*

Wondering what terrible thing was going to happen next, she rummaged through her Rite Aid bag and withdrew her doll and the lavender stalk she'd taken from her mother's garden. She held them tight, praying for a sign that would tell her where to go.

Old Stadium Site

West Oakland

When Gianni drove through the stadium gate, he called out to the red-haired guard whose name, he now knew, was Red: "Happy fuckin' Thanksgiving, asshole." He considered that a friendly yet manly way to greet another guy. Indeed, happily, Red responded in kind: "Fuck you, too, A-hole." But then Red drove out in a seeming hurry, thwarting Gianni's hopes to chum him up.

In fact, having learned that Red and Patty weren't involved, Gianni had wanted to tell about last night's sex, playfully rubbing it in, gloating. That might've even initiated a decent fight with Red to match the enviable "intensity" he'd witnessed between him and Patty.

Still, as overdue for a fight as he felt, Gianni conceded that Red's quick departure was probably a good thing. There was just too much work to do today. Two drainage ditches to dig. More dirt to excavate and replace. Sinkholes to fill in. A half-flat of lettuce seedlings for the garden by the camper. And afterwards, he'd have to drive to the Emeryville scrapyard to drop off the excavated dirt.

So he drove his flatbed, laden with soil bags and landscaping equipment, to the southernmost tip of the stadium complex where an oak tree canopy provided some protection from the spotty rains. Having just driven past scores of people living in tents and old vehicles, he experienced gratitude for his comparatively good fortune. Then he breathed in Patty's lingering scent on his body, sweetly blending with the sweat and soil on his work clothes; the aromatic infusion of earth and sex made him feel alive and vital. *Like a man.*

Reviewing his mapped-out work order, he prioritized the drainage ditches that would divert water from buckled sections of parking lots that had become minor lakes. But the shoveling proved backbreaking, the ground being so wet and heavy. He decided to leave one ditch shallower than it ought to be, planning to return on a better day to correct its grading and depth.

He popped two aspirins and proceeded to his next chore: replacing six inches of so-called topsoil (clay, predominantly, also made heavier by the rains) in a seven-by-seven plot. After loading the excavated dirt onto his flatbed, he sliced open nine bags of soil and poured them in. This step always gratified: standing within soil-clouds that billowed and swirled around him, everything smelling of tobacco and leaves and forests and farms. Of earth. Of life.

After attending to the sinkholes, he drove to the beige camper where the small quiet woman and her daughter lived. He swapped out some soil in their vegetable garden, and planted seedlings of butterhead, romaine, and red sails lettuces. When finished, he whispered, "Paying it forward," as an homage to his parents, who had struggled to live off the land as newly arrived immigrants themselves.

But it being exceptional that neither the woman nor her daughter had come out to greet him, he knocked on their camper door. Odder still, no one answered, not even after he identified himself by the name they'd given him: "It's me, the Nice Man."

Getting no response, he called it a day and walked back toward his truck. It looked so sleek and clean after the laundering rains. Furtive flashes of sun made its black cab gleam, its aluminum siderails shimmer. *Such a handsome devil,* he thought, *if I say so myself.* He'd designed and supervised every stage of its conversion—from an unremarkable Chevy pickup to a landscaper's dream truck. He could fondly recall the day when the steel flatbed fitting was installed. When the post-and-slat aluminum siderails were fitted into the stake pockets. When the rear swing-out gate was bolted on. Then, finally, the toolboxes and gooseneck ball hitch. *My boy,* he thought, stepping onto the flatbed.

After packing his equipment in the toolboxes, he reached for a tarp to throw over his dirt haul. But two of the tie-down cleats were buried beneath it, and it felt like a hassle to clear them. Besides, he reasoned, the drive to the Emeryville scrapyard was short, and the rain had tamped down the pile.

So he hopped off the flatbed and secured the rear gate. Before driving away, he glanced back at the camper, surprised to be feeling gloomy about not seeing the lady or her daughter. He chalked it up to some alone-on-the-holidays effect, and headed for the exit, hoping to run into Red. But when he arrived at the gate, Red wasn't there; his gloom expanded, and he felt inexplicably achy. Then, minutes later, nearing the scrapyard, he decided to invite Patty to drop by again.

ER Doctors' Workstation

Oakland City Hospital

Nora texted Carl from the ER doctors' workstation: *M Here. Where R U? Ready 2 go.*

While waiting for his response, she grew curious about the contents of the scarf-wrapped bundle Daleen had given her. She knew it was probably expected that she not open it; still, technically, she *hadn't* been told. *Besides,* Nora reasoned, *I should know what I'm transporting to a child on behalf of someone I barely know.* So, she unknotted the bundle and peered inside. Her heart ached instantly. She saw applesauce cartons, pudding cups, a half-sandwich, cranberry juice boxes, and cellophane packets of soda crackers—certainly the hospital food that Daleen had been served.

Carl appeared and, noting Nora's reddened eyes and somber expression, asked what was wrong.

"Nothing," she said.

"The evidence suggests otherwise."

"You're right," she said, drying her eyes. "It's just . . . Daleen asked me to deliver this package to her daughter. And it's filled with her hospital food."

Considering her evident distress, Carl decided to spare her the news of Aditya's injury for now. Instead, hoping to strike a positive note, he offered, "It's nutritious."

His off-point comment made Nora realize she required more than rote logic to allay her mounting trepidation about her trek to the stadium. The circumstances concerning Daleen and Yusra were feeling murkier and more desperate by the minute. Longing for the camaraderie of someone fluent in chaos, she decided to phone Jack.

Infirmary, San Sebastian Prison

Marin County

Dr. Jack Griffin, completing his morning shift in the prison infirmary, told his last patient: "Mr. Vaughn, I'm sorry the news isn't good. But I'll make calls to UCSF. They're expert with brain tumors."

"Forget that," replied Pete Vaughn, aka Inmate CDC1244. "And stop calling me 'mister.' I'm not your damn father."

"Okay, *Pete*. But they can at least shrink your tumor to minimize your headaches."

"Did you hear, man? I said *no*."

Jack stared at his patient, wondering whether he was in denial or simply playing tough guy. Perhaps his tumor was impairing his cognition and judgment? "Well, for my edification, can you explain why you're rejecting treatment that would help you feel better?"

"None of your damn business," said Pete, hopping off the exam table. He rapped on the door to summon the guard.

It had been only six months since Jack had begun working at this prison—the same prison in which he'd been unjustly incarcerated. Still, he felt as though he'd discovered his lifetime calling in the practice of prison medicine. Here, he could consistently deliver excellent medical care to people who always needed it. With hope, but in vain, he called out after Pete, "If you change your mind . . ."

Jack put away his stethoscope and entered a progress note into Pete's clinical record. *More accurately, an un-progress note.* Then he leaned back in his chair and reviewed his plans for the remainder of Thanksgiving. *Now the difficult part of my day begins.*

He'd always despised Thanksgivings, even while Richard was alive. But without him, they'd become insufferable. And after having spent considerable time in prison, as either inmate or physician, he'd lost his tolerance—and his gift, really—for small talk. With fingers crossed, he checked his cell, hoping, but failing, to find a colleague's offer of a night shift in the infirmary.

Also ahead: the task of cooking—another interest, and skill, that had withered after Richard's death. Granted, his assignment for tonight's dinner at Carrie's was simple: the garlic mashed potatoes. But he doubted his ability to deliver on Nora's separate but insistent request: "and to bring a positive attitude."

Minutes later, he was on the Richmond Bridge, driving home to Oakland. The Thanksgiving traffic was moving so slowly that clumps of wildfire ash remained undisturbed on his Mazda's white hood. He glanced at the ten-pound sack of Yukon Gold potatoes on the passenger seat and complained, "How's anyone supposed to feel thankful in traffic like this?" Realizing he'd be arriving home later than anticipated, he added, "Thank god I picked you up yesterday." *Wait,* he thought, *I'm talking to potatoes?* But then he instantly reassured himself by recalling inmates who'd befriended even less animate objects: light bulbs, tennis balls, even spoons. *And Tom Hanks befriended a volleyball named Wilson on that deserted island.* Feeling sufficiently right-minded, he glanced back at his potatoes and said, "I'm naming you Chip."

Finally, they crossed the bridge. But during the drive, Jack had developed second thoughts about Chip's imminent stovetop fate. He was relieved when his cell rang, providing a distraction. "Nora," he answered, "tell us you're calling to say that dinner was canceled, and I'll love you forever."

"It's not," she replied. "But seriously? That's your condition for loving me?"

"Of course not!" he said. "But you know how I feel about thanks-fucking-giving."

"Yes. But we agreed to be each other's wingman tonight. Don't even think about bailing out on me like you did last year!"

Jack groaned. "It's different for me. We're going to *Carrie's* and, except for the gray hair, she looks and sounds *exactly* like Lydia! Lydia, who loved you, but despised me."

"Lydia didn't 'despise' you. We've been through this before. She just felt blindsided when you finally came out, after all those years of your friendship. Besides, there'll be lots of wine at Carrie's tonight, unless I get to it first. So, be on time."

"Are you calling just to make sure I'm going to show up?"

"No. Actually, I'm calling for a favor." She whispered, "I'm in the car with Carl. We're driving to the old stadium. I'd appreciate your company."

"Pray tell, why are you going *there*? Wait. Let me guess. They're staging a B-52 dance rave? Another Fleetwood Mac cover band?"

Suddenly feeling foolish, Nora hesitated to explain her desire for his companionship. His teasing only made that worse.

Following an awkward silence, he said: "You know the stadium was shut down, maybe ten years ago?"

"Hey, forget it. It was a silly ask."

"Whoa, now. I love the B-52s. And Fleetwood Mac. Most of all, I love *you*. So, you want my company? I'm there, Nora."

"So, you can still love me, even if dinner isn't canceled?"

He laughed. "Look, it's even convenient to meet you there. We're still in the car. So, just say when."

"Well, *now*. Carl and I should be arriving at the stadium in about ten minutes."

"Okay. We just got off the bridge, so I can be there in twenty. But where exactly?"

"The stadium's between Industrial and Tornwaldt," she said, wondering why he'd started self-referring with the royal "we." "You enter through a gate on 4th, then pass through several parking lots until you get to the D-lot. There's a small—"

"Nora," Carl interrupted. "I couldn't help but overhear your conversation. The most practical advice is that Jack drive to the furthest lot and look for my blue Tesla. It should be obvious, and we'll have arrived at the camper well before him."

Jack smiled at Chip while Nora relayed Carl's advice. He told her, "Copy that. Blue Tesla, D-lot. We'll see you soon."

When he hung up, he realized he'd been so intent on supporting her, especially after embarrassing her, that he'd forgotten to ask for the *why* of her stadium visit.

Old Stadium Site

West Oakland

Patty Dobrovski parked on Industrial and walked up to the chain-link fence surrounding the old stadium. Making sure no one was watching, she pushed aside the plyboard that concealed a passage hole and snuck inside. She kept telling herself to stay calm, but Red's accusation echoed harshly inside her head: *It's your fault, Patty.*

She pulled up her hood, wrapped a scarf across her mouth, and headed for Daleen's camper. The encampment was eerily quiet but for the wind grazing the stadium buildings and the occasional barking dog. People seemed to be ensconced in their tents and cars on this rainy Thanksgiving, and for that she was grateful. But then, as inconspicuous as she was trying to be, she reflexively shouted "Damn!" when she saw that Red's truck wasn't stationed at the gate. *The audacity! Him blaming me for anything that doesn't go right around here, when he doesn't even provide the security I pay him for! And how often does he pull this shit behind my back?* She railed, "Well, I ain't paying you for today!" Then she took a photo of the unattended gate, should she need it as evidence.

She proceeded onward, trying not to stumble over buckled asphalt and cement, PVC pipes, and aluminum cans. Pools of rust-colored water obscured potholes below. Finally, she reached the beige camper and searched its surroundings; but Yusra wasn't there, and the camper's sunroof appeared undisturbed. Still, with slim hope that the girl had somehow snuck inside, she knocked on the camper door, calling out Yusra's name. After getting no response, she held her breath and then unlocked the door. And when she looked inside, her great fear was affirmed: Yusra was missing. *Oh, god. Red's right. I keep screwing things up, and this is my fault, too.* In reflex penance, she quickly tidied up the mess she'd created when she rifled through Daleen's and Yusra's belongings. When finished, she re-wrapped her scarf to cover her lower face, snuck out of the camper, and locked its door. Hoping no one had seen her, she started back toward her car as her cell rang. She answered immediately to preclude another untimely ring: "Whaddya want?"

Jarred by her brusque greeting, Gianni asked, "You upset with me?"

"Sorry," she said. "It's just . . ." She struggled to control her panic. "I try to help people. But it's not easy, let me tell you."

"Well," he said provocatively, "I know how helpful you can be, Patty. You certainly helped me out last night." She scoffed, and he returned: "So, let me help you get rid of your tension." Though he'd aimed to sound clever, he immediately regretted his oily tone.

She knew it was a terrible idea to accept his invitation, but . . . *But a man like this might really understand my personal situation. And I already know he conducts business in a like-minded way.* "All right," she said. "A drink or something later?"

"I like the sound of that 'something,'" he said, again regretting his tone. "I'm free after dumping dirt in Emeryville. We could try the new bar in Fruitvale."

"I'll meet you at your place at seven," she said, feeling slightly less panicked. "That'll give me time to swing by my apartment first, and time for you to clean up."

Guest Suite, Carl's Home

Piedmont

Apprehensive about the time elapsing since Winston left for his "short walk," Fergie went down to the basement garage and saw that he'd taken the Subaru. Because he'd been so somber and contemplative, she assumed he drove to the lake for one of his meditative walks. She'd give him fifteen more minutes before calling him home—

Home? Did I just call this place "home"?

It surprised her, thinking of this mansion—any mansion—as home. Stranger still, to realize how at-home she'd come to feel, living inside this elegant, fortressed bubble. Weighing in Winston's mounting uneasiness, she had to question whether they were paying too high a price for living here—rent-free, thanks to Carl's generosity; but at the expense of losing their insistent identities. Moving to this exclusive neighborhood was proving to be a radical psychological displacement that neither of them had anticipated.

And yet, the situation was providing Winston an unfettered opportunity to write. It was allowing them to build a savings account *finally*.

Noting Carl's Tesla was also gone, she went back upstairs and walked through "his half" of the mansion, looking for who knew what. The main kitchen where they'd shared dinner last night was now impeccably clean. So were the living and dining rooms, the guestrooms and library, the floor-to-ceiling mirrored entryway. In Carl's bedroom, the blankets and pillows were set grid-like in military precision. Across the hallway was Cheryl's old home office, reminding Fergie of a perspective drawing with its books and boxes and file cabinets rigidly squared and arranged—certainly, Carl's handiwork.

She paused a moment, trying to feel a sense of belonging here.

But only feeling greater displacement, she returned to the guest suite in a troubled, contemplative mood. She sat out on the deck, Dianne Reeves' *Quiet After the Storm* playing in the background, and looked searchingly into the rainswept landscape.

Betty's

City Center, Oakland

"I forgot my coupon," Red told the young woman working the counter at Betty's. He was instantly smitten by her radiant smile, her silver nose ring, her cobalt-blue hair.

"No problem," she said, winking conspiratorially. She withdrew a coupon from her jeans pocket and scanned it into the register. "My name's DeeDee, and I got you covered. So, what can I get you boys?"

Red smiled unguardedly. Then he peered down at Luis and said, "Did you hear the lady?"

Luis nodded, but he was afraid. He'd never ordered in a restaurant before. *What should I say? There are too many choices! Can't I just have a hamburger?*

"Hey, little man," said Red. "Don't stress over it." But Luis only cowered behind him.

DeeDee said, "Guess what? Turns out, you guys are our millionth customers for the day. That means you win a prize!" She glanced at the available stock and said, "Your choice: cheeseburgers or quarter-pounders?"

Red's smile broadened so widely, he momentarily imagined it exceeding the width of his face. "Well," he said, trying to contain his unwieldy reaction. "The quarter-pounders, please." He nudged Luis forward and said, "You heard that, little man? It's our lucky day."

"And," she said to Luis, "tell me what you'd like to drink."

Luis mustered all his courage and whispered, "Coka?"

Old Stadium Site

West Oakland

Turning onto Tornwaldt Avenue, Carl said, "I wonder whether this street was named after Tornwaldt, of cyst fame."

"Excuse me?" said Nora.

"For what?"

"I mean, what 'cyst fame'?"

He looked surprised. "I'm referring to the Tornwaldt cyst. It's rather common, Nora. Upwards of four percent of the general population have it and . . ."

She smiled mechanically and braced herself for an onslaught of medical trivia.

He continued, "Though a benign midline nasopharyngeal muco-sal cyst, it can become infected and cause halitosis or eustachian tube obstruction . . ."

While he waxed eloquent about cyst complications, she stared out the window, patiently registering each passing street as they moseyed toward 4th: *17th . . . 16th . . . 15th . . .*

"Still," he said, "in the differential of nasopharyngeal cysts, you must consider Rathke's cleft cyst . . ."

Tornwaldt. Rathke. Why, Nora thought, *do men need to stamp their names on everything—even mucous cysts?* Now arriving on 5th, she relievedly exclaimed: "Fourth is the next street!"

"Of course," said Carl. "Numbered streets are referenced as ordinal numbers and sequenced in an agreed-upon order. That's the convention."

As they neared their destination, more of the stadium complex became visible above the fenceline. "Foreboding" is the first word that came to Nora's mind. The closer they got, the more it looked like a collapsing world. The main coliseum and parking structures were fractured and crumbling. Roofs were caved in, windows were shattered.

Now driving along the perimeter on 4th, she caught glimpses of the interior grounds through the cyclone fence: a continuous sea of rubble and refuse.

When they arrived at the entry gate, they found it slightly ajar, so Nora got out of the car to open it. The air was gummy with soot; it smelled like a high-school chem-lab disaster.

They drove on in silence through the gate. The banks bordering the main entry were rolling hills of trash and industrial waste. Molding heaps of cardboard and newspapers, rotted wood pallets, discarded plastic containers . . . And despite all the detritus in evidence of human life, they saw nobody.

They took the road leading toward the main stadium and entered a landscape of apocalyptic ruin, strewn with gloomy artifacts of lives once lived. Cast-off refrigerators, opened to emptiness. Car tires, traveling nowhere. Tables and chairs, missing legs and backs . . .

Per Daleen's instructions, they turned onto the second service road behind the old stadium that led to the central homeless encampment. While Nora had seen many such camps throughout Oakland, she'd never seen one this large. There were dozens of tents and cars and makeshift shelters, and every inch of space between them was occupied by something. Shopping carts packed with bulging plastic bags. Milk-crates. Water bottles and jugs. Cardboard boxes covered with plastic. Vinyl tarps propped up by metal poles and wooden beams. A fire burned inside an industrial metal drum. And, tacked to an old utility pole, a hand-painted sign proclaimed: "Community of Hope and Dignity."

Nora's heart clenched. What a startling proclamation to make *here*. What radical insistence on optimism and faith. With painful incredulity, she thought, *This is where Daleen and Yusra live. This is where they survive.*

They drove beyond the central residential hub, drawing people's attention along the way. Nora guiltily wondered how many people might be housed for the price of Carl's Tesla or her own Prius.

Finally, they arrived at the narrow road that threaded through rows of dilapidated metal sheds that appeared to be made of rust. When they emerged into a clearing in the D-lot, Nora pointed to an old green bus stripped of its wheels and said: "Head in that direction."

"I know," said Carl, "I remember Ms. Habani's map."

"Of course, you do," she replied, looking around, absorbing the misery, and imagining how difficult it would be to live day-to-day with an unforgetting mind. Seeing this place, and haunted by her own trauma, she wondered: *How could anyone ever feel optimistic or hopeful if they couldn't forget a little?* She asked, "Are you ever burdened by your photographic memory?"

"No," he answered. "But Cheryl used to say it burdened everyone around me." His car's front tires dropped precipitously into a sinkhole, but he continued undeterred: "Did you notice these parking lots are also ordered by convention? Though by letters of the alphabet—"

"Stop!" she said, now spotting the lone orange tent in the D-lot. "We're nearing Daleen's camper."

Carl parked the car, and Nora grabbed Daleen's package for Yusra. They opened an umbrella and trudged several yards through mud and misty rain to the small beige camper surrounded by scrap metal—as had been described. Behind it was Daleen's garden, laced with lettuce rows that coursed between fava beans, beets, cauliflower and broccoli, parsley and chives. And though its lavender was waning, it sweetly scented the otherwise noxious air. Carl said, "I'm surprised these crops haven't been eaten by the animals that must be—"

"Excuse me?" someone said, in a tone devoid of apology.

They turned to see a large officious-looking woman fast approaching. "What are you doing here?" she demanded.

Nora tilted the umbrella to read the woman's face, which was mostly obscured by a scarf and hood. Carl replied, "We're looking for someone."

"Obviously," the woman said, eyeing Carl's Tesla. "Because you two sure don't live *here*. So, tell me what business you got with anyone who does."

"We have no business," said Carl, recognizing signs of escalating conflict between them. He mentally queued up several "remedial communication strategies" he'd been forced to learn at work, choosing "Common Etiquette for Uncommonly Divisive Times." He began: "Hello. I'm Carl Kluft, and this is Nora Kelly. What's your name?"

"Patty," she said, squinting. "And I'm *still* asking what you're doing here."

Although having harbored misgivings about coming here, Nora hadn't anticipated a hostile confrontation with a prickly stranger. She also suddenly realized she hadn't informed Carl about her promise to Daleen to keep this mission confidential. Aiming to preclude his unwitting revelation of it, she blurted out: "We're looking for a family member."

"Yeah?" said Patty, regarding them suspiciously, stepping closer.

Carl took note of the particular tension mounting between Nora and Patty. *They're both flinching, wincing while staring intensely at one another, and speaking with prominent inflections.* Strategizing to intervene with "Polite Curiosity," he asked: "Do *you* have a business here, Patty?"

Nora glanced at the camper, praying for Yusra to emerge so she could present Daleen's signature package. That would not only comfort both mother and daughter; it would also serve as a calling card to legitimize her presence.

"Matter of fact, I have a business here," said Patty. "I manage the nonprofit that supports this community."

"Oh?" said Nora. "Which nonprofit?"

Patty snickered. "Why? Because you know them all?"

"Well, no. But—"

"Tell me who you're looking for," Patty insisted, her hands fisting.

"Yusra Habani," Carl answered immediately.

Nora winced while Patty shouted, "You're lying! You said you were looking for a family member."

"But we are," said Nora.

"I know that girl's family, and it doesn't include either of you."

"Nora is technically correct," said Carl, about to clarify that they were searching for a family member—if even not one of their own.

Determined to keep her promise to Daleen, Nora said: "We're here with good intentions. That's all you need to know." Then she ran toward the camper.

Patty followed close behind, shouting, "No one's there!"

"I'll see for myself," said Nora, knocking on the door.

Short of breath from the pursuit, Patty removed the scarf covering her mouth and panted. Her round face blistered with rage. After catching her breath, she admonished Nora: "I told you so!"

Nora knocked again, though wondering whether she might be frightening any child inside. When she tested the door knob, Patty seethed: "That's it! I'm calling the police!"

Pulling out her cell, pretending to call, Patty internally cursed her bad luck in being left alone to deal with these intruders. What possible interest could they have in the young girl who'd gone missing? Still, she knew she couldn't actually call the police; that'd be akin to shooting herself in the foot. And the only two people who could potentially help her were gone: Gianni, at the Emeryville scrapyard; and Red, AWOL from his job. But then, to her sweet relief, she saw Nora and Carl head back to their car. Believing she'd scared them off, she shouted: "That's right! You liars get outta here!" Then Nora whispered something to Carl, who nodded and proceeded to the driver's seat. But after he positioned himself behind the wheel, Patty saw Nora drop her umbrella and run toward the orange tent.

"Hell!" Patty cursed, fueled by rage, taking off after Nora with such abandon that the aspired-to movement of her legs exceeded their physical capacity; her feet lagged behind her intentions and got caught in a pothole, her right ankle twisting sharply. She screamed bloody murder and struggled to regain footing. Meanwhile, Carl had driven to the orange tent and found Nora staring blankly into it.

"Yusra's not here either," Nora said. "No one is."

"Let's go," he said, noting Patty's limping yet imminent arrival.

"But Daleen's daughter . . ."

"Now!" he said, dragging Nora away.

When Patty arrived at the tent, all she could do was watch Carl's blue Tesla drive away. She doubled over in pain, trying to shift weight off her throbbing ankle, repeatedly muttering, "Fucking Red." If he were guarding the gate like he was supposed to, she could phone him now with orders to detain the car. Still, she phoned him anyway and left a different sort of message: "You're paying for letting the riffraff in! I could kill you, Red!"

Looking desolately around for a stick to serve as a cane, she realized that, despite all the commotion and her yelling, no one had come out of their shelters to check on her or offer their assistance. *Not a one. And after all I've given them?* How alone and demoralized she felt. Foolish, too; for surely, she'd self-sabotaged her mission to sneak inconspicuously into the camp to search for Yusra. Her yelling and cursing had to have alerted residents to her presence. Also, unwittingly, she'd informed Red that she was here. And even more worrisome was the intrusive couple who, whatever their intentions, were unlikely to forget seeing her here. *My god, I'm gonna look guilty if something happened to Yusra and people come here investigating . . .*

Patty limped back toward her car, finding it excruciatingly painful to crouch in order to exit through the fence hole. Her right ankle complained bitterly when her foot alighted on the floorboard and, with forlorn abandon, she sobbed. Wearily resting her forehead against the steering wheel, she wondered where her hard luck was going to take her next. *How am I gonna get out of this hell? Where is Yusra, and why were those people looking for her? Pete, baby—I need you bad. Why'd you abandon me here like this?*

Lake Merritt

Oakland

It happened so fast. Patrol cars converged on the pergola, and police officers poured out, demanding that the crowd disperse.

Winston couldn't believe that on such a cold rainy day—Thanksgiving, no less—homeless people were being forced to leave the sheltering pergola. "But," he told one of the cops, "they've got nowhere else to go!"

"Move on," replied the cop.

"Seriously? They're not hurting anybody."

"Last warning: move along."

"No!" Winston shouted, watching in dismay as the gathering disassembled. "This is wrong."

With a closed-lip smile, the cop gestured for a colleague to come over. Winston said, "I'm also a journalist."

"Look, Hemingway. We warned everyone here an hour ago, and everyone was offered shelter. We're following protocol. They're not."

Winston watched the crowd disperse—up Grand, down Lakeshore—so eerily quiet and submissive. "Hey!" he called out after them, "don't go!" His vigorous entreaty drew several people back.

"That's it," said the cop, cueing his partner to cuff Winston. "Willful obstruction of an officer's duty. Hope you're satisfied."

Betty's

City Center

It was the best burger Luis ever tasted. And Betty's didn't limit the number of relish or ketchup packets! His soda cup was so huge he had to hold it with both hands.

How wonderful it felt to be here. The restaurant was not only heated, it was clean and brightly lit. It had a real bathroom with a toilet that flushed, and a faucet that ran clear water. On top of everything, he and Red were the only customers. And it made him happy to see Red smile back at DeeDee whenever she looked over at them. He dared to fantasize about working here one day.

Red's cell buzzed, startling Luis. Red said, "It's nothing, little man. Just my old phone beginning to charge finally."

DeeDee approached their booth and asked, "Can I get you guys anything else?"

"You been nice to us," said Red. "But we're good. Right, little man?"

Luis nodded, and she asked him: "What's your name, honey?"

Honey? It sounded so sweet. Luis couldn't recall anyone calling him that before. Up close, DeeDee looked like an angel, and he assumed she was of the kind that lived on earth. He grinned impossibly wide and replied, "Luis."

"Well, nice to meet you, Luis. I wonder if—"

"Shit!" Red exclaimed when his phone chimed. Then, "Sorry! A work call popped up. I gotta take it. But I gotta keep my cell plugged in."

"No worries," said DeeDee. "Stay here and take care of business. Maybe Luis can join me behind the counter?" Luis put down the remains of his burger and eagerly followed her out of the booth.

Seeing Luis interacting with DeeDee in such a joyful manner, it dawned on Red that Luis would have a chance for proper care if he simply left him here. DeeDee was kind; she'd see to it that Luis was connected to the right social agencies. However that would turn out, it would have to be better than any existing prospect now.

Yes, after checking this voicemail from Patty, he'd walk out and leave Luis behind. He'd make an excuse—he needed to retrieve something from his truck—and then just drive away.

Red keyed-in his security code and then entered the password for the restaurant's free Wi-Fi. But while waiting for the connection, he made the mistake of glancing toward the counter. Luis was standing beside DeeDee, wearing an oversized Betty's tee-shirt, and smiling directly at him.

ER Observation Suite

Oakland City Hospital

Aditya's abdominal pain was agonizing, and by all accounts—the bloody peritoneal lavage, the ER ultrasound, Carl's diagnostic acumen—his spleen had partially ruptured. Equally painful was his feeling incompetent, having failed to manage an agitated patient and safely time his extubation. And now the chief resident had to be called in, on Thanksgiving, to cover his remaining shift. He glanced anxiously at the monitors for reassurance about his vital signs, dreading the potential prospect of emergency surgery or splenic embolization. He said to Lizbeth, "Some first Thanksgiving we are having together."

"It's Thanksgiving enough for me that you're doing okay," she said. "But I have to go; another GSW came in. Oh, and I asked Marissa to assume your nursing care."

"No!" he said too forcefully, initiating jolts of abdominal pain.

"Aditya," she said, "it's unethical for me to be your nurse." Then she kissed his cheek and left.

He knew she was right. Still, if he couldn't be touched in the ways he'd hoped to be touched by her tonight, it would console him a little to feel *her* hands assessing his abdomen for tenderness, *her* hands massaging his back, her hands checking his IV sites.

The hospital transporter appeared and said, "Aditya Singh? For CT?"

Aditya nodded and held out his wrist band for identification.

"Yup," said the transporter, "it's you." He unlocked the wheels of the hospital bed and pushed Aditya out the door, heading for radiology. Aditya felt every little bump on the floor like an icepick to his belly.

Old Stadium Site

West Oakland

While driving through the stadium's gate, Jack's cell rang. Nora was calling, but he decided not to answer, being so close to where they'd be meeting.

On his way to the D-lot, he was shocked to see so many tents and rundown vehicles on the stadium grounds. They hadn't been visible from the adjacent road he traveled weekly to visit Richard's grave. Occasionally, people peered out from their shelters when he passed. Once, he nearly hit a man who emerged out of nowhere with a jowly, rain-worn dog.

His cell rang again—*Nora, again*—but he was almost there. Besides, the unevenly flooded roadway left no predictably safe place to pull over to answer. But, moments later, when he reached the D-lot, Carl's blue Tesla was nowhere to be seen. "Unbelievable," he complained to Chip, picking up his cell and calling Nora directly.

She answered immediately: "I've been trying to call you!"

He replied with evident exasperation, "Well, I'm at the D-lot, but I don't see you guys anywhere."

"Because we're not."

Jack rolled his eyes at Chip and admonished Nora, "Well, it would've been nice had you informed us earlier about changing your plans. This place is toxic and heartbreaking! We were already at the gate with your first call."

"But we *were* there."

"And what? You suddenly decided you didn't desire my company?"

"Argh! Give me a minute to explain. But first, lock your doors and tell me precisely where you are."

Jack scoffed. "Nora, they don't have street signs or mile markers here. And why are you sounding like such a drama queen?"

"Because I'm worried. Something weird is happening at that camp. There's a missing six-year-old girl, and some crazy lady named Patty is somehow involved. She just chased Carl and me out of the stadium."

"Well," he said, double-checking his doors, "we don't see any 'crazy lady' here."

Noting yet another occasion of Jack using a plural pronoun in self-reference, Nora wondered whether he was still struggling to accept his aloneness after Richard's death. She softened her tone and said, "I'm sorry about all this. But Carl just dropped me at home, so how about coming here so we can talk?"

Jack glanced ruefully at Chip and told Nora: "Can't. I've still got to make the mashed potatoes for tonight. But you're probably prepared, right? Your legendary store-bought appetizers and orange cheese tubs?"

Nora groaned. "Guilty. But, no; I'm not prepared. I'm waiting for Target to open at five. But, just a thought—you could come with me and pick up mashed potatoes at the Target deli. I won't tell. Then we can drive to Carrie's dinner together."

Jack was surprised to experience such relief from a proposition that would spare Chip's stovetop demise. "Sounds great," he said, keying the ignition, winking at Chip. "We'll be at your house in fifteen."

~ ~ ~

"Hang tight, little man," said Red, pressing the accelerator, speeding down 4th toward the stadium while Luis mostly worried about his soda spilling. Upon seeing the wide-open gate, Red shouted, "Fuck!" He hurriedly parked inside and ran back to close the gate. After returning to his truck, he pulled a coin from his pocket and furiously rubbed it between his palms.

"What's that?" asked Luis.

"My lucky quarter," said Red.

Luis sensed something terrible was happening again. He waited for Red to cool down before asking what was wrong.

Red muttered, "Nothing." But, seeing Luis' tortured expression, he added: "You didn't do nothing wrong."

Still, Luis looked worried, and Red felt guilty about having planned to abandon him at Betty's. He said, "Sorry, little man. I shouldn't've yanked you out of Betty's like that. But that call I got was from my boss. And she was pissed as hell I wasn't here."

"You have a job?" Luis asked, his jaw dropping.

Red laughed. "Yeah. A sucky one. But it gets me by."

"What do you do?"

"I work for this woman named Patty. She took over here for her boyfriend, about a year ago. I do whatever she tells me to do. Mostly. But my main gig is guarding this gate and keeping the riffraff out."

Now it made sense to Luis why Red had always seemed to be lurking around and monitoring people. He couldn't wait to explain this to his suspicious uncle once he had the chance. He asked, "What's 'riffraff'?"

"Hah, little man! A riffraff is someone like *me*."

"But you're inside here already," Luis said, confused.

Red put his lucky quarter away. "I'm riffraff everywhere *except* here. But that usually means the jackasses you don't want around. Like the thugs and suits who try to come in here to mess with us—kick us out, arrest us, harass us. Those kinds of things."

Luis liked the sound of this new word, even if it conjured menacing people. Red would never be riffraff to him. And what a happy day it was turning out to be! Now he'd learned about *two* great jobs he could confidently imagine pursuing someday. He gazed appreciatively at the Betty's tee-shirt he wore—

A loud knock on the driver's window. Red grabbed his hunting knife from under the seat; Luis ducked down as instructed. Red looked out to see a tall, blond, middle-aged man with an angular jaw and Olympic smile who was waving at him.

Red cracked open the window. "Who are you?" he asked. "How'd you get inside?"

Jack cocked an eyebrow. "Well, the gate was open. I drove through. And that's my story."

Red closed the window and whispered conspiratorially to Luis, "Riffraff." Then, after telling Luis to stay put and lock the doors, he got out of the truck. He eyed Jack head-to-toe and glanced at his Mazda. "I ain't seen you or your car here before."

"It's my first time," Jack explained. "Well, since a Holly Near concert here in the '70s. No, no—a Prince concert in the late '80s. Anyhow, I have an appointment with a friend in a few minutes. Would you mind moving your truck so I can get out?"

Fuck, thought Red. *Patty will literally kill me if she learns this riffraff got in! She's already ballistic about me being AWOL. But there could be worse hell to pay if I just let him go and he ends up causing trouble.* He stepped intimidatingly close to Jack and said, "You from the police? Immigration?"

"No."

"Don't make me guess! The state? The *what*?"

Jack's smile melted into a perplexed expression. "I'm just a guy who came looking for a friend."

"*You* don't got a friend living here," said Red, ever more suspicious. He checked his cell, relieved to see it'd been sufficiently recharged to allow a call. *I'm fucked no matter what I decide about this guy. Better to let Patty make the decision.*

"Hey, buddy," said Jack. "What's the problem? Who are you calling?"

"You got lots of questions," said Red, backing away.

"All you need to do is move your truck a few feet."

"All *you* need to do is shut up so I can make a call."

"This is nuts," said Jack, pulling out his cell. "Well, I can make a call, too."

Red yanked the phone from Jack's hand and barked, "Relax!"

"I *am* relaxed! Give me my phone!"

Red stepped further back, attempting to complete his call to Patty. But Jack followed, trying to free his cell from Red's grasp. In the tussle, his elbow jabbed Red's eye. When Red fell back, he lost control of Jack's phone; it sailed through the air and smashed against a remnant concrete barrier. Jack ran to retrieve it, but Red jumped him from behind and placed a chokehold around his neck. Jack stumbled to the ground, light-headed. Red warned him to "stay down," but Jack unsteadily got up and lunged toward Red.

MacArthur Maze Area

Oakland-Emeryville Border

Yusra awoke on the blue sofa to the sound of a truck's door slamming. She watched the driver get out and rattle the gate to the scrapyard across the street. A man inside walked out of a booth and met the driver at the gate. He kept shaking his head while the truckdriver tried several times to hand him a piece of paper through the chain-link fencing.

At first, she couldn't hear their conversation. But then they began shouting at one another. Finally, the scrapyard man took the paper, crumpled it up, tossed it over the gate, and walked away. The truckdriver's hands gesticulated wildly, and he repeatedly yelled, "Fuck you!"

Yusra watched the truckdriver pace, occasionally slamming his fist against the gate. He looked scary, and also familiar. *I know him,* she suddenly realized. *He's the man my mom calls the "Nice Man" who changes the dirt in our garden.* She'd always considered it odd, how he'd take dirt out, only to put other dirt in. But whenever she questioned her mother about it, she was only told: "The Nice People here have their own ways, and it is always better not to question them."

Observing him now, Yusra thought such bad behavior *should* be questioned. It didn't seem right to dismiss it as just another entitled oddity of someone in power. She realized her mother must misunderstand the meaning of "nice," because no truly "nice" person would act and curse like him. She'd explain this misunderstanding to her mother when she had the chance, and she'd tell her about the Un-Nice Man and Un-Nice Lady.

Suddenly, the truckdriver stilled and looked in her direction. Then he started toward her, calling out, "Hey, you!"

Yusra gasped and dropped everything except her doll. She ran away as fast as she could, scrambling over bricks, broken glass, rotted wood, rags. She came to a busy street and, despite what her mother taught her, she ran across it without looking anywhere but ahead.

4th Floor Monitored Unit

Oakland City Hospital

How excruciating: forced to lie still in bed and *do nothing*. It was Aditya's first hospitalization, and seeing things from a patient's perspective, he was shocked. Shocked by the large volume of blood they kept extracting from him for testing. His considerable radiation exposure from the scanners. The many strangers who simply barged into his room, often unidentified. He could only eat on their schedule. He couldn't urinate in private. *I feel like an object. Like a damaged needy object that merely inconveniences everyone.* He wondered how often his patients felt the same.

And the hospital room in which he was confined—its aggressive fluorescent lighting, the constant hallway noise, the depressing pallor of the walls . . . *This is no healing environment.*

His ruminations ceased when Dr. Fred Williams unexpectedly walked in. In respect, Aditya tried to sit up; but the immediate agony held him back.

"Stay still," said Fred. "You shouldn't be moving around with that fragile spleen."

"Dr. Williams," he replied, "I'm sorry if my accident necessitated you being called in, particularly on this holiday."

Fred debated whether to tell him the truth: that he'd used Aditya's injury as an excuse to come into the hospital and dodge Carrie's dinner tonight. But remembering how Aditya had helped to save his life two years ago, he decided to confess to disabuse him of any guilt. "Frankly, I needed an excuse to get out of a dinner tonight. I told the host there'd been another 'incident' at the hospital involving an attack on a member of my staff. And protocol required that I be involved."

"But it was no attack, sir. That patient did not intend—"

"I know. And I'm sorry it happened, Aditya."

They stared appraisingly at one another. Aditya, wondering why such an accomplished man needed a lame excuse to skip a dinner party. Fred, imagining how incensed Nora was going to be when she discovered he wouldn't be attending Carrie's tonight—the *second* Thanksgiving in a row.

Fred cleared his throat. "And, speaking of the patient who kicked you. Sorry, but we have to room him with you. The hospital's full, and this is the only remaining monitored bed."

Carl's Home

Piedmont

When Carl drove up to his house, Fergie was waiting on the porch. She waved—more a summons than a greeting. He parked on the street and joined her. Noting furrows in her brow, he asked what was wrong.

"I'm worried about Win. He was moody when he left hours ago. He should've been back by now. And he knows we have Carrie's dinner tonight."

"Have you phoned him?" said Carl, brushing off a porch chair and sani-wiping its armrests before sitting down.

"He's not answering."

"Do you know where he went?"

"I've got a dumb hunch."

"Are you knowingly choosing those words? Because a 'hunch' is a guess or feeling based on intuition rather than known facts. So, if you qualify 'hunch' with the descriptive 'dumb,' it becomes difficult to—"

"I don't know where he is. But if I had to guess, knowing him as I do, I'd guess he's at the lake."

"Then that's a basic hunch, Fergie. No pejorative is called for."

She looked pleadingly at him. "Could you drive me there to look for him?"

"Of course. But I need a few minutes in the house to wash up a little (*a lot*). And I should pack the wine in the trunk for Carrie's tonight, in case our search consumes the time in between."

"A good idea," she said. "I'll pack my lasagna in the car, too."

Nora's Home

Montclair District

Nora anxiously rechecked the time and phoned Jack again with another message: "Where are you? You should've been here by now. And I *really* need to talk with you *now*."

She hung up, feeling bereft of his counsel. *How and when should I tell Daleen about failing to make contact with Yusra? How to prevent her from bolting out of the hospital after hearing that? What, if anything, should I tell her about that menacing Patty who'd been lurking around her camper? And poor Yusra . . . Should I just call the police and social services now? Jack, where the hell are you?*

Nora paced near the fireplace, and, fixing on Lydia's photo on the mantle, said: "I know what you'd say, Lydia: that I'm still Sisyphus' daughter. That I shouldn't have gotten involved in my patient's social problems. That I fucked up again." *And yet,* she thought, *I don't know how else I could've been Daleen's doctor and cared for her. No one would've benefited had I simply refused her terms and walked away.*

Still, Carl's prior warnings kept returning to the forefront of her mind. He'd been right to speculate about potential problems at the encampment, given Daleen's fear and secretiveness. *And now, with Yusra not located . . . Could we be talking about human trafficking? Domestic abuse? Did I endanger Yusra by not contacting authorities yesterday?*

She sank into the sofa, shuddering. It felt like February 2017 all over again. Being here in this living room, under siege, panicked, and imperiled. Grim images ripped from gruesome memories flashed: the killer taunting her in this very room, the cruel beating and baiting, the gunshot. Nora's heart pounded now, her ears rang. She hyperventilated, her hands tingled. Panic was coming to reclaim her.

She grabbed the alprazolam prescribed by Dr. Barteau, and recited internally the advice she'd been given: *Not even two years have passed since you were attacked, and less than four since you lost your family. It will take time . . . (So much fucking time that I don't have time for!) You need to exercise daily/start yoga/join a support group/eliminate coffee/drink less wine/sleep regularly . . . (Yada-yada-yada.)* Then she closed her eyes and reminded herself of Dr. Barteau's parting comment yesterday: *You must remind yourself that the gun isn't actually loaded.*

Contemplating that, Nora realized that two triggers had been pulled on her today: an angry woman chasing her, and a daughter gone missing. She shakily reached for her phone, intending to contact the on-call therapist. But she stopped, remembering today was a holiday, and opted instead for a glass (or two) of merlot to stave off any looming panic attack. *The gun isn't actually loaded . . .*

Finally experiencing the sedative effects from her self-medication, she went to the dining table, opened her laptop, and began to surf the Target website for appetizers she could pick up for Carrie's dinner tonight. But that immediately proved impossible, in view of Daleen's food bundle on the table. All Nora could do was imagine Yusra, hungry and lost, and separated from her worried mother. And how perverse it felt, viewing online ads for gigantic food trays including side "buckets" of dip. Or meat and cheese plates that could feed small villages. Or "social platters" weighted with off-putting presentations of precision-cut veggie sticks and perfectly rounded melon balls impaled with toothpicks.

Nora closed her laptop and decided to leave a final peeved voice-mail for Jack. She reminded him about the not-so-secret location of her spare housekey should he *finally* show up. "But I need to leave the house now."

Indeed, she needed to do *something* to tame her gut-wrenching anxiety over Daleen and Yusra; and their worrying circumstances required urgent responses. It was time, she decided, to drive to the hospital and consult with Daleen about what should be done.

Inn-N-Out Motel

Near the MacArthur Maze

"Lady, like I told you: I haven't seen your little girl since you checked in yesterday . . . Look, I just manage this motel. I'm not a private detective . . . Oh, yeah? Well, in case you haven't heard, it's *Thanksgiving.* And I intend to celebrate it with *my* family . . . No! I don't have time to check every nook and cranny here. She's *your* responsibility, ma'am . . . Okay. Curse me out again, and I'm calling the police. I got a mind to call child protective services, anyway . . . Hello? *Hello?*"

Old Stadium Site

West Oakland

Red pounded on the window, shouting for Luis to "unlock the door!"

Luis let him inside the truck, and Red immediately relocked the door, seconds before Jack began tugging its handle and yelling, "Give me my phone!" While Red tried to call Patty, Luis watched Jack pick up a metal pipe and hold it like a bat; he protectively covered his face with his hands, bracing for shattered glass.

But Jack caught sight of Luis, in time to check his swing. After mouthing "What the fuck?" to Red, he walked to the passenger-side window and saw Luis shuddering. Shocked to see that he'd traumatized the boy, Jack dropped the pipe.

Red appreciated Jack's backing away, and, in a sudden wash of guilt, realized his own contribution to Luis' distress. In a gesture of truce, he put down his cell and held up his hands. Luis uncovered his face and looked indecisively back and forth between the two men. Red told him, "I'm sorry, little man; this never should've happened." Then he got out of the truck to settle with Jack and return his cellphone.

Jack took stock of his smashed cell; it wouldn't even power on. "Fucking great," he muttered. After scrutinizing Red's expression—at once steely but, seemingly, sincere—he said: "The *least* you could do is tell me what this is all about. And who's that kid in your truck?"

"Look, I'm being honest with you: You *really* don't want to know. I'll just move my truck so you can—"

"No. That's not how this is going to work. I want answers. You owe me."

Luis ran up to Red and stood soldier-like beside him, his dark almond-shaped eyes glaring defiantly at Jack. His oversized yellow Betty's tee heightened his olive skin tone and made his body appear miniaturized.

Not wanting to further upset the boy, Jack smiled and said: "My name is Jack. I drove here looking for a friend, but she'd left by the time I arrived. I'm sorry for this . . . whatever 'this' is, between your friend and me. Grown men shouldn't fight like we did."

Red tousled Luis' curly black hair. "He's right, little man. Fighting just always leads to more trouble. I should know."

Pointing to Red's face, Jack said, "You need a few stitches."

Red grinned. "Yeah. I'll see my doctor later."

"No," said Jack, knowing that was unlikely to happen. "I'm a doctor. My bag's in the trunk."

"I'm fine," said Red, shooing him away.

But Luis tugged on Red's jacket and said, "Please let Dr. Jack help you."

Red met Luis' intense gaze, wondering how this little guy could affect him so greatly.

4th Floor Monitored Unit

Oakland City Hospital

When the nurse parted the blue curtain, Tomas and Aditya became visible to one another as roommates. On her way out, she told Tomas she'd return soon with his meds.

Aditya asked the man who was unwittingly responsible for rupturing his spleen: "Do you recognize me?"

"No. We have met?"

Aditya thought: *My girlfriend and I saved your life, and you put mine at risk.* Still, all he said was: "My name is Aditya."

"I am Tomas," he replied. Then they each lay back and companionably stared at the muted TV news. Moments later, suddenly aware that he possessed the only remote, Aditya said: "Sorry. I should turn on the sound."

"Don't bother," said Tomas. "Everybody always sounds so angry. And I can't understand the fast English."

"Well, I can," said Aditya. "That is why I usually mute it."

Tomas smiled weakly and sat up. Then he began disconnecting his IV.

"No," said Aditya, "you should not do that." He wanted to get up to intervene, but he knew that would risk the complete and catastrophic rupture of his fragile spleen.

Tomas persisted. He pulled out the needle, put pressure on the venipuncture site, and knotted the IV tubing to stop its saline flow.

Aditya frantically pressed the call button to summon a nurse while pleading with Tomas to stop.

"I have to go," said Tomas, removing his patient gown. But when he opened his bagged personal belongings, he groaned. "My clothes aren't here."

With relief, Aditya recalled Lizbeth sending Tomas' clothes to bio-hazards, following decontamination protocols. He assumed this would deter Tomas from leaving.

Instead, Tomas looked contritely at him and said, "Sorry, brother." Then he walked to Aditya's bedside and collected his purple shirt, black trousers, and shoes. "I will return these to you somehow."

"I do not care about them! It is unsafe for you to go."

Tomas scoffed. "It's more unsafe for me to stay."

"Mr. Ruiz, we think you are poisoned and—"

"Poisoned?" Tomas closed the door to their room, surprised to discover how weak and unsteady he felt. Eyeing Aditya suspiciously, he asked, "How did you know my name?"

Aditya's thumb had been wearing down the call button, and it seemed futile now to yell for a nurse. He shakily replied, "I'm the doctor who took care of you in the ER."

"I don't recognize you," said Tomas, dressing.

"Please! Yesterday, an ambulance brought you to this hospital. You were very sick. Your nerves were damaged. You had trouble breathing, even worse than it appears now. We ran tests, and we believe you are poisoned by arsenic. We can help you!"

"I don't think so. Unless you can help me put on these shoes." Having no sensation in his feet, Tomas struggled.

"I cannot leave this bed. But I can help you medically. Look, if you are worried about losing your job, I can contact your employer."

"Funny," said Tomas. "Yes, contact my employer. Stop by the prison and explain everything."

"You work in a prison?"

Tomas stared at him, thinking: *Prison is my life. Would you understand?*

"Tell me about your job," said Aditya. "What are you exposed to?"

My friend, thought Tomas, *you don't have enough time to learn about my "job." It's called "survival." And it is anything they tell me to do. I pick, I dig, I clean, I haul, I build things on rich people's land. What am I not exposed to?*

"And exposures also at your house," Aditya continued. Then, acutely embarrassed, he urgently clarified: "I mean, where you live."

My house is a small orange tent for now. But sometimes, it is a warehouse or the back of a truck or just open space. I live wherever they tell me to work, for days or weeks at a time.

"Because," Aditya explained, "wherever you were poisoned, others there could be at risk, too. Your colleagues. Family. Your community."

"You ask many questions," Tomas said, donning Aditya's jacket. "But you seem like a good man. I will pray you get better."

"Wait! At least take my card. My wallet's in the bedside drawer."

Tomas deliberated but, with concerns raised about Luis' health, he took a card and slipped it into his back pocket.

"Call me, please," Aditya pleaded. "We will receive your toxicology results on Monday."

"Sure," said Tomas, heading for the door.

"Where are you going?" Aditya called out, his thumb almost forcing the call button through its casing. "Back to the stadium?"

"To my prison," said Tomas, vanishing beyond the doorway.

Nora's Office

Oakland City Hospital

Nora gasped when she entered her office and saw Fred.

"Sorry," he said. "Didn't mean to scare you."

She set down her purse and huffed, "Well, you *did.*" Then she hurriedly logged onto her computer to check Daleen's recent lab tests, prepping for her imminent visit. She asked, "What are you doing here, Fred? And how often do you sneak into my office?"

"Not often enough," he said, holding up a bag of Cheez Curlz.

"You went through my drawers, too? I'm reporting you to security."

Fred went on to complain about the dearth of such snacks in his household. But Nora stayed focused on Daleen's tests, relieved to find her methemoglobin levels trending toward normal. Still, the question remained: Why was her methemoglobin elevated in the first place? And having just witnessed the so-called living conditions at the stadium,

Nora could entertain several possibilities. Given that the camp's water supply was primitive, she wondered whether Daleen had consumed bacterially contaminated water or vegetables from her own garden. Or, perhaps Daleen was exposed to nitrites; the entire camp could be contaminated by fertilizer runoff from nearby fields. Then again—

"Of course!" she exclaimed, self-interrupting her thoughts.

"You scared *me* now!" said Fred.

"I just figured out why you're actually here! I know you! You made some excuse about having to come into the hospital so you could avoid Carrie's dinner. Right? And you're biding time in my office."

"All right now," he said, clearing his throat. "Guilty as charged."

"Unbelievable! And Vickie and the kids are okay with that?"

He grimaced. "Well, Vickie had to give me some grief, of course. But she and the kids were relieved about not going. Charlie regards Thanksgiving as an appalling celebration of the colonists' war against Native Americans. And Ella—quite the chef these days—was elated. Because then she got to cook a turkey dinner for the family instead."

Nora studied her old friend. As accomplished as he was—renowned clinician, respected chief of staff—he behaved like a frightened child whenever faced with the prospect of seeing Lydia's identical twin, Carrie. She said, "You know, it's hard for me to see Carrie, too. Lydia was my soulmate."

"Nora, this isn't a competition."

"I know. But you didn't go to Carrie's dinner last year, and you promised *me* you'd come this time. I'm still struggling to get back to some kind of normal with friends. So, by you not going . . ."

"But I get angina just imagining seeing Carrie . . . Lydia . . . *whoever*!" He momentarily considered telling Nora the truth about Lydia and him, and finally disburdening himself of the guilty secret he carried about their breakup. Sometimes that secret weighed so heavily on him, it was the only thought his mind could carry. But knowing how it would upset Nora, he merely reached for his inhaler.

"Well," she said, waiting for him to take his medication. "At least tell me the excuse you used to get out of Carrie's dinner."

"I told a white lie."

"A white lie by a black man?"

"You think that's racist?"

"Just . . . what was this 'white lie'?"

With an apologetic grimace, he explained, "I told Carrie I had to go into the hospital because of a 'critical incident.' That another member of my staff had been attacked. She understood."

"Is it even true?"

"Yes. A patient accidentally kicked Aditya and partially ruptured his spleen."

"Aditya?!"

"Hold on! Just saw him, and he's fine. On strict bedrest, 4th floor monitoring."

"How awful. I'll stop by to see him after . . ."

"After what?"

She debated whether to reveal her intention in coming here to speak with Daleen. But that would not only expose their confidential agreement, it would also entail telling Fred about her upsetting experience at the stadium and failure to locate Daleen's daughter.

"All right now," said Fred. "I know you're not scheduled to work today, and you're taking too long to answer. I've confessed why I'm here. Your turn."

She thought, *I'll sound so foolish if I tell him everything.*

He thrummed his fingers on her desk.

"Okay," she said. "I came in to talk with a patient who asked me to . . . to meet with her daughter."

"Oh, her daughter's here, too?"

"No. The patient, Daleen, is here. Her six-year-old daughter Yusra was home—*supposedly*. They live in a camper at the stadium."

"In a homeless camp? You went there to meet the daughter?"

Nora nodded.

He tutted and said, "Sounds fishy. Since when did you become a social worker? Or a pediatrician?"

"It's not like that, Fred." She snatched the Cheez Curlz from him. "Daleen is terrified about losing her daughter. She's afraid Yusra will be taken away by social services or police if they find out she's alone at a camp. That's why Daleen refused to talk to anyone at first! The only way I could obtain the information I needed to diagnose her illness . . . well,

I had to strike a confidential agreement with her. And that required me to deliver a reassuring message to Yusra."

"Nora, I'm just thinking of the million-which ways you made mistakes here. I mean, from the get-go: Suppose after you struck some 'confidential agreement,' Daleen dropped a bombshell on you? Something illegal? Unethical? A secret that made you complicit in a crime or—"

"Stop! I wasn't thrilled about it. But I also wasn't so worried at the time. It wasn't until Carl and I drove to their camper today and discovered Yusra was missing. And then some unhinged woman named Patty chased us out. Then Jack showed up after we'd left, but why hasn't he called—?"

"Hold on, Nora! We're going to count to ten. Then you're going to start from the beginning."

Old Stadium Site

West Oakland

Luis couldn't believe it; his mouth hung open: He was watching a doctor *sewing* Red's face! Four stitches, too! He asked Jack, "You get to do this in your job?"

"Yes," said Jack. "Want to cut this last thread?"

After looking to Red for approval, Luis took the suture scissors and cut the thread above the knot as instructed. Then he stared awestruck at his own hand.

Red said, "Thanks for helping, little man."

"Yeah, you're a great assistant," said Jack.

Luis wondered if life could ever get better than this moment. But, seconds later, he discovered it could when he heard Red tell Jack: "So, that call you wanted to make to your friend? I'd let you borrow my phone if it had any charge. But we can go back to Betty's, I could recharge it, and you could make your call. Maybe get ice for your lip, too."

While considering the suggestion, Jack took stock of his swollen lip and soiled clothes, deciding he was justified in canceling attendance at Carrie's dinner tonight. *Of course, Nora will be mad. But she's responsible for me getting into this mess, and better not give me grief.* Still, on such short notice, he needed to notify her and Carrie soon. And because Betty's was considerably closer than Nora's house, it seemed reasonable to phone them from the restaurant. He told Red, "Sounds like a plan. I'll follow you guys there."

Luis was profoundly amazed. Going *twice* in *one* day to his favorite restaurant! And now he knew about *three* good jobs he might pursue someday.

Lake Merritt

Oakland

"There!" Fergie exclaimed, pointing to her red Subaru. But when she and Carl walked up to the car, Winston wasn't inside.

"Perhaps he's still out walking," said Carl.

Fergie shook her head. "The lake's little more than three miles around. He could've walked it several times by now."

They scanned the shoreline walkway for Winston. Carl said, "I don't see him. But you can't see the entire shoreline from any single vantage point. Why don't you leave a note for him in your car, and we'll drive around the . . . *you know.*"

Fergie looked curiously at him before dashing off the note she left on the driver's seat: *Where are you, Win? Call me. Worried, F.* Then she accompanied Carl back to his car, and they embarked on their search. After several minutes of awkward silence, she asked, "You okay?"

Carl released a sigh of relief. "It's just . . . technically, this isn't a 'lake.' It's actually a natural saltwater tidal lagoon that connects through the estuary and, therefore, to the bay and Pacific Ocean."

She waited a beat. "Feel better?"

"Yes, thanks," he replied, and they proceeded to circle twice around the so-called lake. When they returned to Fergie's car, her note remained undisturbed. She tried phoning Winston again. "This isn't like him," she said. "Something must've happened."

Carl moved closer to Fergie, planning to put an arm around her to convey empathy. "I want to try to comfort you," he explained. "But I don't want to violate your space. Say 'no' if it doesn't feel respectful—" But as soon as he extended his arm, she fell into his embrace.

Grady's Irish Pub

Jack London Square, Oakland

"Hey, buddy," said the bartender. "Last call."

Gianni scowled. "What the fuck? It ain't even three o'clock."

"It's Thanksgiving. We're closing early to get home to our families."

"You're joking. Besides, most people need *more* alcohol on turkey day."

"Says '3 o'clock' real clear on the door."

"Well, what kinda person reads a door?"

The bartender laughed and gifted him a second beer. "This last one's on me. But we're closing in ten."

"Thanks," said Gianni. "Hey. Know anyone interested in dirt?"

"Oh, so you're . . . what? A whistleblower? A celebrity informant?"

"No, man. I mean actual dirt. Like from the ground."

The bartender started overturning chairs onto the tables. "Can't say I do. But it's an interesting question. A geologist, maybe?"

Gianni groaned. "No. See, I got a truckload of dirt I excavated today. My usual guy refused to take it. And if I can't dump it somewhere, I'll have to take a girl out on our first date with a shitload of dirt in the back. Real classy."

"She'll understand."

"Sure," said Gianni, swigging his beer. "What an un-fucking-thanks day it's been. And I also scared a little girl."

The bartender looked troubled. "Meaning?"

"Meaning, I saw this little girl. Not that well, without my glasses. She was alone under the Maze, surrounded by street junk. But when I headed for her, she ran away."

"Imagine that."

"Hey," said Gianni, thumping his glass down on the bar. "The situation doesn't call for your sarcasm. I feel bad about it. That kid looked scared." He tossed a five on the bar and said, "For the beer. I don't want your handout."

After returning to his truck, Gianni fished under the seat where he stored his gun and flask. He looked out at the Oakland Estuary, sipping Jack Daniel's, ruminating about his thirty-odd years of life as a lone wolf. *Where's it gotten me? I'm here alone, in a goddamn parking lot on Thanksgiving.* Though he readily acknowledged that he'd achieved the life he'd intentionally structured for himself, he had to concede that it was beginning to disappoint. It was leaving him feeling lonely and bored. Empty, really. *Do I want to continue like this? No friends, no one to spend holidays with? Do I want to just keep in-and-outing women like I do? And my "job" . . . there's no challenge or future in it.*

He capped his flask and declared new resolutions. The next time the English guy phoned with a work order, he'd give him thirty days' notice. Tomorrow he'd start looking for a job that offered regular hours and opportunities to develop new skills. And now, he'd call Patty to cancel their hook-up tonight and propose a respectable alternative—a proper dinner, perhaps—so they could actually talk.

But Patty didn't answer his call, so he left a message: "Sorry, I can't hook up with you tonight. Call me when you can. I'd like a raincheck to go somewhere decent soon." Then he headed back to the Maze, determined to find the little girl he'd unintentionally scared as his old foolish self.

Nora's Office

Oakland City Hospital

When Nora finished describing her predicament involving Daleen and Yusra, Fred wearily remarked, "Fishy, like I said before."

"That's your expert analysis?" said Nora.

"Well, I'm speechless," he said, shaking his head. "Don't even know where to start! You made an unwise and risky commitment, and then you predictably stepped into s-h-i-t."

"Well, if all you're going to do is judge me, forget it."

"Sorry," he said, sending a conciliatory look. "Try again?"

Nora nodded. "Sorry, too. I know I just dumped a lot on you."

"Won't disagree with that. But, let's triage, like we do in public disasters. Let's prioritize our attention to people based on the severity of their endangerment, maximizing our resources . . ."

But the moment he said "triage," Nora's mind launched into a private orbit, and she triaged her predicament accordingly: *Daleen's already safe, under medical observation in the hospital. So, we should prioritize Yusra's whereabouts and safety.* She blurted out: "So, *before* I speak with Daleen, I should notify the police and social services about Yusra."

Fred scowled. "I just knew you weren't listening to me! You want my opinion or not?"

"Sorry," she said, returning the Cheez Curlz to him.

"All right then. Regardless of what you decide, bottom line is you can't stay silent about a child gone missing. And Daleen needs to know you didn't locate her daughter—she can learn that either directly, from you; or indirectly, from authorities. But if you call the authorities now, they'll come here to question Daleen and initiate a child welfare investigation. And you're right to worry about them taking Yusra from her. Hell, Nora, you don't even know their immigration status, right? It's been scary enough for folks to get care with immigration agents stalking the hospital. So just imagine the consequences for the girl, and what might happen to Daleen's own medical care."

"I know," she said, pacing the room. "And Daleen's upstairs, still waiting on my report. I'm so overwhelmed, I can't think clearly."

Looking sympathetically at her, he said: "Let's take a quick minute. Okay . . . Now, you made it sound like Daleen was two hundred percent certain Yusra was at the camp. So, just saying, you and Carl didn't have much time to search for her. You didn't even get a look inside the camper, right?"

"Only because that madwoman Patty chased us away. She even seemed to have some personal stake in our search."

"Whatever. Point is, it's easy to imagine a frightened child not answering your knock on the door. Or, maybe she was away during the few minutes you were there to . . . I don't know . . . use the facilities? Play elsewhere with her friend from that orange tent?"

"It's just that Daleen was absolutely confident about where Yusra would be in the specific circumstance of their separation. Like they had rehearsed a playbook for it."

Fred's asthma began to flare. After taking another puff from his inhaler, he said: "You've no idea how often I've had to renew this inhaler because of *you.*" She scowled, and he continued: "And, as I asked before while you weren't listening: What about Jack?" Then all he needed to do to establish mutual understanding was give her that familiar look: his coppery eyes widening, his jaw dropping slightly, the right corner of his mouth dropping down.

Nora slapped her forehead. "I've been so upset with Jack for standing me up and not calling back. I just thought he was annoyed with me—for good reason—and doing everything he could to skip dinner tonight. It didn't occur to me that he might've run into trouble at the stadium, too. And it'd be my fault for asking him to meet me there."

"Hold on," said Fred. "Calm down. You and I are going to drive to the stadium and take a *good* look for Yusra *and* Jack. It's only minutes away, and we'd settle two big questions."

"Maybe," she said, deliberating. "I suppose, if we found Yusra . . . healthy and safe, of course . . . then we wouldn't *have* to contact the police, right? And Daleen wouldn't have to worry about losing Yusra."

Fred looked concernedly at her. "I'm not sure about all that, or when to call the police. But I know, for the immediate half-hour or so, we've got a sensible plan to try first. So, why don't we focus on that for now?"

"It's not that simple. If that Patty is still there . . . Her chasing after me . . ."

"Of course," he said, hanging his head. "You were triggered." He couldn't believe he'd been so oblivious. "And here I am, prodding you to go back. Look, I'm perfectly fine to drive out there by myself. Could use a little adventure anyway."

"No. You don't know where to look for the camper and orange tent."

"Then tell me. I know the old stadium by heart. Saw some great concerts and games there. Used to go there a lot as a kid, even; we lived just a couple blocks away."

"It's not the same. It's *completely* changed."

"I expect so. It was shut down about a decade ago. Samantha Greeley's selling the property to Highmark Construction next Friday."

Nora's brow raised. "Samantha Greeley? Your new board member with the 'great legs' and 'Michelle Obama arms'?"

"Hold on! I meant nothing indecent by that. And what I said to you was private, for your ears only."

"Okay. But you seem awfully sensitive about it."

He threw up his hands. "It's just . . . I keep getting email flak from this obnoxious board member. He did wink-winks during our meeting yesterday, implying in front of *everyone*—Samantha included—that I needed to guard against sexually inappropriate behavior toward her. I was humiliated. Now, I'm just afraid to look at her."

"Boys," said Nora, appending a tsk. She planted a kiss on his shiny bald head and said, "Let's drive to the stadium."

Blakeley Apartments

Fruitvale District, Oakland

It felt wrong to use Gianni. But Patty desperately needed someplace to stay now. Besides, he'd happily get "something" out of an arrangement, too. But, contemplating their hook-up tonight, she felt guilty about two-timing Pete. *Still, what am I supposed to do? Pete's in prison, nearly a year already. And if he hadn't acted the fool with his prison cellphone scheme, he'd have been out by now, managing the camp again. But leaving me alone to deal with all the shit there? And with no one dropping off the regular payments? How am I supposed to manage? I got no more money for bread and peanut butter from the Dollar Store for people . . . Red's salary . . . our own apartment rent?* She tugged the key on her necklace—a gift from

Pete—reminding herself to be strong. Then she continued driving to their old apartment, intending to collect their possessions ahead of the end-of-month eviction date she'd been given just yesterday.

But after limping up the front steps, she was shocked to see a padlock on the door. "Hell!" she muttered, banging on the door.

Fighting back tears, she tightened the Ace wrap around her sprained ankle and walked the perimeter of the apartment, trying to see through its windows. But the shades were drawn. Then when she rounded to the back, she stopped and gasped: all their possessions had been dumped onto a puddled backyard, looking like old leftovers steeping in dirt stew. She plucked out a pair of jeans, her favorite tee-shirt, her polka dot sunhat, doubting they could ever be sufficiently cleaned. Looking up to the ash-strewn heavens, she whispered: "Can my life possibly get any more pathetic than this?" Immediately, as if in answer, her cell rang.

She wiped her muddy hands on her jacket and rustled through her purse for her cell. "Thank god," she said, noting the missed call came from Gianni. Surely, it was a sign that pursuing him was rightful; relief washed over her while she entered her passcode to listen to his voice-mail. But then she heard the depressing message: he'd canceled tonight's hook-up. And she'd learned, yet again, how her life could become more pathetic.

4th Floor Monitored Unit

Oakland City Hospital

Lizbeth held out a bag and said, "Happy first Thanksgiving!"

Aditya smiled unpersuasively. "Remember, I cannot eat anything."

"I know," she said, emptying the bag onto his hospital bed. A colorful cardboard turkey spilled out, as did two festive autumn leis, a plastic pumpkin, and a strand of turkey-shaped string-lights. But he continued to appear distraught. "Look," she wearily said, "no one wants to be in the hospital, especially on a holiday. And bedrest and ruptured spleens aren't fun. But I'm here, we're together, and I'm getting tired of your—"

"Forgive me. I'm happy you are here with me. It is only that . . . I have been pressing this call button for nearly an hour, and no nurse ever came."

"Okay. Well, what do you need? I'll get it."

"Too late. I was calling about my roommate."

Lizbeth looked curiously at the empty adjacent bed.

Aditya said, "He got dressed in *my* clothes and left the hospital. He was our patient in the ER with probable arsenic poisoning. The one who kicked me."

"But he was so sick! I'm surprised he could even walk."

"I begged him not to leave."

"Is there someone we can call?"

"No. He never gave the hospital any contact information. And the woman who called the ambulance was anonymous. Besides, he is doing nothing illegal by leaving, and he poses no public health threat."

"Sorry," she said, feeling guilty for having misjudged his mood. "And leaving just a few days before his test results come back."

"Well," said Aditya, "I gave him my card. Hopefully, he will call."

Oakland Detention Facility

Downtown

When Fergie and Winston reached the lowermost step of the jailhouse stairway, he pleaded: "Don't be angry with me, Fergs." He double-checked his pockets to confirm he'd retrieved his cellphone and wallet from the police.

"You could've told me where you were going!" she said. "And you didn't have to get yourself arrested." She brushed off his hand and walked toward Carl's car, which awaited them at the corner.

Moments later, Carl approached Winston and asked: "Are you coming with us? Sitting here on the step conveys that you're not."

"Sorry," said Winston. "I was just thinking."

"Of course, you can do that in a car."

"Not with Fergs being so angry with me."

It was a novel consideration for Carl: that one could be rendered incapable of thinking because of another person's mood. He said, "But as a practical matter, each of us needs to be somewhere else. So why not get in my car, and plan to think afterwards?"

After the three had driven a mile in prickly silence, Winston told Fergie: "I don't know how else to apologize."

"You *genuinely* scared me," Fergie said. "And you had me needlessly searching the lake for you."

"Fergs," he said, "they'd confiscated my cell and wouldn't allow a call. Besides, you should've seen how the police were shoving poor people out of a *public* space into . . . *nowhere*! People who were just trying to survive."

"That's not what this is about, Win."

Carl said, "What else could 'this' be about? 'That' seems to be the fundamental problem."

Fergie flinched. They were right. And she realized her behavior wasn't helping Winston's struggle with his identity crisis. She turned to look at Winston and said, "Sorry. I know you're having a hard time. And maybe I'm defending against that because I'm also just beginning to feel the same." He placed a hand on her shoulder, and they continued on to the lake.

When they arrived, Winston pointed to the pergola and said: "The scene of my crime. And, wow, lots of people returned after all."

Carl asked, "Would you prefer to get out here? Or should I take you to your car?"

They had no need to consult one another; in unison, Fergie and Winston replied, "To our car."

Betty's

City Center

Luis walked straight to the counter, smiled, and said, "Hello, DeeDee."

She smiled back. "What a nice surprise! Hello, Luis."

After tugging his Betty's tee-shirt to straighten it, he asked, "Need any help?"

Before she could reply, Red and Jack approached, each exhibiting facial injuries. Red preemptively explained, "It's nothing. Just a dustup. This here is my friend, Dr. Jack."

"Right," said DeeDee, doubt infusing her voice. "How about putting some ice on your dustups?" Jack thanked her and headed for the restroom to clean up. Red and Luis stood there, smiling helplessly at her. When she broke the spell by asking what they'd like, Red blushed and said, "Uh, mind if we take a booth? I need to recharge my phone for real this time."

"Make yourself at home," she said, taking Luis' hand, ushering him behind the counter.

After plugging in his phone charger, Red walked to the ice machine. He carried back a cup of cubes, which he offered to Jack upon his return. Jack placed them against his swollen lip and, moved by Red's concern, remarked, "You're awfully nice for a tough guy."

"Don't go calling me nice," said Red.

"Okay. But, also, seeing how you treat Luis, I'd guess your parents must be—"

"Don't fuckin' talk about *them*! They kicked me out three years ago. Just back off the personal stuff, okay?"

"Copy that," said Jack, though only made more curious about Red's story of being disowned and living at a homeless camp. And why was this twenty-something street guy with Luis, a seven-year-old boy bearing no physical resemblance? Jack wanted to share that he'd also been kicked out by his parents, but, clearly, it wasn't an opportune time. Instead, he said, "You should be icing, too."

"Save your breath," said Red. "Besides, shouldn't you be calling your friends?" He handed over his phone. "Just needs to stay plugged in while you talk."

But when Jack took the phone, he stared dumbfoundedly at it. Red asked what was wrong and he answered: "I feel foolish. I can't remember Nora's number. It's always been programmed into my phone."

Red put his hand over his mouth but didn't quite succeed in stifling his laughter. Finally, he said, "Sorry, man. It's not really funny."

"Yes, I see how upset you are," Jack said, shaking his head. And try as he might, he also couldn't recall the number for any mutual friend who might provide him with Nora's. He anxiously imagined her incremental irritation while waiting on his visit or an explanatory call. And he still needed to inform Carrie in a timely manner about not bringing the potatoes for dinner.

"Take it easy," said Red. "Target opens in an hour. You could buy a new phone and maybe transfer your old service. Then you call your friends."

"I suppose," said Jack, preferring that plan over driving to Nora's for an intense face-to-face and conversation about *something* now. "It's only an hour's difference, like you said. And I definitely need a new phone."

Luis arrived with two sodas and earnestly inquired, "Would you like something else?"

Jack answered, "Yes, sir. Since it's Thanksgiving, might we have turkey burgers?"

Red guffawed. "Oh, man . . . This ain't Applebee's or some fancy restaurant! They just got normal burgers, from cows."

DeeDee whispered something to Luis, who then announced, "But we have chicken patties."

"Close enough," said Jack. "How about a round for the table? Oh, and house salads, too."

Luis looked questioningly at DeeDee. After she winked and nodded, he answered "Yes" although he couldn't quite imagine how a salad was made from, or into, a house.

Old Stadium Site

West Oakland

Nearing the stadium, Nora cautioned Fred: "Be prepared. It's going to be upsetting. Still, I'm sure the property will sell for gazillions next week. I'll bet your friend on the board with the sexy legs—"

"I asked you not to say such things, Nora. I don't even like you joking about it."

"Sorry, you're right." Then, aiming for more agreeable conversation, she asked: "Remember when you, me, Jack, and Lydia . . ." She composed herself. "Remember when we came here during residency for that Prince concert? In '88, maybe '89?"

"Do I?" he said. He launched into the refrain from "Little Red Corvette," humming the (many) words he couldn't recall. When finished, he said, "Each decade, my mind loses ten percent of all song lyrics."

"Welcome to my choir."

But their conversation turned sober the moment Nora's Prius passed through the gate. Aghast, Fred said, "My god, you weren't exaggerating. This place *has* changed since the day. It used to be . . . magnificent. Inviting. Now it looks like it's been nuked."

They took the main road, driving deeper into a ravaged landscape. Junk piles appeared to float on muddy brown seas, forming gloomy archipelagos. Fred thought: *The new owner must be planning to dismantle this entire place. Can't imagine anything worth salvaging here.* He looked in the direction where his mother and maternal grandparents once lived, only two blocks away; how stunned they would be—*god rest their souls*— to see this place now.

They drove past people coaxing a campfire. A woman with bare bandaged feet walking in a circle. A child dashing across the road, lugging plastic jugs. A rain-matted mutt that growled and bared his teeth. Two small girls stirring a rain puddle with sticks. When they neared the D-lot, Nora pointed and said: "We should look there for Jack. Then Daleen's camper—it's a stone's throw away."

Fred was struggling to take it all in. *How could so many people be living here under such squalid conditions?* His voice broke when he said, "All these people, these kids . . . living like this in Oakland, right under our noses."

"Yeah," she said. "And horrid as it is, still, you wonder where they'll go when your friend kicks them out of this paradise next week."

Her comment stung, somehow making him feel complicit with Samantha's plans. He even heard the defensiveness in his reply: "Sounds like you're blaming Samantha for their misfortune. You really don't like her, do you?"

"I don't even know her, Fred."

"Well, she's a major philanthropist. She supports all sorts of good causes in the Bay Area. The Greeley Foundation is always helping the hospital, too. And her being on the board will definitely boost our fundraising."

"Then I assume she and her foundation have a compassionate strategy to help these people out—literally, 'out,' next week. What's their plan?"

"Don't know," he answered bluntly, privately bothered that he hadn't been aware of the huge encampment. *Samantha may have chosen a buyer who promised affordable housing here, but there'll be a high price to pay for the people living here now.*

When they arrived at the D-lot, they got out of the car and looked around. Fred stated the obvious: "No sign of Jack or his car."

"Maybe that's a good thing," she said. "At least we know he's not been stranded here." She rechecked her cell for messages, and again phoned Jack unsuccessfully.

They returned to the car and doubled back toward Daleen's camper. Fred said, "I hope we find Yusra. If not, you'll be in a tough spot with her mother and the police—sorry to say."

Nora white-knuckled her grip on the steering wheel. "Thank you, Fred! Thanks for such comforting words at a time like this! Jack's missing. A little girl has disappeared." She took a deep breath. *A trigger. A trigger. Remember that the gun isn't actually loaded.*

"Sorry! Didn't mean to upset you."

She silently counted to ten. Twenty. Thirty. But she couldn't gain control over her escalating panic. Her heart galloped, her lungs emptied of air, her brain sizzled, her ears buzzed. She slammed the brakes, switched off the ignition, exited the car, and leaned weakly against it. Fred steadied her by the shoulders and calmly said: "You're having a panic attack. Tell me that you know that."

She nodded, gasping for air.

"Nora, listen. You *can* breathe. Understand?"

She nodded again. But her understanding failed to convince her body. Her vision dimmed; she was about to faint.

Fred insisted, "Breathe with me. Look at me." He placed one of her hands on his chest to help her sync her breathing with his. He breathed in a slow, measured fashion.

Finally, Nora's breathing normalized. The ringing in her ears faded. Her heart decelerated. And to her great relief, she felt her mind escape anxiety's stranglehold. Something other than consummate doom became visible. Standing steady now, feeling the cool misty rain on her face, she looked directly at Fred and whispered, "Thank you."

He said, "God knows, things have been tough on you these last few years. And, far as I counted, you've had at least three triggers pulled on you the last couple days."

Nora closed her eyes and looked inward, privately reciting: *But the gun isn't actually loaded.*

Fred continued, "My asthma is how my body responds to trauma. And you've helped me with that a lot, even saved my life two years ago. So, let me help you now, by driving you back—"

"No. I'm better. And I'm still okay to drive."

"I don't think so."

"Fred, we're already here. So, let's just go check out Daleen's camper."

"You're not thinking clearly. Your judgment's off."

She apposed her thumb and forefinger and said, "Well, imagine telling Daleen we were this close?"

He threw his hands up in surrender.

"Thank you," she said. "Okay. Here's the plan. We find Yusra, make sure she's safe, and give her Daleen's message and food package. Then we swing by my house to check whether Jack showed up, like he was supposed to. And—it won't take long; I hope you don't mind—we stop at Target so I can pick up the appetizers for tonight. Then I'll drop you back at the hospital so you can retrieve your car, and I can visit with Daleen. Then I'll be on my merry way to Carrie's."

Fred frowned, unable to conceal his disapproval of her overly taxing plans. "Too much. And, my god, you can't possibly be serious about still going to Carrie's tonight?"

"Well, I am. Unlike you, I feel obligated to Carrie. And to my friends."

"Stop with the lecture," he said. Then, figuring she'd likely fare worse without his help, he conceded: "All right now. I'm just going to say yes to whatever you propose. C'mon. Let's go find Yusra."

Intersection, Broadway and Grand

Downtown

Tomas Ruiz discovered he couldn't walk without looking at his feet. They were numb, unable to register contact with the ground or to sense the surface irregularities of the streets and sidewalks. At the crosswalk, when he had to look up, he tripped over a discarded beer bottle and fell at the intersection of Broadway and Grand. A young man sidestepped his body. Aggravated drivers honked.

Tomas struggled to right himself and lurched toward the sidewalk. But his foot caught on the curb and he fell again. To get out of people's way, he rolled along the sidewalk until his body abutted a storefront. He lay there, looking up at the cloud-staggered sky while rain sifted through the smoky air and coated his face like balm.

So, this is how it ends, he thought, chilling to the bone. *This is how I die.*

Someone—a man, woman, hard to tell—walked by and told Tomas to get a job.

But I've had so many. My god, so many . . . Every kind of job with dirt, farms, trees, cement . . . trash and hauling . . . painting, roofing . . . I was born with a hammer and shovel in my hands.

A trio of bleary-eyed girls passed, maintaining distance from him; one shot a brief video, another clucked her tongue.

They are afraid of me . . .

A baby in a passing stroller locked eyes with his, her expression indecipherable. Still, something was exchanged between them. *But what?* It made him think about Luis, the brave and loving boy who called him uncle. He feared they'd never see each other again. He felt their orange tent beckoning him home at an impossible distance now.

Arsenic poisoning. That's what the doctor said.

A black van stopped curbside and two men got out. They routed through the pockets of his fancy clothes, coming up empty-handed. "Someone must've gotten here first," one grumbled before running off.

I was lucky to get a good boy like Luis. How different everything would've been had the stranger's hand that had reached for his at the mass gravesite not been Luis'. "Yes," he had told Luis then, "I will be your Uncle Tomas." *Sí, Luis, seré tu tío.*

Now Tomas' vision dimmed and his body became limp. And as his head rested weakly to one side, what a surprise: a golden dandelion that, despite all odds, had insisted its way up through a crack in the sidewalk. It was breathtaking, beautiful, breathtaking.

Old Stadium Site

West Oakland

Holding Daleen's scarf-wrapped bundle, Nora knocked on the camper door, calling, "Yusra?" Then, testing the door knob, she found it locked.

Fred looked anxiously around, reaching for his bronchodilator. Since the wildfires began, his asthma had worsened from hazardous air quality throughout the Bay Area. The additional stress of involvement in Nora's predicament merely amplified the problem.

"We need to see inside," Nora said. "There's a sunroof, but no window."

He shook his head. "I'm not going to do that."

"But Yusra could be inside. Daleen probably taught her to hide—"

"Okay!" he said, trying to maintain calm for both of their sakes. He took out his keychain penlight and, against his better judgment, said: "We'll just settle this now." Then he climbed atop the camper, his jacket and trousers absorbing grime along the way. After reaching the sunroof, he reported: "I don't see anyone inside."

Nora's heart sunk. "But can you see the *entire* interior?"

"It's a penlight, Nora. Not a klieg light. It only shines so far."

"Well, can you open the sunroof?"

"Are you nuts? You're going all Nancy Drew on me again."

"Please? Besides, it's Inspector Jane Tennison, remember?"

"I can't believe I'm saying this: but now I regret canceling Carrie's tonight. I wouldn't be in this position if—"

"Just try, Fred. You're already on the roof."

"Hell," he muttered, jostling the sunroof, and surprised to see it open so easily. But the drop down to the floor looked forbidding. "Nora," he said, "unfortunately, it's at least an eight-foot drop."

"But you're six feet tall! Just sit on the rim, feet inside, grab onto the opposite rim, and lower yourself down."

"I'm supposed to be James Bond now?"

"You'll be fine. If not, remember: I'm an ER doc."

He almost cursed, an impulse checked by his awareness that Yusra might, indeed, be hiding inside. Instead, he amiably called out her name and, getting no response, forewarned: "Okay, Yusra, I'm just coming inside; we're friends of your mom's." Following Nora's advice, he then lowered himself down, surprised by his own prowess. When he opened the door to admit Nora, he expected some acknowledgment of his feat. But she just handed him the food bundle, grabbed his penlight, and searched the camper. She found the sleeping area tidy, furnished with a green army cot and orange milkcrates; it smelled of lavender and mildew. The kitchenette was stocked with cans, and herbal sprays hung from the ceiling. She returned to Fred and shook her head.

"Sorry, Nora," he said, handing back the food bundle. Then he repositioned a nearby workbench and stood atop it to close the sunroof. When he finished, he returned the workbench to its original location, and Nora dusted off his shoeprints with her hand. Fred followed her out of the camper, grazing his scalp against the doorframe as he secured the internal door lock. He closed the door behind them, and checked to make certain it remained locked. But when he turned to Nora, he found her standing motionless, staring at the door. "What's wrong?" he asked. "Did you get stuck?"

Slowly turning to him, she said: "I feel like we just closed the door on any last hope of finding Yusra."

"Hold on now," he said, taking her by the arm, coaxing her away. "We still have that orange tent to check out."

"You're right," she said without conviction. She pointed to the tent while flashing back on her unsettling experience there earlier in the day.

"Well, let's go," he said, nudging her along. "At least there's no 'crazy lady' chasing you away this time."

But when they arrived at the orange tent, they looked knowingly at one another. No lights or sounds emanated from it; the only movement was the billowing of its walls with the breezes.

Fred called out, "Hello. Anyone inside?" Then, getting no answer, he proceeded to open the entry flap, all the while introducing himself as a friend of Yusra's mother. But when he looked inside, he saw no one. He turned to Nora and said, "Sorry, again."

"My god," Nora shakily replied. "I'm scared for Yusra now. And what do I tell Daleen? I should probably go to the police—?"

"Well, I'll be," Fred interrupted, pointing to a couple fast-approaching. "We've got company."

She recognized the blonde woman from the newspapers: Her shapely long legs, regal carriage, and the Michelle Obama arms made evident in a finely tailored jacket. She had to be Samantha Greeley. Nora whispered, "Your new board member?"

"Yes," he whispered back. "But I don't recognize the stocky guy in the hoodie."

Samantha extended a hand to Fred while clearly appraising his dishevelment. She said "Fred" as if it were a question.

"Hello, Samantha," he replied, trying to not view her legs. "This is my colleague, Dr. Nora Kelly."

His "colleague"? thought Nora. *He's definitely flustered.* She smiled politely and said hello to Samantha and her partner.

"Pleased to meet you," said Samantha, eyeing Nora head to toe. She decided not to introduce her partner—*what was the point?*—and said: "I'm surprised to see you two here. May I ask what you're doing?"

Expecting Fred to flub a reply, Nora preemptively answered: "We needed to follow up with a patient living here."

Samantha cocked her head and looked suspiciously at them. "Really? I thought doctors didn't make house calls anymore. Certainly, not to places like this. And, *two* of you? On a *holiday*?"

Fred's asthma began flaring again, reignited by her incendiary doubts. He knew he couldn't truthfully explain their presence without betraying Nora's promise of confidentiality to Daleen. And the truth of their mission would also risk his hard-won alliance with Samantha, sabotaging his arduous efforts to lure her onto the board. He stood speechless before her, now both literally and figuratively sullied—an accomplice to a break-in on her property, and surreptitiously involved in a troubling missing-child situation.

Sensing his discomfort, Nora stepped in again: "You're right, Samantha. House calls have gone the way of the dinosaurs. But 'my colleague' and I are old-school. We wanted to see where our patient lived because she'd developed such a rare illness."

That's not why we came! Fred shouted internally. *What the hell, Nora? I can't have Samantha suspecting we're here to condemn her property!*

Samantha shot her partner a querying look, and Nora watched them negotiate silently. Then the man just shrugged and looked down, partially unveiling his profile from under his hood. Nora saw he was missing his left ear, and his salt-and-pepper hair was pulled or slicked back. Samantha pivoted back to Nora and asked: "What rare illness? And why should it matter where she lives?"

"Sorry," said Nora. "I can't disclose confidential information about patients."

"But I own this place. It's belonged to my family for decades."

"It's just that our patient doesn't have the means or wherewithal to come to *us*," said Nora. She looked askance at the surroundings and continued: "Besides, this place was on our way to a dinner tonight."

Samantha laser-focused on Nora. "You may think 'this place' is a miserable place to live or raise a family. But, tell me, Nora: Where else can these people go? In *your* backyard?" She scoffed. "The Greeley family has *never* charged them *anything* to live off our land. It may not be paradise, but it certainly isn't the worse hell they could be living in otherwise."

Fred cringed. "Please, Samantha; this is a misunderstanding. You and your family's foundation have been remarkably philanthropic. We were honored you joined our board, even if it took some arm-twisting on my part." He waited expectantly for her smile, but he waited in vain.

Nora couldn't stand how "admin" her friend was behaving *again.* Throughout his years of serving as chief of the medical staff, his language had acquired a corp-speak quality that made him sound alien. With misplaced annoyance, she said to Samantha: "And what about you? You're out here today *because* . . .?"

Samantha rolled her eyes, if ever so slightly. "It's basic CEO diligence and oversight. It's me being responsible. The sale of this property is closing next week." She huffishly appended, "It's been in the news for months."

Fred told Nora, "Yes, they're selling to a housing developer. And you've got to admit, new housing would provide a vast improvement to what's here now."

Nora asked, "Will it include low-income units, for people like those living here now?"

Samantha's partner stepped forward and admonished Nora: "You got no cause, lady." But Samantha stepped between them and said, "I don't appreciate your moralistic tone, Dr. Kelly. But if you must know: Our contract with the developer—aligned with my family's longstanding commitment to the community—stipulates the inclusion of low-income and affordable units. And, by the way, a sizable portion of the profits we make from any real estate venture funnels back into our charitable foundation. That, in turn, funds *other* community programs that align with our foundation's civic values." Then, adopting a derisive tone, she said: "So, Nora, remind me about *your* advocacy work with the homeless population."

After glowering at Nora, Fred said, "Let's all step back a minute. We're on the same side."

But Samantha's comment stung deeply, and Nora had to admit: *She's right. Other than handing out the occasional dollar on the street and voting for ballot propositions to fund shelters, I've done nothing meaningful or substantive about homelessness. I live in a comfortable home at a considerable distance from the problem. And though I provide good care to unsheltered patients who come to the ER, still, I'm paid to do that.* She glanced apologetically at Fred, internally conceding Samantha's unmatchable charity. And that's when it occurred to her: she might actually be envious and jealous of Samantha, unfairly projecting onto her. *Samantha the saint. The beautiful and powerful Samantha Greeley with a gazillion-dollar fortune. Fred's Samantha with the "great legs."*

"Right, Nora?" asked Fred.

Nora took a deep breath. "Yes. This has been a misunderstanding. And I regret my part in it."

Samantha flatly replied, "Apology accepted." Then she nodded goodbye to Fred and walked away with her companion.

Once they'd traveled beyond earshot, Fred scolded Nora: "That confrontation was uncalled for! And damn uncomfortable. Risky, too, for me and the hospital. What right did you have, questioning her like that? And to insinuate her property was responsible for a patient's illness? My god, what were you thinking?"

Nora shrugged. "I probably wasn't. Wasn't thinking."

"And look at me! My clothes are filthy because you made me climb—"

"But I am now," she interrupted.

"Now what?"

"Now, *thinking.*"

He was furious. But he also knew that she was unavailable to his rage, watching her begin her familiar inward retreat. He was intimately acquainted with that telling look on her face: so somber, certain, calm, and direct. Her brain was now operating like a masterful symphony. He knew if he waited patiently for her to finish, she'd replay for him what her mind had composed. And, as discordant as that often sounded with what he might prefer to hear, he always trusted it would ring true.

Finally, she said: "I was replaying that old adage in medicine, advising doctors to think 'horses' and not 'zebras' when we hear hoofbeats."

"Yes," he said. "To look for common causes of a patient's symptoms before searching for rare ones."

"So," she said, "Aditya called me this morning for consultation about chelating a patient with probable arsenic poisoning. I was intrigued, of course. But all Aditya could tell me about the man's background was that he lived here, like Daleen. So, within twenty-four hours, we've likely diagnosed two residents from this same encampment with two zebras: methemoglobinemia and arsenic poisoning. And I'm including a third—another resident named Abeo who died last month from organophosphate toxicity. Three rare diagnoses. Three zebras sounding the hoofbeats."

"So?"

"So, there should be an asterisk attached to the old adage. Like, 'this doesn't apply if working near zebra herds.' Because then, it would make better sense to think 'zebras' before 'horses' when you heard hoofbeats." She smiled at him and continued, "And with *three* zebras from this *one* site, we have to assume there's something unique and troubling about this place to make hoofbeats sound more commonly from zebras than horses."

Fred groaned. "You're going from Nancy Drew to Erin Brockovich now? You sure you're not just trying to stick it to Samantha?"

"Please, Fred."

"Sorry. Uncalled for. Still, your suggestion sounds fishy. I mean, it's preposterous to imagine someone buying this hugely expensive property without obtaining rigorous environmental inspections first. And it's *de rigueur* in real estate transactions."

But Nora just stared back, with that same knowing expression, and asked him to accompany her back to the camper. There, she rummaged through Daleen's food bundle for plastic food containers and baggies that she then emptied. "Let's start with the garden," she said.

He wearily watched her kneel and scoop garden soil into baggies. "Are we really doing this?"

9th Floor Ward Room

Oakland City Hospital

Something is wrong if Dr. Nora has not yet brought news of Yusra to me.

Daleen looked out through her hospital window at the ominous soot-laden sky. It reminded her of Yemen, so often dark like this because of war.

Did Dr. Nora tell police and immigration about Yusra? Have they taken her? Maybe Yusra got sick, like me. Is she lying alone somewhere, needing help?

There could be no good reason for the lack of news. And no one here in this American hospital with its clean sheets and enormous televisions could understand or help. *They are oblivious to my suffering. I will have to search for Yusra alone.*

But when she stepped out of bed, she felt instantly light-headed. She fell and couldn't get up from the floor. It alarmed her to notice her skin's lingering blue, heightened in contrast against the beige linoleum.

Finally, footsteps sounded; someone entered her room. She recognized his voice: the intern who'd taken her photograph in the ER. "So, there you are," he said. "I came by a minute ago but didn't see you in bed. Now I know why." He took another photo of her before helping her up and back to bed. "You're not as blue as yesterday," he said, checking the quality of his photo. Then he pulled out his iPad and placed an order for an MRI of her brain. "I'll get you some help," he said, pushing the nurse-call button and leaving immediately.

Target Store

Emeryville

The large boxy building across the street had a huge red target over its entrance, where a large crowd had gathered. Then Yusra saw the doors open and people rushing in. Surely, it was a sign, so she headed to Target, too.

Meanwhile, Jack, Red, and Luis were on their way to the store to purchase a new cellphone. They'd decided to drive in Jack's car to save gas for Red's truck, and left straightaway from Betty's. When Luis mentioned he'd never been to Target, Red assured him he was going to be amazed: "They got *everything* there." Jack thought: *Indeed; soon, even us three together.*

Fergie and Winston had just parked the Subaru in Target's crowded lot. She said, "I can't believe all the people here on Thanksgiving." He replied,

"Well, it's the only major store open now. I hope there's enough food left to take back to the lake." She said, "And remember, it's got to be simple to serve. And we'll need charcoal for the barbeque pits. Oh, and I figured out how to warm up my lasagna and . . . What? Why are you smiling like that?" Winston kissed her and said, "This is the best Thanksgiving ever, Fergs."

A few miles away, Nora and Fred were driving the Mandela Parkway en route to Target for appetizers. To her dismay, they'd not found Jack at her house, and he still wasn't answering calls. The now-established fact of him and Yusra both gone missing washed over her like shocks of frigid rainfall. She shuddered and, suddenly feeling it surreal to be shopping for appetizers, said: "You were right, Fred. I should have just canceled with Carrie. I don't know what I was thinking earlier." He said, "Don't be so hard on yourself. It's been a helluva day. And you've still got your visit with Daleen ahead." Grimacing, she said, "Everything seems out of control, including myself." He cleared his throat and suggested, "Let's take one thing at a time. And right now, I'm starving, and we're not a minute away from Target. So, let's just go in and get some food. You can call Carrie to cancel while I grab a few things."

A block down the street from Target, Gianni parked his truck after failing to find the girl he'd scared away. He looked out the windshield at the crowds swarming the Target lot, undoubtedly planning festive get-togethers tonight. *But me, such a loser that I even scare children off. And now I end up canceling Patty tonight for no good reason. Can't make inroads with Red. Even the bartender gave me grief. And the scrapyard guy rejected me!* He took another swig of Jack Daniel's and headed home, deciding it a good night to get blurry-minded in front of the TV. Along the way, driving by so many shuttered stores and restaurants on Broadway made him feel even more uninvited in the world. But when he crossed Grand, he saw a man lying on the sidewalk, and it made great karmic sense. He parked, grabbed his flask, and headed toward the well-dressed stranger. *All of god's creatures,* he said to himself, imagining some healing camaraderie for each of them. But he got no reaction when he nudged the man and said, "Hey, pal." And when he held out the flask and cheerily offered "hair of the dog," still, the man didn't budge. Gianni squatted down to get a closer look and discovered the man wasn't breathing. He slumped back against the storefront, moaning.

At the hospital, Aditya's cell rang. Lizbeth heard him answer: "Yes, I'm Dr. Singh . . . The police? Why are you calling? . . . Yes, I took care of a patient fitting that description. I gave him my card . . . Well, if he is wearing a purple shirt, black shoes and trousers, then, yes, I believe that is him. But why are you asking these questions?" Still, he knew.

Carl's Home

Piedmont

"I'm sorry to hear that," said Carl. "But yes, I'd still like to come."

On the other end of the phone call, Carrie replied: "Well, it only means more turkey for the two of us!"

"It must mean more than that," he said, "if *everyone* but me canceled for your dinner tonight."

"That's very astute," she said. "No wonder my sister thought highly of you. She always said you were 'one of a kind' and 'brilliant beyond words.'"

Carl felt as though he might faint. "*Lydia* said that?"

Carrie laughed. "Well, that is . . . *was* my sister's name."

After they hung up, Carl walked to his garage in a daze. He opened the trunk of his car and re-counted the wine he'd packed and promised to bring to Carrie's. Then he inputted Carrie's address into his car's GPS and headed out, still amazed that Lydia had mentioned him, let alone in non-caustic terms. *But how, for decades, did I only feel her scalding judgment? How did I consistently misinterpret her attitude toward me?*

Target Store

Emeryville

"Your car stinks," said Fred. "And it's disgusting, eating with all those dirt samples on the backseat."

After popping another cheese cube from the appetizer tray she'd purchased at Target, Nora said: "I take you to dinner at the finest Target lot in all of Northern California, and, still, you complain."

He laughed, nearly choking on a melon ball, then said: "Got to admit, the little sausages were great."

She grabbed another jicama stick. "I felt bad about canceling with Carrie, but she said she understood. Funny thing . . . I was a little hurt when she didn't seem upset that I wasn't bringing my appetizers."

"Yeah, what a mystery. When's the last time you actually cooked anything?"

"Yesterday."

His eyes narrowed. "What'd you make?"

"Stew. First, I took a can of—"

"Forget it. If your main kitchen tool was a can opener, I don't care to hear about it."

She grinned and said, "Old family recipe."

Fred put down his plastic spoon. "All right now. As delightful as this feast has been, it's time to get back to business. And on the way to Jack's house—god, I hope he's there—you need to decide who you're telling first about Yusra: Daleen or the police."

~ ~ ~

Inside Target, Luis roamed the aisles, incredulous. He had to be dreaming or hallucinating, because there seemed to be enough food and clothing here to help *everyone* out. How could that be? Did everybody know about this? His stunning discovery was too much to bear.

"C'mon, little man," said Red, prodding him along. "Try to keep up with us."

Still, Luis lagged behind, struggling to move beyond his disbelief. Jack, sensing that Luis was overwhelmed, said: "My grandfather started a family business of garden and hardware stores. When I was your age, I helped him out after school. I thought it was amazing, too."

Luis stared thunderstruck at Jack. "*You* worked in a store like *this*?"

Jack nodded. "I stocked the shelves and swept floors. When I was older, I took inventory."

Luis' jaw dropped. Before this moment, he couldn't have imagined working in a place that contained everything to help out all the people he knew who had nothing.

Nearing the checkout with their loaded cart, Fergie stopped, pointed, and told Winston: "There's that little girl with her doll who we saw in the cereal section. She's still alone."

Winston said, "She must be lost." But when he started toward her, she startled and ran away.

"Hey," said Fergie, holding him back. "Just stay here with the cart, okay?" Then she walked to the next aisle and found the girl hiding on a low shelf. She stood within the girl's view and pretended to be standing idly by. Then she put her hands in her pockets, stepped back a safe distance, and bent down to lock eyes with the girl.

Yusra stared back at the strange white person: a man or woman? The person wore huge eyeglasses and had blue tattoos around the neck. But why wasn't that person coming after her or trying to scare her? Yusra knew to say nothing, and remained silent when the person asked: "Want to come out of there, honey?" She was surprised when, seconds later, the person just said "Okay" and walked away. When she peered out from the shelf and saw the person waving to her at the end of the aisle, she decided: *That's not a bad Nice Person.* So, she crawled off the shelf and said: "I'm looking for my mom."

Winston received Fergie's text: *Got her. B cool.* In other words, he gleaned: *Don't move suddenly toward the girl and scare her again.*

Moments later, Fergie reappeared with the girl and explained: "This is my friend, Winston. And, Winston, this is my new friend. She doesn't want to tell us her name, but we're going to help find her mom."

"This place is big," he said, "but we'll find her." Yusra shielded herself behind Fergie and smiled shyly back at him.

~ ~ ~

In the electronics department, no matter how passionately Jack pleaded, the salesperson said there'd be no cellphone service transfers today. Too few employees were trying to serve too many last-minute holiday shoppers. Red said, "Give it up, Dr. Jack. You can do that in the morning."

Still, Jack's last nerve was frayed, his lip swelling was irritating, and he almost told the salesperson to "have a happy fucking Thanksgiving." But, aware that Luis was looking up at him, instead he bit his tongue and said: "Luis, if ever you do work as a salesperson, always expect customers to treat you with respect." Then he returned to the salesperson: "Even if they can't help you."

That was amazing to Luis, to learn that a worker was always entitled to respect. He couldn't wait to tell Uncle Tomas, who always said that day laborers like himself were never respected. Someday, perhaps, he and his uncle could get jobs and respect, working at a store like this.

"So, can we go now?" asked Red.

Jack replied, "Yes. No. I mean, wait." He hesitated, realizing he'd be returning Red and Luis to their dreary circumstances. "Hey," he said, "would you guys join me for Thanksgiving dinner at my house first? We could get a turkey here, some potatoes, and greens. And I can drive you back to your truck at Betty's in the morning."

"But you got potatoes in your car already," said Luis.

"Well," said Jack, stalling, "you can never have too many of those!"

Luis begged Red, "Please? Maybe you can call DeeDee and ask her to watch your truck tonight? She lives upstairs above the restaurant."

Red liked the idea, and it provided him with an excellent excuse to call DeeDee. Still, he worried about infuriating Patty again should she discover his overnight absence at the gate. When Jack asked what was troubling him, Red dismissively answered, "Nothing on one level, everything on another."

~ ~ ~

Fergie became anxious after walking all the aisles with the girl and, still, no sign of the mother. *Why hasn't the mother initiated a search by the store's security guards? Why no public announcements about a missing child? Why does this girl flinch every time she sees someone in a uniform?* Fergie texted Winston: *Still no mom. Start checking out. Will catch up.* She asked the girl, "Honey, was your mom shopping for clothes?" The girl shook her head. "For food?" The girl shook her head again, and any further guessing continued to prove pointless. After another walk through the main aisles, Fergie conceded that she should notify store security, as traumatic as that might be for the child. She said, "Honey, how about telling me your name now?" But the girl just slowly backed away.

"Yusra!" someone shouted. The girl shuddered so hard that she dropped her doll. Then she couldn't move, couldn't breathe while Luis ran toward her in a bright yellow tee-shirt. He ran so fast that he almost stumbled. "Yusra!" he shouted, hugging her. "Luis," she sobbed.

"Yusra?" said Fergie, swiftly appraising the girl's age, wondering at the coincidence of Nora searching for Daleen's young daughter with the same name. *But how would a six-year-old have gotten to this store, alone and so far from the stadium?*

Yusra tightly held onto Luis, who exclaimed, "She's my best friend."

Fergie asked him, "Do you know her mother?" Luis said yes, but Yusra placed a silencing finger on his lips. Then he attempted to unsay what he had said: "I mean, no." The two friends looked up at Fergie, maintaining an obvious conspiratorial silence. Then Jack caught up to Luis and happily exclaimed, "Fergie?" Red followed close behind and, recognizing the girl who lived in the camper, smiled at her and said, "Hey."

~ ~ ~

In the parking lot, Nora and Fred were packing leftovers in the car and preparing to leave. Something caught her eye, and she did a double-take: Yes, it was Winston, exiting Target with a cartload of food. Pointing to him, she said, "How odd. You'd think he and Fergie would be leaving for Carrie's about now."

"Well," said Fred, "by the looks of it, maybe they're bringing the entire meal—Nora style."

Nora feigned a smile, donned a rainhat, and said, "Gimme a minute." Then she walked over to Winston, who was transferring bags to his car. She greeted him: "Quite a haul."

Winston said, "Fancy meeting you here! It's for a meal we're fixing at the lake for folks I met today."

"Oh? You're not going to Carrie's?"

He laughed. "Long story. Let's just say we got waylaid, and we called to cancel about an hour ago."

"Poor Carrie! I canceled, too. So did Fred."

"Well, you're welcome to join us and a few dozen others." His phone chimed with a text from Fergie that made him smile and say, "Good news!"

"Happy to hear that," said Nora. "And, thanks for the dinner invite, but I've got to drop by Jack's and then the hospital. Give my best to

Fergie." But heading back to her Prius, she was besieged with worry. *I can't bear to tell Daleen that Yusra's missing. But she should hear that from me. And Jack? Will I end up informing police about two missing persons?* Then her phone rang; Fergie was calling. Nora answered, "I just ran into Winston in the parking lot . . . Sorry? . . . Of course, I remember . . . Yes, Daleen's still in the hospital and, actually, I'm on my way to . . . Her last name? Habani . . . Yes, her daughter's name is Yusra." Then, trance-like, Nora listened while Fergie explained where to meet up inside the store. When Nora returned to Fred, he asked what was wrong. She grabbed Daleen's scarf and said, "Just follow me."

Fred followed Nora into Target. They walked past displays of paper products, gym wear, cotton towels, and bath mats that Nora only saw in a blur. Finally, following Fergie's last instruction, Nora turned the corner around the featured display of Thanksgiving decorations and gasped. Jack was there, standing beside Fergie. But that shock was instantly trumped by another when she saw the small girl with them. *It's definitely Yusra!* The resemblance with Daleen was striking, and they had the same dark questioning eyes. When Nora shakily held out Daleen's maroon scarf, Yusra's eyes opened wide and she ran to take hold of it, whispering, almost inaudibly, "Mom."

Monarch Terrace Apartments

Downtown

When Gianni entered his apartment, he felt as though he were stepping into a cold lifeless shadow. It clung to him and followed him to every room. He caught himself in the hallway mirror—soiled shirt and jeans, muddy boots, earth-rimmed fingernails. "Pathetic," he whispered.

He turned on the TV, grabbed a Bud, and collapsed on the couch. Instantly, he was reminded of his quick tryst here with Patty last night. Then he imagined the one they would be having now, had he not fucked up the plan for tonight. *Still, it felt right to go looking for that girl. I know I shouldn't've been so cocked off when I tried to help her earlier.*

Mostly, he thought about the dead man he found today. *How fucked that anyone should die like that, alone, on a sidewalk, people passing by, ignoring you.* At least the police had responded quickly to his call and been respectful. They even allowed him to drive away with only a warning about the flask. *Still, it feels weird not knowing even the name of a guy I was about to have a drink with.*

Then it occurred to him that Red or Patty might know the man. The police would only say that he'd just left the hospital and had been living at the stadium. *Yeah. I'll ask Red tomorrow if I don't get the chance to ask Patty sooner.*

Now he could focus on the intentions he'd declared after leaving Grady's bar—*at three-fuckin'-o'clock! A new job. New skills and challenges. Relating differently to women. And to guys, too.*

Determined to follow through on them, he grabbed another beer and opened his laptop. Feeling optimistic, he began by consulting the internet for advice about relationship-building. *I can do these things,* he told himself. *I can listen harder . . . talk more about feelings . . . come up with something besides sex to propose to women.*

Visiting Room, San Sebastian Prison

Marin County

Pete Vaughn had just discovered that his headaches improved if he slept sitting upright. And if he turned his head slowly, he could minimize his dizziness. The prescribed acetaminophen—when guards actually cared to distribute it—was sufficient for the pain. *Yes, I got this whole brain-tumor situation under control. No need for barbarian surgeons who just want to cut my brain.*

Sitting behind the plexiglass partition, he smiled at Patty and said, "Baby girl, it's damn good to see you. And coming all this way on Thanksgiving."

Patty pressed her palm against the partition, mirroring his. "I love you, baby," she said.

"Hey," he said. "Why you tearing up?"

Her hand dropped to her lap. "Everything's falling sideways to hell since you've been gone."

"I miss you, too, baby girl. But you got to stay strong." He decided the timing was bad to inform her about his tumor.

She drew a steadying breath. "I been trying, baby. But those people! They're so *needy*. And they been without work since you been gone. I don't know how to find them cleanup jobs or fieldwork. They're real desperate, and I don't have another dime of my own to spare. I'm raiding every food bank, and bargaining at the Dollar Store for bread and peanut butter. And the immigration folks are coming down real hard."

Pete's jaw clenched. Where was all the damn support they'd promised to provide Patty as part of the deal he'd struck in exchange for taking the rap last year? And what was the sense in not helping her find cheap labor for residents, when half the money funneled back into Greeley pockets anyway? He wondered how quickly he could get a message to his people on the outside. "Baby girl," he whispered, "I'm sorry. You're suffering for the mistakes I made. This wasn't supposed to fall on you. You're supposed to be getting help."

"Well, the last time *they* dropped any money in our mailbox was maybe three months ago. And I still ain't been paid back for what I had to put out-of-pocket for our so-called security. My card's maxed out . . ." She stopped herself from telling him how disgracefully they'd been evicted; she saw how angry he'd already become, even holding his head like it pained him.

"It's hard to hear this, Patty. You shoulda told me earlier."

She blinked back tears, thinking, *"Earlier"? Well, you were supposed to be outta here in eight months. But then you had to go selling cellphones in prison and get caught. It didn't have to be this way for me.* "Honestly," she said, "I don't think I can hang on. And people . . . they're getting sick. Going to hospitals. I even lost a child today."

"Someone died?"

"No. I actually *lost* a little girl. Yesterday, I was on my way to visit you, but I'd just taken her mama to the hospital. And I figured ICE or the police or CPS would come looking for her, so I just put the girl in my wagon. But then the traffic was awful . . . my nerves were shot . . . it was raining buckets. I just turned back and took a room at that motel by the Maze." She broke down. "But this morning, when I walked outta the shower . . . well, she was just gone from the room."

His headache fiercely resurrected, and he tried to conceal the pain. "There'll be trouble if someone finds the girl."

"I know! But, maybe we're okay? I mean, she didn't have papers on her. And when I looked through their camper for her mama's, I didn't find any. So, I expect they can't trace her back to us even if someone finds her."

Pete slammed his fist against the wall. "Baby girl, I swear, I was guaranteed you'd have help. Money help and legal help. And by them not taking care of you, they're seriously disrespecting me."

They again touched their palms through the partition and Pete said: "Don't worry. I'm going to contact them tonight. They *will* make things right."

She nodded. But she doubted whether anything *could* be made "right" now in her actual circumstances. It would've been better, she thought, had she followed her instincts and left—him, the camp, the whole outsider way of living—months ago, when he chose to jeopardize his prison release with another illegal scheme. "Well, I hope they do. 'Cuz all I got now is Red, my so-called security man. Even he's been taking liberties, and he's . . ."

"He what?"

"He's blaming me for people getting sick. He told me it's all my fault." She whimpered.

Pete's eyes widened with incredulity. "Baby girl, you got to get perspective. You're not responsible for their misery. In fact, you're *helping* them! I mean, where else can they go? Who else is helping them get jobs? If this Red is holding you responsible, he must think you're god."

She blew her nose, and returned a faint smile.

"There's my sunshine," he said, smiling back. "Hey, but what about that landscape guy who was supposed to help out after they put me away?"

Patty nearly choked, flooded with remorse over last night's dalliance with Gianni. "What about him?"

"Well, isn't he helping you?"

She struggled to meet his gaze. "They called him in a few times. I'm just minding my own business."

"You're right, keeping to your own. Believe me, you can't trust anyone there. But I got this now. Think you can hold the fort a couple more weeks?"

"Oh, baby, I don't see how. You know I'd do *anything* for you, but I got nothing left to give. I'm broke in every way possible. In my spirit, too." *And I'm stuck in the hell you left me in, with not even gas money out.*

He whispered, "I promise to get the word out tonight. And let's give them twenty-four hours to pay what they owe you, or we close down your 'nonprofit.' We let them deal with the problems there." He pointed to the key on the necklace he'd given her last year and winked. "You got a good heart, baby girl, and that key to mine. Just don't let your heart turn so soft that it falls apart. Certainly not before I get outta here."

"But if I just walk away, what about all the people there? And where else would they go?"

"Don't know. But they seem to go anywhere and everywhere in the city. There's places all over the streets for them. Underpasses. Parks, too."

Surprised to be worried about Yusra, her eyes reddened. "I feel like it's more than just me falling apart. The whole thing . . . everything . . . it's all falling apart for everyone. It feels like an apocalypse, and it even looks like one outside."

Pete leaned abruptly back, bowled over by his fury over her suffering. *How dare they treat my girl this way!* Still, he had to admit he was partly responsible for her predicament. He leaned toward her and, in a contrite tone, said, "You got to believe I have your back, even though I fucked up with the cellphone shit. But I won't let you down again. Please, trust me to take care of this." He determined to get his message out tonight. "In the meantime, tell Red to back off and do right by you, or he'll hear from me, too. Settled?" After she nodded, he said, "Good. Now, what are you doing for Thanksgiving tonight?"

Trying to survive, she thought, averting his gaze, daring to hope he'd come through, and feeling relieved she wasn't meeting with Gianni after all.

Samantha's Home

Samantha Greeley gazed appraisingly at her dinner guests: so Northern California tribal in their business-casual attire, comporting with a self-assurance that rubbed up against self-consciousness. And how fashionably intergenerational: Western Financial's CEO sitting beside CoinBytes' COO. Chez Rimbaud's head chef, partnered with Soil-to-Mouth's owner. The Oakland Theater's founder, conversing animatedly with NezGenArt's artistic director.

Midway through the banquet, when she felt comfortable about leaving her guests to carry on without her, she whispered to her tablemate: "We need to talk about the stadium deal."

"Now?" he replied.

She smiled stiffly.

He lifted his wineglass and said, "Of course. But everything's ready and polished for next week's sale."

She did not clink his glass. "I'm having serious doubts."

"But there's no cause, Samantha. We're on solid ground. We've spent years on this deal. All the county and city approvals. The environmental studies. The financing. And Highmark Construction is champing at the bit to begin their housing development."

"Meet me in the library. Two minutes. And be inconspicuous." Then she excused herself to her guests "for a moment" and went to the library, where she waited for Quentin Ocambo. There were hundreds of books here, and so artfully arranged; when would she ever find the time, or interest, to read a few? She lightly petted several of her father's taxidermy mounts, like she used to as a child: the feathery pheasant, the teeth-bared fox, the bulky elk bust, the badly stuffed lumpy bunny. Then she glanced at the legacy wall bearing portraits of family members, who seemed to be staring at her from generations past to the moment in which she looked at them now. She addressed them out loud: "I'm what's left of you all, the last Greeley standing." Then she looked at the vacancy where her own portrait was expected to hang, and decided the vacancy represented her perfectly. "I don't want what you wanted," she continued. "I don't belong on this wall with you."

Promptly at two minutes, Quentin arrived. He closed the door and said, "I can't fathom what might be troubling you."

"And *that* is the problem," she said. "Because it should be glaringly obvious."

"But it's not, Samantha." He set down his wineglass and regarded her with a baffled expression.

"You need it spelled out? Okay. I was at the stadium today, and things didn't look right."

He tutted. "Well, it's no paradise, of course. But still, it's going to fetch us . . . *you* . . . three hundred million."

She gritted her teeth. "You reassured me the property was ready for the sale."

"Because . . . it is."

"Really? Tell me how you know that, Quentin. Validate the expertise I'm getting from your nine-hundred-an-hour fee."

"Frankly, I don't appreciate the way you're speaking to me. Why not get to your point?"

"The *point* is, you're either lying to me now, or you're cognitively impaired. Because we saw tents and cars everywhere. Dozens—maybe hundreds—of people, still living there. You told me last month the homeless camp had been cleared and everyone moved out!"

He stared in shock at her. *Because that's what Martin told me. He assured me . . .*

"And there was no security at the gate," she continued. "We just drove right through and walked around. What the hell's wrong with you, Quentin?"

"I can't believe it. I'd been informed . . ." He shakily sat down to compose himself. *My god, this can't be happening. But Martin lied to me; there's no other explanation.* Thunderstruck, he asked, "What do you mean by 'we'?"

She'd been keeping her relationship with Marty private, knowing it would disturb him—something she had not wanted to risk. But now she was so furious and frustrated with Quentin, she felt like hurting him back. She leaned in close. "Your son and I have been *seeing* each other."

Quentin felt nauseous, and a surge of acid reflux scorched his throat. He shook his head in disbelief. "You can't possibly be dating Martin."

"Well, I am. He's got an eagle tattooed on his—"

"Stop! Why would you do such a thing? He's a sociopath, a loser. He's a . . . a thug. He's using you."

"Using me? I see. You're trying to hurt me back."

"That's not what I intended. He's using you against *me*. And he'll swindle your assets while he's at it."

"Yeah? Well, I'm grateful he accompanied me to the stadium today. It was good to have *someone* actually *demonstrate* concern about my property. And it was good to have an ally when people confronted me."

"The residents?"

"No. Two doctors claiming to be following up with a patient."

He popped an antacid. "It's probably nothing."

"How wrong can you be *again*? It is *something*, Quentin! Those doctors were looking for someone, and they *implicated* my property as the cause for their patient's illness. And I repeat: there was *no security*. I repeat: scores of people and tents were *still* there. And that all adds up to a definite *something*, you fool."

A knock on the door presaged the butler's announcement: "Ms. Greeley, your friend to see you. He said it was important."

Samantha nodded, and Martin entered. "Hi, Dad," he said.

Lake Merritt

Oakland

Over the phone, Fred's wife Vickie inquired whether he'd be coming home. "Or should the kids and I start Thanksgiving without you?"

He replied, "You go on without me."

"All right," she said. "But what's all that noise in the background? It doesn't sound like you're at the hospital. Isn't that the excuse you used to get us out of going to Carrie's?"

"Well, I *did* go in," he said. "But I finished business there. Now I'm at the lake with other people."

"What on earth are you doing there? And what 'people'?"

"I'm with Nora and Jack, and Fergie and Winston. We're preparing dinner for some unsheltered folks."

Vickie tsk'ed and said, "Honestly, Fred, you could've told us earlier. Hang on a minute." He heard her summon the kids—preternaturally aged adults, really—and then a muffled discussion ensued. She returned to the phone and said, "Fred, we're coming down to join you."

"Really?" he said, beaming. "That would be great."

She laughed. "Well, you just made Ella's day. And she wants to bring the dinner she's been preparing for the family tonight. And Charlie . . . well, you know . . . he said he's just happy to experience the holiday in a more 'meaningful' way."

~ ~ ~

Red and Luis were distributing paper cups and plates to the crowd. Red said, "It's cold, little man. You should zip up your jacket." But Luis wanted his Betty's tee-shirt to show, even if he was also wearing his new jacket from Target. He could hardly wait for Winston and Fergie to finish the first round of barbeque so he could serve like DeeDee had taught him.

Yusra, assisting Luis, was wearing her mother's scarf like a shawl. She felt so happy, having learned from Dr. Nora that her mom was safe inside a hospital. And though she'd forgotten to ask whether her mother was still blue, she figured she'd find out soon enough for herself.

~ ~ ~

While Jack was arranging a buffet on makeshift tables under the pergola, Nora approached him and said: "Wish I could stay longer to help. But it's time for me to visit Daleen. The nurses said she ought to be back from her MRI about now."

"Why is she having one?" he asked.

"Apparently, one of our interns found her on the floor and automatically ordered it."

"Is she okay?"

Nora shrugged. "The nurses said the intern didn't perform any clinical exam."

Jack rolled his eyes. "Well, good luck with your visit. At least you'll have good news to deliver! And please call me—I mean, call Fergie—afterwards. We need to figure out what to do about Yusra tonight."

On her way out, Nora called back to him, "Get your damn phone fixed!"

~ ~ ~

Fergie flinched when she heard, "You again!" She instantly recognized the voice, as instantly as she'd know the sound of glass breaking. It belonged to Marla, the woman who worked in the hospital's cafeteria. She slapped Fergie's back and said, "Fancy meeting you here."

Fergie half-smiled. "We're just making dinner."

"Cool," said Marla. "You with a volunteer group or something?"

"No, I'm here with friends. It's my husband's idea."

Marla howled, "A *husband*? Seriously? I had you pegged for a butch, like me!"

"It's my tats and shaved head that confuse people, I think." She called Winston over and introduced Marla as "someone who works at the hospital with me."

He shook Marla's hand and, assuming her to be Fergie's colleague and volunteering with the cookout, said: "It's great to see so many nurses helping out."

But Marla's expression turned doleful; her characteristic bravado extinguished. "Actually," she said, "I'm here because I heard there was going to be food."

Fergie tried to conceal her shame, suddenly hearing Marla's taunts in the cafeteria in an entirely new way. She managed to reply, "It'll be ready soon." Winston stood in awkward silence.

Marla, stung with humiliation, said, "I'll wait in my car. That's where I live."

Samantha's Home

Oakland Hills

Quentin's stomach somersaulted while he was forced to witness his son kissing Samantha.

She responded, "I wasn't expecting you tonight, Marty."

Marty slid his eyes sideways to his father and grinned. "I aim to exceed people's expectations of me."

Quentin tried not to flinch with the provocation. But clearly, he'd been ambushed. And now staring at Martin and his power-intoxicated grin, he was feeling like prey.

Marty told Samantha, "Well, at least we don't need to sneak around *him* anymore." He grabbed Quentin's glass and swallowed its remaining wine.

Regarding his son with a cutting stare, Quentin shouted internally: *You ungrateful bastard! After all I've given you? You've been lying to me all along. You told me you relocated the camp.* He deliberated over telling Samantha that it was Martin who'd been reassuring him about the stadium's evacuation and readiness for sale. That he'd hired Martin almost a year ago—off-the-books, and against his better judgment—to oversee the stadium property and camp relocation. Steeling himself, buying time to figure out what his son was plotting, he said: "I'll admit, your relationship surprises me."

Feigning a look of alarm, Marty said, "Well, speaking of surprises: Did Sam tell you we visited the stadium today? I hate to say it, Dad, but . . . We were both disappointed. The homeless camp is still there. Sam says you told her it wasn't."

Now the awful truth jumped out of the darkness and seized Quentin by the throat. *My son is throwing me under the bus!* He searched Martin's expression for any prospect of truce-making, but only found cold disconnect. *He should've stayed in prison. I never should've helped him out. Nothing good can come of this treason.* Quentin stood, needlessly straightened his tie, and calmly declared, "I'll fix this, Samantha."

Marty's crafty grin returned. "Well, Dad, even if you *could,* that's just part of the problem. I'm here tonight because of more bad news."

"You're going to upset me on Thanksgiving, too?" said Samantha. "Like father, like son?"

"I don't appreciate the comparison," Marty shot back.

Quentin completely agreed with his son's comment, but also recognized some truth in Samantha's. *We are alike, in deep twisted ways. But unlike you, son, I've worked for what I have. All you've ever done is steal and take—from me, from anyone you could. And now, it seems, from Samantha as well. So, I see you, Martin. And I clearly see your double-cross. But I vow this: I will not lose the next round between us.*

"Oh, Marty," she replied dismissively. "Forgive me. You were saying?"

Looking chafed, he replied, "I'm here with a message from Pete Vaughn."

"And?" she asked, checking her watch.

The blood drained so quickly from Quentin's face that he felt suddenly light-headed. *Martin is blindsiding me again. Pete's my client. They must've met in prison . . .*

"And," said Marty, "he wants us to know he's pissed. He says we're not keeping our part of the bargain by paying what we owe. And that we're fucking over his girlfriend, Patty."

Samantha threw up her hands. "What's he and a 'girlfriend' got to do with anything?"

Struggling to contain his rage, Quentin said: "Pete's in prison, doing us a small favor. While he's away, Patty is managing the 'nonprofit' we've been paying to oversee the camp." He looked crossly at Martin and continued: "But *apparently*, she doesn't have Pete's talent for trafficking people—"

"Stop!" said Samantha. "I've told you both a million times: do not tell me the details!"

After sending his father a sideways smirk, Marty told Samantha: "Bottom line? Obviously, my old man has chosen an incompetent to pinch-hit for Pete. Regardless, she told Pete she's not been paid, and he's threatening blackmail if we . . ." He stopped when Samantha placed her hands over her ears. "Sorry," he continued. "Let's just say, Pete intends to make trouble if we don't pay whatever we owe immediately."

Of course, Quentin realized. *Patty hasn't received her money because Martin hasn't been delivering it to her!* He looked away momentarily, absorbing his mounting defeat and humiliation, his murderous rage against Martin. Then, trying to calm himself, he scanned the library, filled with Bert's career commendations and hunting trophies, thinking it was likely the last time he'd ever set foot in this storied room. *I'm sorry, Bert, but the situation you left me in is no longer tenable. What we built doesn't belong to your daughter, let alone to my thief of a son. We took the risk.*

We made the dark bargains and sacrifices. He turned to focus appraisingly on Martin and Samantha, concluding privately: *You* two *vultures deserve each other.* Then, heading out the door, he told them: "I'll fix matters at the stadium, and I'll talk with Pete tomorrow."

After Quentin left, Marty told Samantha, "I don't think my dad was happy to see me."

Samantha scoffed. "I don't understand how he could be so negligent and uninformed about my property. And so unapologetic! That's not like him."

"You're right, Sam; it's completely unacceptable. And though I've had my differences with the old man, still, as his son, I'm personally . . . well, embarrassed by him." He frowned. "But I did warn you, more than once, he was losing his marbles and forgetting things."

Massaging her temples, she said, "And all the innuendos tonight are giving me a migraine. I pay people well to spare me the sordid details, and just fucking take care of business."

"Hey, how about a hug?"

"Not now," she said, reapplying her lipstick. "I'm in no mood. And I still need those people off my property! The sale is next week! And did you check out those two doctors, like I asked?"

"Yeah. I downloaded some files for you."

"Thanks. I'll review them in the morning. I've got guests waiting at the table." She swallowed an oxy and happened to again notice the vacancy that was hers to claim on the family portrait wall. But this time, she imagined it occupied with a portrait of herself as she wished to appear: dressed in a black symphony gown, holding a violin, steeped in the music career she'd always desired. Then, looking at her parents' portraits, she thought: *What irony, on Thanksgiving, to feel so ungrateful to you for saddling me with your sticky family legacy and all its dreary businesses.*

"What are you thinking?" asked Marty.

"Nothing," she answered, sounding thoroughly spent. "Just . . . can you take care of things from now on? And pay off this Patty person. Give her what she needs to move those people out immediately."

"Sure," he said, suppressing his glee. "But what about my dad?"

"I'll take care of him. You just take care of business."

"Dr. Kelly!" said Aditya. "What are you doing here?"

Nora waved to Lizbeth and, seeing the twinkling string of turkey-lights across the headboard, was warmly reminded of Lydia. She said, "Fred told me what happened."

"So, you came by to visit?"

"Actually, I also need to see Daleen Habani. But, for some reason, she's *still* in MRI. She had a fall or a syncopal event earlier, according to the nurses. I just wanted to personally deliver some good news."

"Oh?" said Lizbeth. "You figured out the cause for her methemoglobinemia?"

"Not yet," said Nora. "But I took soil samples—"

A harried nurse burst into the room and, after looking inquiringly around, said: "Dr. Singh! With both Lizbeth and Dr. Kelly here, I can't imagine why you're calling."

He clenched his jaw. "I pressed my call button ages ago. Dozens of times!"

"Sorry," she said. "We're all doing our level best."

"No worries," said Lizbeth, waving her away. "I got this."

After the nurse left, Lizbeth explained to Nora: "Aditya had been calling because he was trying to prevent his roommate from leaving AMA. He was Tomas Ruiz, the man we suspected of having arsenic poisoning."

"He is the patient I consulted you about, regarding chelation ther-apy," said Aditya. "He left before we could start it. And then, about an hour later, he was found dead on a sidewalk."

"My god," Nora gasped. "How awful. I'm so sorry."

"I was on strict bedrest. I could not get out of bed to stop him."

Nora thought about the stadium grounds she had twice visited today. Its aging and dilapidated structures, crumbling pipes, loose wires, cor-roding metal drums . . . a common ground where Tomas, Daleen, and Abeo had lived. *Arsenic toxicity, methemoglobinemia, organophosphate poisoning . . . That land just has to be toxic. But Fred's probably right: no housing developer would purchase that property without environmental clearance.*

"What are you thinking?" asked Lizbeth.

"Well, I'm undoubtedly unhinged," said Nora. "But I collected soil samples from the stadium today. It just seemed like too much of a coincidence: three rare illnesses—"

"Three zebras sounding the hoofbeats!" Aditya said.

Nora smiled. "Yes. So, I called an old friend who is a soils expert at UC Davis to help with testing. I just need to figure out how to deliver the samples to him."

"Let us help," Lizbeth pleaded. "I can drive your samples to your friend's lab, first thing in the morning. And Aditya *really* needs something to do besides fidgeting and driving me nuts."

"Yes, please," he said. "And I can research the property on my laptop."

Nora gazed appreciatively at them. "Well, thanks—that would be a great help. And, Lizbeth, the samples are in my car. If it's convenient, I can hand them over to you now. I'll just send a heads-up text to my friend to expect you in the morning."

Lizbeth silently mouthed, "Thank you."

Lake Merritt

Oakland

Fred couldn't recall seeing his daughter Ella looking so radiant. But radiant she was, in her element, orchestrating a community feast like a symphony conductor. New attendees kept showing up. They moved seamlessly around tables of food platters and serving bowls to which Ella had assigned Jack, Fergie, and Winston as servers. Ella was clearly charmed by Luis, who kept asking for yet another assignment. And Fred's heart warmed to see his son Charlie happily managing the cleanup, easily interacting with everyone here. Fred's wife Vickie approached and said, "Fred, we may've done lots of things wrong, but our kids turned out well." He replied, "You deserve the credit." She said, "True." Then she handed him sodas and said, "Pick up the pace. Lots of thirsty people are waiting on these."

~ ~ ~

When Luis and Yusra were between assignments, they approached Fergie. He asked, "Can you find my uncle in your hospital, too? Like Yusra's mom?" The children looked up hopefully at her, and she replied: "Oh? Is your uncle missing?" The two friends nodded, and Luis said, "And I saw an ambulance take him away." Fergie put her arm around him and said, "I'm sorry. You must be worried about him. Do you remember when the ambulance . . .?" She hesitated, recalling the patient who'd been transported from the stadium to the ER yesterday. "Luis," she said, "what's your uncle's name?" When he answered, "Uncle Tomas," Fergie blanched. She stammered, "Tomas Ruiz?" Luis and Yusra nodded excitedly.

~ ~ ~

Winston asked Red to take over his serving station, and ran after Marla. When he caught up to her, she remarked, "Oh, you—the *husband.*"

He said, "I apologize for being dense and awkward when you mentioned your situation."

She placed her hands on her hips. "My 'situation'? You make it sound like an infection or something. It's my *life.*"

He sighed. "I'm still fucking this up."

She point-blank insisted, "Just say it: homelessness."

After squarely meeting her gaze, he said, "I was upset to hear about your homelessness."

"So, you and your wife come down here, what? Maybe once a year? And you hand out food to make yourselves feel better about people like me?" When he grimaced, she rolled her eyes and said, "Forget it."

"I can't," he said. "Please, with your permission, I'd like to write a news story about your sit—your *homelessness,* for my paper. But I don't want you to feel like I'm using you."

She cocked her head. "You don't determine my feelings. And I can choose to feel used but still give you a story if that might make any difference for people like me."

9th Floor Ward Room

Oakland City Hospital

Concerned by her difficulty in rousing Daleen, Nora asked the nurse, "What happened? She was alert this morning."

The nurse said, "Well, I heard in report she was agitated while they were trying to do her MRI. Screaming even. So, they gave her sedatives to get her inside the scanner."

"Screaming?" said Nora, her jaw dropping.

The nurse shrugged, said that was all she knew, and left.

Nora fumed: *Daleen was probably scared to death, being shoved inside that machine! Did anyone take time to explain it to her? What the hell about patient consent?*

After removing her raincoat, Nora sat at the bedside and placed her hand on Daleen's. She leaned back, closed her eyes, and waited. She also decided it'd been a good judgment call to not sneak Yusra in to see her mother just yet.

Minutes passed, during which Nora reviewed her eventful day. The ride and conversation with Carl (*and now I know a lot about cysts*). Her two visits to the stadium (*meeting scary Patty and leggy Samantha*). Collecting soil samples (*because I must be unhinged*). A panic attack (*thank god Fred was with me*). Her fractured communications with Jack. Aditya's injury. Tomas Ruiz' death. Three zebras sounding loud hoofbeats at the stadium. Thanksgiving dinner in a Target parking lot. And, most wondrous of all, finding Yusra.

But then she began to gnaw on Fred's unsettling charge: that envy of Samantha could be clouding her judgment about her. *Still, I wouldn't want to be her, or have what she has. Maybe I just don't like her. But why?* Answering herself: *It's that way she has of just floating through the world, inside some impenetrable bubble.* Still, why dislike someone for that? *All I know is that I do.* Then, entertaining a fantasy about bursting that bubble, she gamely pulled up images of Samantha on her phone and jabbed her finger against them. There was Samantha at the San Francisco Symphony: *prick!* At the

Sundance Film Festival opening: *prick!* The Oakland Zoo's annual fundraiser: *prick!* Samantha in . . .

In a library?

Nora enlarged the image and read its associated article in the *Oakland Register.* The photo had been taken in Samantha's home library, chockfull of family photos and hunting trophies. *I wouldn't have pegged her as family-minded, let alone interested in hunting—despite the murderous looks she gave me.* Was the library for show? Or, perhaps, a family legacy library?

Curious about the dissonance, Nora googled the Greeley family. She found many entries about Samantha's father, Bert: a business titan and real estate tycoon (*knew that*); avid wildlife hunter (*yuck, but explains the taxidermy*); sports enthusiast (*yawn*); along with his wife, a prominent spokesperson for the American eugenics movement . . .

"Holy shit," she whispered, thunderstruck, scrolling for additional information. After checking several links, she learned that Samantha's parents and paternal grandparents had been prominent West Coast leaders of the eugenics movement. Joining other powerful societal titans of the time, they'd supported efforts to coerce tens of thousands of "undesirable" Americans to be sterilized against their will. The so-called undesirables were mostly immigrants, poor people, people of color, unmarried mothers, and people with physical and mental disabilities. She was surprised to read that the American eugenics movement had lasted through the early 1960s, and shocked to learn that California alone had sterilized more than twenty thousand people—about a third of all sterilizations nationwide.

Nora put down her phone, feeling too dark and demoralized to read more. *Human history 101 . . . a continuum of movements fueled by one group's rabid self-righteousness about eliminating other human beings. Same old playbook, just each one taking a different name and uniform in its time.*

But as she let her mind drift, it soon pulled her thoughts toward a surprising discovery: she was experiencing compassionate stirrings toward Samantha. *I shouldn't have been so harsh and judgmental. Because she must've been morally warped at the get-go by parents who believed that only people like themselves should live and inherit the earth. Still . . .*

Still, the people living on her stadium property . . . many belong to the same groups targeted by eugenics. And they're being targeted for extinction, too—if I'm right about the land being lethal, and those-in-the-know turning a blind eye to it.

Now feeling completely disheartened, she tried to shift focus on the happy fact of having found Yusra today. But reminded of that, she also remembered she was supposed to contact Jack, through Fergie, about plans for Yusra tonight. She texted Fergie: *Sorry. Daleen's sedated. M still waiting in her room. Can U tell Jack?*

Fergie texted back: *OK*

Nora: *How R things?*

Fergie: *Crazy-times-eight but good*

Nora: *Yusra?*

Fergie: *Won't leave Luis' side. Jack prob taking both 2 his home 2nite*

Nora: *Good.*

Fergie: *Luis is asking about his uncle. Thinks he's at OCH, 2*

Nora: *A pt?*

Fergie: *Tomas Ruiz. Can U check?*

Having just learned of Tomas' death—and now, of his relationship to Luis—Nora involuntarily groaned. It was audible enough to awaken Daleen, who said, in a slurred voice, "You came back."

Nora hastily texted Fergie: *Daleen just woke. Got2 go.* Then, trying to still her racing mind, she told Daleen, "Yes. With great news. I found Yusra. She's fine."

"My daughter is fine?"

"Yes," said Nora, opening her purse and withdrawing Yusra's doll. "She asked me to give this to you, to help you feel better and come home."

Daleen held the doll to her chest. And though she long believed she'd become immune to ever crying again, she wept. Although she long believed her past had deprived her of any genuine prospect for joy, she felt joy. When she could manage to speak, she said, "Where is Yusra?"

"She and her friend Luis are staying with my close friend tonight. She was wearing your maroon scarf when I left her."

"Good," said Daleen. "At least I can keep her warm. And dear Luis . . ."

"I was going to photograph her wearing it, so you could see how well she looks. But she refused."

When Daleen just softly smiled, Nora cringed, realizing how foolish she'd been to entertain the photograph. Of course Daleen wouldn't approve such casual documentation of her daughter.

"I know you meant well," said Daleen. "And I'm proud of Yusra for refusing. But, please, what did you tell her about me?"

"I told her you were in the hospital. I said you were sick but getting better, and you'd see each other soon."

Daleen hesitated. "Please, do not be nice. Just be honest. Is all that true?"

When Nora nodded, Daleen's smile widened and she said: "I like this Thanksgiving Day of yours."

~ ~ ~

Part Three

Storm

FRIDAY, NOVEMBER 23

We've got to live,
no matter how many skies have fallen.

D. H. LAWRENCE

Morning

RED FELT DISORIENTED, awakening from an overlong sleep, lying *horizontal,* in a *soft bed* with *pillows,* beneath a *fancy* ceiling light fixture. And there was a second queen bed in the spacious room, in which Luis and Yusra were sleeping. "Oh, hell," he whispered, recalling the circumstances under which he'd decided to stay the night at Jack's house. *But I'm going to lose my job this time if Patty sees me gone from the gate again!* Worse, having left his truck at Betty's, he couldn't even drive directly to the stadium.

He gazed at Luis, who'd refused to remove his Betty's tee-shirt or to stay here overnight without him. *How does that kid stay so sweet when everything around him is so fucked up?* He again considered leaving Luis behind; Dr. Jack could be trusted to find him a good home.

Red google-mapped Betty's and the stadium to determine his travel time. Then he withdrew his lucky quarter, placed it on Luis' pillow, and quietly snuck out.

~ ~ ~

Over breakfast in bed, Fergie finished reading the column Winston had written overnight about Marla. "Win, this is very moving. And disturbing, too. Marla's been living in her car for *two years?*"

He nodded. "Could've been us, but for the grace of god."

"And Carl's, too."

"Still, even if Carl hadn't offered, we would've had an easier time finding housing and jobs. But Marla's been saddled with family caretaking and domestic abuse her entire life. She never got a leg up, let alone a chance at an education or career. She's just kind of stuck here."

"I feel like a freakin' idiot. There I was making 'special requests' in the cafeteria, all the while she was food insecure."

"Give yourself a break, Fergs. You couldn't have known. Besides, she exudes a *lot* of bravado."

Pouring more coffee, Fergie asked, "Where does Marla park at night?"

"Wherever she can. At first, in the regional parks. But when things got unsafe, she started parking in the Walmart lot. Then that got over-crowded, and with too many hostile people. Some guy even tried to rape her. Now, she mostly jockeys for space near the Maze."

"I don't know how anyone working minimum wage can live in this area," she said. "It's crazy-times-a-million! Median monthly rents at three thousand? And home prices over eight hundred thou?"

~ ~ ~

Gianni parked at the gate where Red's truck was usually stationed, deciding what to do. He'd even brought an extra coffee for Red, hoping for a chance to chum up and to ask about the dead man who'd lived here.

Frustrated over his ongoing failure to forge bonds with anyone, he crushed his own coffee cup and tossed it to the backseat. Then, realizing it could prove therapeutic to tackle a fixable problem, he decided to unload his truckload of dirt that the scrapyard had refused. Opportunely, it occurred to him to dump it here, back from where it came: *Like ashes to ashes, dirt to dirt.* It even felt right, as a symbolic and practical act of retaliation against his mysterious boss who'd been paying him so errat-ically for months.

But when he drove behind the main stadium, he was surprised to see Patty. She was talking to some stocky man with a ponytail, who handed something to her before driving away in a black BMW.

Gianni got out of his truck and walked up to her. He said, "I missed you last night."

"Sorry I couldn't call you back," she replied. "I got busy."

Earnestly attempting to demonstrate he could listen, he said, "Care to elaborate?"

But she certainly wasn't going to tell him about her visit with Pete in prison. Instead, she said: "Well, after you canceled on me, I took to bed with a beer. And, speaking of . . . 'Care to elaborate' what *you're* doing here?"

He certainly wasn't going to tell her about his plan to dump the dirt back here. Instead, he said: "I'm coming for the shovel I left in the D-lot yesterday."

She nodded. "I assume you saw the guy who just left in the BMW?"

"I did. What was that about?"

She let out a tired huff. "Took me a while to figure that out myself. Almost didn't recognize it: something *good* finally happening."

Though disappointed she didn't seem to include their hooking-up as any recent good, he said, "I'm happy for you, Patty."

"Yeah. That guy just paid me up and then some. So now I can pay all my overdues. I can even hire you direct, for more work here, if you're interested."

He looked probingly at her. "You're a mystery woman. You finally convinced me Red wasn't your boyfriend, then here you are, looking tight and happy with this new guy. Is *he* your boyfriend?"

"No! But here I am, getting my first piece of good news in a long hard while, and you're talking trash. It'd be nice if you could just be happy for me."

"Wait up now. Calm down."

She looked away, struggling to simmer down. But she was lonely and homeless. She was exhausted and chilled to the bone after trying to sleep here in her car last night, against a relentless backdrop of police sirens, people screaming and shouting, street traffic, dogs barking, trains passing. And without Red guarding the gate, she'd felt edgy and vulnerable. Tonight, though, thanks to the money she just received, she could seek some restful sleep in a motel.

Gianni continued, "I *am* happy for you. But, got to be honest: you don't *look* happy, Patty."

Just how am I supposed to look happy, she thought, *when I got so much damn work to do? And now that I've been paid up, I'll be expected to get it done. But moving all these people outta here? And to where, exactly?* She only said, "I'm just stressed out. Got lots on my mind."

"Well, I can help you with that," he said provocatively—immediately afterwards, catching himself and readjusting his tone. "I mean, how about I take you to dinner tonight?"

She hesitated, doubting the wisdom of trusting him after he stiffed her yesterday. Still, she was going to need his help; he and Red were the only people she had. They also owned trucks that could be used to transport people out of the camp. And, as she had to admit, from prior experience she knew they were *capable* of allegiance. Hoping she might secure their loyalty by paying them in advance, she reached into her pocket and peeled off three hundred-dollar bills from the wad of money she'd just been given. Offering them to Gianni, she said, "I can pay you this now if you promise to work for me this weekend. And, just as you like—no Mr. Tax Man involved."

"Sure," he said, taking the money, feeling prospects for romance dwindle. "But mind saying what for?"

"Just be here tomorrow morning," she said brusquely, turning away. "That's all you need to know."

"So, about dinner tonight?" he called after her, getting no response.

~ ~ ~

Shania Twain blared from the radio, and Fred sang along while his silver Lexus snaked down the winding boulevard en route to work. How exhilarating whenever he took a curve in sync with a bending high note. He was unbelievably happy, remembering the sex he had with Vickie last night—their first genuine attempt in years.

Initially, he'd felt awkward. They'd become unfamiliar with each other's body, and his first maneuvers were halting. He apologized often—his scratchy chin, the inadvertent head butts, excessive body weight pressing on her. Still, what a relief to discover that Lydia, who'd been between them for decades, left him alone. He wanted to tell somebody about his incredible night. But to appreciate its significance for him, that person would need to know about his complex history with Lydia, and the guilt he carried about leaving her. He wondered if he should talk to a therapist, like Nora did—someone without judgment or a personal stake.

Jack's Home

Rockridge District, Oakland

Everything felt magical to Luis. He'd slept in a warm bed, and ate hot eggs for breakfast. Yusra and her mother had been found. He felt reassured by Dr. Jack that they'd find Red at the restaurant or the stadium.

And, for the *second* day in a row, he'd be visiting Target *and* Betty's. Feeling incredibly optimistic, he rubbed Red's lucky quarter and made a wish: to hear good news about Uncle Tomas from the tattooed nurse today.

Yusra draped her mother's maroon scarf across her shoulders, happily anticipating her return visit to the store with the big red target. Dr. Jack was going to help her select clothes to wear when she reunited with her mother. She hoped for a plaid raincoat and red boots.

And Jack would transfer his cell service there, finally reconnecting to the modern world. He'd make his first call, honorifically, to Nora, who was working today. Then they'd head to the stadium and Betty's, looking for Red.

Driving toward Target now, Jack heard Luis and Yusra laughing in the backseat. "What's so funny?" he asked, looking curiously at them in the rearview. "Nothing," said Luis, stifling his laughter, exchanging conspiratorial looks with Yusra.

Jack smiled. "C'mon. Tell me."

Yusra said, "We were just laughing."

Flashing them a skeptical look, Jack said, "But, why? Something must've happened."

Luis and Yusra looked puzzled. Then Luis shrugged and answered for them both: "Because we are happy."

It sounded like such a radical notion that it astonished Jack. But then he remembered the time he was washing dishes with Richard when they inexplicably broke into spontaneous laughter; and how, even later, they could figure no other reason for it, other than feeling happy.

ER

Oakland City Hospital

Fergie heard Nora approaching—*squeak, squeak, squeak*—in her indestructible Keens. "Hey, Nora," she said, without looking up. "Must've had a long night here."

"Yeah, sorry," said Nora. "I couldn't get back to you with an update on Luis' uncle because my visit with Daleen ended so late. But there's so much to unpack and talk about. How about lunch today?"

"Deal," said Fergie. "But warning: I didn't sleep last night, so don't expect sparkling conversation."

"Something fun, I hope?"

Fergie rolled her eyes. "Win was typing nonstop. And, as you may recall, he makes loud editorial comments the entire time: 'That sounds lame!' . . . 'What's a better word?' . . . 'No!' . . . 'Nailed it!' Anyway, then Carl came home around two and began pacing upstairs in his kitchen, making more noise than you in your shoes, and—"

Lizbeth appeared and said, "Sorry to interrupt. But, Dr. Kelly, I wanted you to know I dropped off those soil samples."

Nora said, "And back already? It usually takes a good hour to drive to Davis."

"Well, your soils expert told me he'd be in his office by six. That was perfect, really. I left at five and turned back before rush hour."

Fergie asked Lizbeth, "Hey, don't you have today off?"

Lizbeth replied, "Only if you consider tending to Aditya as 'time off.'"

"Wait," said Fergie. "What's this about 'soil samples'?"

Nora said, "Lizbeth is referring to soil samples that Fred and I collected at the stadium yesterday. An old friend is testing them for chemical toxins. It's informal; he's doing it as a favor to me. But I'll tell you more over lunch." Still, there was already so much to talk about. The news of Tomas Ruiz' death. The question of how, and who, to best inform Luis. And what should be done regarding Yusra and her mother?

"Ah, I almost forgot!" said Lizbeth. "Your expert said the samples were wet, so they'll have to dry before he can test them. But he expects preliminary results on Monday. He also asked if you documented where you collected them, because they weren't labeled and it seemed you might want to know."

Nora grinned broadly. "I remember exactly where I collected them. The yogurt cup contains garden soil, near the fava beans. The plastic clam shell: soil around the lettuces. I filled the sandwich bag with samples near the camper door, and the juice box with soil from behind the camper."

Old Stadium Site

West Oakland

"He's not here," Luis lamented when they arrived at the gate. "He's not here," Yusra sympathetically echoed.

Hoping to alleviate their distress, Jack offered, "We'll find Red. But let's just drive in and look for his truck before checking at Betty's."

Yusra told Luis, "And we could see if your uncle came home."

"No," said Luis, his eyes welling. "He's in the hospital. That's what the nurse with the tattoos thinks."

Still, they drove in silence to the D-lot until Yusra pointed and said, "There's your pretty orange tent, Luis." Jack parked, and Luis ran ahead, entering the tent alone. And while everything looked exactly as he and Red had left it, everything also looked different, as if belonging to someone else now. After spending the last two nights in Red's truck or Dr. Jack's house, he felt oddly ejected from his prior life.

When Jack peered into the tent and saw Luis in the midst of such barefaced poverty, his heart clenched. "Let's go," he said with urgency. "Let's drive to Betty's. And we'll call nurse Fergie at the hospital to ask about your uncle."

But then, like a bullet, Yusra shot into the tent. She grabbed Luis and screamed. Luis asked, "What's wrong?" as Jack dashed outside, in time to spot a black station wagon speeding away. He caught the last two numbers on the license plate: 8 and 5.

"It was the Nice Lady!" Yusra sobbed.

"The 'nice lady'?" said Jack, clearly confused.

Luis said, "The lady who kidnapped Yusra and took her mom away."

Luis' claim rendered Jack speechless. *Who would do such horrific things?* Still, he knew the question was rhetorical, a defense against thinking the unthinkable. He counseled himself to stay strong and calm for the kids' sake, though feeling neither. All he could manage to say was "I'm so sorry." And to his surprise, Yusra ran to his embrace. "Sweetie," he kept repeating, stroking her hair. "I got you. You're safe now." He wiped her tears. "That lady's not going to hurt you ever again. I promise."

"But," said Luis, "the Nice Lady is going to keep looking for Yusra, because Yusra escaped from her."

Jack was floored by Luis' matter-of-fact tone in relating yet another routine horror in their lives. *Terror and trauma are too normal for these kids! And this so-called "nice lady"... "Nice"? My god.* Knowing that Oakland was a hub for human trafficking, he feared the worst. *Whatever the particulars of Yusra's story, I'm in over my head. I should notify the police, not least because of this kidnapping claim. And if Yusra was both kidnapped and trafficked... No, wait... I should call Nora first about bringing Yusra in for emergency evaluation. Yes. They'll have ER protocols for trauma and abuse. Then Nora and the social worker can connect Yusra and Luis and their families with resources for homeless and migrant persons—*

"Dr. Jack?" said Luis.

"Sorry," he replied, "I am just thinking. Do either of you know that woman's real name?" They shook their heads, and he said, "Well, she doesn't sound 'nice' at all. Why do you call her the 'nice lady'?"

"Because my mom says to," said Yusra. "But I don't think she's nice either."

Jack considered pursuing the woman but was afraid of retraumatizing Yusra and Luis should they catch up to her. He took some consolation in being able to assist police with a description of her car and the two numbers he'd gleaned from its plate.

Driving out of the stadium, Jack tried to figure out when he could make his call to Nora without the kids overhearing it. He glanced at them in the rearview and, to his surprise, saw them falling fast asleep despite the horror they'd just experienced. Then, suppressing a moan, it occurred to him how their waking norm had no distance from any stuff of nightmares.

BART Train

Rockridge District

Red hopped the Rockridge BART headed for City Center to retrieve his truck at Betty's. Hopefully, he'd also enjoy a quick visit with

DeeDee. Then, back to his stadium job and, surely, a dreadful encounter with Patty.

Spending the night at Dr. Jack's had been strange. He felt like an alien on a tour of another world, everything foreign to his inner reality. Mostly, he was relieved that Luis was in Dr. Jack's good hands now. *Luis isn't like me. He's sweet and optimistic, and strangers will want to help him. He'll get out of the hell he's been living in.*

Red scanned his fellow passengers on the train: a silent motley crowd of people, each one staring expressionlessly at something—a book, a cellphone, a graffiti drawing, posted public health warnings about herpes—at anything other than a fellow traveler.

He imagined most were heading to work at this hour. Likely to real jobs with regular pay, and for employers who, unlike Patty, treated them with basic respect.

At the MacArthur stop, a wiry man with a gnarly black beard entered and sat next to Red. He smelled like wet cardboard and moldy cigarette butts. He said, "I need ten dollars."

Having little money himself, Red replied, "Sorry, man. I'm just scraping by."

The stranger sniffed him several times and said, "You smell like soap and cologne. I'm living on the goddamn street, pal."

"Yeah?" said Red. "Well, I live in my truck."

The stranger yelled, "At least you got a fuckin' home, asshole!" Then he spat on Red and moved to another seat. None of the fellow passengers reacted.

Red disembarked at 12th Street and walked to Betty's, where he was relieved to find his white truck unscathed, bookended by two yellow school buses. He brushed off his coat, finger-combed his hair, and entered the restaurant.

But things inside were chaotic. Children were yelling and running wild. He watched DeeDee working furiously, carrying loaded trays, replenishing condiments, cleaning tables, backing-and-forthing to the kitchen. Clearly, a bad time to visit. *But god, she looks beautiful.*

He left and drove feverishly to the stadium. After locking its gate and barricading it with his truck, he thought: *Back to normal now. Back to my hell.*

Still, while staring through the windshield at the same old gate, he felt as if something new had opened up.

Ocambo Law Firm

Lakeshore District

Quentin Ocambo hadn't slept all night, ruminating obsessively over Martin's treachery and Samantha's insolence. He couldn't believe he'd been treated so poorly. He couldn't recall ever feeling so livid before. But then, the morning arrived with a fresh assault when Samantha called. *The audacity, the disrespect!* Firing him from Greeley Enterprises, and over *the goddamn phone*!

She insulted him further by conveying her intention to replace him with "young" lawyers who could offer "fresh legal thinking" and "modern insights into the law." She said she'd already scheduled an initial meeting with Palmer & Webley over the weekend! Her news landed in his mind like a poison dart, momentarily paralyzing his thoughts. No one had rendered him speechless like that before, not even his beefiest legal adversaries in court. The only saving response he could marshal in the moment was to summon enough wherewithal to convince Samantha to forgo his firing and, instead, allow him the dignity of submitting his resignation on Monday.

Now, in the immediate aftermath of her call, he stared at his desk photo of Bert and ranted: "She's *your* daughter! *Your* daughter, you left in control, who knows *nothing* about *our* business, and is getting rid of *me*! And she aligned with my son, who is so full of lies, so full of himself. My god, the amplified ignorance and incompetence between them!"

He popped another antacid—*Is there a limit to how many I can take?*—and paced, struggling to compose fitting responses to Samantha and Martin. But their outsized disrespect for him exceeded his capacity for words.

Then, suddenly, it occurred to him that he'd somehow fallen into the weaker position of having to *react* to them. He'd somehow allowed them to shape the battle and force him to assume the defensive position. *No wonder I'm struggling to fight back; I'm on the wrong footing for me.*

Indeed, he realized, that's why he'd failed all night to find satisfaction in planning for revenge. *Revenge is reactive, and only reduces me to a vindictive old man.*

He had to step outside the lines that Martin and Samantha had drawn. He needed to approach them with fierce agency, and take the offensive position. *And my god, why not even make that magnificent! Why not take a final swing for the fences and go out in a blaze of glory? I've nothing to lose.*

Yes . . . Something glorious and operatic in scope that transcends revenge. They may be out to burn me, but I'll raise the bigger torch.

He knocked over Bert's photo, took out a fresh yellow legal pad, and began listing what must be done. Resigning on Monday would leave him with only two days of his security clearances and access to all things Greeley. *Two days to compose my leave-taking score, and script my last grand adventure.*

His to-do list came effortlessly, almost writing itself, each item sounding an operatic chord in a harmonious evolving arrangement:

Change locks—home, office

New passwords—email, financials

Stadium files

The safe

Get Martin's keys to PI

Call Deshawn Palmer

Check stadium yourself!

Visit Pete

Fred's Office

Oakland City Hospital

By the time Fred had arrived at the hospital parking lot, he'd decided to invite Vickie to a romantic restaurant tonight. Moments later, riding the elevator to the C-suite and still humming Shania, he happily imagined another after-dinner dalliance with her. But when he stepped out of the elevator, he saw his assistant standing in the hallway outside his office, sending him a familiar "something's-up" look. When he approached, she whispered "Sorry" and left. Glancing through the doorway, he saw Samantha Greeley sitting on his desk, her long legs flowing toward him.

"Dr. Williams," she said. "We need to talk."

He struggled to fix his gaze on her face, privately cursing Larry Larbor's jinx. *Definitely going to start that psychotherapy.* He said, "Of course. Please have a chair." *Yes, please!*

She sat, waited for him to situate behind his desk, and said: "I've been thinking about your visit to my property yesterday. With your colleague, Nora Kelly."

"Ah. I understand how that could've looked fishy, but . . ."

"'Fishy,' Fred? Or 'fishing'?"

His great good mood came crashing down under the onerous weight of her suspicion. Her tone conveyed accusation and, perhaps, threat? He acutely regretted his involvement in Nora's plans and the compromises he'd made to support her. He stared back at Samantha, debating whether to tell her the truth; that might be safer to admit now, with Daleen Habani improving and her daughter located. *That case should be closed. Besides, seems like I owe her an explanation for my cagey behavior.* He began, "All right now. I'll tell you why we were actually there."

"Good," she said, crossing her legs, one heel popping out of its pump. "Because there have been too many surprises concerning my property these last twenty-four hours—your presence there, included." She narrowed her eyes and leaned in. "I detest surprises, Fred. They're control grabs, really. I pay people a great deal of money to protect myself from them. And, as you know, I'm planning for the stadium deal to close next Friday. It would be unforgivable should a surprise interfere with that."

Fred's chest tightened as he recalled collecting soil samples with Nora yesterday. Although believing they had to be free of hazardous contamination, still, if Samantha learned that he'd participated in collecting them, his relationship with her would be damaged. The hospital desperately needed her foundation's philanthropy and influential membership on the board. *Dear god, I hope Nora followed my advice and abandoned plans to test those samples. But even if she hasn't, it's still early in the day; I can probably intervene.* After clearing his throat, he replied, "Well, no surprises at this end. Nora and I were at the stadium—like she said—in concern for a patient. She'd promised to deliver some food to her patient's daughter. In a Thanksgiving spirit, I believe."

Samantha cocked her head. "And *you* were there, *because?*"

Already feeling compromised after rationalizing his withholding of truth, he now felt pressed between two rival moral aspirations; but honoring his agreements and friendship with Nora was losing out to the public good that would be generated by a new housing development to serve the community. Under mounting pressure, he explained, "I was there to support Nora. She was anxious about visiting the stadium. I shouldn't be telling this, but she's been having panic attacks. PTSD, actually. And she worried she might encounter triggers."

Now slowly heading toward the door, she said, "Sorry to hear that. And, to me, it sounds like she's more than just a 'colleague' to you."

Fred privately berated himself: *Nora would disagree if she knew how I just betrayed her.* He held open the door. "I hope you'll keep what I've said in confidence."

As soon as Samantha left, he called his assistant to reschedule his next appointment, and he headed to the ER to speak with Nora about canceling the tests. Meanwhile, Samantha went to the hospital cafeteria to regroup with Marty. He put down his coffee and greeted her with "That didn't take long."

She sat beside him and said, "Fred was easy. The coffee any good?"

Marty took the cue and got up to order for her. But the woman behind the counter was intensely conversing with two people and ignoring him. "Excuse me," he said, "but can someone get coffee around here?"

Marla shot him a defiant look and said, "In a minute." Then she returned to reviewing some document with the couple—Fergie and Winston—to whom she finally said, "I'm good with this. Go ahead, print it. Just make sure I get a copy." Fergie saluted, Winston shook her hand, and they left.

Marty stepped up to the counter and muttered, "About time." Marla said, "And, such a shame. 'Cuz I think you wanted coffee, right? I'll need to make a new pot. And I'll get to that, soon as I can."

When Marty returned empty-handed to the table and explained the coffee delay, Samantha grabbed her purse and said: "Just hurry. I'll be waiting in the gift shop."

Meanwhile, Fergie escorted Winston to the hospital exit. She said, "Marla seemed happy with your story, Win."

"And that made me happy," he said. "So, I'll email this to the editor. And I'm going to start investigating other story leads from Marla. She even called some friends who agreed to be interviewed."

Fergie watched him leave the hospital, a slight bounce to his step. What a sweet relief to see his assured and purposeful stride again.

Nora's Morning Break

Oakland City Hospital

"Morning, Dr. Kelly," said the transporter who was passing in the hallway, wheeling his patient toward dialysis. After Nora returned the greeting, she overheard his patient remark: "Tell her to try baking soda in those shoes."

Heading to the elevator during her morning break, Nora considered all the remedies people had suggested for her squeaky shoes: baby powder, cornstarch, petroleum jelly, dryer sheets, saddle soap, WD-40—and, again, baking soda. *But what a muck to stick your feet into. I can't imagine—*

Samantha Greeley shot out of the cafeteria, grumbling something about "coffee," and bumping into Nora. She said, "You *again*."

"Well, yeah," said Nora, touchily. "I work here." She knew it was juvenile, but said it anyway, in the same intimidating tone Samantha used with her yesterday: "I'm curious. What are *you* doing here? And on a day like today?"

Samantha smiled mechanically. "I had business with your 'colleague.' Good day."

Nora continued to the elevator, chastising herself (a little) for her behavior. She acknowledged, as Fred had often remarked, that entitled rich people brought out the contrariness in her. *Still, I should have better control over that. (Another goal to add to my list.)* But while pressing the elevator button for Daleen's floor, she was reminded of sitting in Daleen's room when she discovered the Greeley family's involvement with the eugenics movement. Daleen—as a homeless, impoverished migrant woman of color—could've been a prime target of that movement and deprived of giving birth to Yusra. And considering that, Nora's self-rebuke vanished. *Though, in fairness, I need to remember, I don't actually know Samantha's personal views.*

When Nora entered Daleen's room, she was surprised to find her talking easily with Lola, the social worker. Daleen happily announced, "Dr. Nora, Lola is trying to help me leave the hospital tomorrow!"

"Yes, 'trying,'" said Lola, shooting Nora a judgmental look. "But if I'd known *before* this morning about her daughter and their living situation, I could've gotten the ball rolling ahead of the weekend dead-zone we're up against."

"That was not Dr. Nora's fault," said Daleen. "It was my choice, and I hope you understand."

Lola said, "I actually do." On her way out, she half-smiled at Nora and said, "I'm relieved to hear she and Yusra have a backup place to stay with your friend, Dr. Griffin. Because prospects for placement on holiday weekends are always slim." Nora returned a truce smile, and Lola took leave.

Now alone with Daleen, Nora said: "You look great. And, obviously, more alert than last night!"

"I'm ashamed you saw me like that," said Daleen.

"But you had no choice. They drugged you."

"All I remember is them forcing me into that big machine. And holding me down to give me a shot."

Nora cringed, and decided to report the violative incident to the Situation Management and Response Team. And she'd also collar the intern who thoughtlessly ordered the unnecessary MRI that traumatized Daleen.

"It reminded me," Daleen continued, "of other times I'd been forced by people to . . ." She briefly looked away. "Anyway, I always fight back. That is all you can do sometimes."

Nora waited for some overt expression of Daleen being triggered and traumatized, but she only sat quietly. With subdued astonishment, Nora said, "You're stronger than me. If I'd just been triggered like you were, I'd be having a full-blown panic attack now."

Daleen studied Nora's face—a kind face that belonged to someone who inhabited a different world. She said, "In my world, no one has panic attacks. Terror is just always present, so it does not attack. Today, yesterday, tomorrow—it is the same."

Ocambo Law Firm

Lakeshore District

By the time the locksmiths rekeyed the office, Quentin had boxed up the stadium records. He'd transferred computer files to two flash drives: one, exclusively regarding tax and financial matters concerning the stadium that he would hand over on Monday; the other, containing files about long-standing business practices at Greeley Enterprises that he'd relinquish when the time was right. He changed all passwords on his business and email accounts, erased the hard drive, and then phoned the prison to schedule a visit with Pete. He gave a heads-up to his stalwart P.I., Alex Morales, about an assignment involving Martin's office. Finally, he opened the safe and grabbed the folder containing the paperwork concerning the stadium renovation. He also withdrew the two million cash reserve, his fake ID and burner phone, and the .38-caliber pistol.

He put the flash drives in his jacket pocket and stashed everything else in the trunk of his car. Then he drove to the stadium, intent on seeing the property himself. Along the way, he berated himself for having put trust in his derelict son to work as his intermediary. *But "trust" isn't the right word, since I've never trusted Martin. At most, I held a low-odds hope that I could tame his sociopathy by giving him work. Still, I should've known.* He couldn't count the times he bailed Martin out of jail. Or paid off a bartender because of fights, damages, unpaid tabs. Even settled, under-the-table, with neighbors who'd been aggrieved by his son's brute incivility. In fact, had he not made a solemn vow to his now-long-dead wife, he would've allowed Martin to self-destruct on prior occasions. He wondered what she'd think now to see their only "child" returning his charity with a malicious double-cross and intent to destroy him.

When he arrived at the stadium gate, Red came to meet him. He handed over a business card and said, "I'm Quentin Ocambo, lawyer for the stadium's owner. I'm here to check on things."

Red pocketed the card, thinking, *Riffraff.* "I need to clear it with my boss. She didn't give me notice to expect anyone."

"It's merely routine. I'll be quick. And, see, I'm in a bit of a hurry."

"Well, same here, buddy. So, take a breather." Red returned to his truck and phoned Patty.

"You idiot!" she answered. "I'm standing right behind your damn truck. Some security!"

Red saw Patty in the sideview, limping toward his truck. He cursed his bad luck, realizing she must've entered earlier and noticed him being AWOL. When he stepped out of his truck, she greeted him with: "Where the hell were you this morning? I and who-knows-who-else just drove right on through the gate! You have a goddamn job!"

"Sorry. Won't happen again."

She sneered. "How am I supposed to trust you anymore?"

"You can."

"Yeah? Well, I absolutely need you here tomorrow and Sunday, *all* day! No excuses, unless you're dead."

"I'll be here."

"I swear, Red. You better mean it. You'll have a helluva lot more than me to deal with if you fuck up."

He flinched. "What's that supposed to mean?"

She narrowed her eyes, deliberating whether to convey Pete's warning. But Red's allegiance already seemed tenuous, so she decided not to risk scaring him off. Instead, aiming to secure his promise of weekend availability, she handed him wages for the prior week.

"Thanks," he said, perplexed. "But you said you weren't paying me."

"Changed my mind. Just be sure to show up tomorrow morning."

He nodded. "But right now, you got a visitor."

"Who?"

"Some guy. Says he's the lawyer for the owner of this place." He showed her the man's business card.

Patty peered toward the gate to see a silver-haired man standing alongside a royal blue Audi. "What the hell does he want?"

Red shrugged, and she said: "Tell him he's going to need more than a two-cent business card to enter this private property." Then she turned up her collar and walked back toward the encampment, worrying about all the work ahead. Onerous tasks, risky tasks, too many tasks, and without a blueprint. *And, my god, children missing. Residents getting sick. Doctors intruding. And now a damn lawyer! What business does he have here?* She shuddered as her mind whipped up a dozen possible answers. *What was I thinking when I promised Pete to hold the fort while he was away?* Looking beseechingly up to the sky, she implored, "Lord, why'd you give me this heavy cross to bear?"

But nothing other than wildfire soot alighted on her face and outstretched arms. She brushed them off and muttered "Figures," then proceeded to focus on her earthly tasks. First, she needed a decent headcount of the residents, to calculate the number of transports required to clear the camp over the weekend. She also had to decide where to transport the residents. And she desperately needed a good night's sleep.

And yet . . .

How stop-your-heart tempting: all the money suddenly in her pocket. Five thousand dollars, more money than she'd ever seen. It hinted at new options, previously unimaginable. *I could just drive away, and leave all this burden behind. Pete would be hurt. But he's the reason I'm stuck with this cross. He coulda done his time for the migrants and labor trafficking and been out by now, and with me. Why'd he choose to get involved with that stupid cellphone scheme instead?*

Meanwhile, Red had returned to the gate to convey her message. Quentin replied, "You're making a mistake, son. You should let me in."

"I take orders from my boss," said Red, returning the business card.

But Quentin declined to accept it. "Keep it. I've got a hunch you'll need it."

Red smirked. "I doubt it. Ain't never met any lawyer I needed."

Unbelievable, thought Quentin. *This cocky skinny redhead interfering with me!* Under the press of only two days' time before his grand departure from Greeley Enterprises, he scrambled for another approach to obtain the information he needed. Adopting a somber tone, he said, "Well, think about it. But . . . all the people living here? What do you expect will happen to them when the stadium is sold next Friday?"

Red visibly recoiled. *This guy must be wrong. Or bluffing. I'd know if they were selling this place. Patty would've said something.*

Quentin was appeased: at least he knew, by Red's reaction, the camp was, indeed, still populated. He said, "I see you weren't aware of the sale."

"Why are you telling me this shit?" said Red. "And why should I believe you?"

After doffing his fedora, Quentin said: "Just think about what I told you. And better hold onto my card." Then he drove away and headed to the prison for his appointment with Pete.

4th Floor Monitored Unit

Oakland City Hospital

With minutes remaining in her break after visiting Daleen, Nora stopped by Aditya's room. Seeing how distraught he and Lizbeth looked, she asked if everything was okay.

He answered, "Dr. Williams just left."

"With concerns about your injury?"

"No," said Lizbeth. "He came to ask about the soil samples."

Nora's jaw dropped. "How did Fred even know I gave them to you?"

"He said he'd been to the ER, looking for you," said Lizbeth. "You weren't there, and he asked Fergie if she knew anything about them. She told him what I'd reported to you. Then he came here, very upset, and told us to ditch the tests."

Nora scoffed. "It would've been nice if he'd waited to consult with me." Then it struck her: Fred's odd behavior must link to Samantha's presence in the hospital, and his demand to stop testing must relate to her "business" with him this morning. She asked, "What did you tell him?"

"The truth," said Lizbeth, recalling the courage it'd taken to confront him. "I said I'd already delivered the samples, and he'd have to speak with *you* about any cancellation of those tests."

"And *then*," said Aditya, with a burdened smile. "Then he got *really* upset."

He'd been so thrown by Patty's icy demeanor that Gianni forgot to inquire about the dead man's identity. And her rigid business-like manner while offering him money made him feel uncomfortably cheap.

But now driving out of the stadium, he spotted Red's truck barricading the gate, and his dark mood began to disperse. He called out the window, "Been on vacation, Red?"

Red, having had his fill of annoying people for the day, gave Gianni the finger and began to move his truck.

But Gianni got out of his flatbed, held out the coffee he'd brought for Red, and said: "It's cold now, sorry."

Red eyed him suspiciously. "Is it poisoned?"

"Nah," said Gianni. "I just been through some stuff. And thinking a lot."

"I ain't Oprah."

Gianni laughed. "Yeah, I somehow figured that out!" Then he turned serious. "It's just . . . Yesterday, I fucked up everywhere. With everyone. It was an Olympic-level fuck-up day. But when I was driving home, feeling sorry for myself, I saw a guy lying on the sidewalk, and all these people just passing him by. I thought, well, *that* guy is *really* down on his luck, even worse than me. Anyhow, I had my flask, so I decided to cheer us both up a little. But, thing is, when I got to him he was dead."

"Man," said Red, shaking his head. "Sounds awful."

"Yeah, so then I called the police. They came and found some doctor's business card on the guy. It was the only thing on him. And when they called the doctor, they found out the guy was a patient who'd just walked out of the hospital. The police told me he'd been living here at the stadium, but wouldn't say more 'til they reached next-of-kin. Anyhow, I thought you might know him."

Red's face drained of its nominal color. "What'd he look like?"

"Dark. Hispanic, probably. Late forties, maybe. A big scar on his forehead."

"It can't be," said Red, dropping the coffee.

"You know him, then?"

Wondering if Luis had heard, Red nodded.

"Sorry, pal. Can I do something for you?"

Red checked his cellphone to review the route he'd taken this morning from Jack's house. Estimating the time required to return there to speak with Luis, he said, "I got to be somewhere right now. But Patty's still here, and if she finds me gone again, I'll lose my job. Could you cover for me? An hour or two? Just don't let anyone in. I'll pay you."

"Don't want your money, pal," said Gianni. "I'm just happy to do something for you."

Rigby's Diner

Uptown

"I'm so furious with Fred," said Nora. "The audacity! And going behind my back?"

Fergie took another bite of her veggie burger and said, "Again, I'm really sorry for telling him *anything*. He just seemed so desperate, looking for you. Then he popped that weird question about soil samples that took me off any guard. Besides, you'd told me he helped you collect them."

"You've got nothing to apologize for," said Nora. "I'm angry with *him*. And then, bullying Aditya and Lizbeth . . ."

"Well, I'd be upset, too, if a friend—anyone—did that to me."

"And just minutes earlier, in the hallway, I ran into this woman who's got him tied around her little finger. He keeps compromising himself to please her."

"Oh? A romantic situation? Not another Lydia, please."

"I don't think so. Their relationship seems political and financial. Her name's Samantha Greeley, and she just joined the hospital board."

"Of *the* rich and famous Greeleys? Huh. Well, I hope Fred can stand up to her when it's necessary. Anyway, when do you intend to talk with him about what happened? The sooner, the better."

"I need to cool down first. And I have other things I'd like to discuss with you."

"Meter's on. Just no national politics while I'm eating."

"Okay. But brace yourself for bad news."

Fergie nodded, and Nora continued: "Last night, when you texted and asked about Tomas Ruiz? Well, Daleen was just finally coming to. Then, by the time I left her, it was too late to call or text you. That's why, this morning, I asked to talk with you in person—"

"It's killing me, Nora. Please get to the point."

"Well, just before I visited Daleen, I stopped by Aditya's room. He told me about his patient with probable arsenic poisoning leaving the hospital AMA. I didn't know he was Luis' uncle, and . . . well, they later found him dead on a sidewalk. Aditya confirmed his identity this morning."

Fergie pushed her food away, her eyes welled. "Poor Luis. His uncle was his only family."

Nora extended a comforting hand and waited for Fergie's signal to proceed with the conversation. When Nora saw her take a deep breath and nod, she continued: "It's painfully sad. And, clearly, Luis needs to be told. I don't know who's best to do that. Certainly not the police, though they're probably out looking for next-of-kin. Maybe a social worker? What do you think?"

Fergie dried her eyes with a napkin. "Well, even *if* the cops are out looking for Luis, it'd probably take them a while to trace him to Jack's house. So, yeah, maybe a social worker should talk to Luis ASAP. Does Jack even know that Tomas died?"

"I can't imagine how he'd know. But I plan to call him after lunch."

Shaking her head in incredulity, Fergie said, "I was just thinking this morning, how sweet Luis is. Despite everything that's happened to him, he's stayed resilient and optimistic. But I'm wondering what the news of his uncle's death will do to him." Nora nodded and Fergie asked, "Do we know for sure why Tomas died? Was it the arsenic toxicity we expected?"

"We won't receive the confirmatory tests until Monday. And now, because of the unusual circumstances, Tomas' case has also become a coroner's case. Either way, it'll be a few days before we get a definitive answer."

Fergie looked worryingly at Nora. "And if our suspicion about arsenic toxicity is correct . . . Well, there's still the question of how Tomas was poisoned. If by accident, where? If not, by whom and why?"

Jack's Home

Rockridge District

Their trip to Betty's proved catastrophic. Not only was Red not there, but DeeDee had left for the day. Luis suffered a meltdown—a surprisingly dramatic, public one. He became inconsolable, lamenting his aloneness with operatic intensity, crying out to see his uncle at the hospital. Then Yusra, being emotionally attuned to him, began crying over her need to see her mother. Jack became flustered and preoccupied, unable to make his call to Nora. And he had to work to shield the distraught children from curious patrons who began taking cellphone videos of their odd trio. He overheard one patron say, "They can't be *his* kids."

On the drive home, Jack privately rued his ineptitude in caring for children. *A life-saving rescue of a patient with an MI? Can do! An emergency trach for respiratory failure? Can do! But tending to Luis' and Yusra's tantrums? No fucking idea! But Richard—he would've known.*

At a stoplight, he glanced at the kids, whimpering in the back. He decided to phone his housekeeper Zofia as soon as he got home to ask—*beg*—her to stay at the house until things sorted out. Then he'd call Nora and—

What a welcome surprise: When they arrived home, Red was sitting on the porch. Jack pointed to him and exclaimed, "Look!"

Luis sprang from the car and ran into Red's embrace. "Hey, little man," said Red.

"You came back," Luis said, crying in relief.

Jack told Red, "We'd been out looking for you."

"You could've called," said Red, rubbing Luis' head, hugging Yusra.

"Well, my phone service just got activated a couple of hours ago. And, under the circumstances of you *escaping* the house this morning, I thought you might not answer."

Red looked guiltily away, out of Luis' view. Then he told the kids, "Go wash up. Your faces are sticky! I need to talk with Dr. Jack."

But Luis wouldn't budge. Red said, "I *promise* I won't leave. I'll join you in a minute." And once the children were inside and beyond earshot, he said, "Is it true? Did Luis' uncle die?"

"What?" said Jack, his smile instantly vanishing. "What have you heard?"

"Someone I know found a dead guy on the sidewalk yesterday. And from his description and the fact of the guy having lived at the stadium and just leaving the hospital . . . Well, it has to be Luis' uncle."

Jack blanched. "I see. Want to give me a minute to confirm with the hospital?" Red nodded and entered the house; Jack heard the kids' jubilant cries.

Now, in this first private moment, he could finally phone Nora. She answered: "I was just about to call you."

He said, "I need a favor. To check on Luis' uncle who—"

Nora moaned. "That's why I was going to call. Tomas Ruiz was here, but he left AMA yesterday and . . . sorry . . . he was found dead on a sidewalk downtown."

Jack hung up the phone, threw back his head, and whispered: "Dear god, what is it with you and this kid? Can't you give him a break?" Then he braced himself and entered his house.

Visiting Room, San Sebastian Prison

Marin County

"You don't understand," said Quentin. "You may have befriended my son and conducted business with him inside. But any loyalty to you ended the moment he got out."

Pete Vaughn smiled wryly. "That right, Mr. Lawyer?" He was determined to remain calm, having learned the painful way that stress exacerbated his tumor headache. "Because Patty called this morning and told me different. She said *Marty* actually took care of business—something *you* haven't done a long while."

"Let me explain—"

"Frankly, you disrespected me and Patty by not keeping your end of our bargain. You abandoned her in shit circumstances. You made her suffer. That wasn't supposed to happen."

Quentin swallowed forcefully, trying to quell his heartburn. "Please, listen. I paid Martin to manage business at the stadium. I didn't know until last night that he wasn't doing his job. So, I drove to the stadium this morning to apologize in person to Patty, and see for myself what was happening there. But Patty refused to see me. She even instructed the guard not to let me inside."

Pete massaged his forehead as his headache rallied. "Still, it was *you* I had an agreement with, Quentin. Not your son. Be a man. Accept responsibility."

"Granted, I made a mistake. I was merely trying to keep Martin occupied and off the streets and out of . . . here. But you're right. I should've overseen his work. I never had to do that with Alex."

Pete scoffed. "See the irony here? *That* gives me pause about *your* loyalty. Because why would you replace Alex after he done so well by us? He might've been a damn ghost, and I might've never met him. But I always knew he was watching over things. And he always dropped payments on time."

"I didn't abandon Alex. He's working on other assignments, doing important work—"

"I see. So, Patty and my migrants aren't 'important'?"

"I didn't mean that."

"See, here again, you're sounding disloyal. If, like you insist, Marty was incompetent, why put him in charge of us if we honestly mattered to you?"

"Look, the camp needs to shut down this week. Martin told me the residents had done the cleanup and were moved weeks ago to another property Greeley wants to devalue and buy. Clearly, he lied. And all the money that was supposed to go to Patty—he kept that for himself."

"Well, I got no way of knowing you're telling the truth. But I do know I got a message out through *Marty* yesterday, and he got business taken care of *pronto*. That makes me think I can trust him."

Quentin privately counted to ten. "I won't keep defending myself. I was wrong to involve Martin. I've explained what happened. Case closed. I'm here to make you an offer."

"Another fuckin' irony! I'm locked up here in the first place because of an 'offer' you made me—the very one you've been pissing on lately. I took an eight-month rap for recruiting migrant workers and smuggling them in illegally to labor on Greeley properties. And for years, I've moved them around to occupy real estate so you and the Greeleys could buy it on the cheap. You've made millions off me."

"You know I can be trusted. You received the money from our first deal." Quentin hesitated, but decided to say: "And you'd be out enjoying it now, if you hadn't extended your sentence with your foolish prison cellphone scheme."

"Keep your voice down," said Pete, wincing in pain.

After taking a breath, Quentin said, "My new offer is double the original."

"Okay. I'm listening. But I'm not taking another criminal rap for the Greeleys. I want to get out and be with Patty. Make things right by her. And I want her kept out of any trouble with this 'new offer.'"

Quentin nodded and whispered, "It concerns other shady real estate practices at Greeley Enterprises."

"Ha! That's supposed to be hush? What isn't shady about Greeley—?" Pain jolted his right eye and his vision flickered, creating staggered images of Quentin as if from a wonky film reel.

"You're squinting," said Quentin. "Are you in pain?"

"None of your fuckin' business. You got a minute on the clock. Talk."

"All right. Yesterday, Samantha paid a visit to the stadium. As you know, that's unusual; she never sets foot on her properties or wants to know what's what. And it was Thanksgiving, raining. More importantly, Martin was with her."

Recalling Patty's depressing description of the place, Pete said: "You're implying Marty *wanted* Sam to see the stadium."

"Yes. Because he knew the property wasn't prepped for the sale—as was conditional for its prospective buyer. But I'd been telling Samantha otherwise, based on *his* bold-face lies. He schemed for her to see me as negligent, incompetent."

Pete grinned provocatively. "So, your son's trying to take you down?"

"Isn't that stick-in-the-eye obvious? Last night, at Samantha's house for the annual Greeley Thanksgiving, I was ambushed. Samantha took me aside to inform me of her shocking 'discovery' about the stadium. Then—abracadabra—Martin just happens to drop by to deliver your message, acting completely innocent. And he threw me under the bus about the stadium mess. To make matters worse, I was also made aware that he and Samantha are romantically involved."

"Interesting, finally. Go on. You earned another minute, Mr. Lawyer."

"My point is, Martin's been stealing from me and Greeley Enterprises all the while you've been inside. He's been sabotaging the stadium deal and turning Samantha against me, so much so that she's forcing my resignation. So, I'm warning you again: No more dealings with Martin. Your business dealings inside may've gone well. But, outside, he's got more lucrative options, involving more powerful people and bigger stakes. And their interests will trump yours whenever it suits him. My son always takes what he wants, and things like truth and loyalty are just cheap commodities to him. He's double-crossed me, his own father; and he'll do the same to you. Maybe even to Samantha. I wouldn't put it past him."

"Well, he wouldn't have to work hard to pull the wool over her eyes, not with her always turning a blind eye to her own business. She just pays people like us to get our hands dirty, while she gets filthy rich. Anyway, let's hear your new deal."

"In coming days, you'll doubtless hear allegations about Martin's involvement with the stadium. Mostly concerning tax and employment fraud. And because of your long and well-documented 'work history' with him, the police will certainly question you about the truth of those allegations. All I need you to do is confirm that Martin was dropping under-the-table payoffs to you and Patty's nonprofit. That he knew the money subsidized a coerced labor force to provide cheap labor for Greeley properties."

"I don't know," said Pete, shaking his head. "I've known Marty since he was a kid, in high school. You had him working odd jobs at the stadium during the renovation in '89. Well, until he stole that car."

"Yes, one of my many foolish attempts to give him a job to make his mother happy. But, see, that's the strength of your word against Martin—you've known Martin that long and worked alongside him. You've also known him in prison."

Pete laughed. "Marty always bragged about never working legit—for you, especially. He said you and his mom always gave him anything he wanted."

Quentin didn't appreciate being laughed at—directly by Pete, indirectly by his son. Any modicum of regret over retaliating against Martin vanished instantly. He clenched his jaw and said, "Do you understand?"

"Now, don't get upset. Yeah, copy on that: Marty 'working' on and off forever for you and the Greeleys. But I don't know. Why would police believe I knew about Marty's stadium dealings over the last year or so? I've been put away most of that time! And Patty's only received one payment from him."

"I have that covered. We're also going to 'credit' Martin with the payments Alex made the years before."

"So, then . . . a fake paper trail?"

Quentin nodded.

"I see," said Pete. "You're totally pissed at Marty. So you're going to aim a shit fan at him and get out of the way." Holding Quentin's gaze, nodding knowingly, he continued: "Still, shit's kinda messy in a fan. It's near impossible not to get some on yourself, no matter how fast you think you can run."

Confident about going out otherwise, in a blaze of pure glory, Quentin replied: "I'm not worried. Besides, any theoretical risk is worth it. Martin has taken everything from me."

"Wow, you really hate your son."

"That's a separate issue from my warning about him. You and I have worked together for years, doing business by our word and handshake.

And before Martin returned to the picture, we'd always done right by each other, didn't we?"

"You expecting a merit badge for that?"

"No. But I'm expecting you to remember me. *Us.*"

Pete's skull was exploding with pain, and he stood up to leave. "I'll think on it, Mr. Lawyer. Any last words?"

"Last words?" said Quentin, stymied. "I've made you an easy and lucrative offer!"

"Yeah, the money sounds good. The request sounds easy. But, to be honest, I don't want to fuck up and let Patty down again. I can't risk getting involved in something that could extend my time again. I want to get out and be with her, and finally enjoy the money we got from the first deal."

Of course! thought Quentin. *Patty's the key bargaining chip.* He coolly eyed Pete and said, "If you continue to associate with Martin, you'll doubtless incur new charges to keep you imprisoned for additional years and apart from the wealth awaiting you. You will miss the opportunity to be free and reunited with Patty. Unless, of course, she . . ."

"She *what?*" said Pete, with renewed interest.

"Well, if Martin is fingered for criminal activity at the stadium . . . which he will be . . . and since, as even you noted, he began direct negotiations with Patty today . . . Well, clearly, Patty will be viewed as an accomplice—"

"She's a good woman! She just stepped in to help, until I get out. She knows nothing about our deals. It's not her fault I'm in here longer than I was supposed to be. And it's not her fault *you* brought in *your* lowlife son, who apparently fucked things over for her!"

The guard yelled, "Calm down, Pete!"

"Look," whispered Quentin, "I can promise to keep Patty out of everything. But I need you to *immediately* stop *all* communication with my double-crossing, deceitful, lowlife son. And I'll need you to testify that he's done 'work' at the stadium since high school. And those are my 'last words.' What about yours?"

Jack's Home

Red stared at Luis, waiting for his response to news of his uncle's death. But Luis remained silent, didn't even cry. He stared back at Red for a seeming eternity and finally said, "He's gone, like my mom and dad?"

Red didn't know what to say, not knowing what had happened to Luis' parents. Did they die, too? Or had Luis been separated from them, for any of the awful reasons that could break migrant families apart? "Little man," he replied, "I'm just going to be honest with you. Because we're buddies, right?" Luis nodded, and Red continued, "Your Uncle Tomas is gone forever. That's what 'dead' means. Understand? But, your parents . . . well, we never talked about them. So, I don't know if they're gone in the same way."

"They were buried in the ground," said Luis. "I saw the men who shot them dig the hole, and I saw them roll my mom and dad inside it. I was there with Uncle Tomas when it happened."

All the air inside Red's lungs suddenly expelled. "Little man," he said, "I'm sorry. I don't know what to say."

"Say you won't leave me, too," said Luis.

~ ~ ~

Part Four

Whirlwind

SATURDAY, NOVEMBER 24

Old Stadium Site

GIANNI AWOKE IN HIS TRUCK, the sun piercing the windshield and warming his face. And he would've felt wonderful had Red not let him down by breaking his promise to return yesterday. He'd even gotten into trouble with Patty, who, on her way out of the stadium last night, cursed him for covering for Red, angrily asking: "You working for *him* now?" Before he could reply, she flicked her hand dismissively at him and said: "Just make goddamn sure *one* of you stays at this gate. And get rid of that dirt in your truck before tomorrow."

Further dismayed by her unpredictable strangeness, he resolved to abandon pursuit of any relationship with her. *I want to work on friendships; but, man, people gotta meet a few standards. Like, friends should be . . . what? How to put it in words?* It dawned on him that he didn't actually know; he had no relationship experience from which to draw.

Still, at least he'd realized some traits he didn't want in a friend: like Patty's unpredictability and harshness. Her ambivalence, too. *It's a start, and I just made a mistake with her. But she came to me, and mine was a rookie's error.*

And yet . . . *he* had chosen Red but seemed to be failing there, too. *Because a "friend" wouldn't've stiffed me like he did last night. Maybe I just can't do the friendship thing.*

Hungry and searching his truck for food, he only found emptied food wrappers. Realizing he'd eaten all the snacks last night, he considered grabbing a QikBreakfastBizKit at the gas mart a few blocks away. *But if Patty comes by and finds nobody here, me and Red will lose our jobs. And that seems stupid when she can finally pay good money for work.*

He went behind the shed to pee in the drainage ditch, wondering when and if Red was returning, and regretting not having exchanged phone numbers: *like real friends do.* On his trek back to his truck, he saw a royal blue Audi parked outside the gate. A man in a tan fedora called out, "Where's the red-haired gentleman?"

"Who's asking?" said Gianni.

"I'm Quentin Ocambo—attorney for Greeley Enterprises, the owner of this property. Here's my card."

Experiencing a customary mix of nervousness and anger around lawyers, Gianni took the card and asked: "Whaddya want?"

The lawyer—fifty-sixty-ish, tall, neatly dressed—removed his fedora, revealing a shock of silver hair. "I spoke with the red-haired gentleman yesterday. I'm here to continue our conversation."

"Don't know nothing about that," Gianni replied.

Quentin eyed him appraisingly, feeling unnerved by something familiar in his appearance. "When do you expect him back?"

"Can't say."

"I see. Then, mind if I take a walk around the property?"

Gianni hadn't received instructions about handling such requests. Though the man's business card looked legit, he said, "Yeah, I mind."

Quentin tried to appear nonchalant. "Well, like I told the other fellow: keep my card. You'll need it soon enough."

"What the fuck you talking about? You don't know me."

"Perhaps not . . ." Quentin nearly gasped; now the man's voice sounded hauntingly familiar, too. "But what I do know is that this property is occupied by asylum seekers and undocumented migrant workers. Many of them were brought here illegally. And I know they're being used and abused for hard and dangerous labor."

Gianni's hands began to sweat. *Where the fuck is Red?* "I don't know what you're talking about."

"Well, if you can prove you're thoroughly naïve, that would work to your advantage in a court of law."

"What the fuck," said Gianni, pulling out his phone. "I need to call Patty."

Quentin scoffed. "Ah. Ms. Dobrovski. 'Patty' who runs 'Hope and Dignity' here—the fake nonprofit I established for her."

Gianni hesitated, and Quentin continued: "She's already in major legal trouble. And the more you engage with her, the tighter the noose around *your* neck."

Rattling the gate, Gianni shouted, "Get to your fucking point!"

Stepping back, Quentin said, "All right, son. It's still early, so you have time to avoid what will otherwise become a very bad day for you. And, for that matter, for anyone working or living here."

Rather than phoning Patty, Gianni googled Quentin; his picture popped up, and his name firmly linked to the Ocambo Law Firm and Greeley Enterprises. He looked up to see Quentin grinning.

"Those photos don't do me justice," said Quentin. "But, as you see, I'm legitimate. What's your name, son?"

"My name's Gianni. And don't call me 'son.'"

Quentin tried not to flinch, but it was obvious now. *My god, that name . . . that voice . . . the thick black hair and crooked mouth. He has to be Tony Moretti's boy!* "Okay," he managed, covertly absorbing the shock. "But, tell me, Gianni. Are you aware this property is being sold to a housing developer next week?"

Gianni's jaw-drop conveyed his answer. Quentin nodded knowingly and said, "So, clearly, the camp should've been cleared out by now. The final walk-through with Highmark Construction is scheduled for Friday. And they won't sign, not with a large, entrenched encampment here. Or they'll impose such costly penalties on Greeley Enterprises—"

"But where are these people supposed to go?" Gianni charged, thinking of Red, thinking of the lady and her kid with the garden.

Quentin shrugged. "They're usually relocated to other properties to do construction, landscaping, agriculture, cleanup—whatever work Greeley Enterprises needs. And the ones living here now should've been moved out weeks ago. They were brought in originally to clean up the stadium and leave. It's basic labor trafficking."

"But, of *human beings,* man?" Gianni felt nauseous. *But if what he's saying is true, I want no part of it. Fucking assholes making money off the people living here!* He thought about his own parents who'd emigrated and were worked to early deaths through hard labor for subsistence pay, trying to provide him with a better life. Although "Moretti Landscaping" was always a shoestring business, it was also a lifeline for his father, who so generously tossed it to him. "You're saying," Gianni managed, "the Greeleys are making a killing by working these people to death. And I'm thinking, if you're the Greeleys' lawyer . . . you gotta be as much of a lowlife as them. Lower even, 'cuz you probably always make sure they get away with it."

Privately, Quentin rued: *This wouldn't be happening if Pete were out of prison like I'd planned. He'd have quietly moved everyone out by now. But, no; he had to ruin things with his damn prison cellphone scheme. Then, his foolish insistence that Patty should "hold the fort" for him. My god, that woman is useless.* He said, "These people here are used to the way things are."

Gianni rattled the gate again and shouted, "How's that any kind of excuse?!"

Quentin felt rattled himself—thrown off-guard by meeting Tony Moretti's son and hearing his accusations. *How to justify things for this young man?* "Look," he replied, "it's not only about *labor* trafficking. Sometimes people are moved around merely to manipulate property values."

"What the fuck is that supposed to mean?"

"They're just moved to property that Greeley wants to purchase. Once they drive the purchase price down sufficiently, Greeley buys. Then the residents clean up the property, and they're relocated elsewhere."

Gianni shook his head in disgust. "I don't know why you're telling me all this shit. But I see from where I stand, that you're covered in it." He spat on the ground and turned away.

"Wait!" said Quentin. "I agree with what you said. And I want to help you."

Gianni glared at him, waiting.

Quentin Ocambo had always wondered what a "come-to-Jesus moment" might feel like. An avowed atheist, he'd always been flummoxed—amused, really—whenever plaintiffs or defendants invoked the phrase during legal proceedings. But now, staring back at Gianni, whose glare cut through the veneer of his own being, he thought he finally understood. No godly figure materialized; no stirrings of the celestial sounded. But there in the visage of Tony Moretti's son was truth itself, genuine, unvarnished, transcendent, and piercing him—if only fleetingly.

4th Floor Monitored Unit

Oakland City Hospital

Surprised to see Nora entering his room, Aditya said, "I heard footsteps, but no squeaking."

She laughed. "Because it's Saturday; I'm not working. I'm here to pick up our no-longer-blue patient. She and her daughter will be staying with Jack a few days. Thought I'd just stop by to say 'Hi.'"

"My hemoglobin has been stable, and my CT is clear. So, I, too, am going home today—as soon as Lizbeth arrives with clothes for me."

"Remember, take things easy. No sky-diving or boxing tournaments. Don't return to work before you're ready."

"No worries," he said. "But, where will Ms. Habani and her daughter go after Jack's? Back to that camp?"

"I don't know," she said worriedly. "Right now, it's one day at a time. And the days have gotten so long recently! But a social worker is on the case now, trying to find a safe disposition."

"Do you still think she and Mr. Ruiz got sick from that camp?"

"I do. Along with the third patient who lived there and died last month from organophosphate toxicity. Still, at the moment, I have no definitive proof of ground or water contamination. Not 'til Monday, at least."

"Well, in the meantime, I have done some internet sleuthing. It is amazing how far you can travel in cyberspace while you are stuck in bed. Anyhow, we discovered that the stadium . . ." He stopped, glanced toward the doorway, and said, "Lizbeth! I was just about to tell Nora about the Regal Chemical Company."

Lizbeth waved at Nora and said, "Yeah, talk about fascinating ancient history! The Greeleys tore down Regal Chemicals and built the stadium on the same land."

"What?" said Nora, her mind reeling. "How 'ancient'?"

Lizbeth grimaced, wondering how old Nora might be. "Sorry, I didn't technically mean 'ancient.'"

Aditya keenly took over. "The Regal Chemical Company made pesticides. At one point, it was the second major US supplier of insecticides, herbicides, and fungicides. The Alpers family owned it. And, so, when its sole heir, Winifred, married Bert Greeley in 1950, its ownership transferred automatically to Greeley Enterprises. Anyhow, it was torn down immediately. And within a year, they had built most of the main coliseum."

Nora's jaw dropped. "That's definitely 'fascinating.' Back then, in 'ancient' times"—she smiled at Lizbeth—"they didn't require environmental inspections when real estate changed hands. 1950–51 was at least a decade before Rachel Carson published *Silent Spring*. And *two* decades before the EPA even came into existence, under Nixon."

"Yes," said Aditya. "The first environmental inspection of the stadium that I could find was performed in 1989. The Greeleys had to commission it before they could sell off parcels of adjoining land—which they wanted to do in order to finance the stadium's renovation. And that 'Screening Site Inspection Report' documented extreme contamination of the land and groundwater with toxic pesticides and solvent residuals."

Nora let out an exasperated sigh. She'd done a cursory check of her own after Fred had challenged her judgment about soil testing at the stadium. "But I checked the national EPA website, and California's EnviroStor database. The stadium property isn't listed as a hazardous waste site."

"That's because," said Lizbeth, "the Greeleys then became obligated to clean up their property—something called a 'land remediation.' The chemical cleanup took two years. But when the property passed reinspection in 1991 and was certified as nonhazardous, they could proceed with the land sale and could begin the stadium renovation."

"And we know," said Aditya, "the property was reinspected this year as well, ahead of selling to Highmark Construction. It passed environmental inspection again."

Lizbeth haltingly concluded, "So . . . it looks like the stadium property has been healthy for the last twenty-seven years."

Aditya, noting Nora's embarrassment, offered: "Still, it is always good to check those databases—even though we know many contaminated sites are never reported or officially listed, for one reason or another."

Nora felt foolish, hearing the evidence, while also recalling Fred's resonant admonition. Absorbing Lizbeth's and Aditya's sympathetic gaze, she felt embarrassed for having drawn them into her amateur soil-testing escapade. She sighed and said, "I was probably too desperate to find a reason for our patients' illnesses." *And, perhaps, as Fred insinuated, to stick it to Samantha Greeley?*

Aditya said, "I know you will figure it out. Oh, and we downloaded all those environmental reports. Would you still like to see them? I can email them to you."

"Sure," said Nora, turning away, heading to the hospital elevator, thinking: *I should've looked at the EPA and EnviroStor sites first . . . or just listened to Fred's sensible warning. Still, it made—makes?—sense to suspect the stadium's ground and water. And there are so many known hazardous sites surrounding the stadium . . .*

Now in the elevator, heading to the 9th floor to pick up Daleen, Nora stared plaintively at her distorted reflection in the chrome doors. *I'm nuts. What was I thinking? I actually imagined the Greeleys capable of knowingly exposing people to hazardous chemicals?* At Floor 5: *Fred's going to say, "I told you so."* Floor 6: *How "ancient" does Lizbeth think I am?* Floor 7: *As Aditya asked, where will Daleen and Yusra go after leaving Jack's?* Floor 8: *Should I apologize to Samantha for my behavior?* Finally, at Floor 9: *But why did three people residing at the stadium sicken or die from toxic exposures?* The doors opened.

Carl's Home

Piedmont

"What's Carl doing now?" asked Winston, working on his laptop.

Fergie had been staring out the window, watching Carl. "He's sweeping ashes off the driveway."

"It's amazing how far they've traveled from the wildfires. Is he wearing a mask?"

"Yeah. Two."

"You know that big housing development at the stadium site?" he said. "Where we'd hoped Marla might be eligible?"

"Oh?" she said.

He wondered whether she was listening. "Well, it appears *technically* true that Samantha Greeley obtained a pledge from Highmark Construction to include affordable units in the new housing development. But guess how many of the fifteen hundred apartments were promised?"

"Dunno."

"A measly eighty! A whopping five percent! And who knows if even *that* will happen? Because Highmark can just choose to pay an in-lieu impact fee to Oakland instead. Even then, most of the time, Oakland doesn't collect the fee from the developers." After waiting in vain for her outrage, he closed his laptop and said, "What's up, Fergs?"

She turned from the window and joined him on the couch. "I keep thinking about Luis and Yusra."

He put an arm around her. "It's mind-blowing what those kids have endured."

"I feel helpless, Win. At least you can write about the atrocities and bring them to public attention."

He looked stunned. "Excuse me? You actually save people's lives! And your ER's where poor and homeless people show up. You take great care—"

"But that's my job. I get paid to do it. Besides, I'm talking about making a difference in a bigger-picture way. I do my work, one person at a time. Like drops in the ocean."

His face lit up. "Why not work with me on some stories that matter to you?"

"Because I can't write."

"If you can talk, you can write."

But she appeared unconvinced. He pressed, "You can read . . . do research. You can come with me on interviews. I'd love your company."

She tutted.

"You're tough to woo," he said. "Okay. So, you're thinking about Luis. Why don't we pursue a story that bears witness to his uncle's death? One that sheds light on the bigger picture of homelessness and powerlessness? There's more than four thousand people living homeless in Oakland, with four thousand stories that should be told."

Fergie went to the refrigerator for yogurt. "You need to understand that exposing details about Tomas Ruiz could put Luis at risk. We don't even know Luis' immigration status. If he's illegally here and your story leads immigration to him . . . god, imagine Luis in one of those horrid detention centers."

Winston walked to the window and saw Carl removing his gloves and facemask. "I know that, Fergs. I'd . . . no, *we'd* be careful about that."

"In the ER, we never ask patients about immigration status. Gets in the way of their care. They either clam up or leave. Or they lie, because they think they have to in order to get any help."

"It must be tricky to diagnose and treat people accurately if you're working on partial, or even false, information."

Fergie nodded. "Lots of sick people don't even come to us in the first place, because they're afraid of being deported. And when they finally do, it's often on a stretcher because they waited too long at death's doorstep—like Daleen and Tomas. And by that time, it's often too late to make a difference."

Winston waved back at Carl, who was now hosing down the driveway. Then he suddenly turned to Fergie, a provocative smile on his face.

"What?" she said, blushing.

"Well, I think you just outlined the big-picture story that's waiting for you to write it."

Jack's Home

Rockridge District

Yusra washed her face and brushed her teeth twice. Then she sat on Jack's big leather couch with her mother's maroon scarf across her shoulders. She asked Jack again, "When is my mom coming?"

Jack patted her hand and said, "One minute less than the last time you asked, sweetie. My friend Nora, the nice lady doctor who brought your mom's scarf—"

"She is no Nice Lady!"

"What?" said Jack, alarmed. "Why do you say that?"

But a knock on the door intervened, and Jack got up to answer. Yusra gasped when her mother stood radiant in the doorway, reminding her of a saint she saw in the stained-glass window of a sanctuary church where they once slept. She ran to her and held her fiercely as Nora walked in.

"My daughter," said Daleen, overwhelmed with joy, though barely able to stand.

When Yusra finally let go, she stepped back and observed, "You're not blue anymore." She turned to Nora and smiled.

"Welcome, Daleen," said Jack. "I've prepared a guestroom for you and Yusra."

"It has its own bathroom!" said Yusra, still amazed that one house would contain five.

Jack said, "Can I get you something to eat or drink?"

"No, thank you," said Daleen. "But I should lie down, if that is all right. And maybe I could have some time with Yusra?"

"Of course," he said. "I can show you to your room."

But Yusra was already leading her mother away.

When Jack and Nora were alone on the couch, he exhaled fully and said: "There hasn't been so much life in this house since Richard died."

Nora rested her head on his shoulder. "You're sweet to offer your home to them and Luis. The social worker was cautiously optimistic about finding them shelter after the holiday weekend."

He shook his head in incredulity. "It used to make sense to Richard and me, to own a four-bedroom home. We kept a master bedroom and guestroom, and converted the other two into personal offices. But after he died . . . this home mostly housed space. 'Emptiness,' actually." He steeled himself and continued, "Anyway, Zofia is coming tonight and staying a few days. Thank god! I'm thoroughly incompetent with kids. I've no idea how to handle them. But, Red? You should've seen him. He knew exactly how to be with Luis and tell him about his uncle's death."

"And Daleen's here now. Once she's steady on her feet, things should get easier with the kids. By the way, where's Luis?"

"With Red, who stayed here last night to comfort him. But this morning, when Red said he was leaving to spring a guy named Gianni who covered for him at the stadium last night, Luis insisted on going with him. They left about an hour ago."

Nora frowned. "Luis is so young, and has no one there now."

He has Red," said Jack. "And he's returning here tonight after they eat at Betty's. I have no idea what happens tomorrow."

Old Stadium Site

West Oakland

When they arrived at the stadium, Luis said, "I thought your friend Gianni was supposed to be here."

"Me, too," said Red. "But I can't say I blame him for leaving. I should've sprung him last night. He was doing me a favor by covering for me."

A fist pounded on the windshield, and Gianni shouted, "Open up!"

Red jumped out of his truck and said, "Sorry, Gianni! I didn't have your number, so I couldn't call last night. And I was into something big—"

"Will you shut up for a second?" said Gianni. He looked nervously around and, spotting Luis in the truck, asked, "Who's that?"

Red whispered, "Luis. He was living here with his uncle—the guy you found dead."

"Aw, fuck!" said Gianni, shaking his head. "It's all so messed up."

"Yeah, so, when you told me yesterday about his uncle, I had to go see the little man."

"Hey, no need to apologize." He patted Red's shoulder. "You're a good man."

"I owe you big. I won't forget the solid you did me with Patty. Speaking of, has she been by?"

Gianni scoffed. "No, but she did have an interesting gentleman caller. A lawyer—get this—named 'Quentin Ocambo.' Sounds like a fancy cocktail, right?"

"Shit. He was here yesterday, too."

"I know. Because he asked for you. But don't worry. I didn't say anything. He doesn't even know your name."

"What did he want?"

Gianni deliberated briefly. "It's funny. About an hour ago, I was here wondering if I should give up on you, Red. But I didn't. Instead, I decided to trust you had a good reason for stiffing me last night. And now, look: turns out I was right. I was right to trust you, and that feels good to me right now."

After Red grinned and gently punched his shoulder, Gianni pointed up 4th Street and said: "I parked there, right after Ocambo left. And I've just been waiting for you since, to warn you not to come back. In fact, we should get out now, before Patty shows up."

"Sorry, Gianni. But I really need the cash."

Though bracing himself for rejection, Gianni decided to take the risk and proposed: "So, here's that solid you owe me: to trust me on this." And to his astonishment, Red nodded.

Fred's Home

Berkeley

Fred sat at the kitchen table, trying to appear nonchalant. But Vickie was moving merrily about the house, and, still, neither of them had said a word about having had sex the other night. It seemed to him the occasion should merit an honorable mention at least. *Or was it a fluke? Pity sex, maybe? Worse—is she actively trying to forget it?*

"Hey," said Charlie, opening the fridge.

While the lone "Hey" wasn't much, it was one word more than Fred usually heard from his son in the mornings. "Hey," he coolly returned, afraid to sound wanting more.

But then Charlie asked, "Know where Ella's at?"

Fred put down his coffee and stared inquiringly at his son. *What's happening to my family?* He cleared his throat. "Well, being Saturday, she's probably with her study group." Since returning to the family fold, he'd dutifully mastered his kids' complex schedules and adapted to Vickie's house rules. He added, rather proudly, "From eight to eleven, I believe. Then she's got track 'til one."

Charlie laughed. "Just testing you, Dad!" On his way out, he said: "You're getting better at it."

Fred let out a sigh of relief. How exhausting to be always on stage inside his own home, constantly working to earn his family's approval. And these last two days were particularly excruciating, waiting on Vickie's appraisal of his performance in bed.

"Oh, Fred," she called out from the living room.

"My god!" he whispered, his heart racing. *She's summoning me!*

"Fred, darling?" she said in her sing-song voice.

"Coming," he said, hurriedly checking his shirt for toast crumbs. But before he could rush to her, she appeared in the kitchen doorway with Carl. His high hopes for romance sunk precipitously. She said, "Carl dropped by to see you. Isn't that nice? I'll leave you two in private, so you can talk."

"Oh . . . Carl," said Fred, wistfully watching his wife depart. "Didn't expect you."

"You said to drop by sometime," said Carl.

"So I did," said Fred. He pushed aside his newspaper and invited Carl to sit. "Would you like some coffee?"

"No, thanks. I've had my twelve ounces already."

Thrumming his fingers on the table, Fred said, "All right now. What brings you here?"

"I want to talk about Lydia."

Fred gulped. "What? Hell, no! My god, not *here.*" He prayed that Vickie hadn't overheard Lydia's name mentioned.

"I thought it would be better to speak about her in a private setting."

"*This* is not the *right* private setting," whispered Fred.

Carl said, "But I thought everyone knew about your relationship with Lydia. Even Vickie and your kids."

"Please," Fred said. "It's complicated. We need to keep our voices down."

"Okay," said Carl. "It's just that, during Thanksgiving dinner with Lydia's sister Carrie—I was the only guest—I learned some things about Lydia. Things I'd been wrong about, including her perception of me. And since I've been learning how to be more emotionally attuned, I was hoping we could discuss my misinterpretations. I would ask Nora, but I see how much it still pains her to talk about Lydia."

Vickie re-entered and cheerily inquired, "What are you boys whispering about?"

Fred preemptively blurted out, "Hospital stuff! Work."

Carl registered Fred's acute discomfort and willful deception. *Coupled with his body language—clenched mandible, piercing stare—he's sending a "covert communication" to me.* He knowingly nodded to Fred and said, "Yes, 'hospital stuff' and 'work.'"

"Yeah?" said Vickie, catching the drift, knowing each of them, in their unique ways, to be amateurs at deception. She playfully inquired, "Like what?"

Fred grabbed the first thing that came to mind: "Just hospital board stuff. Boring stuff. *Bored* already."

She sat down at the table. "Well, try me."

"All right then," said Fred. He cleared his throat, biding for time. "For example, we have a new board member." After a long pause during which she and Carl stared expectantly at him, he added: "Samantha Greeley. Of *the* Greeley family. They own the old stadium site that's selling off to Highmark Construction next week. We expect good things to come from that—a massive housing development that should benefit our patients and service employees."

Carl felt acutely unburdened with the conversation's shift; he'd been focusing all his energy on not lying to Vickie about their hushed conversation. Besides, with this new topic, he could offer interesting information about one of the most storied Bay Area families. He said, "I met Bert Greeley in 2010, the year before he died, at a fundraiser for my wife's research initiative. His daughter, Samantha, was with him. She was about to turn forty and told us she was planning a celebratory Caribbean cruise with her friends."

"Oh?" said Vickie. "And what about Bert's wife, Samantha's mother?"

"Winifred—nee Alpers, of *the* Alpers family—wasn't there because she was dead."

"Oh . . . sorry," said Vickie.

"She'd died during childbirth in 1971. And I regret to say, at that time, my field of obstetrics wasn't as advanced—"

"Hold on," said Fred. "Did Samantha's mother die while giving birth to her?"

"Fred, I just told you. That's what 'during childbirth' means."

Vickie looked sideways at Fred and said, "Darling, he's right. That's what it means."

Fred's finger-thrumming resumed as he flashed on his last two encounters with Samantha. Both were unsettling and had taken him by surprise. Gazing back at Vickie, he wondered why his relationships with women seemed to entail intense psychic struggles that always left him feeling thickheaded. *With you, of course. Our daughter Ella. Samantha Greeley. Lydia.* And now, even Nora, to whom, he conceded, he should apologize for being so oppositional to her well-meaning inquiry about her patients' environmental safety. Finally, he said, "I was just surprised to learn how young Samantha was when she took over the family business."

"Family *businesses*—plural," said Vickie. "They own half the city."

"Actually," said Carl, "that's an overestimation."

Fred grinned and told Vickie, "He's right, darling."

Old Stadium Site

West Oakland

Patty parked on 4th and snuck through an entry hole in the fence. If anything were to go sideways during the camp evacuations, her car would be safer on the street, especially if any riffraff caught wind and decided to show up. *Those busybodies with their obnoxious video cameras and hateful slogans. At least me and Pete been giving these people some protection and support.*

Despite recent rains, the skies remained dappled with wildfire ashes drifting in from the north, and the air smelled sweetly of pinewood and fir trees. She inhaled deeply and fantasized herself sitting near a cozy fireplace, just like happy people did in movies or on TV.

She felt confident now about the plan she'd finalized after her mind-restoring sleep in the motel. With Red's and Gianni's help, the camp evacuation was certainly doable over the weekend. Right now, she'd give the residents notice to pack up. Five would fit in Red's crew cab, and six on Gianni's flatbed; with three transports in the afternoon and three at night, she could evacuate sixty-six people today. And by starting earlier tomorrow and adding three morning runs, they'd move out the ninety-some remaining people to clear the camp by Sunday night.

But . . . déjà vu: On her way to the D-lot, she saw no one guarding the gate. And to her mounting distress, Red's and Gianni's trucks were nowhere to be seen.

The air suddenly smelled acrid and burnt. She trembled with fury and panic. Already, she'd accepted the money and spent too much of it. She'd assured Marty Ocambo she could deliver on the evacuation. And Pete had intervened and was counting on her.

She struggled to steady her hands to phone Red. When he didn't pick up, she felt too anxious to leave a message. Then a desperate call to Gianni, who also didn't answer. Dumbstruck, paralyzed, all she could envision was the menace she'd seen in Marty Ocambo's eyes.

Betty's

City Center

Jack's mention of Betty's had stimulated Nora's appetite. So, after leaving his house, she headed for the restaurant, not caring whether a patient might spot her taking out a cholesterol-drenched breakfast sandwich with home fries. It was the therapeutic meal she craved.

After placing her order with the blue-haired woman at the counter, Nora leaned against the soda dispenser and began skimming Aditya's emailed documents. How stunning to see the damning environmental report of the stadium's widespread contamination in 1989. And, in contrast, the stellar reinspections in '91 and 2018. But there they were, in black-and-white, issued by Epitome Soil Testing Lab and approved by the EPA. By all accounts, the toxic stew left by Regal Chemical had been dutifully cleaned up by the Greeleys. *God, I've been foolish. Wrong about the stadium, wrong about Samantha and her family business. And now I've got to apologize to her, and Fred, as well.*

She grabbed her takeout, planning to enjoy it at home. But the aroma of well-seasoned grease made her stomach growl. So, seated behind the wheel of her car, she tore into her Sausage-N-Bacon-N-Egg special.

But then someone tapped on her window. With a mouthful of sandwich, she looked out to see a thirty-ish-year-old man with a leathery face and crooked grin who stood by his dirt-laden truck. He said, "Nice Prius you got."

Taken aback, she locked the doors, tossed her sandwich onto the passenger seat, and turned on the ignition.

Realizing his misstep, he said, "Sorry! Don't go. My name's Gianni. I just like your car."

But she drove away, heading home with a new grease stain on the car seat.

Saul's Delicatessen

Berkeley

Alex Morales sopped up the egg yolk on his plate with a poppyseed bagel and asked his tablemate, "You going to eat that?"

Quentin offered up his plate of potato latkes. "Go ahead."

"Thanks," said Alex, heaping on sour cream. "Anything wrong?"

Quentin replied, unconvincingly, "No."

Alex scoffed. "You recall, I'm a P.I. I've done work for you for ages. No use lying to me."

"And you're an old friend, as well. A loyal friend and business accomplice since '89."

"Hmm. You're being awfully precise with your timeframe. And sounding . . . sentimental, actually. You traveling down memory lane, Q?"

Smiling appreciatively, Quentin handed over a thick envelope and a set of keys to his son's business office. "Thanks for agreeing to take care of this. I appreciate the favor."

Alex grinned. "Wow. Giving me *keys*? You're making this job easy for me."

"They're the originals, from the landlord. I've been paying the rent on Martin's office all along—whatever the hell he does there. But he'll be gone Monday at the tracks, as usual." He put on his fedora, preparing to leave.

"Stay," said Alex. "For old times' sake. Really, what's on your mind?"

Quentin glanced away, weighing the risk of jeopardizing his chances for his grand finale if he spoke his burning concerns. There was Samantha firing him—and so ingloriously, over the phone. His storied legal career forcibly terminated, unceremoniously and shamefully. His son gleefully stabbing him in the back. *But the less Alex or anyone knows, the less likely my plans can be disturbed. Still, if I tell him nothing, he'll become suspicious.* He tried to sound blithe: "You're right about memory lane. Holiday season sentimentality, I suppose. Lately, I seem to be reminiscing about my life's work for Bert and Greeley Enterprises."

"No. You've *constantly* thought about that, regardless of any season. I don't remember you having any life of your own."

"True," said Quentin, reflecting on Thanksgiving dinner at the Greeley mansion. "The other night, I was in Bert's old library. Well, Samantha's now. It'd been years, but, yes—memory lane—seeing all the Greeley and Alpers portraits on the walls again. You know, Samantha still hasn't hung up hers."

Despite a mouthful of latkes, Alex managed, "I've seen pictures of her on the internet. She's beautiful—in a traditional sense, at least. Can't see why she'd hesitate to include her portrait with other family royalty."

"Well, she's never been very family-minded." Then, recalling the hunting trophies he'd seen again that night, Quentin asked, "Remember all the times you refused Bert's invitations to go hunting?"

"I never could stomach murdering animals for sport."

"Well, it wasn't about murdering animals for me. It was about spending time with Bert. He was a father figure to me. He taught me the business from the inside out. Samantha was never interested in a relationship with him or the business—let alone hunting."

Alex put down his fork. "Skilled as I am at finding and connecting the dots, I'm not following your hops down memory lane. What's the thread here, Q?"

Quentin nodded. "It's just interesting what trophies each of us chooses to pursue in life. Me? I've got diplomas on the wall, a fancy house and car, bloated bank accounts. Bert—he married well, made fortunes in business and real estate. And he loved sports, especially hunting; he spent millions developing the stadium property that's about to sell. Anyway, Bert also prided himself as a serious moral philosopher in his pursuits. When it came to hunting—or, as you say, 'murdering animals'—he held strong moral views about the optimal way to control wildlife populations. He advocated for 'lethal control'—an approach using lethal methods, like hunting, trapping, or fishing."

Alex grimaced. "As opposed to natural regulation? Like, changing wildlife habitats or environments? Relocations?"

"That's right."

"Well, as a vegetarian, I strongly disagree. And I'm glad I never stepped foot in Bert's library with all those stuffed animals. Makes me sick just to imagine that. In fact, I'm done here. Let's go."

When they stood together outside the restaurant, Quentin said, "You're the only person I trust anymore."

"Can't say it feels that way," said Alex. "Seems to me, a trusting friend would tell a trusted friend what was troubling him. You've been purposively vague and curiously sentimental. So . . . *what*? Are you sick? Dying?"

"I just wanted you to know how I felt."

"Okay, just forget it," said Alex, turning away. "I'll TCB at Marty's office on Monday."

Nervous about leaving Alex irritated, Quentin scrambled for something to say to secure his allegiance. "I met Gianni Moretti face-to-face today. Of 'Moretti Landscaping'? You dropped off payments to the family's postbox for years."

"You mean," said Alex, "until you handed over my stadium job to Marty."

Quentin was thrown by their conversation's abrupt return to this tenacious complaint. Staring pleadingly at Alex, he thought: *I can't leave you angry like this. I need to trust you'll do this last job for me.* He said, "I regret hiring Martin to replace you. It was wrong. My moral compass was off, but now it's righted in a better direction." When Alex merely returned a skeptical look, Quentin held out new bait: "I'm a broken man. Martin not only betrayed me. He persuaded Samantha to fire me."

"She's *firing* you?" said Alex, feeling sorry for Quentin but also vindicated for astutely calling out his opaqueness. "After all these years?" Quentin soberly nodded, and Alex said, "Sorry, Q. That's rough. Should I be worried about you? What are you going to do?"

Now confident that he'd gained Alex's binding sympathy, Quentin replied, "Don't worry about me. And I'm not just rolling over. Despite the odds, I intend to take a final swing for the fences to even the score— perhaps, even, to win if I'm that lucky. But you helping me with this last job gives me a sporting chance."

Samantha's Home

Oakland Hills

Gazing at the Oakland cityscape from inside her glass-enclosed deck, watching wildfire ashes swirling around, Samantha imagined she was living inside a snow globe. Safe but distant from the world, comfortable but confined in her bubble, it resonated with her experience of life as a Greeley.

Marty appeared, still in his robe, and said, "Morning, Sam. What're you doing out here?"

"Experiencing distance, I suppose," she said. "From the world. From my own life." *The life I would've chosen, filled with music and art.*

He raised a brow. "Too heady for me at this hour."

Too heady for you at any hour, she thought, fantasizing, yet again, about being in a relationship with someone capable of meaningful dialogue. Certainly, she had her pick of other men—women, too, for that matter—who could provide that; and she could've chosen someone with a less fraught background. Still, she had to admit that her relationship with Marty had evolved in other, wholly unexpected ways. She'd become attached to him, beyond the initial lure of his thick-muscled shoulders and thighs, his rugged face, his macho strut. She'd even experienced occasions of surrendering to him when her disdain for the family business became intolerable;

he could step in for her then, with his fearlessness and bravado, and she could trust him to "just take care of things." In essence, she'd found someone to compensate for her; and someone whom she could compensate in other ways. They could use each other.

"But, hey," he continued, "I'm going to grab a waffle before I drive to the stadium. Want me to pop one in the toaster for you?"

"No. The maid brought poached eggs and fruit an hour ago."

Lucky to have missed that, he thought, hungering for butter-soaked waffles. He kissed her and said, "I'll call when I get a clear picture of the progress there. Don't worry about anything. I'll take care of business."

"Before you go—did you find out anything new about those two doctors? What you gave me before was useless."

"Yeah," he said, biting his tongue. "Nora Kelly's been struggling with panic attacks. She wrote about that on some touchy-feely health website. And Fred Williams—well, being on his board now, you must've heard about the scandals at his hospital. The murders in 2017. The fraud and opioid abuse. Anyhow, I downloaded that stuff and printed it out. It's on your desk."

She already knew about Nora's PTSD, via Fred. And the hospital scandals had been widely reported. She dismissively looked away and said, "Just call me with news of the stadium."

"I will. Mind if I take the Beemer today?"

"Go ahead. I'll get a driver for tonight."

"Where you going?"

"I'm interviewing lawyers from Palmer & Webley over dinner. I'm looking to replace your father ASAP."

"Well," he huffed. "Don't you think I should be there, too?"

Betty's

City Center

"What you going to do with the kid?" asked Gianni, unwrapping his Betty's special stuffed with bacon and cheddar.

"His name's Luis," said Red. "And I honestly don't know."

"He seems awfully sweet on that blue-haired woman. Maybe he'll marry her."

"You're a jerk. And her name's DeeDee."

"Hey," said Gianni, manually deconstructing his sandwich, "want this tomato and lettuce? I don't know why they always gotta ruin a good burger with this kind of shit."

"No! But I want to hear about the lawyer. Man, this better be worth it, because I'm sure I just lost my job. So, go on, while Luis is hanging with DeeDee."

Gianni slid a fingernail between his front teeth to pick something out. "Did I get it?"

"Gross! Don't ask me stuff like that. I'm not your dental hygienist."

"Well, didn't mean to offend. I've just always hated anything stuck in my teeth—since I was a kid, actually."

"You know, I'm not your therapist either. Can you just jump to the bottom line?"

"Sure. I can do that. But the bottom line is not straight."

After an overlong pause during which Gianni picked at his teeth, Red said: "That's it! I owed you a solid. But I paid up. I left my job to come hear you out. So, we're square now, right? I'm going back—"

"Calm down, pal. I was only thinking now about maybe not involving you. I mean, I've come to like you, Red. And I'm thinking, maybe because you're looking after the kid now . . . Well, maybe you should forget things with the lawyer. And, I agree: you paid me back. We're square."

"How the fuck can I 'forget things' I never heard about? And Luis is no business of yours. So, shit or get off the pot!"

Gianni leaned back and folded his hands on the table. Red, noticing his fingernails so solidly rimmed with dirt, recoiled. "You could grow a fucking garden in those fingernails. And you clean your teeth with them?"

"Okay," Gianni laughed. "Let's talk. This lawyer—Mr. Fancy Cocktail, 'Quentin Ocambo'—he shook me up today. He told me all this shit about the Greeleys using people at the camp to make money. 'Basic labor trafficking,' he said—like it was *just business*! Or moving them around like pawns to screw up property values. It was sick. Then he says, if I want to stay out of prison, I had to stay away from Patty and the stadium. And when I asked what the fuck that meant, he asked just how much did I want to know."

"And you told him *what?*"

"To fuck off, of course. And that I didn't need to talk with no stinking lawyers."

"That's it? That's what you dragged me out here for?"

"No," said Gianni, cocking his head. "Because then he says, 'Let's talk about what you do around here.' I said I didn't know him and had no cause to trust him. That's when he offered to be my lawyer—for free! He said lawyers had to keep client information confidential because of 'attorney-client privilege.'"

"Fuck. This is making me nervous. And Ocambo seems legit. I checked him on the internet, and he's been lawyering for the Greeleys forever. So, shit, something real is happening at the stadium. What did you tell him then?"

Gianni stared affectionately at Red. "I told him I needed to consult with my pal first." Red blushed and Gianni continued: "Then he asked if I was referring to the red-haired 'gentleman' he met—ha, that's you! I just said, 'Maybe.' So then he told me he gave you his card, too. And he offered to represent us both, for free—if you wanted."

"Why the fuck would we need his help? And what does he want from us?"

"That's exactly what I asked him! And he said we should meet tomorrow to talk everything over."

"I don't know," said Red, glancing worriedly at Luis.

"Well, wait. I'm not done. Because then he says, if I promised to keep an open mind about accepting him as my lawyer, he'd give me a free get-out-of-jail card right then and there. Frankly, I respected him doing business by his word, man-to-man."

"What's the get-out-of-jail card for?"

Gianni whispered, "He asked if I knew what was going down today with the people living at the camp. Of course, I said something smart-ass about them getting a day older, like me and him and everyone else. But then he looked at me so intense that I got the creeps, and he said: 'Care to guess the customary prison sentence for human labor trafficking and harboring illegals for commercial gain?' Well, immediately, these light bulbs went off inside my head. And he must've seen that because he said, 'And that's just the tip of the iceberg. So, here's your free get-out-of-jail card: avoid this stadium and any dealings with Patty Dobrovski.' He said Patty was clearing out the camp this weekend ahead of the stadium selling off next Friday. And then I remembered Patty insisting about you and me being there—us, with our *trucks*. Hell, Red, she was going to use us to move illegals and migrants to some new shithole!"

Red felt his life spinning in an orbit beyond his control. Human labor trafficking? Of the people he'd watched over, as best he could? People like Luis and Yusra? People like himself.

"You okay?" asked Gianni, finishing his fries.

"Yeah. I'm just having a hard time wrapping my mind around everything you said. You think Patty would actually do that shit? She can be a mean pain in the ass, but, still, it's hard to believe she would . . . or could . . ."

"Well, don't ask me. I'm the least qualified person on the planet to analyze *that* woman! Any woman, for that matter. Even a few minutes ago, when I got here before you, I was just trying to be friendly in the parking lot, and I told this lady I liked her Prius. But you shoulda seen how scared she got."

"But, if it's true about Patty . . . I feel sick knowing I was working for her."

Gianni looked concernedly at him, wondering how to disburden him of worry. "You make a good point, Red—questioning if it's true. 'Cuz we don't really know, do we? So, tomorrow, maybe I go alone to meet with Quentin Ocambo to hear what he's got to say. I'll demand the evidence and find out about the 'lucrative deal' he's offering us."

"What 'lucrative deal'? And why still meet with him if you already decided not to work for Patty anymore?"

Gianni smiled. "We're on the same wavelength *again,* 'cuz that's precisely what I asked him." Noticing Luis and DeeDee approaching the booth, he hastily added: "But then Ocambo said he'd already given me my *one* free card; and if I wanted any more help, we'd have to talk in person tomorrow."

San Sebastian Prison

Marin County

Prison guards surrounded Pete's body, which lay limp on the floor. Bloody froth dribbled from his mouth; urine seeped through his trousers. His cellmate grumbled, "What took you so long?"

"Shut up," barked Baldwin, one of the guards. He turned to his colleagues and said, "Take Vaughn to the infirmary. He's had a seizure."

"Big fucking genius!" said the cellmate. "And, know what? You could've actually *seen* him seizing if you'd come here half an hour ago."

Baldwin cupped a hand over his pistol, walked up to the cellmate, and whispered, "Care to repeat? I couldn't hear you too well over there."

As they carted Pete's body away, the cellmate railed: "You let him flail around on a *cement* floor, you moron! Banging his fucking skull! Biting his tongue! There's blood and piss everywhere! He even shit in his pants."

Baldwin grinned. "Okay. I heard you really well this time. Thanks for the report." He left and locked the cell door.

"Hey!" the cellmate called out. "What about the stink in here?"

Old Stadium Site

West Oakland

What a great day, thought Marty. Three butter-soaked waffles in his belly. Driving a sleek black Beemer, cruising down Broadway. And, later tonight on the DVR, the Ultimate Fighting Championship with his sure bet on Blaydes.

What a fucking great day, savoring Samantha's ever-expanding reliance on him. He'd finally earned standing as her closest business confidant, now serving as her "full service" man. It shouldn't take long before they married; then he could relax and comfortably pursue his own interests.

What an unbelievably fucking great day. A day of mythic import, even. Finally, his patronizing almighty father had received the come-uppance he deserved: the gods had banished him from Greeley paradise! *Yes, the tables have finally turned, old man. Now I'm in the power seat, and you're the loser and incompetent minion.*

Turning onto Tornwaldt, he imagined the camp evacuation to be in full swing. He'd paid Patty handsomely for the job (pocketing only a twenty-percent cut). And what could be so complicated about hiring guys with trucks? Then tonight, he'd triumphantly report to Samantha that, unlike his deadbeat father, he'd taken care of business.

But upon his arrival, he found the entry gate open and unattended. He drove through and headed for the backlots, searching for Patty, expecting to see residents bustling for eviction. But nothing looked different. And no trucks, no Patty, not even Patty's car.

"What the fuck's going on?" he asked no one in particular. *There's got to be a reason. Maybe trucks already left with some migrants? And maybe Patty's taken some in her car? But why . . . why are there still so many tents and cars?* He phoned Patty, but she didn't answer.

Think, think, think . . . Okay, she's not answering because she's still driving. Yeah. But, then, why not tell me yesterday she'd be doing some transport herself? And why leave this place unguarded during a risky operation? Then, realizing Pete probably knew of her plans, he phoned the prison; but they told him Pete wasn't available for the call.

Something's definitely very fucked up. He again phoned Patty but left a message this time: "I'm at the stadium, and it's dead here. What the hell's happening? Where are you? Call when you get this!"

He waited in the Beemer for a call-back, but the minutes felt like an eternity in hell. Overwhelmingly frustrated, he slammed his fist against the horn. And to his great dismay, he saw people streaming out of every tent and vehicle in sight.

~ ~ ~

Part Five

Earthquake

SUNDAY, NOVEMBER 25

Patience is bitter,
but its fruit is sweet.

ARISTOTLE

Carl's Home

Piedmont

WHEN WINSTON TOSSED the *Oakland Register* onto the bed, Fergie exclaimed, "Your story's on the front page!"

"Still," he said, "I wish Marla's story wasn't the reason for it."

"I know," she said. "But her story will impact readers. It may not solve homelessness here, but it'll move the needle for some readers. It may even help Marla."

"Speaking of—don't forget to pick up a copy for her on your way to work."

Grabbing her backpack on the way out, she said, "I won't. And, hey, let's celebrate your publication when I get home."

"How about doing me one sex favor for every one hundred words of text?" he said as the door closed behind her.

He walked to the window and waved while she pulled out of the driveway. Then Carl popped into view and waved back; a minute later, he appeared at the door and surprised Winston with "You summoned me?"

"Oh," said Winston. "Well, I suppose I wanted to show you my story in today's paper."

"I've read it online," said Carl. "It's upsetting to learn about Oakland's forty-seven-percent increase in homelessness over the past year. And about the woman you featured who lives in her car while working *full-time* at *our* hospital. It's unethical that we don't provide employees like her with living wages to support basic housing needs."

"Yes, ironic. A hospital ought to be fundamentally concerned about promoting human health—its employees included."

"Nora and I visited a homeless camp at the stadium on Thanksgiving. I had a partial look—but I'd estimate close to two hundred people living there." When Winston appeared surprised, Carl said, "Remember our discussion during lasagna dinner? I told you and Fergie that I planned to accompany Nora there."

"Of course," said Winston, slapping his forehead. "On a search for Yusra, your blue patient's daughter. And, by the way, Fergie said the two of them were staying at Jack's for now. With Luis, too."

"Who is Luis?"

"Sadly, the nephew of Tomas Ruiz—the man found dead on the sidewalk on Thanksgiving."

"I wasn't aware he'd died. He was Aditya's patient who accidentally kicked him and ruptured his spleen. He's the patient they suspected of being poisoned by arsenic."

Winston's jaw dropped. "Arsenic? Luis' uncle?"

Speaking louder for Winston's purported benefit, Carl said, "Yes, arsenic. Yes, Luis' uncle."

"My god . . . that's worrying. And how can it be that so many people are still living at the stadium? It's been widely reported the stadium property is selling off in a few days. Where will all the people go?"

"Fred may know. He's discussed the sale and future housing development with Samantha Greeley, the stadium's owner."

"Thanks," said Winston. "I think I'll call him. Because I want to follow up today's column with others about unsheltered populations in the East Bay. And, wow, Fred sure has friends in high places."

"I didn't say they were friends," Carl said and left.

Having forgotten to ask Carl for Fred's number, Winston phoned Fergie instead. She answered, "You know I hate being called at work for something that can wait. It's crazy-times-ten here, Win, and . . . yeah, another O.D.'s coming in."

"Please?" he said. To which she responded, "Why?"

"I want to ask him about stadium stuff."

"No freakin' way! I'm not participating in *that* again. Fred went ballistic when I told him about Nora sending off some soil tests from there."

"Soil tests?"

But she only replied "Gotta go" and hung up.

Winston paced in the living room. The hallway. The kitchen. He couldn't keep up with his own racing questions. So he phoned Nora and asked, "Would you mind telling me about the soil tests?"

"Yes, I'd mind," she replied. "It's embarrassing."

"Please? What were you looking for? Why?"

Nora groaned. "Evidently, I was looking for *trouble*. And, why? At the time, I was convinced the stadium was toxic and sickening people. But my tests were a waste of time."

"Oh, the results came back negative?"

"Technically, no. They're due out tomorrow. But yesterday, I saw two certified environmental inspections documenting the property was clean as a whistle—both this year, and in 1991."

Winston hung up, even more confounded, and he realized he'd again forgotten to ask for Fred's number. He tried not to feel sorry for himself; but there he was, longing to drive to the stadium to investigate, but stranded without the car. Perhaps, he thought, when Fergie came home, he could persuade her to accompany him there for their first shared writing venture. *Hopefully, she'll forget about the romantic evening I proposed.*

But then he felt like an idiot. *What the hell am I thinking? No, the stadium investigation can wait. I should take time with Fergs to celebrate the good occasions in our lives.*

Still, how great it feels to rediscover my desire to write.

Oakland Estuary

Jack London Square

Red arrived early to speak privately with Gianni, ahead of their meeting with Quentin Ocambo. They sat on a bench outside the Last Chance Saloon, facing the Oakland Estuary.

"I thought about it all night," said Red, rubbing his forehead. "I still don't know."

Gianni patted his back. "That's okay, pal. I get it."

"I mean, if it's true what Ocambo said about human labor trafficking and harboring illegals, wouldn't it be better for us to know nothing more about that?"

"Maybe. On the other hand, if they bust Patty for that . . . and who knows who else . . . I think they'd still find out about us working with her. You don't need Sherlock Holmes to prove that. And then, we'd have to convince them we didn't know what we were doing at the time—'Honest, officers.'"

"But we didn't!"

"That's right, Red. But truthfully, with our backgrounds, who's going to believe us? Or maybe you believe the criminal justice system is always fair."

Red frowned. "Course I don't."

Gianni tossed a stone into the estuary and watched it ripple the water. "Well, then, maybe you should meet with Ocambo. 'Cuz even if you don't want to hear about Patty's shitscapade and his 'lucrative offer,' you'd still need a lawyer when they start questioning you about working for her."

"I'm fucked either way. And, god, I don't have a job anymore."

"Sorry, pal. I can cut you in on my hauling and landscape gigs, but there's barely enough to pay my rent. And sure as hell, I won't be working the stadium anymore."

"Appreciate the offer," said Red, "but I'll find something." Then, remembering the homeless man on the train, he added, "I'm lucky to have my truck."

Gianni gave Red a stick of gum, and they sat chewing, gazing at the ferryboats a while. Gianni said, "You could stay with me 'til you get settled. My apartment's small and . . . well, messy. I keep all my landscaping stuff inside."

"That's nice," said Red. "But stop worrying about me." Still, privately, he worried where he could go after leaving Jack's, once Luis felt secure.

"Suit yourself. But my offer stands. And, hey, how about grabbing a beer after we meet with Ocambo?"

"Can't. I promised Luis I'd be back by afternoon."

Gianni's face lit up. "I just got another brilliant idea!"

"You're certainly full of . . . them."

"Ha! I know what you meant. Full of *something*, right?"

Red smiled.

"Well," said Gianni, "there's something Ocambo *can* help you with: adopting Luis! Or, becoming his guardian, I guess. You're old enough."

Shaking his head with incredulity, Red said: "C'mon, man. You know it's more complicated. You gotta have money, a safe place to live—"

Gianni scoffed. "Don't see why, if biological parents don't need any of that to have kids."

Red stiffened, pointed up the wood-planked walkway, and whispered, "Ocambo's coming."

Samantha's Home

Oakland Hills

Marty sauntered into the breakfast room, where Samantha was waiting at the table, ready to serve questions. She said, "When did you get home last night, Marty?"

"Two, I think," he answered. "And, 'Morning' to you, too."

"Where were you?"

He scratched the scarred site of his missing ear—a tell of his nervousness. "I texted you around eight to say I was hung up."

"Yes. You texted precisely in the moment I was being seated for dinner with attorneys from Palmer & Webley."

"Shit! I forgot. Sorry, Sam. It's just . . . There were problems at the stadium. Some not-so-good surprises."

She gazed icily at him, thinking, *He knows I won't ask about them. But now he's holding the reins on whatever's happening there.* She said, "So, did you take care of those problems, Marty—as you promised?"

He cringed. "They're not exactly fixed yet. What happened was—"

"Stop! You *know* I don't want to hear details. I just want to hear you made the problems disappear."

"Okay. But, see . . . I spent the whole day looking for Pete's girlfriend, Patty. I even drove to their old apartment; there was an eviction notice on the door. I phoned her a million times. And every time I checked the stadium, nothing was happening with the camp. I couldn't get a call through to Pete. It was rough, Sam. So, afterwards, I just needed down-time . . . a drink. I went to my office, had a beer, and just forgot about our dinner meeting."

"Sit."

"Mind if I pour a coffee first?"

"I said, 'Sit.'"

He feigned a look of bemusement. "Okay, you're the boss."

"Yes, I am, Marty. And the boss needs to know whether you can handle the reins. Do you have *any* idea what's going on with my property?"

He looked away from her disdainful expression. "What's going on is . . . well, *nothing*. Nothing's going on that's supposed to. I'm thinking Patty stiffed me. And maybe Pete was in on it, and that's why he stopped taking my calls. You remember he was mad at us. Hell, maybe he even encouraged Patty to mutiny."

Samantha paced around him. "You expect me to believe this woman 'Patty' would do something that fearless and stupid, and think she could get away with it?"

"Well, I . . . *we* gave her five grand. That's a lot to someone who's desperate. I mean, she's alone, evicted, her man's in prison. Could've seemed worth the risk to take the money and run."

"You're quite the amateur psychologist."

"C'mon, Sam. Don't be sarcastic."

"And Pete? Why would he suddenly turn on us, especially *after* we paid her up? Your father *never* had trouble with him, as far as I know. Quentin just took care of business—"

"Yeah, okay."

"Don't interrupt! Your father took care of the planning commission, the city council, the permissions, the environmental inspections, the contracts, the protestors . . . everything! Some of us have worked on this stadium deal for years."

"But you saw the property! You can't consider that 'taking care of business.' You were right to get rid of my dad, and just in time. There's no way Highmark Construction would seal the deal after the walk-through on Friday. Besides, you getting new lawyers who don't look a century old will help—"

"You don't know what they look like, because you didn't show up for our dinner meeting!"

Marty's foot began tapping the floor. "I said I was sorry."

"And tell me," she said, her eyes narrowing. "Why haven't you pursued those nosey doctors we ran into?"

"Babe, I gave you the stuff from the internet."

"That was so pathetically basic! It told me nothing new! Your father would've dug up serious, useful information. You're not being resourceful, Marty." Her fists clenched. "Remember those doctors talking about some sick patient and their suspicions about my property as the cause? And you, being such an astute amateur psychologist—didn't you notice how coy and cagey they were behaving? *Deceptive,* really?"

"I did. The guy seemed nervous. The woman was feisty."

"So, if they were suspicious enough about my property to be there on a *rainy fucking Thanksgiving* . . . what do you think they might plan to *do* about their 'feisty' concerns?"

He released a slow, controlled breath. "I don't know, Sam. Maybe check the soil to see if they were right."

She rolled her eyes. "And?"

"And . . ." he began uncertainly.

"*And,* so, if they discovered something, do you think they might've reported it? Could that self-righteous bitch have alerted public health agencies? Could investigators have come to the stadium and frightened Patty away?"

"Stop sounding patronizing."

"Well?"

Reminded how his father always spoke to him like this, Marty stared icily at her. "I suppose it's possible when you lay it out that way. The gate wasn't guarded yesterday when I stopped by. So, other people . . . investigators, inspectors . . . could've just entered the property, too. Also, I have to say, it seemed that lady doctor had some psycho-negativity against you."

"Stop with your two-cent analyses. Are you even getting my drift about what needs to be done? Or must I spell out *everything* for you?"

"No. Hey, I got this!"

"I hope so, Marty. Because you're beginning to disappoint me."

"I've been thinking . . ."

"It's about time."

"Don't be mean." He reached for her hand, but she brushed it away. "What do you expect me to do, Sam?"

"Well, at a minimum, not completely blow the stadium deal!" She huffed and said, "Just *think*, Marty!"

"Look, this is new to me. I'm doing my best. But you want to be mad at someone? Be mad at my dad—he's the one been managing business at the stadium until just a few days ago! I inherited Patty and any lame-brained problems from *him*."

"You always have an excuse, don't you?" She grabbed the last of the coffee. "We lost the sale of our waterfront property just last year because of all the protestors *still* defending the homeless camp there! Look, my bottom line? The stadium sale must go through on Friday as planned. We're talking about a three-hundred-million-dollar deal. Do you think you can do what's necessary to make that happen? Or need I summon your dad back to work?"

The Marina

Berkeley

Finally, a sunny cloudless day, perfect for strolling the Berkeley Marina. The San Francisco Bay gently stroked the shoreline, and colorful kites skimmed a royal blue sky. And, for the umpteenth time, Luis asked Jack: "When's Red coming back today?"

Jack looked into Luis' worried eyes and said, "As soon as his meeting with his friend is over." Luis nodded and returned to Yusra and Daleen, who were walking ahead. Then Jack turned to Nora and said, "And *that* can't be soon enough."

Nora smiled, moved by Jack's sweetness and patience. She'd never seen him interact with children. "How did things go at the house this morning?"

"Well, obviously, Daleen's back on her feet. Yusra slept through the night. And Luis . . . such a great kid . . . but he begged Red to stay the night again. I'm just worried about what's going to happen with him."

"If it's any consolation, I'm meeting *unofficially* with a social worker tomorrow. She's going to lay out options for him—and for Daleen and Yusra, too. I can drop by after work and we can all discuss them together?"

"Perfect. I can make it home from work by four. Let's make it an early dinner at the house?"

Nora nodded, and they strolled arm-in-arm in silence a while. She looked at the bay, relieved that, while in Jack's company, she no longer needed to fend off flashbacks of her daughter and husband drowning. When she glanced back at him, she found him staring at Luis, a sweet expression on his face. She asked, "What are you thinking?"

"Oh. About something that happened at the house last night, after you left."

"Tell me," she said. It'd been a while since she'd heard him sound so light.

"Well, my savior housekeeper showed up and started dinner. For the kids, it was a Disneyland-level spectacle. They'd never seen most of the kitchen tools or spices Zofia was using. They were amazed—especially Luis, who fancies working in a restaurant someday." He wiped his eyes, Nora put an arm around him, and they continued on the twisty path ahead.

Old Stadium Site

West Oakland

Marty Ocambo wasn't keen on being disrespected, especially by women. If so much weren't at stake, he'd have put Samantha in her place. But he understood the risk in "disappointing" her further.

While devouring a 7-Eleven coffee and breakfast burrito, he tried again to phone Patty and Pete. Failing both, he headed to the stadium.

All the while he drove, Samantha's humiliating remarks weighed heavier on his mind.

But once again at the stadium, he saw no Patty, no trucks, no bustle in the camp. He drove the Beemer to the end road in the furthermost lot and, thinking of Patty and Samantha, he shook his fist to the sky and roared, "Fuck!" He hurled rocks against the Beemer, denting its hood and grill. Then he kicked the doors, finally injuring his foot, and he howled out in pain.

The pain oddly functioned as a distraction, allowing him to feel something other than rage. Then he leaned against the Beemer, thinking: *There has to be a way to fix this.* He considered driving to the prison to talk in person with Pete, who probably knew why things were going south. *But waste of time—if he's not taking my calls, he's not going to take my visit.* Perhaps he could ask his old buddy to help him transport people out. *Yeah! Me and Kevin can just rent a U-Haul and clear this place by tomorrow night!* And those nosey doctors—*Sam's probably right; hell, they basically flat-out said they were here investigating.* He pulled up the information he'd downloaded for Samantha and refreshed his memory of their names: Nora Kelly and Fred Williams.

~ ~ ~

In hiding, several yards away and inside Daleen's camper, Patty Dobrovski shuddered when her phone lit up. *Marty calling again.* She sat on the floor, hyperventilating. She was afraid to move. To sleep. To let down her vigilance.

She jolted when she heard a man roar "Fuck!" somewhere nearby. Then loud clunks sounded . . . thuds . . . a howling scream . . . a car pulling away . . . silence. Her nerves wrapped tighter around her wildly vibrating mind, strangulating her thoughts.

She kept reminding herself of Pete's instructions: to stay low and calm until she heard from him, and "remember to eat." Staying low wasn't difficult with her psychic paralysis. But calm wasn't possible. And she had no appetite to help keep her promise to eat. Last night, when she'd opened a peanut butter jar that she found in the back, she saw spoon streaks in it, reigniting her guilt over Yusra. *Lord, what have I wrought? The world's collapsing on us all! Pete, tell me what to do!*

Oakland Estuary

Jack London Square

"I'm glad you both came," said Quentin, sitting on the bench alongside Red and Gianni, taking in the lively estuary. "Every time I come here, I see something new—a restaurant, a bar, a shop. And right now, looking at you two, I see new opportunity."

"Before you start," said Gianni, "Red's not sure he wants to get involved with . . . well, whatever your 'opportunity' is. I told him about that attorney-client privilege thing. Still, he needs to know if he's already in some kind of trouble and how to get out of it."

"Honest," said Red, "I had no idea about *any* kind of human trafficking there. Or harboring illegals. I just thought we were all stuck in a shitty place and helping each other out."

"Son, it won't look that way to others," said Quentin. "I saw you myself, providing gate security at that camp. I also witnessed you interact with Patty Dobrovski and refer to her as your 'boss.' You took orders from her to bar me from the premises—which you had no legal right to do. And I'm sure encampment residents can attest to you working under her direction—"

"But I only watched over the people!" said Red. "I tried to protect them from riffraff."

"What 'riffraff'?" asked Quentin.

"You know—people who just want to cause worse trouble for people like us. Thugs. Police. Druggies. Thieves. *Lawyers.*" His stomach knotted.

Gianni said, "It's true. Red's been like the protector for 'Hope and Dignity.'"

"Ah, yes," said Quentin, "the name of Ms. Dobrovski's so-called nonprofit."

"Now, why'd you say that like it was something dirty or bad?" said Gianni. "Look, we've been freaked out by what you said about her yesterday. But before that, we didn't know her to be anything but . . . well, *halfway* decent to the people living there."

"Yeah," said Red. "I mean, I had my run-ins with her. Lots of them. And I blamed her for not taking good enough care of people. Hell, so many of them were getting sick! There was hardly any food, and no clean water, especially the last few months. And no jobs for anyone."

"I believe you, son," said Quentin, resting a hand on Red's shoulder, suddenly realizing that he'd never spoken those particular words to his actual son. "Still, that won't spare you legal trouble over your associations with Patty and the camp." Then, looking at Gianni, he said, "And regarding her nonprofit? It wasn't legit."

Gianni tsk'ed. "Nah. This can't be true. *Patty* and fake nonprofits? *Patty* and human trafficking?"

Red said, "Sometimes she even buys food for people from the Dollar Store. She . . . it was too late . . . but she got Luis' uncle to the ER when he was sick. And she drove Daleen Habani there herself."

Quentin was surprised to be experiencing . . . *What? What is this odd feeling? Paternal, maybe?* These two young men, unlike his actual son, sounded credible and guileless, thoughtful and kind. He even felt a pang of guilt for disabusing them about Patty. He replied, "I know what I'm talking about, because I'm responsible for the smoke-and-mirrors around her nonprofit. I set it up as a conduit for cash transfers from Greeley Enterprises so Patty and her boyfriend could take care of business."

"I *knew* she had a boyfriend!" said Gianni. "Who is he?"

"He's in prison," said Quentin, "on charges of human trafficking and smuggling people across the border—all labor-related, far as I know. And while he's been away, Patty has been *trying* to manage the stadium camp. But that's when I took my finger off the pulse of all things stadium and hired my son Martin to oversee Greeley interests there. I didn't know until the other night he'd been pocketing the money that should've been going to Patty to maintain the camp."

"Damn!" said Gianni. "Is your son the big guy, missing an ear, she was talking to on Friday? He drove a Beemer, and I know he gave her money."

Quentin sighed dramatically. "Yes. Martin was finally paying Patty, expecting to motivate her to clear the camp so he could appear the hero and make a fool of me."

Red clutched his stomach and doubled over.

Gianni said, "You're upsetting my pal, Mr. Lawyer. And, damn . . . What the fuck about *you*? You just admitted to helping Patty fake things so illegal crap could happen at the stadium in the first place!"

Quentin found himself thinking: *They're so upset already, and haven't a clue as to how terrible things actually are.* Sensing them pulling away, he urgently proposed, "Hear me out on the money you'll make if—"

"Let's go," Gianni told Red. "This guy's bad news."

"Wait," said Quentin, realizing that money alone wouldn't do, and grasping for different bait. "I knew your parents, Tony and Celia."

"What?" said Gianni, turning back. "Who the fuck are you?"

Got him, thought Quentin. *Reel him in.* "I employed your father on behalf of the Greeleys. I helped him launch his landscaping business."

Gianni stared doubtingly at him. *My parents barely spoke English, and I don't remember them ever involved with any lawyer.* And because they'd also conducted business in the shadow immigrant economy, it was impossible to imagine Greeley Enterprises legally engaging their services. He replied, "That makes no sense. I don't know what you're up to, but . . ."

"Your father was paid under-the-table. I began working with him in 1989. You were three years old at the time."

"Nah. I *never* heard of you. My dad maybe couldn't write and keep normal records, but he talked business to me all the time. And I definitely would've remembered *your* weird name."

"There's a reason you didn't," said Quentin, reaching for the minimum truth required to keep Gianni engaged, realizing: *This catch requires a deep hook into his feelings.* "After two years, your father told me to stay away. You were five then, and coming of age to understand things. He didn't want you exposed to me or the Greeleys."

Red, amplifying Gianni's exasperation, charged, "You're implying G's dad was crooked?"

"On the contrary," said Quentin, turning to Gianni. "I'm saying I treated him badly. I involved him and his workers in things they couldn't possibly understand. Tony was a good man, a smart man. He was a detail man who also always saw the big picture. So, when he learned the stadium property had received a clean bill of health in '91 . . . well, he *knew*."

"Knew what the fuck?!" shouted Gianni.

The disparaging expression on Gianni's face reminded Quentin of Tony's searing look upon discovering he'd been betrayed. And it threw him once again—although, again, for only a fleeting moment. Quentin replied, "Please understand, I was young when I started working in '89 for the Greeleys. Bert hired me specifically to deal with 'issues' delaying his stadium renovation—"

"No one cares about you!" said Gianni. "Get to the point."

"The point," said Quentin, stalling. *It's that I've got less than forty-eight hours to get you on board as "whistleblowers." What's it going to take?* Then it dawned on him what to say: "No one was surprised to learn the stadium property was contaminated with hazardous wastes and chemicals when it was inspected in 1989. It'd been developed decades earlier on the site of a pesticide factory. Still, the land had to be remediated—or 'cleaned up'—before Bert could sell off parcels of the property to offset renovation costs. So, I drove to 6th Street and picked your father out of the day-labor line to head the cleanup. I gave him the go-ahead to hire a crew—"

"Did he know about the contamination?" asked Gianni, his fists clenching.

Quentin shook his head. "Not until two years later, when the *Oakland Register* reported about the stadium passing its reinspection in '91. A guy on your dad's crew who spoke Italian translated the report for him."

"And?" said Red, stepping closer.

"And . . . of course, Tony added things up. So, when I saw him the next day, he made me promise to stay away from him and his family. He shoved his stadium ID badge and work records into my hands and told me to leave. I still have the maps he drew, plotting out the work he and his crew did."

"You son of a bitch," Gianni muttered, trembling with rage.

It wasn't how he preferred to lure Gianni or Red into his plan; still, Quentin thought, rage offered a unique potential for seduction. He said, "I'm sorry. I'm an old man, wrestling with an epiphany, seeking forgiveness and justice. But I'm resolved to make things right."

"Unbelievable!" said Red. "You pathetic self-centered fuck who got rich off hurting people like G's dad. And now you're dragging Gianni out here to ask for forgiveness? Go to a fucking confessional!"

"Gianni," said Quentin, "I tried to make amends to your father. But he adamantly refused to see me. So, secretly, I secured work for him over the years—safe, well-paying jobs at other Greeley properties."

"To keep his mouth shut about what you did!" said Gianni.

"No, son." *Actually, yes.* "He didn't even know it was me. And my P.I. secretly dropped off payments to him in a postbox. Then, a couple years ago, when I—I mean, my middleman—called with a lucrative landscaping job, you picked up instead and said he'd died and—"

When Gianni's fist raised, Red held it back and said, "This scumbag lawyer ain't worth it. And he couldn't even keep his promise to your dad to leave you alone! Because, look—here he is, dragging you into a new shitstorm at the stadium."

Quentin pleaded, "But don't people deserve second chances? I'm here, asking for one. I want justice for you and your father, Gianni—even if that also benefits me by alleviating my conscience. Justice delayed, perhaps; but justice, finally. In truth, I'm willing to sacrifice everything to make the Greeleys suffer for their crimes and pay reparations to the people they've hurt. And, yes, I've been their malevolent handmaiden; but I still hold the keys to their kingdom, and I can let the daylight in now." *At least until Monday.*

"You sound unhinged," said Gianni. "And I don't think you even know what 'justice' is."

Now Quentin relaxed. He'd finally got them hooked in a dynamic that he could control. "If you work with me as whistleblowers, you'll both become incredibly rich. You'll have enough money to support *your* version of justice, however you see fit. You'll be in a position to help so many others."

Gianni scoffed. "You're pranking us. You really expect us to believe what you say after all your lies? Can you even hear yourself, old man?"

Red said, "And I lost my job because of your bullshit. Hell, I can't tell what's real with you."

"Okay," Quentin said. "The human trafficking to provide cheap labor . . . harboring illegal immigrants . . . the forced camp relocations to manipulate property values favoring the Greeleys—all real. But let's *all* be honest—you two *personally* know about labor exploitation and tax evasion. Now, Patty may not have been the mastermind behind the crimes. But, as I've said, the legal finger could easily point at her and each one of us. So, help me attain the justice I seek, and I'll make certain you're not only freed of this mess; I'll make certain the Greeleys pay for their ill-gotten gains."

Gianni and Red stared at one another, deliberating. After Red nodded, Gianni turned to Quentin. "Okay. But we got a pre-condition." Red didn't flinch, but was curious what that was.

"Your pre-condition?" asked Quentin.

"You help us support people in the camp to defend against getting thrown out."

"Deal," said Quentin. "And I've got a pre-condition of my own. I'm going to need all your workmaps tonight."

Nora's Home

Montclair District

Spending the day with Jack and his new household had been lovely. Still, how good to be home now with Bix on her lap, a glass of merlot, the calming silence—

A door creaked.

Nora whispered to Bix, "Did you hear that?" as he instinctively jumped off her lap and ran out the door to hide on the deck. She froze, listened hyper-attentively.

Now she heard the familiar groans of the entryway floorboards. Then a footstep . . . another . . . another . . . each progressively louder. She reflexively grabbed her cellphone and wineglass and ran out to the deck, too. She quietly slid the glass door shut. Then she crouched behind a lounge chair and silenced her phone.

A tortured minute later, she saw someone enter her living room—a bulky figure in dark clothes. A man, definitely; with a ponytail evident in silhouette. She watched him rifle through paperwork on her dining table until something appeared to catch his eye; he picked it up—a sheet of paper—and stuffed it into his pocket. When he disappeared into the kitchen, she fumbled in the dark, trying to activate her cell's 911 button. Then he suddenly reappeared in the living room, carrying a wine bottle and the carton of potato salad she'd earmarked for tonight's dinner. On his way out, he abruptly stopped and glanced toward the deck; she flinched, became breathless, watched him return to the dining table and grab her laptop. He headed again for the exit, and, again, paused. This time, as if entertaining an afterthought, he knocked over her grandmother's porcelain vase, shattering it across the floor.

Betty's

City Center

He had to see her. He needed to be reminded of the capacity for goodness in people. So he stopped by Betty's, hoping to find DeeDee.

"Hey, Red!" she exclaimed. "Where's Luis?"

Red felt like falling apart, but willed himself not to in front of her—anybody, really. "He's staying with Dr. Jack for now."

"Okay," she said. "But, how are you? You look tired."

He dug his fingernails into his palms to distract himself from his torment. But he'd just discovered he'd been unwittingly involved in illegal activities with morally bankrupt people. He'd just discovered he'd been complicit in financial set-ups that made rich people richer, and poor people poorer. He'd lost his job at the stadium and, with that, a place to live in his truck. Feeling cornered, he and Gianni had agreed to a risky liaison involving Ocambo that aimed to "make things right." And if Ocambo's plan failed, he knew he'd have to flee—without Luis, without her. He shakily replied, "Yeah, I'm probably just tired." *Of everything, DeeDee; of everything.*

"I get off in an hour. Want to hang out and talk then?"

"Yes," he blurted out.

She smiled and handed him her key.

Marty Ocambo drove to the stadium, one last time for the day. Still not finding Patty, he parked the Beemer, finished his purloined potato salad and wine, and tossed the empties out the window. He phoned Patty and Pete again, leaving no message this time around. *Yeah, they're definitely stiffing me. There's no other explanation.*

He stared through the windshield at the ever-darkening sky, furious that they'd made him their dumbstruck victim. It also rattled his self-confidence, and gnawed on his ego. He dreaded the humiliation he expected to face when returning to Samantha's tonight.

But why would my pal Pete suddenly turn on me? Then, catching his reflection in the rearview, he saw that he'd done the same to his own father. He told himself: *I guess I'm good at burning bridges. Pete. Patty. Dad.* Even his old buddy Kevin had refused to help him out with the U-Hauling because of previous betrayals. He shuddered to think that his bridge to Samantha might be burning now.

His cell rang, Samantha was calling, and he had no positive news to convey. Still, he answered, they stiffly exchanged greetings, and he reported about his fraught day. An uncomfortable silence ensued. Finally, she said: "So, you've spent the day, accomplishing nothing. The homeless camp is still there. You can't locate Patty. Pete won't accept your calls. Your 'old buddy' refuses to help. And you've discerned *nothing* about possible interference from vigilante doctors—"

"Hold on," he said, happily remembering the paper he'd pocketed in Nora's living room. "I have something. Gimme a second; it's dark out here."

"You sound drunk, Marty."

He pulled out a penlight to read the paper. A drop of blood fell on it from his vigorous scratching at the site of his missing left ear. "So, that lady doctor with attitude, Nora Kelly. I found this list on her dining table—"

"No, Marty! You didn't break into her house? Don't tell me that."

He scoffed. "Fine. I won't tell you. But, anyway, get this: the paper's got 'soil samples' written on the top! And then . . ."

"Then, *what?*"

"Sorry. It's just kinda weird. Then it lists four things. Says, 'yogurt fava, clam lettuce, bag door, and box back.'"

"Fuck, Marty! That makes no sense."

"Tell me about it! But maybe there'll be something on her laptop to explain it."

"You . . . you stole her *laptop?* She's going to notice it missing, you moron."

He gritted his teeth, and the strain in his voice conveyed his anger: "Do not speak to me like that, Sam."

"And Fred Williams," she persisted. "Did you break into his house, too?"

"No," he said, trying to refrain from adding more fuel to the bridge that was most definitely burning between them now. "I drove to his house, but there were too many people inside. But, c'mon, Sam—we hit pay dirt at Kelly's. You were right about her! It looks like she was actually investigating your property—just like she told us."

Nora's Home

Montclair District

Detective Darinda Johnson told Fergie and Winston, "I think Nora should stay somewhere else tonight. I mean, it's not even been two years since we were all here in this house with that psychopath. You honestly think she's going to be okay? She's nearly catatonic."

Fergie removed her thick bifocals, rubbed her bloodshot eyes, and nodded. "We're staying with her tonight. Besides, as you heard, she refuses to leave."

Darinda asked, "Does she have a therapist you can call? A psychiatrist?"

"Yeah," said Fergie, "a psychiatrist. But I only know her as 'Frenchie.' That's what Nora and Lydia always called her."

Sweeping up the broken vase, Winston offered: "I can check the medicine cabinet for a doctor's name. Or phone Fred or Jack—they might know."

Darinda handed her card to Fergie and, on the way out, said: "So, here we are again. Call or text me with any development, okay?"

Fergie went to Nora's kitchen to cook something for everybody. But, as expected, she found only processed or frozen foods, and everything seemed to contain meat. At least there were eggs, two weeks outdated, but still. *How can a doctor eat like she does?*

Minutes later when she carried the omelet into the living room, she found Winston sitting on the couch with Nora and eyeing her anxiously. He stiffly explained, "Nora keeps repeating something about 'the gun not being loaded.'" Fergie almost dropped the serving plate.

He continued, "And she remembers seeing a guy in the living room while she was out hiding on the deck."

Fergie sat beside her and said, "That must've been horrifying, Nora."

"The gun wasn't actually loaded," she replied.

Stopping herself from gasping, Fergie said, "So, the guy had a gun?"

Winston said, "That's important. We should notify Detective Johnson."

"No," Nora insisted.

"I agree with Win," said Fergie.

Nora visibly shuddered, then managed: "No. I didn't see a gun."

Sensing Nora's readiness to talk, Fergie asked, "Are you remembering what happened?"

Nora closed her eyes to focus on the memory. "I was on the couch. I heard the front door open. Then footsteps approaching from the entryway. Bix ran out the door to the deck, and I followed. I closed the door and hid. But I could see inside . . ." She took a fortifying breath and opened her eyes. "There was a man inside my living room."

After a brief silence, Winston asked: "Was he alone? What was he wearing? Did you see—?"

"Win!" said Fergie. "Slow down."

"He was big," Nora said. "Stocky. Wearing dark clothes, but . . ."

"Take your time," said Fergie.

Nora pointed to the dining table, suddenly remembering: "He took a sheet of paper from there. My laptop, too."

Winston, aware that Nora hadn't activated her home alarm system—the system he'd installed for her almost two years ago when she was attacked—correctly anticipated her answer to his next questions: "Did you have a security password on your laptop? And maybe a backup of your hard drive?"

Nora shook her head. "Okay," he said, wondering how such a brilliant physician could be so inattentive to cybersecurity health. "Do you remember your laptop make and model?"

"A PC. It was silver."

He suppressed an urge to roll his eyes while pulling out his cell. "Well, I'll notify Darinda about the laptop and—"

But Nora stood up suddenly and bee-lined to the table. She began sorting through her paperwork, hoping to determine what had been pilfered. Fergie, trying to help, observed: "You got all these papers about arsenic . . . methemoglobinemia . . . soil testing . . . EPA Superfund sites. And, huh, menus for appetizers and cheese platters."

"That's it!" Nora exclaimed.

Fergie looked worryingly at her. "You don't actually think the guy stole a food menu?"

"No. But food . . . soil . . . Daleen's vegetable garden. He stole my list of the soil samples I collected at the stadium."

Winston's eyes widened. "You sure?"

"I'm positive. After Lizbeth mentioned I hadn't labeled the samples she delivered to Davis, I wrote it all down so I wouldn't forget. That list was here on my table."

"Do you remember the list?" asked Fergie.

"No, but . . . look here, on my cell . . . I scanned it so I'd have it on hand whenever UC Davis called with the results."

After examining the list on Nora's cell, Fergie said: "It's titled 'soil samples,' but I doubt whoever stole the list will be able to make sense of it. It's only because I remember you laying it out for Lizbeth in the ER that I can get its drift."

Winston turned to Nora and said, "But the guy also stole your laptop. A laptop, without password protection. Does it contain clearer information about those samples?"

"No," said Nora, the fog of panic lifting from her brain. "Still, all the files and shortcuts on my desktop would suggest what I'd been researching. Soil testing for hazardous waste and chemicals. The Greeleys. The old Regal Chemical Company. The environmental inspections of the stadium that Aditya emailed to me. So, all the dots are there, and so close together that they practically connect." She turned away, thinking: *And the intruder's targeted interest in my list . . . it means someone else is curious about the stadium, too. Maybe I was right to suspect a health hazard after all. Still, we won't have results on the soil tests and Tomas' arsenic levels until tomorrow.*

"This is crazy-times-a-million," said Fergie. "But something about the stadium soil seems awfully important to somebody." She inhaled deeply, reminded of the fracas into which she'd been unwittingly snared: "And remember how Fred blew up when he couldn't stop you from testing the soil, Nora. And now . . . now a guy breaks into your house and steals your list."

"No," said Winston, "you can't believe the two are connected! That *Fred* conspired with a thief to break into Nora's home?"

"I agree with Winston," said Nora. *I understand Fred worrying about disappointing Samantha, as appallingly corp as that may be. But the intruder tonight was a thug, destroying my grandmother's vase for pure sport. And he, or whoever hired him, must've had reason to worry I may have collected actual evidence.*

"I'm not suggesting *that*," said Fergie, turning to Nora. "I'm suggesting Fred could've been trying to discourage you from getting involved all along, only because . . . Well, clearly, he's been having his own stressful experiences around it, so maybe he was trying to protect you. He's been . . ."

Nora nodded knowingly. "I can finish your sentence. He's been—as have you and Winston—*very protective* of me these last couple years." She picked up her cell and said, "But it's time for that to change. And it's time for me to return the favor."

"Who are you calling?" asked Winston.

"Fred," she said. "Because he was with me when I collected the samples. So, whoever broke into my house tonight might also be targeting him."

DeeDee's Apartment

City Center

Red was asleep, seated upright on the couch, when DeeDee entered her apartment. His mouth hung open. The porcelain whiteness of his face and hands popped luminous against the black upholstery. His corona of orange-red hair reminded her of sunsetting skies.

She tiptoed to the kitchen and set down the quarter-pounders she'd packaged for him and Luis. Then she sat in her blue armchair and watched Red sleeping. She breathed in and out with him, syncing her breaths with his chest's rhythmic movements. Then she closed her eyes and synced her breathing with the sounds of his. She felt deep, comforting peace.

A-1 Property Management

Fruitvale District

Sitting in his so-called business office, Marty finished the last warm Corona from the bookshelf. He kept rereading the cryptic document he'd stolen from Nora's dining table, trying to divine its meaning. But in concert with all her desktop files pointing to the Greeleys and the stadium, he had to admit Sam was right: *Nora Kelly is up to something.*

After pulling information from Nora's "Personal Data" folder—her Social Security number, bank passwords, ATM codes—he leaned back in his desk chair, trying to determine his next best move, scratching the excoriated site of his missing ear.

I've got to keep Sam happy. Or I'll lose everything—the clothes, the Beemer, the whole fucking happy-ever-after with her. But all I seem to do these days is piss her off. Still, she's pissing me off, too! So fucking disrespectful! He experienced a fleeting moment of glee, recalling the damage he'd done to her car earlier.

But back to numero uno: I won't make her happy if I don't get those people off her property. So, everything else—these dumb soil tests, Nora Kelly, Patty and Pete—they're lower priority now.

Encouraged by his self-counsel—and bolstered by wine and beer—he confidently asserted: *I can do what is needed all by myself. I'll just rent a U-Haul in the morning and move those people out. Shouldn't take but a few trips, and Monday's not too late for a deadline. That'll make things right between me and Sam. And she'll see me succeed where she thinks my dad failed.*

My dad . . .

It suddenly occurred to him that the legal documents pertaining to the stadium and its sale were in his father's possession. Over the prior year of "working" for him and occasionally meeting at his law office, he'd often seen the stadium files on the desk and even furtively thumbed through them. *If I can get hold of them before my old man transfers files to Sam's new lawyer, then I can get hold of the environmental inspections. They're supposed to be fine—Dad said so. But sure as hell, I can't ask him for anything now. Still, if I can show them to Sam tonight, she'll relax about the doctor's soil testing and let me off the hook.*

He felt triumphant: *several* saving epiphanies within mere minutes of applying his nimble mind to complicated problems. If only he had one more Corona to celebrate!

Ocambo Law Firm

Lakeshore District

Quentin had added five extra hundreds to the envelope he'd dropped into Alex's postbox an hour ago. It was amazing—not only how well his plan was proceeding, but how spontaneously better it kept becoming. Admittedly, it was a bit of a thrill—the clever plotting, the growing satisfaction of victory and revenge, the glory nearing his reach.

And his work was done for the day. He cursorily reviewed the documents he'd drawn up: statements for Gianni and Red that he'd present for their signatures tomorrow. Then he slipped them into his briefcase and waited inside his darkened office.

Minutes later, as expected, he heard someone trying to jam a key into the new lock on his office door. A pause. Another failed attempt. Then forceful kicking of the door, and fist-pounding on it. A loud curse followed: "Fuck you, old man!"

It was, predictably, Martin. Now Quentin knew for sure that Martin, without permission, had duplicated the old keys and stolen into the office whenever. Tonight's attempted foray undoubtedly concerned the stadium deal. Quentin popped an antacid and waited for his son's retreating footsteps.

But then his cell rang. Martin was calling. Quentin flinched and hastily silenced the ringer. *Did Martin hear it?* His mind raced; gastric acid backwashed into his throat. Finally, he heard the explicit chilling answer: "See you soon, Dad."

~ ~ ~

Part Six

The Sun, the Moon, and the Truth

MONDAY, NOVEMBER 26

Infirmary, San Sebastian Prison

Marin County

SEVEN A.M., and already his voicemail was full, mostly with urgent requests to come to the infirmary. Jack grabbed his work cell and stethoscope and hurried through security checks to arrive at Pete's bedside. The nurse reported that Pete had suffered three seizures over the weekend and, during moments of clarity, had demanded to speak *only* with Jack.

Jack reviewed the clinical chart to confirm Pete was receiving optimal antiseizure medication. Still, he knew that medication alone would ultimately fail; Pete's aggressive brain tumor required surgical intervention.

After repeated nudging, Pete awoke. In a slurred voice, he said: "What took you so long to get here?"

"Hello, Mr. Vaughn—I mean, *Pete.* Sorry, but I wasn't working the holiday weekend."

"Today's Monday?"

"Yes. And it seems you've had three seizures."

"So, I heard." He yawned. "But if today's Monday . . . Oh, fuck. It's maybe too late."

"For surgery? No, we have time."

"Not *that,*" said Pete. He signaled for Jack to come closer and whispered: "You're my doctor, right? And you gotta keep things confidential between us, right?"

"Yes, and yes," Jack responded warily. "But confidentiality isn't *absolute.*"

"What the hell does that mean?"

Jack felt as if he might faint from the overwhelming stench of Pete's breath. He backed away a little and said, "Well, confidentiality doesn't apply to *everything* someone might tell me. Imagine, for example, if a patient told me he'd murdered or—"

"Nothing like that, man. C'mon. I got nobody on the outside to lean on anymore. And my lawyer's a lying douchebag. So, I need you to do me a favor."

Jack scoffed. "I'm not your gang member, Pete."

Pete's unsteady gaze struggled to alight on Jack's face. "I changed my mind. I want the surgery. My douchebag lawyer . . . let's say, *motivated* me the other day. Then, if I make it through surgery, I'll finish my time and get back with my baby girl."

"Sounds like a plan. I'll call UCSF."

"Wait. For everything to work out, I need you to deliver a message to my girl."

"Why don't you just phone her? Or ask her to visit?"

"It's not like that. She's . . . terrified. Paranoid. Paralyzed, actually. A lot of bad shit just went down on her, and people are out to get her. And it's all my fault, see? Besides, she knows the phone lines here are tapped."

Jack scoffed. "I can't get involved like that."

"C'mon, man. Her name's Patty. She's in hiding. Laying low. She's suffering, and I can't stand it no more. You're supposed to be a goddamn healer. So, heal me! Get a healing message to her! My life ain't worth anything without her in it."

Jack's moral compass wobbled wildly. His professional ethics encouraged pursuit of the greater good for patients, but that didn't entail having to run personal errands for them—especially if doing so might entail crossing lines into murky legal territory.

"Doc," said Pete, "you're wasting time thinking. All you gotta do is go tell her in person, 'Time to bingo.' That's it."

Jack's jaw dropped ever so slightly. The request sounded so cloak-and-dagger, a melodramatic trope from an old B-movie. "Pete, I can't do that. It's . . . too . . . too *something*."

"Just go to the old Oakland stadium and—"

"What?" Jack exclaimed. He'd recently visited the stadium *twice*. He was providing room and board to several people who'd been living there.

"I said, 'the old stadium in Oakland.' You can't be so posh that you don't know it."

"Of course, I know it."

"So, just go—*now*. She's hiding, like I told her to. In a beige camper with a garden, in the D-lot. Just tell her from me, 'Time to bingo.'"

Cafeteria

Oakland City Hospital

"I wondered whether you were coming," said Nora, offering the extra coffee she'd ordered.

Fred sat across the table from her and said, with formality, "Well, I'm here."

Nora looked appraisingly at her old friend, wondering how he could behave so coldly toward her. Recognizing her injured expression, he said, "Well, if I'd been allowed sleep last night, maybe I'd be in a friendlier mood."

She said, "Last night was *terrifying* for me. I had another panic attack after some thug broke into my house! He even stole my laptop. So, if you could try to be a little more understanding . . ."

"Sorry, Nora; I just can't. Because after you called the house last night, my family freaked out, paranoid that someone was going to break in! *Then* the police stopped by to check on us in the *middle of the night*. No one slept in my house. And all this happened because you were so damn insistent on playing Nancy Drew and sticking it to Samantha Greeley."

"You're joking! You know that's not true. I collected that soil because I thought I could find the cause for people getting sick, dying even."

"Don't know about that. You're never at your best around people with money and power. You disliked Samantha from the moment—"

"Excuse me, Fred, if I don't swoon over a great pair of legs with big bank accounts." She felt so suddenly distant from him, she could barely see him as the friend he'd been.

Staring crossly at her, he counted to ten. "Did you invite me here to have this fight?"

"No. And I may as well get it off my chest now. I wanted to tell you in person, in a neutral setting—not your office or mine—that I received results from those soil tests an hour ago. And . . . you were right. They turned up negative. I'd also learned over the weekend that professional environmental testing—"

He scoffed and, unable to refrain, said: "Told you so!" Secretly, however, he was greatly relieved. In his most paranoid of moments, he had worried about the tests revealing toxic chemicals. That would've disrupted the stadium sale and embittered Samantha toward him and, therefore, the hospital. The prospect of new affordable housing for service employees would vanish, as would any laudatory recognition of his role in securing it.

Nora appeared stunned. "Did you just say 'Told you so'? And with that grin on your face?"

He hadn't been aware of grinning.

She said, "I can't understand why you'd be happy with the test results. Because something's still sickening people at that godawful camp, and it would've been good had we discovered it!"

"Please, keep it down."

"And not just for medical reasons, Fred! It would've given people like Daleen and Luis a legal recourse to seek compensation to help them escape their fucked-up circumstances."

"Hold on! You don't know that. Besides, most of those encampment residents are probably there *illegally*. Since when did you become an expert on immigration law?"

Nora threw her napkin down on the table. "And since when did you become so *completely* corp?" She stormed out of the cafeteria, trying to hold her head high, trying to hold intact her breaking heart.

Quentin's Home

Temescal District, Oakland

Finishing what was likely to be his final cup of coffee in his home, Quentin mentally reviewed the tasks remaining on his evolving to-do list. Obtain signatures from Gianni Moretti and Douglas "Red" O'Brien on their statements. Get the spare keys to the Audi. Compose resignation letter for Samantha. Confirm bus schedule pickup. Pack.

He walked to the back garden to take a last look at the three dozen rosebushes he'd inherited from his wife—*god rest her soul.* He'd spent considerable time and money maintaining them and defending them against hungry deer: *At least one promise to her that I was able to keep.*

But now, dear wife, I relinquish them and our son to their fates.

A-1 Property Management

Fruitvale District

It was a popular misperception that a P.I.'s work must be "interesting and exciting." At least, that's what P.I. Alex Morales was thinking as he scanned the one-room office of "A-1 Property Management." Filled with beer bottles and snacks, he thought: *It's got to be a ruse—an urban man-cave for Marty.* Besides, there was no nameplate on the door. No phone, printer, office supplies, file cabinets.

Alex saw a silver laptop on the desk; on it, a "Property of" sticker bore the name "Nora Kelly" and a phone number. Its battery was depleted, and he couldn't find a cord, so he took several photographs of it. Then he proceeded to examine papers on Marty's desk: child-like drawings of airplanes . . . guns and swords . . . a cat (or cow?). Outdated newspapers. Napkins pilfered from local takeouts. *Absolutely nothing interesting or exciting here.*

Well, to the mission now, he told himself. Then he reached into his satchel for the two envelopes Quentin had given him—the first at Saul's, and the second dropped into his postbox last night. He withdrew their documents and set out to plant them here, as instructed.

But, still bothered by Quentin's odd behavior at the restaurant—his self-deprecating comments and sentimentality, his caginess and smoothed-over desperation—Alex hesitated. *What do these documents have to do with Quentin taking some last "swing for the fences"?* Then his curiosity—or, honed investigator's instincts—got the better of him: Against his professional ethics and customary practice, he decided to examine the documents.

Well, well, he thought, thumbing through them, *this is actually interesting.* He saw an environmental inspection of the stadium property, dated 1989, documenting extensive contamination of the land and groundwater with DDT, nitrates, toxaphene, arsenic, and sundry other chemicals he couldn't pronounce. But it was also accompanied by two clean reinspections of the property subsequently performed in 1991 and 2018 by Epitome Soil Testing Lab. *What's the point of planting these?*

In the second envelope was a stack of invoices addressed to Marty for soil purchases and dumps, attached to mapped drawings of work projects by "Moretti Landscaping"—the same company he used to furtively pay at Quentin's behest. While some were recent, others were dated 1989–91. *Why on earth would Quentin be making these under-the-table transactions visible now? Why establish a paper trail between Moretti and Marty?*

Then he opened a small spiral notepad. It was filled with handwritten entries for "cash received" by Marty during the prior year for "stadium property management"—a job that had once been his. "But, what the fuck?" he said aloud, seeing that Marty got twice the pay.

Alex angrily tossed aside the notepad, feeling that he'd been treated like dirt himself. *You betrayed me, Q. You replaced me as the stadium go-between with your parasitic, incompetent son—and at double the pay.*

Habitually scratching his beard while thinking, he suddenly recalled Quentin's comment about feeling betrayed himself. *So, is all of this about payback, Q? Are you turning on Marty now, with something more than the usual wrist-slap? The cut must've been deep this time around. How many times did you—and I—save his sorry ass over the years? From the time he was a teenager, "working" odd jobs for you, while stealing and lying and dealing . . .*

Though he rarely stole a private moment while on assignment, Alex took a minute to reconsider his relationship with Quentin. It'd been friendly though business-like since 1989, until about a year ago when Marty reappeared, expecting the usual handout, and Quentin blithely handed him the stadium gig. *A gig I'd done flawlessly since '89, never once exposing Quentin or the Greeleys, let alone my own identity. How could Q not have known how I'd feel about that? How could he be so oblivious? Even at Saul's the other day, he still didn't apologize directly.*

Still, beyond those grievances, he was feeling most bothered by Quentin's casual attitude about killing animals for sport, with the self-interested aim of befriending Bert Greeley. And by his lack of moral qualms over lethal control—exterminating creatures who'd become inconveniences. *You have to question the character of a man like that.*

Alex stared warily at the documents he was tasked with planting at Quentin's behest. *So, he's expecting me to pave some crooked paper trail with these. A trail, I'm sure, leading to trouble. I could be implicated if things go wrong. And here he is, once again, oblivious to how his decisions affect me.*

Now unbearably suspicious about what he might be enacting for Quentin, and doubtful about obtaining a truthful explanation from him, Alex spread the documents across the desk. For his own personal insurance policy, he scanned them into his phone. When he finished, he headed out to find Nora Kelly and discover her importance to Marty.

Cafeteria

Oakland City Hospital

At the ER entrance, Winston kissed Fergie goodbye and said, "Have a good day at work. And thanks for letting me have the car."

"No worries," she said, heading into work. "Carl will drive me home tonight. Say 'Hi' to Marla for me."

Winston nodded and proceeded to the cafeteria, intending to ask Marla what she'd thought about the story as published. But near its entry, he heard familiar squeaks signaling Nora's approach, and he cheerily exclaimed "Hi!" A millisecond later, he noticed she was in tears.

"Not now," she said, exiting the cafeteria, hurrying away.

A moment later, Fred also bumped into Winston on the way out. "Don't ask," he said, taking the hallway in the opposite direction.

Somewhat thrown, Winston entered the cafeteria. Marla smiled and said, "Your story was okay. But you could've mentioned I was single."

He laughed. "I'm sure that's just a matter of time. A *short* time."

She gave him the stink eye. "Obviously, you got no idea how *impossible* it is to meet someone when you got no place to live. No place to hang with them, get to know them. Hell, no place where they can just *find* you. Google Maps doesn't keep tabs on my car." She grimaced. "At least, I hope not."

"I'm embarrassed to say, I hadn't thought of that problem before."

"Well, yeah. Then there's the problem of no cell reception in the kinds of places I got to park most nights. I couldn't text or call a sweetie if I had one. Don't even got a mailbox to receive anybody's valentine! Look, I appreciate your optimism, but it's gonna be a *long* time before Ms. Right *can* find me."

"Sorry," he said, absorbing Marla's distressing remarks.

"Well, don't just be 'sorry.' Write about that someday. People don't understand."

"I will. But right now, I'm off to interview the family you put me in touch with who live at the dump. Afterwards, I'm checking out an encampment at the stadium. I've been wanting to do that for days, but something's always interfered."

"The 'Hope and Dignity' group, right?"

"You know it?"

After settling a customer's bill, she said: "Anyone who's been here on the street a while knows it."

"Is that something you're willing to talk about?"

Marla nodded at a regular who wordlessly handed over two dollars and left with his tea. She told Winston, "Well, the H-and-D folks are managed. And they're moved around the Bay Area every so often, to do labor on the cheap for higher-ups. They've been at the stadium a while now. Migrants, mostly. Lots of illegals. Some homeless locals."

"Have you stayed there?"

"Once." She scoffed. "But didn't last a week. They let me park there, but they worked me *real* hard—like everyone else living there. The work was all shit jobs . . . dealing with dirt and pollution, trash and hauling. But, see, I already had *this* job in *this* cafeteria. It just didn't pay enough to make rent. Anyhow, they told me I could stay at the camp and keep this job if I worked there nights. But, man, those latrines they had me cleaning . . . really, just plastic work buckets full of nasty stuff."

Winston cringed. "Sounds horrible. And unsafe."

"That's right. And H-and-D gave me a flimsy pair of gloves—*one* pair I was supposed to wash when they got dirty. As if ever they weren't."

Recalling his conversation with Fergie about contagious diseases spreading within neglected communities, he said: "So, you're talking iffy sanitation at the camp. And, I assume, no clean running water? People must get sick a lot. They must have a hard time recuperating, too."

She rolled her eyes. "Ya think? Then all the people living in their safe, pretty houses—they got their heads in the sand, thinking they're safe from us. But when we're sick, we still go out in public—to parks, grocery stores, schools—hell, lots of us *live* in public. We take the bus, ride BART, go to the library. And lots of us have other shit jobs—like me, here in this cafeteria—that we *got* to do if we want food on the table."

"Even if you're sick, right?" he said, expecting, and receiving, another eye-roll. "So, you described the stadium camp as 'managed.' Is that common?"

"No," she said. "I can't speak for all the camps in Oakland; there's about a couple hundred, right? But the few that I've been to? *Lawless.* Wild West lawless, sometimes. Especially dangerous for women and children. For anyone not right in the head, too. Some were run by thugs. Some made you pay five or ten bucks a night to sleep on a *public* side-walk or bench. Shit . . . So, one good thing about the H-and-D camp, they kept thugs out. And they didn't put up with public drunkenness or hard drugs, or people peeing and shitting anywhere. And, I got to say, they made sure the women and kids weren't sex-trafficked at least— that's a big deal."

"You keep mentioning 'they.' Who's 'they'?"

"Not sure. But that short while I stayed at H-and-D, a big white lady named Patty was in charge. And a scrawny kid . . ." She chuckled. "A scrawny kid with red hair who was 'security'! I swear, I could've sneezed and knocked that child over."

"Oh . . . 'security'? Think I'll have trouble getting into the camp today?"

"Well, besides that child guarding the gate, the camp's surrounded by fencing topped with barbed wire. But everyone knows it's got holes that people sneak through. Just got to know where they are."

Nora's Office

Oakland City Hospital

Nora sat at her desk, trying to compose herself after her upsetting encounter with Fred, with five minutes to spare before her shift began. How to make sense of the negative soil tests she'd just received? *There has to be something toxic in the soil or water with people getting so sick. And Samantha acting twitchy about my visit . . . someone breaking into my house, stealing my list and laptop . . .*

And yet . . .

Not one, but two professional inspections by Epitome Soil Testing Lab confirmed the stadium is clean.

She dashed off an email to her soils-expert friend at UC Davis: "Again, thanks for testing those samples for me. I know my testing method was amateurish. But please humor me again: Is it possible for contaminated soil to pass testing by *professional* inspectors and agencies?" Then she pulled up Epitome's website on her desktop as the day's first cardiac arrest summoned her.

Oakland Estuary

Jack London Square

Morning sun bounced off the estuary and flashed storefront windows. Gianni adjusted his shades and complained, "The bad thing about some mornings is they're too bright. Your eyes take longer than the rest of your body to wake up." When Red didn't respond, he said, "We can do this."

Red said, "I guess I realized I'm afraid to risk what I got to lose. I didn't understand how much that was until now."

"Look at me," said Gianni with momentousness, and Red met his gaze. "Now, I don't like this Ocambo A-hole, and I wish I'd punched him. But I prefer him telling the truth about what happened to my dad and his guys. And I want justice for them. What Ocambo's proposing to do about that sounds as right to me as anything can at this point. And us becoming millionaire whistleblowers in the process, well—yay for us and all the good stuff we'll do with the money."

"So, then, we're signing on?"

"You can still back out, pal. I want you to be two hundred percent comfortable. Besides, it wasn't your dad that him and the Greeleys fucked over."

"Well, it may've been your dad, but it's not only been him." Red stared at an outbound ferryboat heading to San Francisco and fantasized about sailing away with DeeDee someday, somewhere, anywhere. "It's about all the people living at the camp, too. I always just accepted things were *normal* awful for them and me. I didn't know the Greeleys were actively fucking us over. And, god, I hate knowing I played some part in it. Human trafficking and labor abuse? Man, I just wish us fighting back could be about *those* things. Us whistleblowing for 'tax evasion' and 'employment fraud' feels lame."

"Still, if the plan works, we'll be able to help everyone. Hey, do I got a poppyseed stuck here in my teeth?"

Red looked, and shook his head. "But I don't really trust that lawyer. Seems Ocambo's up to something besides 'justice' and 'making amends.'"

Gianni grinned and looked sideways at Red. "Think we should tell him I been recording our conversations?"

"What?!"

"Hah! We've been sharing a wavelength again, pal. 'Cuz, I agree. We gotta play defense with him. He's not as honorable as us."

"You got everything on your phone?"

"Yep. His shit about what he did to my dad and his workers. Harboring migrants and labor trafficking. Him asking for my workmaps to prove the Greeleys' shadow employment and tax evasion." Gianni slapped Red's shoulder and said, "Me and you, pal! Go, defense!"

Red elbowed Gianni to signal him of Quentin's approach. "Sorry I'm late," he greeted them. "I brought the statements." He handed paperwork to each of them and said, "Sign by the yellow tags. I'll make copies for you and place them with the legal documents you'll be delivering to the lawyer tomorrow."

Perusing the originals, Gianni said, "I'm still pissed over what you did to my dad and his crew."

Red said, "And the shit way you've been treating migrants and homeless people."

"I apologize again, gentlemen," said Quentin. "As I've hoped to convey, I'm doing my level best to make amends. But should I worry that you're both so 'pissed' you won't follow through with our agreement?"

Gianni spoke through the side of his mouth: "Some people are actually good for their word."

Quentin stared overlong at them, wondering how it might've been to have had a son like one of them—ragged, crude, intellectually simple; but motivated by heart and principle. *So unlike Martin. And, actually, unlike me. But would I have been bored with a son like that? My character made soft and weak?*

"Hey," said Red, "the way you're staring at us is creeping me out again."

"Sorry, son," said Quentin. "I was just . . . regretting I won't be around to celebrate with you when all's said and done."

"Well, this better end in a reason to celebrate," said Gianni. "Me and Red aren't fond of lawyers and courts. You want to at least tell us where you're going?"

Quentin shook his head and took back their signed agreements, wondering whether his plans were going to work out to allow him to see Tony's boy again. He said, "Do you have any last questions for me?"

Red shrugged. "Everything's too unreal to have real questions right now." Gianni added, "And just thinking about us becoming millionaire 'whistleblowers' . . . I can't wrap my mind around that. So, I guess we got no questions."

Quentin nodded and handed over his spare car keys to Gianni. "You'll find more than enough in the trunk of the car to tide you gentlemen over while things play out through the courts. Do you remember where the car is located? And the lockbox code?"

Gianni scoffed. "Course I do."

"Good. And here's the business card of my attorney at Palmer & Webley—*your* attorney now, too. Deshawn and his firm will handle your case and provide financial assistance with your settlement. When I meet with him in person later today, I'll give him these original statements so we can proceed swiftly. Tomorrow, he'll be expecting you to deliver the documents in the trunk of my car—just remember not to pick up the car before noon. After he receives them, his firm will have everything it needs to work your case and prosecute the Greeleys."

You-Hawl Car & Truck Rentals

East Oakland

Marty Ocambo pounded on the glass door of You-Hawl Rentals, although a clearly posted sign read: "Open 9-to-5." He kept yelling at the clerk inside, "I can fucking see you!" and "Open the damn door!" Then, with great vigor: "I'm gonna kill you, bastard!"

A patrol car arrived and two police approached. One asked, "Sorry, who'd you say you're going to kill?"

He cursed at them and spat on the glass door. But when he looked inside, he saw the clerk smiling back in galling victory.

Jack's Home

Rockridge District

Luis insisted on clearing the breakfast table. He was intent on mastering the dishwasher and garbage disposal today, and Yusra was happy to assist. Jack's housekeeper, Zofia, pointed to the pair and told Daleen: "With them around, I have no work to do!"

Daleen smiled. "May I help with the dinner tonight?"

Zofia said, "I'd love your company, if you feel up to it. But it's going to be simple. Dr. Jack is picking up rotisserie chickens on his way home from work. Dr. Nora's arriving around four."

With some hesitation, Daleen said, "And I believe she is bringing information from the social worker."

The two women exchanged pained looks, and then silently resumed watching Luis and Yusra.

Nora's Office

Oakland City Hospital

After reading Nora Kelly's outdated LinkedIn profile, Alex drove to Oakland City Hospital. He grabbed an empty wheelchair in a hallway and pushed it, as if on a mission, past an ER security guard, to whom he complained, "I wish people wouldn't just leave these around everywhere." He slipped into Nora's office and closed the door. On her desktop computer screen, he saw the same environmental reports he'd been tasked to plant in Marty's office. Its browser opened to the website for Epitome Soil Testing Lab. Her last sent email, to someone with a UCD.edu address, asked if, and how, contaminated soil could still test negative for toxins. He rifled through her desk drawers, surprised to find such robust stores of Cheez Curlz, and then snuck out of the hospital with his head spinning.

Upon returning to his car, his cell rang. He debated whether to answer Quentin's call. *But I got to admit, things are getting more interesting by the minute.* He picked up. Quentin immediately asked whether he'd "taken care of business at A-1 properties."

"Mission accomplished," Alex replied.

"Good," said Quentin. "Because I'd like you to check on another matter."

"No. We agreed A-1 was my last job."

"But it's part of the same mission. Look, I'll pay double. Do you remember Pete Vaughn's girlfriend, Patty Dobrovski?"

Alex stroked his beard, thinking, *Now it's getting wild.* Puzzle pieces were just dropping from the sky. He chose to respond provocatively, aiming to rattle Quentin and shake more clues from the proverbial tree. "You're confusing me with your son. If you recall, you chose Marty to deal with Patty and the stadium's oversight. And at twice what you paid me."

"I see," said Quentin, a long pause ensuing. "So, then . . . you read the documents." After another long pause, he said, "I had expected you would."

Alex felt skeptical about Quentin's claim. *Why this time would you expect that of me?* Hoping to extract additional information, he continued his provocation: "It was fucked up enough, you taking me off the stadium detail. But, paying Marty *double*? That's not right."

Quentin sighed. "Come on! You know I always paid you in cash and never kept records. So, Mr. P.I., having seen the documents, didn't you think it strange—?"

"Still, *twice*?"

"I did *not* pay him double. I inflated those so-called payments and recorded them in a ledger under 'cash *received*' by Martin. But the figures and ledger are fake. They're just meant to establish a paper trail between Martin and the stadium."

"What's this all about, Q? Frankly, I've had it with your caginess."

"I understand," said Quentin, trying to contain his anger over being questioned by Alex, while still needing his help.

"Why have me plant *good* environmental reports about the stadium in Marty's office? What's the point of that? And why suddenly resurrect old workmaps from Moretti Landscaping?"

"Please, this truly last request is urgent. And simple. I just need you to scout the stadium and report back whether Patty Dobrovski is there. I'll text you a photo of her from Pete's trial so you can identify her. But I need to know now, or a deal I made will fall apart."

"A deal with who?"

"Look, I have to go. But meet me at the Italian place tonight—Lopato's, seven o'clock. I promise I'll explain everything. Come, for old times' sake, too."

DeeDee's Apartment

City Center

He was supposed to meet Gianni at the hardware store. But Red was drawn by irresistible urges to DeeDee's apartment door. He also wanted to apologize for running out of her apartment yesterday, immediately after awakening on her couch.

"Hey," she said, still in her nightgown. "I was hoping you'd come back."

Her heart-stopping smile rendered him momentarily speechless. "Sorry about yesterday. I must've needed the sleep, but I shouldn't've bolted. See, I was already late for Luis, and he gets bent out of shape—"

DeeDee took his hand. "I miss the little man. Maybe you can bring him around soon? We could hang out."

Suddenly, his worry about having hurt her was supplanted by a worry over kissing her. But if he didn't kiss her now, he might never get the chance, given the potential risks he'd be facing in an imminent battle with a huge corporation and wealthy family. He only replied, "Luis would like that."

Taking his other hand, DeeDee pulled him into her apartment. He thought he might faint. His mind became vacant, and everything inside his body vibrated. He whispered, "I never kissed a girl before." She leaned in close, kissed him softly, and said, "Well, that's no longer true."

The Greeley Foundation Building

Lakeside Drive, Downtown

Samantha's assistant Juliana entered the office with an armful of folders. "Morning," she said. "These just need your signature."

"Thanks," said Samantha. "Oh, and our meeting this afternoon with lawyers from Palmer & Webley—make sure the files from Quentin's office are available in the conference room."

"What files?"

Samantha's brow furrowed. "I told Quentin on Friday to have them sent here immediately. We're no longer using his services."

Juliana looked perplexed. "That's odd. Because he was here in the office just minutes ago. And he said nothing about any files."

"But I terminated his services! What was he even doing here?"

"Well, I don't know. Maybe meeting with real estate or financials? He stopped by my desk like usual to say hello, and he made me *promise* to tell you the same. Then he left . . . took the elevator. But he left no files with me."

"Was he carrying anything *out* of the building?"

"Not that I saw. And I'm sorry, Sam. But I never received a memo that you'd fired him."

"Tell in-house counsel to come here immediately."

Juliana grimaced. "If you'd like, I can contact them at home. But they both called in sick today. That's why I didn't suggest Mr. Ocambo might've been meeting with them."

Samantha's face turned crimson. After dispatching Juliana to alert security about Quentin's illicit visit, she swallowed two ibuprofens, hoping to quell the brewing migraine behind her eyes. *What the hell was Quentin doing here? What did he take? The man is sly—a quality that's served my family well. But now? Now he's using his cunning to manipulate me! I should've sent out a broadcast memo on Friday that I was firing him. I should've sent security to his office to retrieve the foundation's files. I was an idiot to fall for his song-and-dance and let him "resign in dignity" today!*

She scanned the folders on her desk—*Highmark Construction; Media Releases, Stadium Sale; Board Minutes*—and pushed them aside. All she could think about was Quentin's mysterious and provocative presence. *He was so blatantly here today! And making sure I knew that. Is he trying to intimidate me? Was he sneaking out records, flash drives, keys, documents . . . ?*

Now the migraine jackhammered against her skull. She switched off the lights and lay down on the couch, suddenly remembering her intention to contact Marty to check on his progress at the stadium. But she already had an intolerable headache to abide.

Carl Kluft peeled off his nitrile gloves and deftly discarded them in the biohazards bin. After disinfecting his hands twice, he faced his patient and said, "Your IUD won't cause further problems. Are there other needs I can help you with?"

His patient replied, "Yes. Will you marry me?"

"No," said Carl. "It's unprofessional and unethical to get romantically involved with a patient."

"I'm sorry, Dr. Kluft! I was joking."

"Oh?"

"Yeah. It's just something people say sometimes when they're grateful. You know, like, 'You can have my firstborn.'"

No patient had ever made either of those comments to him; yet, surely, many had experienced gratitude. Still, offers of marriage or firstborns sounded odd and wrongheaded. Intrigued by this exchange, he headed to the doctors' workstation to confer with Nora. But finding her staring pensively into space, he instead said, "You look worried."

Nora was pleased that he'd accurately interpreted her expression. Indeed, she was waiting, with slim hope, for the social worker, who'd be bringing suggestions for Daleen, Yusra, and Luis. She said, "Yes. I'm worried, but—" She pointed to the doorway in which Aditya and Lizbeth appeared.

"Hello," said Aditya. "We have good news. We just left my surgeon's office. She said I can return to work on restricted duty." Lizbeth turned to Carl and said, "And we were just telling her about you, Dr. Kluft— how grateful we were for your quick diagnosis and help."

Carl decided to test the waters: "So, do you want to marry me? Or give me a child?" When Lizbeth only looked uncertainly at him and replied, "Uh, no," he knew he'd been correct earlier in experiencing those comments as misguided.

"Also," said Aditya, addressing Nora, "this morning, we received test results for Tomas Ruiz. They came back *very* positive for arsenic."

"It makes sense," Carl said. "Clinically, your patient had a classic toxidrome induced by arsenic."

"What's a 'toxidrome'?" asked Lizbeth.

"It's a constellation of clinical signs—especially vital signs, mental status, and respiratory, neurologic, ocular, and skin findings—that are characteristic of illness caused by general classes of poisons," Carl replied. "Your blue patient certainly has a toxidrome—though you have yet to identify the poison inducing her methemoglobinemia."

"And like Nora's patient who died last month from exposure to organophosphate insecticides," said Aditya. "He had a classic toxidrome reflecting the cholinergic excess—bradycardia, profuse salivation and lacrimation, miosis, diarrhea, and emesis."

"Well," said Lizbeth, "I only wish we had known in time to make a difference for Mr. Ruiz. And I suppose this also means Luis should be checked for arsenic, especially if your soil tests come back positive."

"But they didn't," said Nora, chagrined. "And I might've figured that out beforehand had I taken the time to do the research on the stadium inspections like you and Aditya did."

After everyone left the workstation, Nora sat wrestling with self-doubt. *They were all trying to be so polite, after all the fuss I made—clandestine soil testing, corporate environmental crimes, zebras' hoofbeats . . . Pure hubris! My ridiculous pursuit also hurt my friendship with Fred. And I've failed Daleen, not finding the cause for her illness.* The only pinpoint of light she could see was her dinner tonight with Jack and his new household.

Michpay's Hardware

Lakeshore District

Gianni startled when someone pounded on his truck. It was Red, his arms stretched out, and smiling like a fucking lunatic! Gianni got out and said, "I hardly recognize you, pal! I never seen you smile like this."

Red said, "I guess I never had cause, G!"

Gianni delighted in Red calling him "G." *A nickname, like pals make up for each other.* He slapped Red's shoulder and said, "Well, spill the beans!"

"I think I'm in love. It's never happened before. So, maybe I'm wrong. But I'm guessing . . . this is maybe what it feels like."

"Trust me! You're in love all right! Just listen to yourself."

"It's that woman at Betty's with blue hair."

"Which one?"

When Red appeared thrown, Gianni guffawed. "Just messing with you! C'mon. Tell me about it while we pick up our stuff. I threw a tarp over the dirt in my truck, so I'll haul the hardware. But we should put the food in yours. Just don't eat it all before we get to the stadium!"

San Sebastian Prison

Marin County

Pete Vaughn lay strapped on a gurney while the ambulance crew prepared for his transport to San Francisco. Jack said, "Good luck. And I'll stay in communication with your neurosurgeon."

"And you're telling Patty, right?" said Pete.

Jack believed that if he explicitly said no, Pete would cancel surgery. He said, "I promise to do what I can." He thought, *And what I "can" do doesn't embrace carrying out your request.*

"Not good enough. Yes or no? You gonna tell her?"

This is absurd, Jack thought, imagining a return to the stadium to deliver some cockamamie message about "bingo" to a woman named Patty who was "laying low" inside a camper. He said, "I'll think about it." *Believe me, I'll think about this odd request for the rest of my life.*

Pete collared him, pulled him close, and whispered, "And you gotta tell her today. If you don't, you'll have her blood on your hands."

A guard loosened Pete's grip on Jack's collar, and the EMTs wheeled him out.

Noonish

Marty Ocambo tore up his losing tickets and tossed them into the vacating stands at Golden Gate Fields racetrack. He shot a contemptuous look at the happy couple in the next row who were still celebrating their big win. "Get the fuck outta here," he muttered to them under his breath.

He lingered in his seat, thinking he couldn't possibly be in a worse mood—not after losing so big . . . after being detained by police this morning and banned "forever" from You-Hawl . . . unable to reach Sam. And with no one willing to help him clear the camp, he was beginning to panic over ruining the stadium sale and losing favor with Samantha. He grabbed someone's half-empty beer can from the ground and gulped it.

My dad's the only person who could bail me out now. But fat chance of that happening now.

Looks like Sam was right about that, too; I should've waited to end things with the old man.

"Fuck it," he said, tossing the can perilously close to the celebrating couple.

Still, the old man's got to get me out of this hell. And if he refuses . . . Well, I'll get satisfaction enough, finally knocking the arrogant smirk off his face.

~ ~ ~

Meanwhile, Samantha's migraine was escalating. She popped an oxycodone and checked her phone messages. There was Marty, sounding exasperated, but leaving no useful information except to say he'd be working late in his office tonight. *What a barefaced dodge,* she thought.

Her assistant Juliana reappeared, a strained expression on her face. "Sam, some good news: security reported nothing missing from the building. And they reviewed all the security footage; it looks like Mr. Ocambo simply came and went. It tracks him from the elevator, crossing the lobby toward the restrooms, and, just two minutes later, he's at my desk saying hello. Then he enters the elevator and leaves the building."

"Okay," said Samantha, vigorously massaging her temples. "Have his office files arrived yet? I absolutely need them for our meeting with the new law firm."

Juliana frowned. "Sorry. That's the not-so-good news. Security had to wait on a warrant to search Mr. Ocambo's office. And, well, they found it'd been emptied out."

~ ~ ~

In his office, Fred struggled to review the pharmacy budget, but was feeling too remorseful over how he'd behaved toward Nora over coffee. *How could I have been so cold to one of my oldest friends?* Still, he knew the answer: his desire to appease Samantha had prevailed, fueled by expectations for her foundation's generous charity to the hospital. *Hell, Nora's right; I've become thoroughly "corp."* He pushed aside his paperwork, and called Nora to invite her to an "apology drink" at Grady's after work.

~ ~ ~

Winston took advantage of dining solo by ordering a cheeseburger for lunch. It'd been weeks since he'd consumed red meat; Fergie would never approve. He even waited to finish before phoning her with his updated plans. When he relayed what he'd eaten, she called him a caveman. And she reiterated how much she hated receiving trivial calls at work. "Wait," he said, "I called to tell you I'm going to be home later than expected. I haven't even been to the stadium yet." Fergie suggested he come home instead, and visit the camp tomorrow. But he insisted otherwise: "No, woman. Me caveman. Have red meat. Me go tonight." She hung up without saying goodbye.

~ ~ ~

Red and Gianni received the word from Quentin that his P.I. didn't locate Patty at the stadium. So, they drove to the camp and hurriedly distributed their truckloads of supplies to the residents. Boxes and bags of cleaning products, batteries, flashlights, towels, and emergency survival kits from Michpay's Hardware. Food and bottled water from the nearby Food Palace. They warned everyone about Patty's plan to kick them out. Red handed over padlocks to the two guys he'd only ever known as "the Cousins." Then he and Gianni drove out, planning to reconvene at Betty's.

Old Stadium Site

P.I. Alex Morales had rationalized his reporting back to Quentin that he hadn't "found Patty" at the stadium: it was, technically, true. Still, he hadn't actually searched for her. Instead, with his curiosity piqued by Quentin's "urgent" and secretive need to know Patty's whereabouts, he parked his silver Mazda on 4th near the stadium gate and waited, on the lookout for the consequences of his report.

Glancing at himself in the rearview, he thought, *You're not too old for a fresh start.* His clear caramel eyes still sparkled; his coppery hair and beard were full and stylishly trimmed. And, perhaps he imagined it, but since distancing himself from Quentin, his face appeared freshly disburdened. And for the first time in many years, he realized he was being drawn into a genuine mystery—*Something honest-to-god interesting and exciting.* His career as a P.I., largely in servitude to Quentin and the Greeleys, had entailed little more beyond yawning errands, menial tasks, and rote cash-under-the-table transactions. The major risks he'd faced involved papercuts, speeding tickets, guard dogs, and an occasional gut punch.

Yes, he was feeling lighter by the minute, detaching himself from Quentin. Quentin, who'd acted in rote complicity with Bert's revolting hunting philosophy. Quentin, who treated people like pawns in business transactions. And now freed from his blind loyalty to Quentin, he could begin to see himself pursuing work that was interesting, and, perhaps, even good.

All the better, too, that Quentin *seemed* to be leaving. He'd left enough clues: his hints at endings and final chances, his severance from Greeley Enterprises, his perplexing sentimentality, his break with Marty. *I'll have a better chance at a fresh start if he's not around.*

Alex leaned back against the headrest, reviewing his day, culling salient facts. *Quentin claimed he expected me to look at the documents, but knowing that was never my style. Do I believe him about that, or is he playing me with some convenient lie? And why would he be okay with me discovering he was setting up Marty for some kind of fall? No . . . he's probably pissed off about it all. And why choose this particular time—finally!—to punish Marty? Do I buy his claim about not paying Marty double? Whatever . . . the bottom line: He should've had the decency to let me in on what he's up to, because he's implicated me in it. Will he actually tell me the truth over dinner tonight? Will he even show up? And—*

Two loud trucks arrived and pulled up to the gate. Alex looked out to see a white crew cab and its red-haired driver; the other, a black flatbed, driver unseen. Two male guards allowed the trucks in. Twenty minutes later, the trucks exited; Alex turned on the ignition, planning pursuit. But then a red Subaru pulled up, and a black-haired man in a Warriors jacket got out. Alex watched the guards push him away while padlocking the gate. He cracked open the window and heard the man claim, "I'm a journalist!" before he finally backed away, his hands held up in surrender.

A journalist? thought Alex. *Now what the hell is he interested in?* Then, recalling what he'd seen today on Nora's office computer: *Why is Dr. Kelly interested in this place, too? And what's Marty's interest in her?*

The Subaru passed, and Alex ducked down. Then he furtively set out in pursuit, trailing the car onto Tornwaldt, where it parked. From a safe distance, he withdrew his binoculars from the glove compartment and watched the self-proclaimed journalist search along the fenceline. Then all of a sudden, the man disappeared. Alex got out of the car and ran to the vanishing point, where he found a hole in the fence and entered.

Midafternoon

The news of Pete's intraoperative death shook Jack so violently that he hesitated to drive across the bridge. They'd just spoken so intimately; their conversation was still warm. *"Yes or no? . . . time to bingo . . . promise me."* Jack could still feel Pete's desperate grip on his collar . . . still smell his pungent breath . . . still hear the neurosurgeon's leaden report: *Brain herniation . . . surgical complications . . . uncontrollable intraoperative sei-zures . . . death, finally.*

But Jack's shift was over, and bridge traffic would soon become unbearable. He was also hosting dinner tonight with Nora, and had promised to pick up rotisserie beforehand. So, he braced himself and slowly headed out of the employee parking lot.

~ ~ ~

Samantha was also feeling shaky, edgily awaiting the lawyers from Palmer & Webley, whom she'd intended to sign. *Why are they late? And where are Quentin's stadium files—if not here or in his office?*

Finally, at least, the pain medications began to kick in—though, perhaps, too powerfully. And now, ruminating about her ominous predicament, she had to concede that Quentin and her father had been right: she really should have familiarized herself with the family business. Had she done so instead of passing its management onto well-paid others, she wouldn't be stuck in this vulnerable and uninformed position right now. And yet, self-admittedly, by the wildest stretch of her imagination, she also couldn't imagine having sacrificed any more of her one precious life to the soul-crushing machine that was the all-consuming family business.

Then a knock on the door. Juliana entered, clearly distraught, and reported, "I don't understand, Sam. No one at Palmer & Webley is even answering the phones. I've double-checked all my emails and texts, and there's nothing from them about canceling today. The appointment was solid as a rock! Do you think, under the circumstances, we should postpone Friday's signing with Highmark Construction?"

Samantha dismissed the suggestion and told her to leave. Alone again, she paced the conference room, wondering what could possibly account for the chaos around the stadium sale. *Something is terribly wrong. No, everything's terribly wrong.* She walked unsteadily back to her office and searched her father's old rolodex for the name of the private investigator he and Quentin had relied on: "Morales, Alex—PI."

~ ~ ~

At Quentin's home, Marty pounded furiously on the door after failing to fit his old key into the new lock. He tossed a potted geranium through the front window, triggering the security alarm. While he fled, he repeatedly vowed to "kill the old man!" The home security service dispatched local patrol to the address, as it also notified Quentin about the attempted break-in.

Quentin examined the home-security-cam footage on his cell-phone—as expected, featuring his hapless, hothead son. Earlier, he'd seen the video-feed from his law office: the police and the Greeleys' security team forcing open its door, and staring at the emptied safe and file cabinets. He was pleased. *Everything's proceeding on track.* He patted his coat pocket containing his two flash drives, ready to take the next step toward his grand finale.

~ ~ ~

Carl dropped by the ER to pick Fergie up and drive her home. But she appeared upset, and he said so. Still, lacking confidence, he asked, "Am I right?"

"Yes," she replied. "It's just . . . Win's investigating the homeless camp at the stadium. It was important to me—and, I thought, to *him*—that we do that together."

"I have a solution," he said. "Let's grab something to eat, and then I'll drive you there so you can join him. Just call and tell him you're coming."

Fergie smiled and said, "Brilliant!" He needed no confirmation on his take of her reaction.

Jack's Home

Rockridge District

When Nora arrived at Jack's, Zofia ushered her into the living room and reported: "Dr. Jack called to apologize. He's going to be late because of some emergency with a patient."

Nora wished she'd known, because she'd declined an apology drink with Fred in order to arrive here on time. And now, being made to wait for Jack's unpredictable arrival, she'd also have to sit on the social worker's recommendations while in the company of the people it most affected—suggestions for Daleen and Yusra, and the "solid bet on a good home for Luis."

Immediately, she overheard Luis exclaim from the kitchen, "She's here!" Then he rushed in, wearing his Betty's tee-shirt, with Yusra following.

"Welcome, Dr. Nora," he said. "Would you like a water?"

Nora smiled so hard that it broke her bad mood. "Yes, thank you," she replied, and the children ran back to the kitchen.

Hearing the commotion, Daleen came in to greet Nora. "We have been looking forward to your visit."

Nora's expression turned somber. "I'm sorry. But I may as well tell you while the kids are out of the room. I didn't find the cause for your illness. I was mistaken."

"Do not be so hard on yourself. I'm grateful you cared to try."

"Still, I should've been more circumspect. And less cocky. Because my fixated search to prove my theory only gave you false hope. I really thought I could tie everyone's illness to stadium contamination. And, well, then we'd also know how to prevent others living there from getting sick or dying."

Daleen frowned with the inference about Tomas. "Mr. Ruiz was a good man. He took care of Luis as if he were his own. Did you find out what caused his death?"

Nora nodded. "We received confirmation today. He was poisoned by arsenic."

"Arsenic? But how?"

"I don't know. But that's another reason I regret having been singularly invested in the stadium being the source of all evil. I should've been thinking more broadly. Still, even in retrospect, it just seems to make sense, knowing the stadium was built on the site of an old pesticide factory."

"Oh? That could explain my illness, as well as Tomas' poisoning?"

"In theory, yes. Because the old Regal Chemical Company manufactured pesticides against all sorts of insects and critters and microbes. And many of those chemicals or the solvents they used to manufacture them were hazardous for humans as well. Like arsenic, for example. Or chemicals like dipyridylium, naphthalene, and nitrates that could trigger methemoglobinemia—the illness you suffered. Also, a month ago, I cared for a man living at the camp who died from organophosphate poisoning—another toxin that easily could've been left in the ground by Regal Chemicals. So, to me, it seemed beyond coincidence—*three* people, living on the same land, developing rare diseases that could logically be ascribed to environmental pollution by a pesticide company."

"Your theory sounds more than reasonable. What changed your mind?"

Looking sheepish, Nora said, "Evidence. *Actual* testing of stadium soil. I received the results of my own tests this morning: no residual toxic chemicals or pesticides. And besides—"

Luis and Yusra delivered Nora's water. Yusra asked her mother, "Would you like a water, too?" Luis whispered something to Yusra, which prompted her to add: "Ma'am."

After the children returned to the kitchen, Nora told Daleen: "As I was saying . . . besides, the stadium property had passed two professional environmental inspections since 1991, including one this year." She let out a tight laugh. "And then—talk of the obvious!—there was your beautiful, *thriving* garden in front of my very eyes."

Daleen laughed, "Well, yes. I am lucky with the garden now. But not lucky at first, when nothing would grow. Not even weeds!"

"That's odd," said Nora, her brow furrowing. "How did you turn things around?"

"I wish to claim, by my gardening skills. But no. I had luck only after they started replacing soil in my garden. Then my vegetables began to grow. Unfortunately, so did the weeds!"

"Wow, that's . . . amazing! And how nice that someone would do that."

"Yes. Even now, they continue to add new soil and compost."

"Who is this 'they'?"

The children reappeared with Daleen's water. Daleen smiled and said: "Yusra, Dr. Nora wishes to know about the Nice Man who exchanges the dirt in our garden."

Late Afternoon

Jack couldn't believe he was driving to the stadium to fulfill a dying— now, dead—man's last request. It seemed so noir and beyond-duty, but also the right thing to do. At least delivering the message—cryptic as it was, "Time to bingo"—shouldn't require more than ten, twenty minutes tops. Unless . . . "Oh, fuck!" he shouted, realizing the girlfriend was likely unaware that Pete had died. *No! I can't be the one to tell her!* He considered turning away but couldn't; the urgency of the request and his promise to fulfill it—as well as the threat of "blood" on his hands—held sway.

He continued cursing as a verbal catharsis while proceeding onto 4th. And that's when he saw it: the Nice Lady's station wagon that had spooked Yusra! He slowed down to confirm that its license plate included the numbers he'd committed to memory: 8 and 5. Then he wrote down the remainder of the plate and considered calling the police. But sundown was approaching, Nora was waiting at the house, and he was about to deliver painful news to Pete's girlfriend. So, he decided to prioritize his original mission and then hightail it home. But the stadium gate was padlocked, and someone other than Red was standing guard.

~ ~ ~

Meanwhile, in Jack's living room, Yusra was trying to discern what her mother *really* wanted her to tell Nora about the Nice Man who exchanged their garden soil. She'd always been told to maintain strict secrecy about their lives. And, more recently, she'd determined on her own that her mother misunderstood the meaning of "nice." But to raise that now would only embarrass her mother in front of the doctor. Hoping she wasn't about to fail her mother's expectations, she told Nora: "The Nice Man takes our old dirt away from the garden and he gives us new dirt."

Nora smiled uncertainly. "That's interesting."

After checking her mother's expression and receiving a supportive nod, Yusra continued, "Yes. He digs up the dirt and puts it in his truck. Then he fills the holes with dirt from bags."

Daleen wrapped an arm around Yusra and added, "I do not pretend to understand him. He does the same thing in other areas of the camp, too; not only our garden. Takes dirt, gives dirt. We do not question him or the other Nice People who run the camp. It is always better for us that way."

Luis eagerly offered, "I met the Nice Man! His name is Gianni. He's Red's best friend! And he doesn't like lettuce or tomato on his hamburger."

Hearing the Nice Man spoken of within the context of friendship with Red, Yusra's eyes widened, opening to the possibility of seeing that the Nice Man might be, as her mother had deemed, actually "nice."

Nora's eyes widened, too—for a different reason. A new pattern was developing from threads of information provided by Daleen, Yusra, and Luis. *No vegetables, and no weeds . . . but then, ta-da!—vegetables and weeds. Soil removed, but soil put back in.*

Daleen asked, "What are you thinking that makes you smile like this?"

Nora held Daleen's gaze for an overlong moment. Then she said, "Yogurt fava, clam lettuce, bag door, box back."

~ ~ ~

Red was kissing DeeDee an umpteenth time when Jack phoned, requesting help getting through the stadium gate. But Red was learning about DeeDee's life. Her estranged family and upbringing in Cleveland. Her best friend dying in grade school. Her recent boring job as a receptionist at the hospital's research institute. And he was longing to hear more, *everything* about her. He wanted to experience this being-in-love for as long as possible, before pressing circumstances might endanger everything. He asked Jack, "Why?"

He replied, "I need to talk with someone inside."

"Not a good idea, Dr. Jack. Some bad stuff could be going down there tonight. You should get outta there *immediately*."

"Believe me, I wish I could. But I promised to deliver a message."

"To who?"

"Can't say. It's confidential, involving a patient. Can't you just tell the two *gentlemen* here to let me in?"

Red sighed. "It's complicated. And risky. Look, just wait for me. I'll be there in ten."

Moments later, when Gianni saw Red descending the staircase from DeeDee's apartment, he knew something was wrong. He put aside his Betty's special and asked, "What's up, pal?"

Red zipped up his jacket. "I gotta be somewhere for a quick minute. And you got a sesame seed in your teeth."

"Thanks," said Gianni, picking the seed out. "It must be awfully important if you're trading time with your sweetheart upstairs."

"Someone needs my help. And I owe him big. Please, just don't ask me about it."

Recalling the last propitious time he covered for Red, the decision was easy. Gianni nodded and said, "Be careful."

~ ~ ~

Fred was nearing his home when he received a call from Nora. "Hello," he cheerily answered. "Changed your mind about that apology drink tonight?"

Nora brusquely returned, "Where are you?"

"Oh? Well, almost home. But doesn't matter. I'm happy to drive back to Grady's."

"We need to talk about the soil samples."

He groaned. "C'mon. I apologized, you apologized. Let's move on."

"No. Those samples we took—"

"The samples *you* took."

"Fine. Listen. *I* took those samples from places where *clean* soil had been *planted.*"

"Hold on. How would you even know such a thing?"

"Because I told Daleen and Yusra where I'd collected them. They're positive I took them from spots where a 'Nice Man' removed dirt that he replaced with clean soil. And Luis said the man was a friend of Red's named Gianni."

Fred pulled over and switched off the ignition. "You're claiming you sampled healthy soil."

"Yes. And that's why the tests came back clean."

He withdrew his bronchodilator from the glove compartment. "Fishy. Where are you going with this?"

"Well, to the stadium. To get new samples. Legitimate samples. And hopefully, with you, *now.*"

Recalling their recent fraught foray there, he said, "Why not go with Jack if you feel compelled to go now? You're already at his house for dinner, right?"

"Yes, but he's been delayed by some patient emergency. Please! I need help with this. And before you ask, Fergie doesn't have the car tonight—"

"But can't you wait 'til tomorrow?"

"No, because the testing takes several days. And you told me the stadium deal closes on Friday."

Fred internally revisited his anxiety about offending Samantha should she become aware of his collaboration with Nora's dogged investigation. He tried dissuasion again: "But what makes you confident you'd know where to take 'legitimate' samples this time around?"

"Because this time, Daleen is coming with us. She can point out sites that she's never seen rigged. And her being with us should preclude anyone's suspicion about our presence there."

Switching on the ignition, and turning back toward Jack's house, he said, "Nora, I expect this to pay off my entire penance to you."

Law Offices, Palmer & Webley

Trestle Glen District, Oakland

"Samantha's office has been calling all afternoon," said Deshawn Palmer. He poured two snifters of brandy and carried them to his desk.

"I'm not surprised," said Quentin, clinking glasses with Deshawn. "I suspect even *she* can tell that her perfect little world is crumbling." He removed one of the flash drives from his coat pocket and set it on the desk. "The stadium data—it's all here—tax evasion and employment fraud writ large. You'll receive the original documents after noon tomorrow, including signed statements from our two witnesses: Gianni Moretti and Douglas O'Brien aka 'Red.'"

Deshawn took the drive. "Thanks. This is great. I should also thank you for rescuing our firm from signing with Greeley Enterprises. It came rather close."

"Yes, well, the place is quite the snake pit."

Regarding him curiously, Deshawn said: "As you know, I had dinner with Samantha on Saturday. And, well, she didn't seem *that* horrible to me. But you seem to *deeply* dislike her."

"Your point?"

"Okay, then. It's hard for me to believe you're abruptly turning against Greeley Enterprises because of sudden misgivings about tax evasion and financial irregularities."

While sipping his brandy, Quentin measured a response. Finally, he said: "Very astute of you. It is more complicated. Taking care of the Greeleys has been my life for near as many years as you've been alive."

"This case is the case of a lifetime for me. I'm aware of the enormous gift you're giving my firm. You're even providing two witnesses on a silver platter, and extensive documentation! I'm confident my firm will provide the legal muscle you need to carry these allegations to the end zone."

"Glad to hear that. I'm counting on you to stay in the game until we win."

"Of course! You have more than an iron-clad contract with our firm. You have my word. And, as your personal attorney as well, it'll be easy to keep you apprised of developments in the Greeley saga." He buzzed-in his assistant and asked her to start printing out documents from the flash drive. After she left, he told Quentin: "But you still haven't answered my question about Samantha."

Quentin stood up and walked to the aquarium in the middle of the office. "You have some beautiful fish here. Rats were the only wildlife I ever had in my law office."

"Metaphorically? Or figuratively?"

"Both," said Quentin, staring at the fish. "Tell me. Are you familiar with the term 'lethal control'?"

"No. Not that I recall, at least."

"A good lawyerly answer!" Quentin returned to the desk and held out his snifter for a second pour. "It's about controlling wildlife populations when they get out of hand or become undesirable. Using lethal methods, like fishing or hunting, to keep the numbers down."

Glancing nervously at his fish, Deshawn asked, "Should I be concerned?"

"You're funny. But no, not about them."

Deshawn shifted uncomfortably in his chair.

"I was discussing lethal control with a friend the other day," said Quentin, with a slightly bemused expression. "And he was deeply offended by the concept. A vegetarian, naturally. But the point is: he *felt* something about it. He held a *moral* viewpoint about it. And throughout his life, he'd made ethically consistent choices about not fishing or hunting or trapping; about not eating meat. But me? It's funny. I never once thought to question it. I'd join Bert Greeley on hunting expeditions as a means to an end, hoping to gain his favor and advance up the corporate ladder."

"Sorry," said Deshawn, "I'm not getting your point."

"Not your fault. I'm being discursive. But the same day I had that conversation with my friend, I also happened to meet Gianni Moretti—one of our two witnesses. And while we were talking, I suddenly realized he was the son of a man I badly betrayed many years ago. The point being, that made me feel—actually *feel*—a sting of conscience. Thank god it was fleeting. But it made me wonder why anyone, like my morally minded friend, chooses to live life vulnerable to such stinging disturbances."

An indecisive smile appeared on Deshawn's face.

Quentin put his snifter down and looked directly into Deshawn's eyes. "You inquired about my problem with Samantha. Well, then. Here we go . . . I may have done some 'sketchy' things while running Greeley Enterprises with Bert. But I put aside any so-called moral qualms about them in order to achieve great things: a massive real estate empire, a Fortune 500 business, hotels and golf courses all over the world. But Bert and I did the work that was necessary to make it all happen. And we let our hands get dirty in the process. So, to be terminated from Greeley Enterprises by some woman who never lifted one of her well-manicured fingers to build anything . . . To see her *triumphant smile* during my humiliation and ruin . . . To watch her and my treasonous son *claim all the rewards,* with no respect or understanding of what Bert and I had to do . . ."

Deshawn sat rigid, unblinking.

"Sorry," said Quentin, reeling back his anger. "But I'm putting all my cards on the table now. I gave you this 'case of a lifetime' and asked you to be my personal attorney because I wanted to preempt your firm's imminent engagement with Samantha Greeley."

"Yes, you made that strategy clear when you first called," Deshawn stammered. "You also convinced me Greeley Enterprises was a can of worms; no, a 'snake pit.'"

Disappointed with Deshawn's fainthearted reaction, Quentin hesitated about handing over his second flash drive. He wasn't convinced Deshawn was capable of the outrage required to destroy Greeley Enterprises, all legal expertise aside. Recalling Samantha's disparaging remarks to himself, he pushed: "To take down Greeley Enterprises, you'll need more than 'fresh legal thinking' or 'modern insights into the law.' You'll need a deep moral understanding of their crimes to burn with the passion this case requires."

"Hey," said Deshawn, "that's awfully radical. But . . . seriously, take them down? Don't get me wrong. As a law-abiding taxpayer, I'm offended whenever wealthy corporations evade tax—"

"'Offended'?" Quentin scoffed. "I need a lawyer who's biting at the bit to launch a ruthless offense. What must I do to ignite your fire over this case?" *Indeed, what's the carrot here? I don't have enough time to engage another firm.*

"I'm just not sharing your perspective, Quentin."

Privately, Quentin bristled with the irony: *How am I ending up with some soft lawyer who needs to "share" a perspective?* After furtively popping an antacid while Deshawn looked momentarily away, he said: "All right, then. Listen to this. The Greeleys paid impoverished people—homeless people, migrants—next to *nothing* to perform dangerous and dehumanizing forced labor. They moved those people around to construction and demolition sites, hazardous dumps, fields and farms. Sometimes, just to drive down property values so the Greeleys could buy properties on the cheap. The Greeleys took advantage of people's desperation and profited handsomely! They should be criminally prosecuted for the economic human trafficking!" He took a deep breath, pleased by his performative rage; to himself, it sounded rather convincing.

With a doubtful expression, Deshawn replied, "Well, I understand and share that sentiment. But we both know those business practices are commonplace, if despicable. We both know the shadow economy is enormous and vibrant. Labor trafficking is nothing new. It's difficult to prosecute employers for—"

Quentin slapped his second flash drive onto the desk. Deshawn asked, "What's this?"

"Part two of your 'case of a lifetime,'" said Quentin.

"But didn't you just give me all the tax and financial—"

"This is different," said Quentin, tapping a finger against the drive, hammering out each charge: "Environmental crimes. Soil-testing fraud and data falsification to cover up contaminated properties. Human endangerment. Real estate fraud. Harboring illegals. Exploiting migrants. And, like I said, human labor trafficking."

Staring thunderstruck at Quentin, Deshawn finally managed, "What the hell? And *other* kinds of human trafficking? Sex trafficking? Debt bondage? Women and children—?"

"I wouldn't know," said Quentin. "I've stayed focused on Greeley business and real estate."

Deshawn's stomach flipped. He wondered what was happening—and whether he truly wanted to know. "We . . . we talked about obtaining immunity for you; but over tax evasion, labor abuse, and shareholder fraud. You're already courting legal and ethical violations by leaking the Greeleys' business crimes and coming to us for representation. But now . . . hell . . . you're telling me about flagrantly criminal federal offenses?"

Quentin grabbed the drive and returned it to his pocket, smelling fear and retreat in Deshawn's reaction. *If this boy scout is that freaked out and afraid of compromising himself . . . if he notifies authorities or calls the police on me . . . I'll never get my chance at a grand finale.*

Deshawn asked, "What are you doing?"

"Leaving," said Quentin, retrieving his fedora, heading for the door. He'd protectively hold onto the second drive for now, maybe adding it to the document box that Gianni would be delivering here tomorrow.

"Show me that 'part two' now!" Deshawn demanded, his fist thudding on the desk.

Now reassured of Deshawn's capacity for rage, Quentin stopped at the door and secretively smiled. He then turned to Deshawn and said, "You'll see it in due time. When you do, know that I won't give a damn what you think about me. But I will expect you to work with prosecutors to see Samantha punished to the fullest extent. And I want my son made accountable for his complicity with Greeley crimes."

"Is that all?" Deshawn sarcastically shot back. "Maybe you'd like a coke with that?"

Old Stadium Site

West Oakland

Winston followed Marla's directions to the green bus belonging to the Boudreaux sisters. They were sitting outside, smoking weed. "Hi," he said, "Marla sent me. My name's Winston Wang. I'm a journalist with the *Oakland Register.*"

The ostensibly older sister, Vero, replied: "Well, we're here, honey. Been waiting on you."

He withdrew his cellphone and said, "Thanks for agreeing to speak with me."

Ruthie, the younger Boudreaux—and obviously pregnant—grabbed his cell and said, "Uh-uh. No pictures. No recording."

Winston held out his hand. "Okay. But, want to return my cell?"

"No," she said. "I'll hold onto it 'til we're done. We trust Marla. But we don't know you, got me?"

"Hey!" Vero exclaimed, pointing to somewhere behind Winston. "Look who's here!"

Red approached and was taken by surprise to see Winston. He said, "I recognize you from the Thanksgiving cookout at the lake."

Winston nodded. "Hello, Red."

Ruthie Boudreaux put an arm around Red. "Winston's gonna interview us and make us famous!" Vero kissed his cheek and said, "Where you been, baby?"

"Hanging at Betty's tonight, waiting on whatever happens next," Red said, declining their offer of a joint. "I just thought I'd stop by and check on my favorite sisters."

Ruthie said, "You're so full of shit! Truth—why are you here?"

"I had to sneak a friend inside for a visit. I'm just waiting on him to finish so I can take him back out."

"Who's he visiting?"

"Don't know. He made me drop him off near the D-lot. Said it was a 'patient' thing."

"Oh?" said Winston. "So, a doctor or nurse?"

"You know him," said Red. "Dr. Jack, who was with us at the lake." He then turned to the Boudreauxs, pointed to their bus, and said, "I like what you did with the sign." They had spray-painted a yellow "B" in front of "Riter's Day Care" and blacked out some letters to make it read: "BRiter Day."

Vero laughed and said, "You know we're always about trying to make things 'brighter' for everybody. But you're looking down, Red."

"Yeah, well . . . You heard about Patty's plan?"

Ruthie said, "Everyone knows about that now. It's sick! But we're prepared, thanks to you and your friend Gianni. You think Patty might try to do her evil here tonight?"

Red shrugged. "Don't know how. I was told she wasn't here. Then we padlocked the gate, and the Cousins have been guarding it since."

Winston, his head spinning, said, "What 'plan'? Who's 'Patty'? And what's Jack doing here?"

"So many questions," tsk'ed Vero Boudreaux. "But you're supposed to be focusing on me and my sister." She turned to Red and said, "And thanks for all those goodies you dropped off today. So nice!"

"Well, me and Gianni just delivered them. The lawyer who works for the owner of this place bought everything. Even the padlocks."

Vero's eyes narrowed. "That makes no sense. If sicko Patty's trying to throw us out so the owner can sell this place, why would the owner's lawyer be helping *us*?"

"Yeah," said Winston, "why would Greeleys' lawyer—?"

"Because me and Gianni are helping *him* out," said Red. "He wants to set things straight about shit that's been going down here a long while. Matter of fact, he's who told us about Patty's plan. But we had demands of our own. Like, him making sure Patty wasn't here so we could drop off those supplies today."

"No way," said Ruthie, shaking her head. "That lawyer doesn't sound straight-up one bit."

~ ~ ~

Alex had tracked the journalist to the Boudreauxs' green bus, and peered out from behind a stash of car tires, straining to hear his conversation with the two women. A red-haired man soon joined the threesome: *It's the guy who drove the white truck through the gate!* Then he faintly heard vigorous knocking that sounded from another direction, and a man's insistent claim: "I know you're inside." Alex snuck closer to see a tall blond man knocking on a beige camper door. Now he was torn: *Pursue the journalist or the blond man?* But the answer declared itself when the man at the camper said, "Patty Dobrovski? I'm here for Pete Vaughn."

Jack's Home

Rockridge District

While Daleen gathered plastic containers from Jack's kitchen, Nora phoned Lizbeth and explained why she was returning to the stadium to collect new soil samples. Then she asked Lizbeth whether she could deliver them to UC Davis in the morning "again."

"Of course," said Lizbeth. "And if it's convenient, you can drop them off here tonight." Aditya grabbed the phone and said, "Nora, I overheard what you told Lizbeth. I want to say how sorry I am for not even considering the possibility of false-negative tests. I should have trusted your diagnostic instincts and been more open-minded."

Nora said, "There's no need—"

"But there is," he insisted. "My competition with you has only made me foolish. May I ask, though, why you suspect they might have been false negatives?"

"Well, Daleen and Yusra provided the clue. They spoke about a man who'd been swapping out soil at the stadium—and precisely where I'd collected my samples." Her heart sunk with the weight of her suspicions about the man named Gianni who'd won the affections of Red and Luis. "So, I realize it's a longshot . . . but that made me wonder whether Epitome's sampling in 1991 and 2018 could've been performed where soil had been exchanged, too."

"But the stadium property is 170 acres, Nora. How could one man have planted enough clean soil to cover all the possible locations where Epitome would choose to sample?"

He's right, she thought. *That's not possible. But my choice of where to sample was motivated by concern for Daleen. Could Epitome have been somehow "motivated" where to sample, too?*

After a prolonged pause, Aditya said, "Nora?"

"Sorry," she said. "It's just occurring to me how . . ."

"Is there something I can do to help?"

"As a matter of fact, yes. Could you review all the environmental inspections—from '89, '91, and 2018—and text me ASAP the precise locations where soil and water were sampled each time?"

After receiving Aditya's enthused "Yes!" Nora bid goodbye to Yusra and Luis. Then she and Daleen got into her Prius, and, with its engine running, they waited for Fred to arrive and hop in.

Old Stadium Site

West Oakland

Alex saw the tall blond man enter the beige camper. Then he snuck up to it and pressed an ear against its door, trying to hear the conversation inside. At first, all he heard was keening: *A woman's voice; it must be Patty's.* Then short bursts of sobbing alternating with fragile silences. She then several times insisted "He can't be dead," each time followed with the man responding, "I'm sorry." Finally, a stable silence prevailed. Then the man said, "Pete asked me to deliver a message."

Alex held his breath and pressed harder against the door. But his cellphone unexpectedly rang. He fumbled to silence its ringer as the couple inside shouted "Who's there?" and the headlights of Nora's Prius caught him. Then the camper door flung open, hit him in the head, and knocked him over.

Jack appeared in the doorway, visibly on edge, and saw Alex on the ground. Simultaneously, he saw Nora approaching, with Fred and Daleen trailing behind. His jaw dropped, then he called out, "Nora?"

Alex unsteadily stood up, surrounded now by four strangers. Jack demanded, "Who are you? What are you doing here?"

"Wait," he replied, checking his forehead for bleeding. Turning to Nora, he asked: "Did I hear right? You're 'Nora'?"

"We'll be asking the questions!" said Fred.

But Alex persisted: "Nora Kelly, right? And your laptop is missing?"

Fred moved toward him, assuming him to be the thief who'd inflicted so much grief on Nora and his own family. But Nora intervened: "No, Fred! He's not the guy who stole it. The thief was bigger. And he had a ponytail."

Though his forehead badly ached, Alex couldn't suppress a grin. *Now, this is definitely interesting and exciting.*

"What's so funny?" Nora fumed.

"Nothing," he replied, trying to tame his odd excitement. "My name's Alex Morales." He opened his wallet and displayed his ID. "I'm a P.I. The guy with your laptop is named Marty Ocambo."

Her voice trembling, Nora asked, "Who's he? And why did he break into my house?"

Fred was guilt-stricken, witnessing Nora's distress and considering his less-than-empathic support. *And,* he worried, *is what's happening now going to trigger her again?*

Alex answered, "Marty Ocambo is the inept, narcissistic, untrustworthy, psychopathic boy-child of the Greeleys' main lawyer—Quentin Ocambo. He's also the grifter boyfriend of Samantha Greeley, who owns this place. But why he B&E'd your house to steal your laptop? I was hoping *you* could tell *me.*"

"Nora," said Fred, "remember that stocky fellow with Samantha the day we came here? Could he be this 'Marty'?"

Nora braced herself and looked away, struggling to break through her defensive resistance to remembering that night. *Both were big men . . . Same body habitus . . . The man with Samantha had his hair pulled back, so maybe a ponytail, too?* Looking back at Fred, she said, "Maybe." Then she told Alex: "He also stole a document from my home, listing where I'd collected soil samples here . . ." She stopped, stepped back, and said, "Wait. We don't know you. We've no reason to trust you."

Patty, overhearing the conversation outside and assured of Marty's absence, emerged from the camper. Sniffling, her face swollen, she managed to say, "Alex is a good guy. Pete said he was a man of his word." She nodded respectfully to Alex, seeing him for the first time.

Alex nodded back. "So, *you're* Patty Dobrovski. The one holding the fort here."

But Nora pointed at her and said, "You're the woman who chased me away!"

Daleen said, "Actually, she is the Nice Lady."

"What?" Jack exclaimed, staring wide-eyed at Patty. *The woman who kidnapped Yusra? But why is Daleen so calm?*

Daleen continued, "Still, I do not know why she is in my home. And, Dr. Jack, your presence here is also surprising."

Patty collapsed into Jack's uncertain embrace while Nora looked questioningly at him. He began to explain: "I came here to deliver a message to this Nice . . . to Patty."

"In person?" asked Fred, incredulous. "Now?"

"It's confidential," said Jack. "Concerning . . . a patient."

Patty lamented, "He came . . . to tell me . . . my Pete died."

"Wow," said Alex, stuck on surprise. "Pete's dead?"

Nora shot him a disapproving look. Then Daleen walked up to Patty and said, "I'm sorry. You two always looked happy together."

Patty smiled feebly. "Good to see you looking well, Daleen. You were awfully blue and sick when I took you to the ER."

"So, that was you," said Daleen. "I was too sick to remember anything. But thank you. I would not have survived otherwise."

Jack felt his rigid judgment against the Nice Lady begin to bend. Still, he needed to ask her: "What happened between you and Yusra?"

Patty moaned, faced Daleen, and confessed: "I'm sorry! I didn't know what to do with Yusra while you were in the hospital. Tomas was too sick to care for her. My god, I tried . . . I took her to a motel. But then I lost her! I looked everywhere, and couldn't find her. I still don't know where she's at."

Daleen's eyes widened. "But Yusra is fine. She is with me now."

Acutely disburdened of guilt, Patty felt the coiled tension in her body violently release. And now, without the safety-net prospect of a future with Pete, she felt herself falling, falling, falling . . . dropping out of the grim life into which she'd been born, bereft of possibility.

Meanwhile, Alex looked on, privately sorting his observations like puzzle pieces: *So Patty was here after all, though I told Quentin otherwise . . . Pete Vaughn died; I doubt Quentin knows that yet . . . But this also means Pete's taken his secrets with Quentin to his grave, unless . . .* He glanced at Patty: *Unless Pete confided in her about them.* Then, looking at Nora: *And this doctor spoke about collecting soil samples here . . . I saw on her office computer that she'd emailed someone, asking about falsification of soil testing . . . And if Marty stole her home laptop . . . Hell, this Dr. Kelly is definitely on the scent of something rotten happening here.*

After collecting herself, Patty thanked Daleen "for the accommodations," explaining she "just needed a safe place to hide for the night." Then she handed back the key to the camper, dried her eyes, and announced to everyone: "I need alone time now. I'm sure you understand." She ambled off, a limp to her gait, and headed toward her car.

Still, Alex's antennae were buzzing. He needed to find out if Patty knew about Quentin's secret dealings with Pete. "Wait up," he said, starting after her.

But Fred reproached Alex with: "Give her time to grieve, man. Her partner just died." And Nora actually stopped him with an arresting claim: "You're the only person who hasn't explained his presence here."

Alex halted, again torn between competing pursuits: either interrogating Patty, or staying to answer to—and question—Nora. His cell rang again—a second call from old man Greeley's office.

The Greeley Foundation Building

Lakeside Drive

Samantha slammed down the receiver: the P.I. wasn't picking up *again*, though he'd served at the beck and call of Quentin and her father! Palmer & Webley was standing her up. The irresponsible absenteeism of her in-house counsel today. And Quentin's infuriating antics! *The disrespect! The rudeness! So flagrantly unprofessional and disloyal, all of them!*

And, as always, Marty—bumbling, incompetent Marty, whose bad-boy swagger was proving to be nothing more than beefy bluster. She'd been foolish to hope he could take care of business in the background, like Quentin had. Even now, in this time of her need, he was nowhere to be found. *He's probably drunk in his stupid office. It's probably the only thing he ever does there.* She eyed her father's pistol in the desk drawer and—

Juliana appeared and fretfully announced the unexpected arrival of the police. Detective Darinda Johnson asked, "Ms. Greeley—do you know where Martin Ocambo is?" Samantha barely suppressed a laugh and asked why. Darinda answered, "We have him on video, attempting a break-in at his father's house and threatening to kill him." Her partner Tom added, "The *second* time today he's threatened to kill somebody."

The detectives left with Samantha's promise that she'd notify them should she hear from Marty. But, when alone again, she began pacing with rage. *I should've told them to look in his stupid caveman office! Why should I protect the bastard?* She took two oxycodone and a bourbon to wash them down.

Some vague time later, Juliana returned. "Just checking on you, Sam. It's been a rough day. And, did you decide about rescheduling Friday's signing with Highmark Construction?"

Samantha said, "It's late. Just go home."

"You sound . . . funny. A bad migraine?"

"Yeah. A bad migraine."

After Juliana departed, Samantha walked unsteadily to the vacant lobby. She bitterly envisioned the smug expression on Quentin's face when he'd been here earlier, bidding Juliana to inform her of his illicit presence. *But why was he here? And why did he need me to know that? By security's account, he stole nothing . . . He was here for only two minutes . . . He walked toward the restrooms . . .*

Samantha shook her head, trying to clear its boozy fog. *Okay, think . . . Whatever he was up to, he accomplished it within a two-minute roundtrip walk from this desk.* She pressed the timer on her cell and set out to re-create his probable route. Walking toward the restrooms, she searched the hallway for evidence of his treachery. But nothing appeared to be missing from the display cabinets . . . the floating shelves and console tables . . . the wall coverings—

She stopped cold. Her mind momentarily blanked. There was, she realized, a framed photograph of herself that newly hung on the wall. And she knew. *Quentin didn't take anything from Greeley Enterprises; he snuck something inside.*

It was brilliant—she had to give him that—to hang something so inconspicuous that no one else would find it remarkable being here. *No one, of course, but me.*

She recognized the photo, taken from an *Oakland Register* article about the pending sale of the stadium property. *So, you're furious with me for dismissing you over the deal. But you were flagrantly negligent in its oversight! What was I supposed to do, Quentin? Besides, Marty told me about you losing your marbles.*

She shakily took down the photo, and an envelope from the back fell to the floor. She read the letter inside:

Dear Samantha,

This letter serves notice of my resignation from Greeley Enterprises, effective November 26, 2018.

I wish I were resigning under more optimal circumstances, and with the dignity usually afforded a career-long employee who loyally served—and helped create—a family dynasty such as yours. Still, I will admit, leaving Greeley Enterprises with your strong-armed encouragement is proving liberating for me. Though it may sound counterintuitive, your complicity with my son's fevered drive to destroy me has been a gift; for it has finally freed me from any sense of duty or obligation toward him. I sincerely hope—and I intend to see—that each of you gets what you deserve.

In that regard, concerning you, I feel you deserve to know.

You deserve to know about the widespread corruption within Greeley Enterprises over which you titularly reign. You've profited enormously from the family businesses, all the while insisting upon your blissful ignorance about them. But now I rip off your blinders.

You also deserve to know *that you can no longer afford your seeming indifference about business operations, because no amount of money or well-paid minions can protect you from the revelations I've put in play over the ensuing days that will force your accountability in a most public way.*

Frankly, I believe you've more than suspected the systemic corruption—yet just enough so that you could defensively distance yourself from your father and Greeley businesses. Enough so to always claim you didn't care to know what was in the trough from which you've lavishly feasted. And enough so to use people—like me, Pete Vaughn, and my foolish son—to carry out your will and the company's dirty work in the shadows, so all the while you could make believe your hands were clean.

But the pretense ends now. I've apprised my new attorneys at Palmer & Webley about rampant criminal activities at Greeley Enterprises. (Yes, I preemptively hired them out from under you after your unwitting heads-up to me over the phone.) I've provided them with evidentiary support for my whistleblower claims that will force you to account for the malignant underpinnings of Greeley real estate operations. I've provided evidence about corporate fraud and tax evasion that will be shared with federal and state agencies. Suffice it to say, the evidence against Greeley Enterprises is ample and stomach-turning; even the small taste I shared with your in-house counsel today gave them cause to call in sick.

You will perhaps assume that my actions are motivated primarily by revenge. After all, you certainly dishonored and disrespected me. And you cast me aside in choosing to ally with my sociopathic son. But that assumption wouldn't be correct.

Instead, it is shame that primarily motivates me. I've not been able to forget about Thanksgiving, when we last saw each other in your library and discussed the stadium sale. Since then, I've been haunted by the cold triumphant look on your face when you informed me about your liaison with Martin. And while I believe you didn't understand at the time that your anger toward me was manufactured by his lies, still, you knew the news would sever my relationship with him. And that is my shame—that it was you, not me, who wielded the power to finally free me of my son.

My shame in that matter aside, you may inform Martin that I concede defeat in this particular battle. But also tell him that the war between us remains his to lose.

Sincerely,

Quentin Ocambo, JD

PS: Although, as written, I'm not "primarily" interested in revenge, I do maintain a strong secondary interest in it.

PPS: The accompanying photo of you will fit perfectly with those of your family on the library wall.

Old Stadium Site

West Oakland

Because Quentin had told him Patty wasn't at the stadium, Red was startled to see her limping past the Boudreauxs' bus. And how sad and feeble she looked, deflated of her bloated self-importance. She certainly didn't appear to be marshaling forces to clear the stadium out. *Still, what's she doing here?* Then it dawned on him: *She's coming from where I dropped off Dr. Jack. So, it's her he must've come to visit! Yeah, and with a message from "a patient"—so, from someone in prison, like her boyfriend.*

He excused himself to Winston and the sisters, and hurried back to the D-lot, where he and Jack had arranged to meet up. Jack was arriving simultaneously, and he greeted Red: "Mission accomplished. I was about to text you."

Red said, "So, you delivered your confidential message?"

Jack nodded. "And it was wild. Least of which, because Nora, Fred, and Daleen showed up. Hey, come back there with me to say hello."

"Why are they here?" Red asked fretfully. When Jack merely shrugged, Red charged, "You're keeping secrets from me!"

"I'm not! It's just . . . I don't want to involve you."

"Seriously? 'Involve me'? I'm so fuckin' involved already, I can't be no more involved!"

"Hey, take it easy. It's going to be okay."

"No, it's not! I'm up to my eyeballs in shit! I'm drowning in it! I got a lawyer breathing down my back. I'm trying to help people who need it in the worst way. I ain't got a job or a place to live anymore. And Luis, little man . . . Then, I fall in love, and I know I'm going to fuck everything up with her. Oh, god . . ." He doubled over, heaving.

Jack held Red tight, surprised to be feeling so paternal toward him. And he didn't let go whenever Red halfheartedly pushed him away.

~ ~ ~

Meanwhile, Nora and Fred were sampling soil under Daleen's guidance. Daleen targeted some sites where she'd tried, unsuccessfully, to help fellow residents grow vegetables; others, too, that were predictably associated with children developing odd rashes and diarrhea. Nora collected additional samples near Luis' orange tent. All the while, Alex kept offering to help, but Nora remained cautious and declined; if it weren't for wanting to retrieve her laptop afterwards, she would've asked him to leave.

When Jack returned to their company with Red, Nora noticed that Red's eyes were swollen, and Jack appeared subdued. She asked, "What's wrong?"

Red had difficulty looking into her tender eyes. He blurted out, "We shouldn't be here. There's nothing but disaster brewing. I only came because Dr. Jack needed in, to bring his message to Patty, who—"

"Oh," said Nora, hoping to slow him down. "You know Patty?"

Having just listened to Red's abbreviated version of his complex predicament, Jack answered: "He's been working for her. Apparently, she's planning to eject all the residents here."

"But, honest," said Red, "I didn't know that! She . . . she tried to get me and Gianni to kick everybody out, with nowhere for them to go. God, I almost took her damn money to help her!"

Alerted by his raised voice, Fred, Daleen, and Alex approached. Nora held up her open palm to them, signaling that things were in control.

Then, trying to comfort Red, she told him: "But that hasn't actually happened. The residents are still here."

"It's just a matter of time," Red countered. "Because Patty *was* here—even after the lawyer told us she wasn't! And even after me and Gianni got padlocks for the gate. She's *here,* and she's hellbent on kicking everybody out!"

Nora didn't know where to start: *Lawyer? Padlocks? "Disaster brewing"? And another mention of Gianni's name tonight.* Deciding what Red most immediately required was reassurance over Patty, she said: "I doubt Patty's even thinking about this camp tonight. Because Jack just informed her that her boyfriend died, and she seemed very upset by the news."

"And," said Jack, recalling where he'd spotted Patty's car on the street, "she headed off in the direction of her car. So, she's probably gone."

Red wasn't appeased. With a doubtful look, he asked Jack: "You said you came to bring a message to Patty. But why is everyone else here?"

Nora said, "Well, I'm here because I think this property remains contaminated by the pesticide factory that stood here before the stadium. I think people are getting sick, dying even, from residual toxic chemicals. And one problem is . . . this friend of yours, 'Gianni.' We learned tonight he's also the 'Nice Man' who replaces dirt with clean soil here. And I believe that's why the soil I recently tested came back clean." She startled when Red clenched his fists, his face reddening.

Fred tried to turn down the heat, calmly explaining: "And Daleen and I are helping Nora collect soil from places not known to be rigged."

"'Rigged'?" shouted Red. "You gotta be joking! Gianni would *never* do that. You don't know him!"

"Sorry!" said Fred. "Didn't mean to—"

Red punched the air and asked Nora, "You think Gianni's some kind of fortune teller? You think he could've predicted where you were gonna take your damn samples? Besides, it's not even him that decides where he swaps dirt anyway!"

Remembering Quentin's mention of having met "Gianni Moretti," Alex barged in: "Are you referring to Gianni Moretti?"

"Who the fuck are you?" said Red.

Jack focused his gaze on Alex and said, "He told us he was a P.I. searching for Patty, right?"

Alex remained silent, realizing he didn't want to overtly lie to these seemingly well-intentioned people. But Nora sensed his evasiveness and said, "And yet, you didn't follow her when she left."

"Well," he stalled, internally groping for a plausible but honest excuse. "Fred was right about her needing to grieve. I can track her down tomorrow."

Nora eyed him suspiciously. "Okay. Then explain how your search for her relates to your knowing about my stolen laptop." In unison, her friends looked expectantly at him. He hesitantly replied, "They're *separate* jobs."

Stepping up to him, she said, "No. Too much of a coincidence. And you've been awfully eager to help us tonight."

Her physical closeness caused his mind to blank momentarily. Then he said, "Because you all just seem genuinely well-intentioned about this place and the people living here."

She shook her head. "Your interests *are* connected. There's common ground—in the fact of you being here now, you pursuing the woman managing this camp, and your interest in my stolen laptop. That common ground is the *actual* ground we're standing on now. So, one obvious question that comes to mind: Were you coordinating with Patty to rig soil testing here? Do you know the location of my stolen laptop because *you* stole it?"

"No!" he said with offense, stepping back, and trying to keep confidential his professional services for Quentin and the Greeleys. But under the intense glare of everyone's suspicions, he already felt exposed. Besides, this woman, Nora, was putting a human face on Marty's break-in and theft. A redheaded man was suffering over the mistreatment of the encampment residents. And a resident named Daleen was embodying toxic effects of a potential environmental scam. Feeling no loyalty to Quentin now, he exhaled dramatically and said: "It's time for me to give up the ghost." But, seeing Nora's expression turn quizzical, he realized he'd just blurted out a private joke under duress. He quickly appended, "I mean, *me*. I'm the P.I. who's ghosted for the Greeleys' main lawyer."

Half in anger, half in fear, Red asked, "You work for Quentin Ocambo?"

"I *did*," said Alex.

Jack asked Red, "Isn't that the lawyer you mentioned who's 'breathing down' your back?"

Red nodded. "He asked me and Gianni to be whistleblowers against Greeley Enterprises. We signed the papers today. He said we got immunity, and we could stop the labor trafficking of people, and them getting screwed."

"So, it is true," said Daleen. "We all knew they were using us. Sometimes they would come in the middle of the night and make us pack up everything to start work somewhere else. And we all knew those places—like this one—were unhealthy. But we were afraid to question the people who let us stay here . . . anywhere they moved us, really." Remembering Yusra's defiant questioning eyes, she privately vowed: *But that won't ever happen again, my daughter.*

Nora pointed accusingly at Alex and said: "You've been *working* for the Greeleys' lawyer? And it just happens that his son stole my laptop?"

"Fishy as all hell," said Fred, now wrestling with fresh doubts about Samantha. "Let's get out of here."

But as everyone turned away, Alex pleaded, "Please, don't go! I can help. I *want* to."

Dusk

After a quick meal at Rigby's, Carl and Fergie drove toward the stadium. Concerned about Fergie's gloomy silence, he said, "Still no answer from Winston?"

"No," she said, worried that Winston was sabotaging their first joint writing venture.

Hoping to distract her, he said: "There's an interesting story about one of the streets bordering the stadium."

"Oh?"

"Yes. Have you heard about Tornwaldt cysts?"

Gianni worried; too much time had elapsed since hearing from Red. And when DeeDee descended the staircase from her apartment, the usual light in her eyes extinguished, he knew she was worried, too. She sat in his booth and asked where Red might be. When he shrugged, she said, "You must have some idea."

Her tender concern for Red amplified his own. "All I know," he offered, "is he had to go somewhere to do somebody a quick favor. I wasn't supposed to ask."

"Well, before he left, he was on the phone with Dr. Jack. And Red told him he'd be 'there' to meet him in ten minutes."

"Where?"

"Wherever it was, it upset Red to know Dr. Jack was there."

Ten minutes away? thought Gianni. *And keeping it secret from me? It's got to be the stadium.*

Old Stadium Site

West Oakland

Jack, Fred, Daleen, and Red were deferring to Nora whether to accept Alex's offer of help. But she hesitated; already she was drowning in a sea of murky facts, struggling to reach the light-filled air above. *Can I trust this man who worked for the Greeleys' lawyer?* But when she scanned her friends' wrought expressions, all eyes on her, she adopted an alternative view: *Maybe I'm operating with an upside-down metaphor. Instead of struggling to swim up toward light, I should be heading to the shipwreck below.* She took a deep breath and pivoted to face Alex: "Why would Quentin Ocambo encourage Red and Gianni to become whistleblowers against the Greeleys? As their lawyer, he's bound to be implicated in any Greeley corporate crimes."

Alex had been anxiously holding his breath. Now relieved that Nora seemed amenable to remain in dialogue by her questioning, he exhaled audibly. "Because Quentin's furious over Samantha Greeley firing him."

Glancing sideways at him, Nora said, "You're suggesting, he's so upset over losing a *job*, that he'd try to take down Greeley Enterprises?"

"And self-incriminate in the process?" said Fred dismissively. "Too fishy."

"It's more than that," said Alex. "Quentin also claimed his moral compass had flipped in some better direction."

"I don't buy that," said Nora. "Morals aren't pancakes. People can't just flip them over." *Unless they're delusional. Or lying.*

"Still," said Alex, "it's Greek tragedy level. Samantha also replaced Quentin with his treasonous son, Marty; and now Marty has Samantha's ear." He regretted his choice of metaphor, but no one seemed to notice. "And *that* happened because Marty duped Samantha into believing Quentin was feeble-minded. But it's for *all* those reasons that Quentin is hell-bent on destroying Marty and Samantha, as well as Greeley Enterprises."

Jack tsk'ed and said, "Retaliation is understandable. But, self-destruction?"

Nora felt the accumulating weight of information driving her deeper toward the wreckage. *Keep diving . . . Tug every line . . . Toss one out to this P.I. to see how he reacts.* She abruptly asked Alex, "Were the environmental inspections of this property fraudulent?"

To everyone's surprise, he outright replied: "I don't know. Maybe."

Fred said, "You're choosing to remain vague, standing next to Ms. Habani, who nearly died—?"

"Wait," Red interrupted. "Ocambo said he paid Gianni's dad and his guys to clean up the stadium a long time ago."

Referring to the documents he'd planted in Marty's office, Alex said, "Well, any cleanup would had to have happened between '89 and '91. Because the original inspection in '89 confirmed this place was a toxic cesspool. Herbicides, fungicides, insecticides, and all the solvents used to manufacture them—they were everywhere. In the soil, the groundwater, and the sediment. But the '91 reinspection stated this place was clean, as did this year's inspection."

"Well," said Nora, "I want to believe that. But too many people are getting sick here. And the surrounding neighborhoods have such unusually high rates of respiratory diseases and cancer . . ." She shook her head in disbelief. "I read those documents, too. That pesticide factory just dumped its wastewater into an underground septic tank and on-site drainfield that had *no containment.* That's why in '89 they found those chemicals off-site, too. Like all along Tornwaldt, where the wastewater discharged into a ditch. The toxins even reached the Bay River—four thousand feet away—through storm drains on this property."

Fred looked angrily away, remembering family members and friends who, because of poverty or skin color, had been forced to live in this toxic blighted neighborhood surrounding the stadium, this so-called fenceline community. *Their early deaths, their chronic heart and lung diseases, their odd cancers . . . several generations who lived near this deadly fenceline. Of course, all the toxins here bled out into their homes, their land, their water. Blatant environmental racism and genocide!* He remembered staying for weeks at a time with his grandparents, who had lived two blocks away in a house jam-packed with oxygen tanks and medication bottles. Then, wondering, too, whether his own asthma had been triggered by his exposure to this place, he blurted out, "But we were told this area was safe to live in!" He abruptly turned to Nora, and they held each other's gaze for a steadying moment.

Daleen, inspired by her daughter's exemplary courage, said: "Well, if this place has been clean since 1991, why must this Gianni *still* be exchanging soil here?"

That's right, Nora thought. *But it also begs Red's question: how Gianni could have predicted where to swap the soil I would happen to test.* Then, while glancing at Red, whose conviction about Gianni was palpable, the answer became obvious: *Gianni wasn't strategically swapping soil around Daleen's camper! He chose those sites to exchange, guided by the same motivation that guided me where to test: we each cared about Daleen and her daughter. Still, it's curious—why does he also swap soil in other locations?*

Red told Daleen, "You gotta believe me. Gianni's a good guy. Me and him snuck in today after the lawyer told us Patty wasn't here, so we could warn everybody about her plan to kick them out. We brought in food and water. Padlocks, too, to keep Patty and her riffraff out. And Gianni told Ocambo that we weren't going to sign his fucking paperwork unless he helped us do all that. *That* was Gianni's 'pre-condition.'"

Nora asked, "Can you be more specific about this 'paperwork,' Red?"

"Me and Gianni signed witness statements about employment fraud and tax evasion—stuff the lawyer says he's confessing to himself. And he made Gianni hand over his invoices. Well, not regular ones. But drawings, like maps, showing where Gianni did jobs here."

"Well," said Alex, *fascinated and excited* to be riding this roller coaster. "That explains the landscaping workmaps I . . . 'discovered' today."

After shooting him a wary look, Nora turned to Red. "You said Gianni didn't decide where to swap soil. So, who does?"

"Don't know. Gianni says some guy calls him on a burner phone, and tells him what to do and where. He's got an English accent. But he pays twice, sometimes three times more than Gianni's regular jobs."

Alex asked, "And in cash, no doubt?" *But who's this English guy? Someone Marty hired to do the work he was too lazy to do himself? Or maybe Quentin had to replace me with two people—him and Marty?*

Red nodded. Nora smiled sympathetically and said, "It sounds like you and Gianni got caught in the eye of a storm." Then, registering the collective fatigue among the group: "Look, it's getting late. Maybe we should call it a night."

"Wait," said Alex. "Aren't you coming with me to retrieve your laptop? Marty's office is just minutes away." He hastily added, "I've shown you my ID. Your friends have met me. Come."

Sensing her conflict, Fred offered: "Well, I'd be happy to drive with you in your car, and we can follow Alex to the office. Then you can take me back to Jack's so I can pick up my car." Jack added, "And Daleen and I can drop off the soil samples with Lizbeth on our way home."

But Nora felt guilty over having *again* upset and inconvenienced her friends. And she was feeling newly emboldened about prying more information out of Alex. "No, thanks," she said, "I'm fine going alone."

The Eastshore Freeway

Oakland

For Marty Ocambo, it was the last straw: being stopped by a patrol officer for the vandalism and failed break-in of his father's house. "C'mon," he pleaded to the cop who'd chased down his fleeing Beemer. "My dad doesn't care. Just ask him."

"I don't think so," she replied. "Driver's license, please."

"But if I don't take care of some important business now, I'll lose *everything.*"

The patrol officer clicked her teeth and surveyed the freshly dented Beemer. "Step out now, hands where I can see them."

But Marty couldn't allow anything to interfere. *Not now. Not after every shit thing I've been through.* And he couldn't risk the officer discovering the gas cans and fire sticks in the trunk. So, he sighed theatrically and pretended submission. He slowly pushed open the car door while the officer began stepping back. But then he slammed the door as he switched on the ignition and sped away.

Outside the Old Stadium Site

West Oakland

Red protectively escorted everyone out through the gate. Jack drove off with Fred and Daleen and the new samples. Nora drove Alex around the block to retrieve his car, planning to follow him to Marty Ocambo's office to recover her laptop.

But when she turned the corner onto Tornwaldt, she was taken aback to see Winston getting into his Subaru. Alex said, "Well, I'll be damned. That's the guy I was tailing earlier. Claims to be a journalist."

"Because he is," she said. "And he's a friend. Are you giving him trouble?"

"No! I saw him trying to get through the stadium gate earlier. He was pleading his case as a journalist, but they weren't letting him in. I figured he knew something, so I followed."

"He's writing about homelessness," she said, pulling over. "And—"

Alex, on instinct, said, "Text him I'm coming over." Then he dashed out of the car and ran up to Winston.

Winston had just turned his cell back on, his head swimming with stories from the Boudreaux sisters, when Nora's text popped up: *M parked behind U. Friend Alex coming to C U.* He looked in his rearview and recognized Nora's car, simultaneously noting the arrival of a tall bearded man at his window. He also saw a string of texts from Fergie: *Text me . . . Worried . . . Call! . . . They won't let us in . . . Know UR inside, saw our car on street . . .* He wanted to text her back, but the man insistently called out, "Mr. Journalist!" When he opened his window, Alex asked, "So, you're a real journalist?"

Meanwhile, Nora stayed in her Prius, using the downtime to reply to Aditya's *Call me ASAP!* text. She phoned and apologized: "Sorry. I had no time to call until now."

"No worries!" Aditya said. "But, mission accomplished. I made a chart of all the locations where they tested soil and water at the stadium! I emailed it to you. I hope it helps."

After they hung up, Nora opened his email and began reviewing his chart. *If I can somehow match these sites to the sites where soil was exchanged, at least we'd know that Epitome's testing was rigged. Still, if Gianni's involvement was innocent, then who is behind—?*

A knock on the car door. It was Alex. Nora opened the window and complained, "You scared me!" He leaned in close. The overhead streetlight draped dramatically over his face, highlighting his fresh forehead injury and creating dramatic angular shadows under his lips and brows. His coppery hair and beard glowed. She felt awkward meeting his gaze.

He smiled. "Did you ever have one of those days that shook you so hard, you simply fell right out of your old life?"

Yes, she thought, *more than once.*

"Well," he continued, "that's what today's been like for me. I'm feeling . . . reborn."

She felt even more uncomfortable with his unbidden "sharing" of such deeply personal sentiments. It made her again question the wisdom of following him to a strange Fruitvale office. Still, he'd proven himself helpful and informative—*and my friends can identify him.*

"Anyhow," he said, "we should get going. I've got dinner tonight with Quentin. He promised to talk; we'll see."

"Wait," she said, backing away from the window, recalling his peculiar remark about "discovering" documents in Marty's office. "Did you *break* into the office of the man who broke into *my* house?"

"No! His father gave me the keys, with his blessing. He pays Marty's rent—*naturally.*"

"We're done," she said, closing the window, planning to call Detective Johnson. *I don't know what I was thinking, going along with him. The police should be retrieving my laptop.*

"Just give me one minute," he begged, stepping back from the car, keying a number into his phone.

She held up her phone to him, showing her finger poised on the 911 call button. But then her phone rang, and she saw him smile. She answered and said, "How did you get my number?"

"Same place. Marty's office. It was written on your laptop. You should be more careful."

"What hubris!"

"I'm just being transparent. And I'm on your side. Look, all your friends can ID me. And I just AirDropped *every document* I scanned in Marty's office to your journalist pal . . . the environmental inspections, the invoices, the maps, the—"

"What maps?"

Alex continued to stare at her through the car window, increasingly mesmerized by her passion, *fascinated* by her complexity, *excited* to be sharing this pursuit. "The landscaping maps," he said. "Probably the workmaps Red talked about, drawn by his friend Gianni."

Nora's eyes widened. She got out of the car and said, "Show them to me."

He pulled up the scans of the workmaps and handed over his phone. She held his phone next to hers, comparing the two screens a while. Then her jaw dropped. She could correlate the locations of Epitome's test sites—in 2018, to recent soil swaps by Gianni; and in 1991, to those by his father and crew. When she suddenly looked up at Alex, she appeared radiant and awestruck; it caught him off-guard, and all he could manage to say was "What?"

"They match," she said, her eyes glistening, her heart skipping a beat.

~ ~ ~

Red had decided to check in with the Cousins before returning to Betty's. He remained troubled over having seen Patty inside the camp. The shorter Cousin, who'd just re-padlocked the gate, told Red: "Hey, we understood your warning. So, if you just saw Patty inside, it wasn't 'cuz she got past us."

The taller Cousin said, "We'd never let you down like that, Red. And sure as hell, not the people living here."

Moved by their loyalty, Red smiled and said, "She must've gone through one of the fence holes."

"Well, we didn't see her," said the shorter Cousin, grinning. "But we did see a hot chick with great tats who kept wanting in. She was with some talky guy."

"Yeah?" said Red apprehensively. "What did they want?"

"She said something about her husband being inside. The guy was just talking all kinds of stuff. Even something about cysts."

Red thanked the Cousins and walked away, heading toward his truck, consumed with worry. Then, suddenly, a car revved up, and the Cousins shouted his name. When he looked up, he saw a black Beemer barreling toward him.

~ ~ ~

It seemed so obvious in retrospect: that you could drive everyone out of the stadium without trucks or You-Hawls (or people like Patty). *You just had to create the proper incentive for people to leave on their own,* Marty realized.

Yes, he'd drive through the gate, start a couple of fires in the backlots, then leave and call the fire department. If the fires didn't drive the residents out, the fire department would forcibly evacuate them from the camp.

He checked his rearview—the cops still nowhere in sight, successfully shaken off somewhere along the freeway—and then headed for West Oakland, taking side streets toward the stadium. Turning onto 4th, he pressed on the accelerator and barreled toward the entrance, gleefully imagining the colossal dent he'd add to Samantha's Beemer when it popped the gate open. He had a split second to react to Red crossing in his path. He didn't expect padlocks on the gate.

Alex's Car

Fruitvale District

After checking the rearview to confirm that Nora's Prius was still following, Alex picked up his cell to return the calls from old man Greeley's office. But no one answered.

Driving onward to Marty's office, he chastised himself, believing he'd made Nora uncomfortable by expressing his feelings. *Women are harder to decipher than any case I've ever handled.*

Still, how invigorating it had been to work in camaraderie tonight—definitely more enlivening than sleuthing around as a lone ghost for a corporate lawyer. And how darkly illuminating as well: to realize how habituated he'd become to providing blind service to Quentin, rarely questioning its reach into the lives of actual human beings. But today, his unwitting complicity with Greeley Enterprises became glaringly obvious. He'd met a sickly woman who lived at the stadium, and he heard about her neighbor's death from arsenic poisoning. He watched doctors digging in dirt for the truth. He heard Nora lay out her informed suspicions about soil switches to rig environmental testing, and he met a companionable journalist who seemed to genuinely care about the people living at the stadium.

His neurons were firing, his heart stirred. He shook his head in amazement. *I'm getting more than I hoped for—work that's not only interesting and exciting; it's fascinating . . . and actually meaningful.*

Stopped at a traffic light, he began to take further stock of what else had happened tonight. What a shock to learn of Pete's death. *Caused by stadium contamination, too? Or a hit job, maybe? And was Quentin somehow involved? And then, Patty—what does she know about Pete's secret arrangements with him?*

Tomorrow, he'd track Patty down. For now, he'd retrieve Nora's laptop and, hopefully, allay her misgivings about him in the process. Then he'd have his dinner with Quentin tonight. *And there'll be more on the menu than he expects.*

The Greeley Foundation Building

Samantha scanned her office walls, hung with the ornate tapestries she'd collected over the years to replace her father's hideous hunting medals, business commendations, and photo ops with political cronies. *And still,* she thought, *they're inadequate.* For indeed, she could see right through them now.

And she had to admit: she'd been brilliantly outmaneuvered by Quentin. Not only had he ruinously tricked her; he had expertly trapped and cornered her in this loathsome office, as if she were another of his—and her father's—hunting trophies. He'd pushed her against the proverbial wall. And her reign over the family legacy was about to end in epic disgrace.

Such a pathetic way to be destroyed, and because of a life I never wanted.

She flung her coffee mug against the wall, spattering the tapestries. Then she leaned back in her chair and stared thunderstruck at the ceiling, wondering how her big, beautiful world could have been destroyed so abruptly. But in a flash of unbidden recall that illuminated the thudding answer, she was reminded of her encounter with Quentin on Thanksgiving.

She took a long, bracing breath. How obvious in hindsight now: Their last in-person meeting was the turning point. Her icy dismissal of him was the lynchpin.

Even at the time, she knew it was harsh and impulsive. But there were guests waiting at the table. She'd been convinced of his dotage. And his colossal ineptitude in preparing for the stadium sale was outrageously negligent.

And, yet . . .

It was Marty who strong-armed me to visit the stadium that day. Marty who convinced me about Quentin's alleged cognitive decline. Marty who kept insisting I tell Quentin about our relationship. It was Marty who just happened to barge into my house while Quentin was there, clearly intent on humiliating him.

And I allowed that all to happen.

Marty played me like a pawn. I was collateral damage in his war with his father.

After swallowing another bourbon, she slammed the shot glass down on the desk like a gavel. *Marty engineered the turning point.*

She withdrew her father's .38-caliber from the desk and slipped it into her purse, along with her bottle of oxy. She added Quentin's stinging letter that she would force Marty to read aloud. After arranging for a taxi, she walked unsteadily out of the office, ignoring the landline that was finally ringing with a call-back she no longer required.

Outside the Old Stadium Site

West Oakland

The crash was thunderous, the screams were curdling; Fergie and Carl heard them a block away. They dropped everything, rushed out of Carl's Tesla, and ran toward the commotion.

~ ~ ~

Winston had been sitting in his car, feverishly thumbing through the documents Alex had AirDropped to his phone. *So much money . . . references to soil removal and dumps . . . hand-drawn maps . . . commissions for landscaping . . . payments in cash—*

He winced, suddenly remembering to call Fergie, and feeling guilty about his self-absorption in this rapidly developing story. But she didn't pick up. He left a hurried message: "I'm okay, don't worry. Just *lots* happening. Coming home now." He resigned himself to her cold reception upon his late return; but the story he'd been handed was the opportunity of a lifetime for any journalist. His mind spun wildly around new facts and what-ifs about the stadium. He happily imagined staying up all night, researching and writing the complex story. He'd also call his editor to propose the evolving investigation as a series of reports and—

A window-rattling explosion sounded. Every muscle in Winston's body clenched. "Fuck!" he shakily cursed, turning the car back toward the stadium to investigate. But coming up fast on Industrial, he slammed the brakes. Carl's blue Tesla was parked on the street, its doors wide open, with no one inside. He got out to look. Fergie's cellphone was on the passenger seat, her backpack on the floor. "Fergs!" he yelled with raw fierceness.

His hands trembled; he fumbled a call to 911 as serial explosions sounded. He looked up the smoke-filled street to the intersection and saw Carl dragging a body along the sidewalk. Winston tore through the smoke, running toward Carl, shouting "Fergs!"

But Fergie's first-responder instincts had already delivered her to the center of the calamity. *Click*—she'd seen Red, limp on the ground, and instructed Carl to drag him to safety. *Click*—she'd eyeballed the two guards behind the crashed-in gate who had denied her entry, and assessed them as safe to wait. *Click*—she saw a body squeezed behind the airbag of a crumpled black Beemer; running toward it, realizing she'd left her phone in Carl's car, she shouted for someone to "call 911!"

~ ~ ~

Gianni's speeding truck fishtailed as it rounded a corner en route to the stadium, its tarp flying off the flatbed. Whatever had drawn Red urgently there couldn't be good. *Did Patty find some way to kick out the residents after all? Why would Dr. Jack be there? And why couldn't Red confide in me?*

And then he saw it: orange flames searing the sky, billowing black smoke plumes. He got out of his truck and saw a man dragging Red's body along the sidewalk. He shuddered from a flashback of finding Tomas Ruiz' body on the sidewalk. And then he ran toward Red as fast as he could.

~ ~ ~

The Beemer exploded. Multicolored pyrotechnic tongues of fire lashed against the dusky sky. Successive detonations sounded a percussive, threatening litany. The air boiled in the intense heat.

A-1 Property Management

Nora waited edgily in her car for Alex to retrieve her laptop from the darkened office building. Though largely reassured about him, she took a photo of his license plate through her windshield and texted it to Jack: *For evidence, in case.*

But she immediately felt silly, realizing: *It's not him I'm afraid of. This sense of danger is coming from inside me. I'm afraid of . . . what? That I'm feeling too much, wanting something more?*

She seismically flinched when Alex's flashlight flickered through the street-facing office window. "Damn!" she muttered, trying to calm down. "This is nuts!" She tried to discharge her nervous energy by rubbing a rag against the newest grease stain on the passenger seat, and then looked—in vain—for her car's lost phone charger.

Then a yellow taxi pulled to the curbside. Nora watched Samantha Greeley spill out of it and stagger up the steps to the office building.

Jack's Home

At Jack's house, Daleen and Yusra heard the familiar sounds of bombs exploding, and they reflexively sought cover under the bed. Luis peered through the kitchen window at the wild auburn sky, worrying that the wildfires were encroaching, wishing Uncle Tomas were with him, fingering Red's lucky quarter. Jack, having just bid goodbye to Fred, was still standing in his driveway; he looked apprehensively toward the source of the explosions, speculating about another domestic terrorist attack.

When Fred heard the blasts, he pulled over in his car, several blocks away from Jack's house. *More gunfire and gangs? Another refinery accident?* He phoned the hospital to check whether they'd received alerts

about incoming trauma. And while he waited for a response, a sputtery black station wagon pulled up alongside him. He recognized Patty
behind its wheel, a confused smile on her face. *Poor woman,* he thought.
Must be in shock after what Jack told her tonight.

Patty Dobrovski was trying to remain focused on the road, though
thoroughly shaken by Pete's death and the message he relayed through
Dr. Jack. She placed a hand over her necklace key as if to steady her
heart. How incredible to discover that—as doubtful as she'd been about
his desire to be with her—Pete had come through in the end. He'd
relayed the safe word, and now she was free to leave her burdensome life
at the stadium behind. Within days, she'd arrive in Florida; then she'd
drive to the bank in Four Corners to "bingo." She'd collect all the money
from their security box. She'd have a better life.

Outside the Old Stadium Site

West Oakland

The first thing Red saw when he regained consciousness was Gianni
and Carl bending over him and frowning. He thought he was having a
weird dream.

Further down the block, Winston grabbed Fergie and, despite her
protestation, pulled her away from the flaming Beemer. When they
stumbled and fell onto the street, he held on, despite her insistence on
returning to tend to victims. "Fuck you, Win!" she kept repeating, her
anger fueled from an unspent reservoir. "I know," he kept repeating, "I'm
sorry."

Simultaneously, the Nextdoor sites ignited: *Loud explosions, fire in
West Oakland. Anybody know anything? . . . Sirens, lots, W Oak . . . Terrorism? . . . Another Richmond oil refinery? . . . Domestic terrorism . . . Build
the wall! . . . Really? Idiot! . . . Terrorism . . . Suspicious white/black/brown-
skinned man . . .*

The patrol officers who'd been pursuing Marty had previously
phoned-in the car chase, so police and ambulances were alerted. The fire

trucks came quickly, and a safety zone was secured around the Beemer to keep the growing crowd of onlookers at bay. An officer repeatedly warned a rubbernecker with a selfie-stick to move away from the fire, but he dismissed her and continued to snap selfies. Witnessing the interaction, Fergie's jaw dropped: the scofflaw was the arrogant hospital intern who'd taken photos of Daleen! Fergie broke free of Winston's hold; she ran back to the crash scene and knocked the selfie-stick out of the intern's hand. When his phone sailed into the fire, the officer just smiled at her and looked away.

Police Headquarters

West Oakland

At headquarters, Detective Darinda Johnson was mulling over the news about Marty's fleeing car and its subsequent explosive crash into the stadium gate. She guiltily wondered whether the violence could've been prevented had they detained Marty after the You-Hawl incident this morning. But everyone at headquarters was accustomed to his father springing him—always, immediately, and threateningly. *Still, look at the consequences—all the destruction and chaos Marty caused, even losing his own life.*

Her partner, Detective Tom Burka, offered: "Pal, there was nothing you or anyone could've done to stop that guy. He had a short fuse and was going to explode at any minute. Besides, we've been through stuff with him a million times, and his daddy always gets him out." Attempting to lift her mood, he added: "You gotta admit, his death makes our paperwork easier. His death threats at the You-Hawl. The vandalism and B&E. Resisting arrest, reckless endangerment, hauling explosives." When she didn't react, he tried another approach: "Hey, I'll go with you to notify next-of-kin, once we get official ID on the body. Course, we know who it is."

She said, "I appreciate you trying, Tom. But I'm okay. Go on home. The body's so burnt, the ID confirmation is going to take a while." When he didn't budge, she added, "Besides, I want to go back to question

Samantha before official word's out that Marty's dead. She played so dumb today. But I don't know . . . She was Marty's girlfriend. And she owned the Beemer that he filled with explosives and crashed into her property. She's *gotta* know *something*."

"Well," he said, "let's go talk with her."

A-1 Property Management

Fruitvale District

"Where's Marty?"

Alex almost dropped Nora's laptop. He pivoted around and recognized the intruder. "Samantha Greeley," he said, "what a surprise."

"Who the hell are you? What are you doing in Marty's office?"

He sized her up: *Imperious (as expected), drunk and/or stoned (no surprise), pissed off (but why?).* When she reached into her purse, he feared she was going to phone police about his apparent break-in. "Wait," he said. "My name's Alex. I'm a P.I. who's worked for your lawyer."

Samantha scoffed. "You mean, for my *hangman*—Quentin fucking Ocambo."

"Sorry?" he said, wondering what Quentin had done to antagonize her.

Tottering, she sat down and charged, "And *you*. I called *you* twice today."

"Ah," he said, "so *you* made those calls. I recognized your old man's number, but hadn't seen it in a while. Quentin sometimes called from it when he conferenced with your dad. Anyhow, I called back about fifteen minutes ago, but nobody answered."

"Because you were too late," she slurred, scanning Marty's office, repulsed by its disarray. "Marty . . . what a loser. And so lame. I mean, 'A-1 Property Management'? That's the clever name he chose for this dump?"

Alex was intrigued. "Look, I'm just here to retrieve this laptop. Marty stole it from a nice woman—"

"Boring!" she guffawed. "I already know about it. I told Marty he was an idiot for stealing it. And 'nice woman'? No."

Alex almost flinched when Nora appeared in the doorway, and he furtively gestured for her to stay back. He said to Samantha, "Your turn. Why are *you* here?"

"To see Marty, of course. He's supposed to be here tonight. And since he's not answering his phone . . ."

Alex crouched down to establish eye-level contact with her. "So, why did you call me earlier?"

"Let me count the reasons," she said. "One: Because Marty used me and fucked me over. Two: He lied to me to turn me against his father, and now his father's coming after me with all he's got! Three: Both of them are hanging me out to dry for company crimes I didn't know about." Her brow knotted. "What number was I on?"

"Enough!" said Nora, barging in, unable to stand back any longer. Thinking of Daleen, Yusra, Luis, Tomas, Abeo, and imagined countless others, she charged, "You can't possibly be *that* ignorant about Greeley Enterprises!"

After blinking several times as if to clear her vision, Samantha exclaimed, "Oh, the nosey doctor is here! Well, this isn't so boring after all." She stood up to meet Nora's glare and said, "Four. I was on the number four." Then she fell feebly back into the chair.

"Hey," Alex whispered to Nora, "she's on the verge of passing out. We better prioritize our questions."

Nora nodded, shook Samantha's shoulder, and asked: "What do you know about falsifying environmental inspections of your stadium property to facilitate its sale?"

Samantha sneered. "What are you talking about?"

"You must be aware of the fraud."

"No, no, no," Samantha sang, "I don't know, know, know." Her head dropped to her chest.

After lifting Samantha's chin, Nora looked into her lightless pinpoint pupils and said: "I don't believe you. Your family tore down Regal Chemicals to build the stadium in 1950 while the land was *still* contaminated with pesticides and industrial solvents. The 1989 inspection confirmed that. And I know about the two clean reinspections afterward, but I think they were rigged. I think your property was *never* cleared of the toxic chemicals that continue to sicken people. Kill them, even!"

"Why say such nasty things?" said Samantha.

"Because they're true."

"Boring again."

"'Boring'? How dare you!"

"Look," said Samantha. "I don't know what you're talking about. I pay lots of people lots of money so I don't have to bother with such trivia. But, sure . . . okay . . . I wouldn't be surprised if what you said was true."

Nora and Alex exchanged shocked expressions. Then Nora half-asked, half-exclaimed, to Samantha: "You wouldn't be surprised to learn the environmental testing of your property was rigged?"

Samantha laughed. "Well, I wouldn't put that past my father. Or family. You wouldn't either, if you knew them."

Alex said, "But your father's been dead for—what?—about seven years? So, maybe he could've orchestrated rigged testing in '91. But certainly not post-mortem in 2018."

Samantha mumbled incoherently. Then her eyes rolled back, she nodded off, her purse dropped to the floor.

Nora took Alex aside and said, "I can't believe I'm about to say this. But it's possible that Goldilocks really doesn't know a damn thing."

"Yeah," he replied, incredulous. "Some people never have to flush their own toilets. Still, ignorance shouldn't let her off the hook for Greeley Enterprises."

"And such *blissful* ignorance. With the money and privilege to afford it."

He nodded. "Still, in my business—and, I suspect, yours—when you're trying to diagnose a problem, you've got to put aside biases and strong emotions to focus objectively on the puzzle. So, putting aside Samantha's privilege and snark . . . I saw her looking around this office and commenting on it as if she were seeing it for the first time. That makes me wonder: Why come now? What motivated her to show up on this particular day, in this particular moment?"

Building on his remarks, she said: "And arriving so inebriated and angry as well, her visit must be personal." Then, casually picking up

Samantha's purse from the floor, she was struck by its heft and peered inside. She winced. "Yep. *Definitely* personal. There's a gun inside."

Alex shuddered. He hadn't considered that possibility when Samantha reached into her purse earlier. Seeing the pistol now, he shakily acknowledged, "She could've used it on me . . . us." Then he grabbed the gun and emptied its bullets into his pocket. "Hell," he said, returning the pistol to Samantha's purse, "Marty sure knows how to piss people off."

But Nora was sitting at the desk, already preoccupied with the letter she'd also found in Samantha's purse. Alex immediately recognized the distinctive letterhead: "Law Offices of Quentin Ocambo, Esq." She held it out so they could both read, all the while Samantha snored indelicately in the background.

When she finished reading, Nora tsk'ed and said, "Well, this 'letter of resignation' reads more like a poison pen letter. No wonder Samantha's strung out and furious. And this letter is dated today, so her coming here now . . ."

"And with a loaded gun . . .," he said.

"It appears she's holding Marty somehow responsible for her predicament," she finished.

Alex patted his pocket containing the bullets. "And how cosmically ironic—we may have saved his life."

Concerned now that Marty could arrive at any moment, she hastily rummaged through the documents on his desk, thinking: *Someone tells Gianni where to swap soil at the stadium. And twice, Epitome just "happens" to test the same spots. If Gianni isn't corrupt, then who . . .?* She eyed Alex suspiciously and asked: "Did you ever work for Epitome?"

"No," he said with offense. "Not that I know of, at least. But Quentin never told me much. He just gave me instructions, and I always worked alone." He smiled tentatively. "Well, until tonight, with you."

To his disappointment, she only returned a wary expression. "I'm bothered. You, working for the Greeleys' lawyer. You, 'finding' my laptop here. You, *planting* documents in this office. Then, the coincidence of Samantha and me showing up here simultaneously. Who—and what—are you setting up?"

He froze within her icy stare. The truth, he knew, risked aggravating her doubts about him. Still, he chose truth anyway. "I found your laptop when I came here to plant documents for Quentin. They all concerned the stadium property—mapped work orders, environmental inspections, cash ledgers. But honestly, when I walked through this door, I had no idea about any of that. Only after I looked, which I normally wouldn't, did I suspect Quentin of roping me into something shady to frame his son. So, for my own protection, I scanned the documents into my phone—the ones I AirDropped to your journalist friend. And as far as any 'coincidence' of you and Samantha being here? Clearly, she came of her *own* intoxicated accord, and you were *supposed* to stay in your car while I—"

"Still, after suspecting what Quentin was doing, you chose to go ahead and help frame his son?"

"Look. I don't like Marty. But I also don't want him taking the rap for something he didn't do. That's his father's style—not mine."

"But you're complicit."

Alex sighed, thinking: *Now I've fucked up everything with her. She sees me as someone who lies. Breaks into offices. Plants evidence. Frames people. A P.I. who overlooks a fucking gun. Worse, perhaps—someone who overshares his feelings.* Finally, he replied, "Yes, but it's complicated. I knew Quentin was furious with Marty and Samantha. So, yeah—I suspected that whatever I was planting here was intended to hurt Marty. But I expected that to be personal, inside the father-son zone. Besides, Quentin had been acting odd—*sentimental.*" When Nora appeared unmoved, he continued: "So, when I read the documents and saw how impersonal and technical they were . . . well, I got curious. And, stymied, actually—I mean why have me plant *benign* property inspections of the stadium here?" She crossed her arms and remained silent. He went on: "And it was interesting that money was involved. Because Quentin *never* denied Marty *anything,* whatever the cost. Sure, Marty had to ingratiate himself to get what he wanted. But Quentin seemed to enjoy the control, and they related through that sick power dynamic—until now, I guess, with Marty's uprising." He threw his hands into the air. "Bottom line, Nora? I just got curious as all hell."

"So," she said, intrigued by his reasoning, "you justified planting documents because you 'got curious'?"

He wasn't sure whether she was conveying judgment or—*Dare I hope?*—companionable curiosity. "Yes," he said. "For the first time in years of my work, I felt like I'd stumbled onto a genuine puzzle. A puzzle that also mattered. It compelled me." He hesitated. "And I'm guessing you understand that."

She uncrossed her arms, wondering whether she'd ever heard any man express appreciation for her curiosity and love of mystery. "So, what makes you think Quentin's recent sentimentality is sincere? And sentimental over what? His son, his life, his work, his what?"

"Not sure. But he wasn't just sounding sentimental or nostalgic. He was also reflective—ruminating about hunting and business philosophy, personal regrets, career choices. That intrigued me, too. So, I rationalized my behavior. I decided I was planting seeds when I planted the documents. I was curious about what was going to grow. And then . . . well, things grew fast. You and I bumped into each other at the stadium. I heard you speculate about soil rigging, and I started wondering how the documents I planted might be related. Then you get a chart of Epitome's testing sites, and I have scanned workmaps of the soil swaps, and together we figure out that Epitome's test sites must've been rigged—"

"Whoa!" she said. "Aren't you supposed to be having dinner with Quentin?"

"Hell," he said, realizing the time. "In fifteen minutes! But we should both leave if Marty is expected to show up here tonight. Besides, now we're assured from Quentin's letter that Goldilocks *really* doesn't know anything."

"But we can't leave her like this," said Nora, shaking Samantha's shoulder and getting no response. "I saw oxy in her purse, and there's enough alcohol on her breath to disinfect even this office."

Old Stadium Site

West Oakland

While the fire raged, most encampment residents stayed inside their shelters, fearing another raid by immigration or police had begun.

Winston watched in awe as Fergie worked the disaster scene with such calm authority. Then he phoned his editor and began to live-report the breaking story.

After obtaining Gianni's promise to accompany Red to the ambulance paramedics for evaluation, Carl retrieved his doctor's bag from his car and returned to the stadium entrance. He informed the officers in charge that he was entering the camp to address any possible obstetric emergencies. When they barred his entry, he dismissively stated: "Don't be unreasonable. People inside are certainly stressed by the sirens and commotion. As a medical professional, I suggest you step aside and not make things worse." He dusted ashes off his coat sleeves and walked through the gate.

Gianni helped Red to his feet and said, "Man, you scared me! Seeing you on the street like that . . . Shit." Red, buoyed by his concern, said, "Sorry. Won't happen again." Gianni half-smiled and, as he'd promised Carl, suggested they check in with the paramedics. But Red shook his head and said, "Let's check on people inside first and . . ."

His mid-sentence stop startled Gianni. "What the fuck, Red! Can you talk?"

Red was staring slack-jawed down the block, suddenly flooded by memories of events just prior to his concussion. He managed, "There was a fancy black car. A Beemer, coming at me fast. Or maybe . . . maybe not at me. Maybe I just was in the way? I jumped and . . ."

"It can't be coincidence," said Gianni, remembering seeing such a car inside the camp on Friday. "The lawyer's son drives one. And, like I told you, he's who gave Patty the money."

Struggling to reclaim his memory, Red said, "Yeah, about Patty . . . fuck . . . I saw her inside the camp tonight."

"I dunno, pal. You just took a bad knock on the head. Ocambo told us she wasn't there, remember? Then we padlocked the gate, and everyone was on lookout for her. Maybe you're hallucinating?"

"I'm positive I saw her. And, it's hard to believe, but I even felt bad for her. She looked kinda broken. Dr. Jack just told her that her boyfriend had died."

"I see," said Gianni, recalling Quentin's mention of Patty's boyfriend being imprisoned. "So you must've come here to let him inside, not knowing it was Patty he'd come to talk to?" Red nodded, and Gianni continued: "Well, that's a kick. She was here after all! Hey, you think she's still inside?"

"Doubt it," said Red, recalling Patty's limping, dejected trek toward the fence. "It looked like she was just kinda 'walking away,' you know? Besides, her car wasn't inside, so I'm guessing she was heading out through a fence hole." Pointing up the street, he said, "Speaking of, let's go in through the one there. There's too many cops and riffraff at the gate."

Detectives' Car

Oakland

"What crummy timing," said Darinda, putting down her phone. "We got the official ID."

Tom, turning the car around, said, "Hey, it won't take long to notify Marty's father. And I doubt we'll need any Kleenex for it. We'll get back to tracking down Samantha soon enough."

While they drove toward Quentin's home, Darinda stared blankly through the window, thinking: *So, Samantha's not at work now. She wasn't at home. Her house staff had no idea where she was. Her car was in Marty's possession. She's not answering her cell . . .*

"A penny for your thoughts," said Tom.

She smiled appreciatively. "That's more than they're worth."

"Just put it on my tab."

"All right. It's silly. But, truth? I can't understand how someone like Samantha Greeley ends up with a loser like Marty, someone that crude and unhinged. She's so wealthy and beautiful, in a white-girl kind of way."

He chuckled. "Where's this heading? Better turn off your mike."

"Well, how does something like that happen?"

"I dunno. Love is a stranger to me. But someone like her? She doesn't risk *anything* when she hooks up with *anybody*. She can play with whomever she wants. She's lawyered up and has the money to pay off *everybody,* and get out of *everything.*"

"I'm trying not to pigeonhole her. I'd like to think more objectively about this case."

"Then, do that. Free Samantha Greeley from pigeonholes!"

Taking a deep breath, she closed her eyes, centered herself, and said: "So, I'm thinking . . . Her boyfriend used her car as a weapon. Seems he targeted her property. The attack was clearly premeditated and violent; maybe not creating the particular violence he'd planned, but violent still. So, it looks very personal. Are we dealing with a crime of passion? Could Samantha be missing because he . . .?"

"You're right," he said. "Let's put out an APB on Samantha Greeley."

A-1 Property Management

Fruitvale District

Cautioning Alex about his imminent dinner with Quentin, Nora asked, "If he's so vindictive, aren't you worried about meeting with him? He's aware you've uncovered things you weren't supposed to know. And look how viciously he's retaliating against his own son, let alone setting out to destroy Samantha and Greeley Enterprises."

Alex shrugged off her concerns, but was pleased to hear them. "I *have* to go. Quentin promised to explain everything over dinner. And he *knows* everything. He's *been* Greeley Enterprises since Bert died. Besides, we'll be in public view inside a restaurant."

"But can't you postpone meeting him—?" She'd been staring at Samantha, still slumped in the chair, when it occurred to her why Alex *should* go. "No, you're right. It may well be our only chance to question him."

"Our"? thought Alex. *How wonderful that sounds.* "Well, he certainly left a handful of clues that he might be leaving for good."

She nodded. "It's suggested throughout his letter to Samantha. Cutting ties to her, and Marty, and Greeley Enterprises. It would also explain his urgency in finagling Red and Gianni to sign some kind of 'statement' today." Her brow furrowed; she appeared to turn inward.

"What?" he said.

"Nothing, really. Just . . . If Quentin flees right after dumping his toxic secrets about Greeley Enterprises, he won't suffer any fallout. Others will be left to pay the consequences and clean up after him. So, within a personal realm, he's reenacting the stadium's history."

Alex refrained from saying, "I love how you think." Instead, he said, "So, we need to question him tonight, before he gets away scot-free. We've got to hold his feet close to the fire." Then his face lit up and he brightly insisted, "Come with me."

"You're not serious."

"Why not? I *know* you'd like to question him, too. In fact, he's never met you. So, you can just walk into Lopato's a few minutes after me and ask for the nearby table. Then you see and overhear what you can of my conversation with him. Use your phone to record it. Even text questions to me!"

"That's preposterous. I'm not a—" She stopped herself, thinking: *Why am I hesitating? If I'm right about the stadium soil hoax, and this lawyer who's "been Greeley Enterprises" is escaping . . . With the stakes being life-and-death for so many people . . .*

"Please come," he said. "Clearly, I'm a much better P.I. around you."

"Like I said, we can't in good conscience leave Goldilocks like this."

He rolled his eyes. "We also can't allow Goldilocks to own *every-thing*! Not this opportunity, not *our* time. What about calling 911?"

"She doesn't require that acuity level. Besides, one of us would have to wait for the ambulance and talk to the EMTs. Just . . . go."

"Well, can you call somebody to step in?"

Nora immediately thought of Darinda Johnson. But even if she did step in, the prospect of playing detective with Alex remained somewhat outlandish and daunting. "I can't," she said, disappointment suffusing her voice.

He frowned. "Okay. But after all this, don't forget to take your laptop." Then he paused in the doorway and, before dashing out, said: "I hope you change your mind. I'll stall as long as I can."

Old Stadium Site

West Oakland

After reassuring the encampment residents about the cause for the outside commotion, Red and Gianni headed for the exit. Gianni said, "Wow, everyone was so scared."

"Yeah," said Red. "And they're used to living on the edge."

"And *us*—man, we almost got bitten by rats like a million times! Then that twitchy guy who pulled a knife on us. But then, that scared little girl we found hiding in that old freezer . . ."

When they reached the gate, they looked out at the formidable crowd that had gathered at the crime scene. An acrid smell wafted from the smoldering Beemer and the adjacent junkheaps that had incidentally ignited. Two ambulances remained, and the street had been pooled by fire hoses. Red saw Fergie and Winston at a distance, both interacting with a camera crew from the *Oakland Register.*

Considering the extensive damage done, Red said: "It's hard to believe people do such evil things. That idiot riffraff in his fancy Beemer, taking his anger or his *whatever* out on the people living here."

"Yeah," said Gianni. "Some people just always see targets on other people's backs. But at least we know the lawyer was honest about one thing: his son's a definite A-hole."

With smoldering rage, Red said: "If we hadn't padlocked the gate, just think of all the people who could've died if that A-hole made it *inside* and crashed his car. With all the chemical shit in the ground, the explosion could've triggered an apocalypse."

"Hey, don't get worked up. *That* wouldn't've happened because—remember?—the fuckin' lawyer had my dad and his guys clear out the chemicals and pesticides a long time ago." But when Red merely returned a worried expression, Gianni asked, "What's wrong?"

Red recalled dozens of spontaneous combustion incidents he'd helped extinguish inside the camp, and the strange glowing fire that twice snaked along a sewage stream for days. And he thought about

Nora's visit here tonight, and the case she'd made for a cover-up. He hesitated and then said, "I'm not sure they actually cleaned the shit out, G."

Gianni looked offended. "Hey, if my dad did the work, it *was* cleaned out!"

"That's not what I meant," said Red, steeling himself to deliver upsetting news. "A lady doctor I know—her name's Nora—she was also here tonight with some friends. They were collecting soil to check for chemicals because she's positive someone rigged the tests by putting clean dirt in—"

"No!" said Gianni, his face falling. "She suspects *me*?"

"I told her you'd never pull that crap!"

Gianni's jaw dropped. "So . . . what, then? D'ya think someone's setting me up for it? Did I fall for some dumb bullshit again?"

Bracing against a more sinister possibility, Red said: "I don't know about that. But if Dr. Nora's right about chemicals still being here, well . . ."

"Just say it, Red!"

"Then you've been exposed to them big-time all year long. Exposed, like your dad was. And like everyone else living or working here."

Gianni stared back blankly while his mind roamed a dark, wordless territory. Finally, after mentally revisiting their conversation with Quentin, he managed: "If that doctor's right, then . . . well, then, *that* is what my dad 'added up.' *That* is what the lawyer actually meant." He clenched his fists and paced. "When my dad was told what the newspaper said about the stadium being cleaned up, he would've known it wasn't true. He would've known the work he did with his crew couldn't've 'added up' to that cleanup. *That's* what my dad figured out. The damn cleanup was a damn cover-up!" He punched the air and turned to Red, tears on his face. "Ocambo used my dad and his guys for show. And he put their lives at risk."

Red placed a steadying hand on Gianni's shoulder. "It's sick, G. I'm sorry. No wonder your dad told Ocambo to fuck off, and tried to keep him away from you."

Gianni turned away, closed his eyes, and imagined a conversation with his father. *Dad, I wish you could've told me what happened. And still, after all you did to provide for our family and protect me, I'm in the same situation with the same lawyer who's doing the same shitty thing to me. I . . . we can't let him get away with it. I won't let him fuck us over again.*

"Hey," said Red, "you okay?"

Gianni looked clear-eyed at him. "We made a huge mistake in making any deal with Ocambo."

"I know that now."

"And Ocambo's lowlife middleman . . . calling me in here for jobs, probably setting me up . . . I want to kill them both."

"Hey, G, let's calm down—"

"Remember Ocambo's bullshit about wanting justice? Well, I'm going to show him a different view of how that looks to someone like me." He briskly hugged Red and said, "I'm asking you for a solid: Don't follow me and don't call me, okay?" He ran toward his truck as Red called out, "What are you going to do?"

~ ~ ~

Fergie was drenched in sweat, soot, and . . . *what?* Winston smiled and said, "You look hot, Fergs."

She rolled her eyes. "I'm exhausted. Tonight's been crazy-times-infinity."

"But, hey," he said. "We put out *our* first story *together.* My editor's going to post it tonight. I wish it was about something else, but . . ."

After wiping grunge off her cheek, she announced, "I've decided to stick with nursing and human bodies. Investigative journalism is too messy."

"Let's go home and sleep on that. And clean up. By the way—have you seen Carl?"

"Twenty, thirty minutes ago, he came by to give me my cell and backpack. He said he was driving some woman from the camp to the ER for an obstetric emergency." She pointed toward the gate and said, "Hey, Red's still here, sitting on the curb. But he should've gone to the ER, too." They walked over to him and asked how he was doing.

"I'm nervous," he answered.

Fergie said, "Don't worry. We'll take you to the ER. Concussions can be serious, but if we get you checked out—"

"No," he said. "I'm scared about what my friend Gianni's going to do. I told him what Dr. Nora said about bogus soil tests. It made him so angry, I'm afraid he's gonna do something stupid."

"Like?" said Fergie.

"He wouldn't say. That's why I'm guessing it's pretty bad. But, if I was that lawyer or his middleman, I'd be scared right now. Gianni thinks they've been setting him up for fake soil testing. And that the lawyer screwed him and his father."

Winston flinched. *Marty Ocambo just died at his own hands, intentionally or not. And now the lives of his father and some middleman might be at risk, too?* "Red," he said, "I'm hoping we can prevent any more violence and death tonight. So, who's this middleman you're referring to?"

"Don't know. Some British guy who phones in jobs for Gianni. Gianni said they never met, and they use burner phones for business." He doubled over and moaned. "It's my fault. I shouldn't have said anything. And I'm not even sure if what I told G is true."

Winston pulled Fergie aside and asked, "Actually, how sure is Nora about the stadium being contaminated? Because the P.I. she introduced me to tonight gave me environmental inspections—from '91 and 2018—and they looked fine."

Fergie grimaced. "I'll call Nora and ask. But first, since Red's concerned about Gianni doing 'something stupid,' we should alert the police. And Red still needs a medical eval."

Detectives' Car

North Oakland

Darinda put down the phone and shook her head in amazement. "Tom, that was Nora Kelly. She's located Samantha. Let's head to Fruitvale."

Tom dutifully turned the car around. "How the hell did she find her?"

"Nora said she 'bumped into' Samantha when she was retrieving her stolen laptop from Marty Ocambo's office."

"What? And she didn't tell you she was going to do that? How'd she even know her laptop was there?" Darinda shrugged, and he continued: "Well, she's interfering with police work, and she's playing with fire. She gets *too* close to danger and *too* often for her own good."

Having witnessed Nora suffer two major traumas, Darinda had to agree. *Still, Nora sounded strong on the phone just now.*

"And then?" he said. "Samantha just *happens* to be there, too? After *we* couldn't find her? How does Samantha even relate to the stolen laptop—?"

"I don't know, Tom. But I'm just going to trust Nora. She said she had an emergency and had to be somewhere, but Samantha was nodding out and needed attention. Or 'protection,' maybe? Doesn't matter. We'll find out soon enough."

"Well, I've got questions for your Dr. Kelly. And what? Should we ask her to locate Quentin Ocambo for us, too?"

"Just check your attitude when we get there, okay? And remember Samantha's been out of it, so she won't know Marty's dead."

"I'll be gentle," he said, laden with sarcasm. "Hell . . . You know I got your back, Darinda. But you're giving Kelly a long rope. She shouldn't be interfering in a theft investigation, even if it involves her own property. And if we put out an APB on Samantha because we thought *she* might be in danger . . . well, Kelly being with her . . . she could've placed herself in harm's way, too."

A-1 Property Management

Fruitvale District

Nora's head was spinning after Fergie phoned with all the dizzying news. The crash and explosions outside the stadium. *(Thank god the car didn't make it into the camp!)* Marty Ocambo, dead. *(So much for thinking Alex and I were saving his life.)* Carl escorting an encampment resident with an obstetric emergency to the ER. *(How wonderful he was there to help.)* Red with a concussion and worried about inciting Gianni to go after Quentin and his middleman. *(I'm glad Fergie notified the police, and I hope she can at least reassure Red about the rigged soil testing being true.)*

But given all that Fergie had shared, Nora was feeling bad for having withheld information about Quentin's location. Still, she was determined to give Alex at least twenty minutes to question him at the restaurant; she felt she owed him that, and would want that herself in his position. *Besides, it's merely speculative what Gianni is up to, and Fergie's notified the police to boot.*

Nora stared at Samantha—finally, no longer snoring—and wondered how she was going to react to news of Marty's death. *And to the fact that you won't be able to shoot him now.* Checking the time—*Alex's dinner with Quentin should be starting now*—she anxiously awaited Darinda's arrival.

She walked to the window, peering out for the detectives' car, eager to dash out to the restaurant the moment they arrived. Just beginning to sort through Fergie's shocking news, she realized that Quentin and Alex were likely unaware of Marty's death. *Should I text that info to Alex now, or wait until—*

A loud rustling noise distracted her. She pivoted around to find a gun pointed at her. Samantha said, "I knew you were trouble the moment we met. And such a fucking self-righteous know-it-all."

Shockwaves roiled Nora's mind, adrenaline turbocharged her body. But she stood still and strong. She watched Samantha's grin extend into a toothy smile as she pulled the trigger and . . . *Click.* Samantha scowled, pulled the trigger again. *Click,* again.

The women stared at one another, absorbing tectonic shifts in power between them. Samantha fell back into her chair, a capitulating expression on her face. Nora inhaled deeply, the adrenaline now flowing like baptismal water, and she shakily said, "The gun isn't actually loaded."

Intersection, Broadway and Grand

Downtown

Gianni parked his truck on Broadway and Grand, and looked out to the sidewalk where he'd discovered Tomas' body. This was the only place he could think to be, in hopes of calming down.

His fists were still throbbing, having beaten against doors—to Quentin's office as posted on the business card, and to his home address as listed on the internet. He'd called the British guy multiple times on the burner phone, never getting any response. "Where the fuck are they?" he muttered.

When he checked his personal cell, he noted a long string of texts from Red, pleading to make contact. He shook his head, thinking: *I can't, pal. Don't want you involved in any of this. Fact, I shoulda kept you out of everything in the first place, just like I thought.*

Then he grabbed his flask and got out of the truck. He walked to the spot where he found Tomas, vividly recalling how he had looked. After taking a swig of Jack Daniel's, he ceremoniously poured a little on the spot and toasted: "To you, buddy. To you, and to my dad, and to all the people like us they keep using up."

And then, feeling clear-headed and right-minded, he understood what he needed to do.

Lopato's Trattoria

Temescal District

Savoring the last of the calamari appetizer, Quentin said, "Thanks for meeting me here."

Alex sat across the table, worried that his stalling over an entrée choice was becoming obvious. *Nora should've been here by now if she's coming.*

"But you're awfully quiet," Quentin said. "You all right?"

"It's just a little odd," said Alex. "We've worked together a long time. But tonight, I feel like you're a stranger."

Quentin nodded and signaled the waiter for another basket of warm ciabatta. Then he topped off Alex's wine.

"Thanks for remembering I like pinots," said Alex.

"Remembering is easy," said Quentin. "It's forgetting that's hard."

"What do you mean?" asked Alex, instantly regretting the question, fearing its potential to spark a conversation he'd prefer to postpone until Nora's hoped-for arrival.

Fortunately, Quentin lifted his glass to the light and, leisurely studying the wine, seemed to take another step down memory lane. "I was young in '89 when I began working for Bert. Naïve, too. I sold my soul to him and his family business."

Alex impatiently drummed a breadstick on the table. "I'm not here to listen to your old-man regrets. If you're expecting me to cry—"

"Of course not. I benefited immensely from that bargain—money, power, social prestige. The right political connections. It was all so shiny. And, god knows, the work provided a great escape from my son and his coddling mother—god rest her confused soul."

Alex thought, *Nora was right to question whether Quentin's feelings were sincere. He's certainly working overtime to generate sympathy and manipulate mine.* He felt like shouting, *I know you fucking used me! You made me complicit in all the shitty stuff you did to profit yourself and the Greeleys!* Instead, still stalling for Nora, he said: "Before I forget, you want your keys back to Marty's office?"

Quentin flicked his hand dismissively. "To 'A-1 Property Management'? Such an uninspired name for a business, especially a fake one. Yet so typically Martin. He's not very bright."

"Don't know about that," said Alex, his patience fraying. "Because Marty did stick it to you."

Leaning back in his chair, Quentin assumed a contemplative pose. "That's premature. There's still time on the scoreboard. And besides, I've benefited from Martin's double-crossing chicanery. I'm feeling liberated for the first time in decades."

Alex stared back, thinking: *Liberated to do what?* A breadstick broke in his tense grip.

"Is something bothering you?" asked Quentin.

Alex wiped his palm free of bread crumbs, conceding that he, too, was reaching a breaking point. He could no longer wait to confront Quentin, and began by calling him out: "You're trying to make me believe that you're genuinely sharing some epiphany about your life." *But I know you're not. You're only scheming to escape responsibility. I know you're trying to set up Marty and Sam and Gianni to take the fall. I know the Epitome test sites were rigged; you had to have known.* He checked his watch again. *Where the hell is Nora? This conversation is about to explode!*

"Well," said Quentin. "It sounds like I'm failing."

"That's right."

Quentin smiled appreciatively at Alex. "Well, I always said you were the best P.I. that money could buy."

A-1 Property Management

Fruitvale District

As Detectives Johnson and Burka ascended the steps toward A-1 Property Management, the door burst open and Nora rushed out, clutching her laptop. "Thank you!" she said, passing them on the stairway, heading to her car. "Samantha's inside, first door to the right. She doesn't know Marty's dead." Tom started after her, but Darinda held him back and called after Nora: "Where are you going?"

At curbside now, Nora shouted back: "An emergency. I'll call when I can." She paused just before entering her Prius, looked squarely back at Darinda, and said, "The gun isn't actually loaded."

Darinda nodded knowingly and Nora drove away. Tom said skeptically, "Hope you know what you're doing, Darinda."

Lopato's Trattoria

Temescal District

Alex's conscience stung from Quentin's barbed compliment, characterizing him as "the best P.I. that money could buy." It made him feel even more tainted about his complicity with Greeley transgressions. *Is Quentin intending that? Or does he mean to sound threatening? Maybe both?*

The server set down two Caesar salads. Alex removed the anchovies from his and furtively checked his phone for any message from Nora.

He was surprised to feel so affected by her no-show. *What is it exactly? Disappointment? Hurt?*

After the server left, Quentin continued the conversation: "Regardless, I do have an epiphany to share."

"Go ahead," said Alex. "Share."

Quentin regarded Alex with a probing look, wondering how he could so coldly dismiss his friendly overture. "Well," he said, "the stadium being torn down and replaced with something new? That's provided me with a powerful metaphor that's birthed a personal epiphany."

"That so?" said Alex, feigning interest.

"Bert Greeley built us both. And as goes the stadium, so go I."

~ ~ ~

Meanwhile, Nora had arrived at the parking lot. She recognized Alex's Mazda, illicitly parked in a reserved space. She stole a moment to check her appearance in the rearview, hoping she didn't look too wild-eyed to perform the role of a casual diner. Then she hurried toward the trattoria while taking a quick mental inventory: *Quentin likely won't know about his son's death, let alone Pete's. Or that Samantha's in police custody. Or that we've read the letter he wrote to her—*

A text popped up from Fergie: *Red just said G has gun in truck. And still not answering his calls*

Nora looked pleadingly up to the heavens. *What a fucking mess! Just what the world needs—another angry man with a gun! So many people could get hurt. And if he somehow tracks Quentin here, Alex and innocent patrons could get caught in any crossfire. Hell, I could get caught!* She visualized herself minutes earlier, standing within the crosshairs of Samantha's gun, and whispered, "The gun isn't actually loaded." Then she entered the restaurant.

~ ~ ~

Alex nearly choked on his pomodoro when he saw Nora enter the trattoria and follow the maître d' to the adjacent table. And when she nonchalantly set her cellphone at the table's edge, he felt instantly emboldened to, finally, pounce on Quentin. Staring pointedly at him, he said, "And aren't you and the stadium also toxic and dangerous?"

Quentin put down his wine. "That's awfully harsh, Alex."

"It's just the epiphany I'm having."

"That so?" said Quentin, his forehead furrowing. Then, as if searching for a clue to Alex's contrariness, he studiously scanned the restaurant; when his gaze momentarily netted Nora, Alex's heart skipped a beat. But then Quentin straightened his already-straight tie and said, "Look, I didn't realize until today how upset you've been over me handing the stadium assignment to Martin. But, of course, you deserve compensation. And I'm offering that to you now. How much will it take to make things right between us?"

Alex bit his tongue, thinking: *How obtuse can you be to think that's what I care about?* He replied, "Actually, I'm here because you promised to tell me 'everything' over dinner. I'm interested in knowing what you're up to."

Leaning close, patting Alex's chest in a seemingly friendly gesture, Quentin said: "You're not wired, are you?"

"You know I'm not."

"Because you seem angry, and you're sounding like an inquisitor. And it's never been like you to question me."

Nora stealthily shot Alex a supportive look. He, feeling its salutary effects, replied: "I need to know what you've implicated me in. I'm not Pete Vaughn, and I won't be taking any rap for you. I'm not Marty, and I won't be framed by you. I'm not Samantha, and I won't be turning a blind eye to you." Now he leaned in close. "I intend to figure out what's been happening at the stadium. And if you're skipping town as shit hits the fan, I want to know where I'm standing in your shitstorm."

After swallowing a forkful of Bolognese, Quentin nodded. "Fair enough. But you have to admit, Martin and Samantha deserve a serious comeuppance. And Pete's no dupe. He knows how to strike a bargain. If he hadn't screwed things up for himself, he would've been out of prison months ago, living handsomely off the 'compensation' from our original deal. Anyhow, when he does get out, he and his hapless girlfriend will be rich. I can arrange the same for you, Alex."

"But I don't want what Pete wants," said Alex, scrutinizing Quentin's expression for any flicker of awareness about Pete's death. Detecting none, he said, "So, start explaining."

"All right. But where to start? Perhaps with your hurtful accusation about me and the stadium being 'toxic and dangerous'?"

"Yeah. Start there."

Quentin grinned. "Well, you'd have to be a moron to expect otherwise. About the stadium, that is. Bert built it in 1950 on the former site of a pesticide factory, for god's sake! No one was talking about environmental testing and safety back then. That only became an issue in '89 when Bert wanted to sell off parcels of the property and had to obtain an inspection. *That's* when the stadium contamination became a 'problem.' And that's what he hired me to fix."

Alex's stomach churned, trying to digest Quentin's callousness. "You're wrong," he said. "Maybe the contamination wasn't always an official regulatory or legal problem. But it was *always* a common-sense one. How could anyone not see a problem with human beings living and working on land saturated with toxic chemicals?"

Nora momentarily closed her eyes, looking inward, trying to make fuller sense of things. *We know Epitome's testing sites were rigged to match soil swaps. Still, we don't know by whom. And, still, we don't have actual proof that the stadium is contaminated.*

"Your tone, Alex," said Quentin, snappishly signaling the waiter for more water. "It's sounding judgmental. And hasn't the stadium passed inspections *twice* since '89?" He eyed Alex censoriously. "Why, *you* even saw those reports. *You* even planted them in Martin's office."

And now Alex heard it loud and clear—the calculated threat of blackmail behind Quentin's words. Trying not to appear defensive or intimidated, he replied, "We know Epitome's soil testing was rigged both times."

Quentin regarded him with a scornful expression. "Now you're sounding paranoid. Conspiracy-minded, even. Well, perhaps that's just a sign of the times in which we live." He sighed theatrically. "And by the way, who is this 'we' you speak of? You've always worked alone."

Alex stiffened and fixed his gaze on Quentin, fearful of prompting attention to Nora. But his odd reaction was precisely what alerted Quentin. He glanced over at Nora, eyed her cellphone at the table's edge, and stared icily back at Alex.

At that moment, Nora's server arrived, wedging herself between the two tables and obscuring Nora's view of the two men. Preemptively, the server told her, "Thanks for your patience! It got busy all of a sudden. Are you ready to order or would you—?"

"It's fine, and I'm ready," said Nora, trying to restrict the chit-chat. She speedily declined serial offers . . . of bread . . . water . . . house wine . . . cocktails . . . "something else to drink?" Then, after cutting off a recitation of "entrées not on the menu," she blurted out: "Just give me the daily special, please."

"Sorry," the server replied. "We don't have daily specials per se. We like to think every day is special here. But may I recommend . . .?"

"Yes, thanks," said Nora to whatever was first proposed. And finally, with the order settled, the server left. But now Nora saw that Alex and Quentin had vacated their table.

She tossed money onto her bread plate and rushed out of the restaurant, in time to see Quentin's royal blue Audi speeding out of the parking lot—with Alex inside. She fumbled with her cell, afraid of accidentally erasing her recording, and intending to phone Darinda; but its battery had died. Then she jumped into her Prius and took pursuit.

The MacArthur Freeway

Oakland

"Where are you taking me?" asked Alex.

"To hell, with me," said Quentin, one hand on his gun, the other on the wheel.

Fully apprised of Quentin's marksmanship, Alex kept his hands on the dashboard as commanded.

"But don't ever forget—you had a choice," Quentin continued. "I offered you a way out—a golden parachute, actually. You could've been filthy rich."

"Like everyone else you just pay off? Everything's transactional with you. You've got no moral—"

The car turned so abruptly onto a freeway exit ramp that Alex couldn't catch its signage. Quentin laughed and said, "An old trick you taught me years ago!"

"What the hell!" yelled Alex, after his already-bruised forehead thudded against the dashboard.

"No need to shout," said Quentin. "Besides, no one can hear you out here. Certainly not that woman who was seated at the next table." He glanced at Alex, who maintained silence. "Well, she must be *special*. Because, god . . . you used to be a great P.I. But that set-up in the restaurant? So sloppy and amateurish! And then you, coming along with me to protect her—yes, she must be very special to you."

Alex shuddered, grasping that Quentin might've actually shot Nora had he not gotten into his car. He managed to say, "Whatever you're up to, you won't get away with it. You've left evidence everywhere. And Nora's seen you—"

"So that's her name," said Quentin. "Old-fashioned, but nice." He exited onto an unmarked road that led toward an expansive industrial park. "And, FYI, I plan to 'get away with it.' One way or another, I'm taking my last swing for the fences. And regardless of what happens, I'm going out in a blaze of glory. I don't give a damn what that costs—even if it costs my life. Now, how's that for 'transactional'?"

Alex resigned himself to his entrapment, forced to surrender his cell to Quentin and having no control over the locked doors. For the first time in his life, he regretted not joining Bert and Quentin on their hunting excursions and learning how to handle firearms. Hoping to create a distraction, he asked, "What exactly do you mean—'going out in a blaze of glory'?"

After taking a service road and heading into a sprawling complex of storage lockers, Quentin said, somewhat wistfully: "A grand parting gesture in the world, to mark the end of my grand tour." Then he stopped the car in front of a large storage unit. "I refuse to go out, bowed and whimpering and insignificant. And if I must be destroyed for that to happen, it will be by my own hands—no one else's." He smiled wanly at Alex and said, "I hope you don't need reminding—I'm an excellent marksman and hunter. So, don't even think about running when I unlock the door."

Nora lost several precious minutes when Quentin whipped his car onto an exit ramp and she couldn't slow in time to take it. She was forced to wait on the shoulder, several yards beyond, until the freeway cleared; then, holding her breath, she backed up to the ramp and floored her Prius—vowing to purchase a sportier car next time around. But finally, she spotted a lone car trailing behind a slow bevy of trucks. When it passed under a streetlight, she identified Quentin's royal blue Audi.

She followed at a safe distance, driving past buildings all utilitarian in design. A block-shaped paper-shredding facility. A squat gas station with a single pump. A boxy bus terminal, dimly lit. Then a blunt maze of storage lockers. Finally, she saw the Audi stop in front of a large industrial storage unit. She switched off her ignition and headlights, and waited anxiously to see what would happen next.

Blaze of Glory

Nora flinched when Quentin got out of his car and stepped into its headlight beams. He held an arm extended and, gun in hand, pointed to the passenger side—ostensibly at Alex. Recalling Alex's remarks about Quentin's marksmanship and lethal control philosophy, she felt chills rattling her spine. She flashbacked to the internet pictures she'd seen of the hunting specimens inside the Greeley library and lamented, "Oh, Alex." Cursing her missing cell charger, she helplessly watched Quentin enter a code into the storage unit's lockbox before returning to his car. Then, after the massive metal door slowly lifted, he drove inside.

She knew she had to do something, anything. *Should I drive for help? Sound the horn to distract—?* But then a gunshot sounded from within the storage unit. A man ran out. An engine started, and a black truck emerged from behind the storage units. When it sped by, she saw it was a flatbed carrying a load of dirt. *The driver's the man who hassled me at Betty's!*

Flush with adrenaline, Nora dashed out of her Prius and toward the locker. She slipped inside, under the now-descending door, terrified about finding Alex shot. *It's my fault. I put him in danger. Playing detective—*

Instead, she saw Quentin sprawled on the floor, bleeding, groaning. Alex appeared to have wrested the gun from his hand; he turned to her wild-eyed and exclaimed, "Thank god, it's you!"

She braced herself against Quentin's Audi so as not to collapse from the shock. Finally, she managed, "You're okay?"

"Physically, yeah," said Alex, in shaky possession of the gun. "But Quentin's been shot in the leg."

While Nora stanched the bleeding from Quentin's thigh with his tie and pocket square, Alex rifled through his pockets. He retrieved his own cellphone and tossed everything else onto the floor: a wallet, keys, a bus ticket, a flash drive, and two cellphones. He told Nora, "No hidden weapon—and this time, I'm sure."

This isn't possible, Quentin thought. *This can't be happening.* He locked eyes with Nora and demanded, "Just fix it so I can walk."

She eyed him disparagingly, refraining from replying: *I'm not your damn servant.* Instead, she asked Alex, "What happened?"

Pointing to Quentin, Alex said, "I thought he was going to kill me! But when we came inside, a man ambushed us and shot Quentin before Quentin could shoot him. And the shooter was *the* mysterious Gianni, because Quentin shouted out his name when the gun went off."

Quentin bristled with mention of Gianni's name. *To think I actually called him "son"! That he'd turn on me—shoot me! Ungrateful little . . .* He tried to stand, but couldn't get off the floor, and sat there clutching his thigh. *Such a humiliating position to be in now! And, damn it, Bert— I wouldn't be in it if you'd left me in rightful control of the business!* Then, squaring Alex in the crosshairs of his annihilating gaze, all he saw was how disrespectful and traitorous he'd become. *I offered you a fortune to make things right between us, but that wasn't enough for you!*

Though unnerved by Quentin's feral stare, Alex continued: "Then Gianni freaked out. He said he was sorry, that 'it wasn't supposed to happen this way.' And he just ran out of the locker."

Red was right, thought Nora, *to be concerned about Gianni going after Quentin and his middleman. But now it sounds as if Gianni didn't intend to shoot. What, then, was he after?*

Quentin forcibly shut his eyes and softly banged his head against the wall, thinking: *Gianni. Tony Moretti. Bert. Alex. Martin. Who needs you? Fuck you all. Every man for himself now.* Then he so thoroughly steeled himself that every bit of him turned into solid armor, and he abruptly looked up at Nora with a smile that made her skin crawl. "So, you're Alex's special friend Nora."

"Just ignore him," said Alex. "He's baiting you. Let's call the police, an ambulance—"

"Not yet," said Nora. "His wound is stable."

Alex eyed her with concern. "Even so, there was a shooting. And Gianni's on the loose with a gun."

She shook her head. "It sounds like Gianni didn't intend to shoot anyone. And he saved your life, Alex. If he hadn't been here . . . well . . ."

"Still," said Alex. "That doesn't give us license to—"

"Please," she said. "I gave you time to question this man earlier. I want a minute now. Besides, I know the police have already been called out on Gianni."

"This is absurd," Quentin protested. "That man attempted murder!" Then the thought came easily to him: "And Gianni Moretti is a *career criminal.* I've got evidence to prove that in the trunk of my car. I even have a signed confession from him. But *that's* why he came after me tonight! Go ahead, open the trunk."

But Nora just coolly stood there, scrutinizing him for clues as she would a patient whose illness she was trying to diagnose. *So, you used Gianni and Red. You worded their whistleblower "statements" in some pliable way to serve as "confessions." But . . . what's your endgame? And, confessions to what?*

Meanwhile, Alex had picked up Quentin's wallet and bus ticket. He found a fake ID, and the ticket displayed an imminent departure time from the nearby station. "We were right," he told Nora. "He had plans to leave."

"Look," said Quentin. "This seeming fiasco need not end tragically for any of us. And forget Gianni. I've got two million dollars in the trunk, and we can split it if you both—"

"You must be joking!" said Nora. "You're actually trying to bargain with us?"

"Everything's transactional with him," said Alex.

"Fine then," said Quentin. "Take it all. All I ask in return is a sporting chance to escape."

Alex raised his fist, but lowered it after catching Nora's cautionary look. He seethed, "You were going to kill me, you bastard! And you expect us to let you go? You think I care about you taking a last swing for the fences or going out in your stupid blaze of glory?"

"What do you mean—'last swing' and 'blaze of glory'?" asked Nora.

Quentin scrambled internally, trying to discern the optimal currency to bargain his way out. Waging his bet on moral sympathy—*given these two bleeding hearts*—he replied: "My last swing is my last chance to obtain justice. To see my son punished for the harm he's inflicted on the people living and working at the stadium under his toxic stewardship. To see Greeley Enterprises pay for their environmental and corporate crimes. And, on a deeply personal note, I want Martin and Samantha to see that it's *me* bringing *them* to justice."

Alex, recalling Nora's comment about the pretense of people flipping their morals like pancakes, said: "I'm not buying that."

Repulsed by Quentin's odious attempts at manipulation, Nora struggled to remain calm and analytical. *Is this man completely amoral? Is anything he says true? Does he care about anyone but himself?* Though believing she knew the answers to these diagnostic speculations, she decided to place a telling bet; she nonchalantly informed him: "Your son Marty is dead."

He flatly replied, "Okay."

She studied his expression: it was as neutral as his reply, and as devoid of discernible sorrow—just as she had wagered.

But her brusque announcement had jarred Alex; on a leap of faith, he chose to believe that her cold delivery was strategic. Still, independently, the news of Marty's death rattled him, as did his witness of Quentin's unemotional reaction. "So," he managed, "you won't get your chance to see Marty 'brought to justice' after all."

When Quentin merely stared blankly back, Nora followed with: "And the police already have Samantha. Meaning, your vindictive little victory lap around Marty and her is officially canceled."

"We'll see," said Quentin, already recalibrating his options. *The crimes I've exposed and acknowledged some responsibility for . . . They're minor corporate transgressions, everyday tax fraud and labor abuse. Besides, I'll be granted whistleblower immunity with all the evidence I'll continue to offer. That's not so bad—staying, being heralded as a hero who exposes the evil Greeley empire.* He took in a deep breath, as he also took in the gift of his son's death: *Now the serious crimes can be pinned on Martin alone. He can't challenge my version of events or framing of him; and Samantha's too ignorant of everything to have a say.* He slowly exhaled, happily realizing: *And I no longer need to risk getting burned in a blaze-of-glory exit in order to destroy them and Greeley Enterprises.*

"What've you got to smile about?" asked Alex.

Not conscious of smiling, Quentin answered: "I'm *musing,* actually, about the overwhelming evidence against Martin's involvement in serious Greeley crimes. You, of course, planted some of that in his office." When Alex looked shamefacedly away, Quentin winked and continued, "And I seriously doubt you'd want the world to know about that."

Nora slapped her forehead. "Unbelievable! You're trying to pitch a new deal by threatening Alex with blackmail?"

Quentin was basking in an ever-brightening outlook for shifting the bulk of the blame for environmental testing fraud and human endangerment onto Martin. Everything was falling neatly into place. "If we play our cards right, no one need worry."

"Look," said Alex, "unlike you, I intend to take responsibility for whatever I did. But it's hard to know what that entails with you being so fucking deceptive and—"

"You're not seeing things clearly," said Quentin. "None of us has to get hurt if we merely allow the evidence to speak for itself." On top of it all, he'd recently negotiated a new bargain with Pete: In exchange for the promise of money and Patty's protection, Pete would end communications with Martin and testify against him when the time was ripe. Pete would confirm that Martin was always 'on the take' with Epitome Soil Testing Lab—whether working for Quentin in '89 or now. "And," he said, "as extra insurance, Pete Vaughn will back up the evidence against Martin—"

"That's not going to happen," said Alex. "Pete's not going to lie for you or take another rap, no matter how much money you throw at him."

"Pete?" Quentin scoffed. "Clearly, you don't know him."

Using the same brusque delivery as before, Nora said, "He's not going to help you because he died on the operating table today."

Quentin fell silent, dispassionately appraising her, trying to decide whether she was telling the truth.

This time, Nora nearly gasped, shocked by his emotional vapidity. *Not a flicker of feeling about Pete's death, let alone his own son's.*

Stymied by Quentin's seeming obliviousness to his *own* dire predicament, Alex stroked his beard and said: "Actually, it's you not seeing things clearly, Q. You've been caught. *Trapped*, really."

"You forget you're talking to a master hunter, Alex. See . . . I'm on record acknowledging my role in tax and employment fraud at Greeley Enterprises—my own 'whistleblower' allegations. But there's no 'paper trail' to connect me to the particular environmental crimes that you appear to be interested in. I believe any existing evidence will clearly point to Martin, who won't be around to deny anything. And whatever Pete knew about those crimes . . . clearly, that's taken to the grave now."

He's so disgusting! Nora shouted internally. *So repellant, I can barely think straight.* But when she turned in outrage to Alex, she was instantly reminded of their conversation in Marty's office. Holding Alex's steady gaze, she took a moment to tame her emotions in order to focus more objectively on the evolving puzzle. Then, while taking a sweeping glance around the storage unit—at Quentin's car, the bus ticket, the wallet containing a fake ID—she slowly turned back to Quentin. She said: "It makes no sense that you'd have plans to leave town—not if you were cocksure about your legal immunity . . . your framing of Marty . . . the absence of any paper trail between you and Epitome." She regarded him now with a piercing, clinical stare. "So, there must be something *else* . . . Something awful you haven't admitted yet. Something you'd *need* to escape from if it became known, because you couldn't realistically expect immunity for it."

"Of course!" chimed in Alex. "And *that's* what he's been waiting on to take his 'last swing for the fences.'"

Nora's head tilted as she looked inquiringly at Quentin. "But a last swing you don't appear to be taking now."

Quentin listlessly replied, "It's moot now. I've changed my mind. Martin, Samantha, Greeley Enterprises . . . I'm actually satisfied with how things have worked out for them."

"I don't agree that it's over," said Nora, shaking her head. "Your 'last swing' was also the lynchpin to trigger your Plan B—the scorched-earth strategy you were willing to implement even if it risked losing your life in a 'blaze of glory.' So, I'd really like to know—"

"I don't have time for this," Quentin said, trying to stand up. His effort was thwarted by Alex's hand pushing him back down.

What's the "something else"? thought Nora. *Where's the lynchpin?* Her attention alighted on the flash drive on the floor, and she was about to pick it up when Quentin lunged for one of his cellphones—the further of the two on the floor. Alex kicked them both aside; they slid several feet away, along with the drive.

"This is a foolish waste of time," said Quentin. "Everyone can get what they want, if you two just let me handle things."

"How can anyone in good conscience agree with that?" asked Alex.

"Your conscience isn't the only moral concern here," he shot back. "Come on. This is easy! I stay and become the *consummate* whistleblower against Greeley Enterprises. They're held responsible for the environmental transgressions that matter to you. Then, you obtain reparations for the people you seem to care about. And I'll be considered a hero—a white-hat lawyer, forced to resign from Greeley Enterprises after exposing its soulless crimes in pursuit of justice for its victims. The underpaid, overworked, unprotected poor and homeless people who've been abused and misused will be—"

"You don't give a damn about those people!" said Nora.

Feigning offense, Quentin replied, "Well, that's not how it has to *look*. Besides, name even one other private entity in Oakland that has consistently allowed people to live rent-free on its properties. Under my compassionate legal stewardship at Greeley Enterprises, people without home or country have been—"

"Getting sick, even dying!" she shouted. "I know that stadium is contaminated. And I know you're behind it."

Feeling confident about his brightly revised vision of his future, Quentin said: "It's time to call the ambulance and police."

"Nora, please," said Alex. "That's the only agreeable thing he's said."

"One more minute," she said, pacing before Quentin, mulling over his egregious pretense of caring for people. Then, suddenly, within that harsh light, she saw several puzzle pieces illuminate. She stared fiercely at him and said, "You and the Greeleys are made of the same rotten cloth. You believe other people are disposable. You use them like throw-away objects."

Quentin huffed. "For such a self-righteous bleeding heart, you're actually standing over a man with a gunshot wound, but you won't call—"

"I'm not worried," said Nora. "Your wound is superficial, like you."

Alex was inclined to call an ambulance, despite Nora's protestation. But then he saw her become perfectly still while turning inward and furrowing her brow—just as she'd done in Marty's office. And moments later, when she emerged from the depths of her stillness, she looked at Quentin and said: "It's not only that you and Greeley Enterprises haven't *cared* about poor and marginalized people. You've actually *facilitated* their extermination."

"Now you're sounding hysterical," chided Quentin.

"Wrong," she said. "Because 'hysterical' means being irrational and paranoid. So, see, it's you and Bert Greeley who've been hysterical. You've been *irrational* about people who don't look or sound like you—people of color, foreigners and migrants, women . . . the sick and disabled. You choose to hold beliefs about them that aren't reasoned or reality-based. And you're *paranoid* about them, in no small measure because of the demonizing stories you've fabricated about them. You're threatened by them, afraid they'll deprive you of something—especially if the playing field were made level."

He tsk'ed loudly, but she leaned in closer and continued: "That's why you feel fine about using them as disposable commodities and working them to death. And that's why you 'allow' them to live rent-free on your lethal property."

Quentin yawned. "Your point?"

"My point," said Nora, now struggling to control her temper. "Your lethal control mentality . . . The eugenics mindset of Greeley Enter-prises . . . Your grotesque profiting from environmental genocide . . ." She took a deep breath. "*Your* arrogant belief that *you* have the right to target certain people and animals for their elimination, and *your* phenomenally extreme indifference to other human beings . . . Only someone like you *could* have knowingly rigged soil tests and not given a damn about lethal consequences for people. So, my point is, it *had* to be *you.* And that is the 'something else' you would've had to expose if you'd decided to pull the lynchpin on Plan B."

When he merely responded with willful silence, Alex reflexively took a step back, struck by Quentin's monstrous lack of remorse. The thundering truth of Nora's words was all he heard for a torturous while. Finally, he said, "She's right, isn't she, Q? You bribed Epitome. And you told them where to test, because you knew where the soil was rigged."

"You have no proof," said Quentin. "And I—"

A thunderous crash sounded. The storage unit's door buckled in. Sirens wailed. Police rushed in with drawn weapons. Alex protectively threw himself over Nora, and they dropped to the floor. Darinda Johnson shouted, "Hands up where I can see them!" Tom Burka summoned the medics for Quentin.

Darinda watched Nora shakily stand with Alex's assistance. "Did you hit your head? You look dazed."

"I'm fine," said Nora, though without returning eye contact. Her speech was hesitant, and she appeared to be searching the floor for something. "How did you know where to find us?"

"We'd put out an APB on Gianni Moretti after Fergie's warning. It wasn't hard to find his truck, tearing down 580. When we pulled him over, he told us what'd happened here. We came, fast as we could."

"Huh," said Nora, fixing her attention on Quentin's flash drive and cellphones.

"Gianni was scared shitless," Darinda continued. "He claimed he didn't intend to shoot anybody. He just wanted Ocambo to confess and apologize for crimes against his father. He wasn't expecting Ocambo to be carrying a gun, so he freaked out; he shot first, before Ocambo could, and then he ran out."

"He tried to kill me!" Quentin insisted, as EMTs assisted him into a chair. "Because I have proof that he and his father committed testing fraud with environmental inspectors. He conspired with my son—"

"Where is Gianni?" asked Nora, silencing Quentin's protest.

"Outside, in one of the cars," said Darinda.

"Would you bring him here for a minute?"

Darinda winced, expecting Tom to blow a gasket if she even appeared to entertain the request. Instead, he shrugged and said, "Fine by me."

When Gianni was escorted in, hands cuffed, he blurted out blanket apologies to everyone, including Quentin, who repeatedly demanded, "Get that killer away from me!" During their fraught reunion, Nora again searched the floor, this time knowing precisely what she needed. She picked up the cellphone that Quentin had chosen not to reach for earlier, despite it being closer to him. And, ignoring an officer who warned her against touching anything, she snatched Quentin's flash drive from the floor.

"Let her be," Tom instructed his fellow officer, who dutifully—if uncertainly—stepped away from Nora.

Quentin's jaw clenched as Nora began walking slowly, purposively, confidently toward him. When he stirred, Tom placed a hand on his shoulder to weight him in the chair. Standing now several feet away, Nora held out the flash drive and told Quentin: "This will document the falsified soil tests and fraudulent cleanup of the stadium that you and the Greeleys orchestrated." He stared stonily back while she continued to speak with icy precision: "Exposing this was going to be your swing for the fences at the last minute. It was going to set flame to Marty and Samantha and Greeley Enterprises. And though you were hoping to escape the fire, you were also willing to go down in your blaze of glory— just as long as you destroyed everything and everyone else."

She focused on Quentin, waiting—in vain—for him to react. He maintained his stony expression even when she held out his phone and said: "And now I understand why you chose not to reach for *this* cell when you tried to make a call earlier." She glanced at the screen and nodded. "Yes. It appears that someone's been trying to call you, maybe a dozen times today. I think it's rude not to return the call, don't you?"

He evenly hammered out each word: "You. Have. No. Idea. Who. You're. Dealing. With."

She slightly cocked her head. "But I do." Then she switched on the speaker phone and played the most recent unanswered voicemail. The furious (and curse-proficient) voice clearly belonged to Gianni, who repeatedly demanded "a fucking call-back!"

"What the fuck?" said Gianni, his jaw dropping, a cloud of confusion crossing his face.

Nora watched Quentin's eyes narrow, as all the while they filled with rage. *He's only capable of feeling personally wronged,* she thought. *He's oblivious to the suffering that he's inflicted on so many people.* Exasperated now, and intending to see him somehow affected, she took her own swing for the fences and said: "Let's see what happens when we press the call-return." And after she did, the burner phone inside Gianni's pocket rang.

Gianni tried to break free of the police, lunging toward Quentin, shouting: "*You're* the fucking middleman, too! You faked that accent like you faked everything else!" Turning to the restraining officers, he said, "He lies about everything! I got him recorded on my phone. He's trying to frame me! He used my dad . . ."

But Nora heard nothing of the ongoing commotion. Staring at Quentin, she only heard the dark pulsing truth beating in the room, all the while the police scouted the storage unit, searched Quentin, examined the Audi's trunk, took possession of the phones and gun, secured the crime scene . . .

Remaining laser-focused on him, she didn't notice Alex's admiring expression, Tom's respectful nod, or Darinda's appreciative grin. She just waited . . . patiently waited . . . holding Daleen and Yusra and Luis and Tomas and Abeo in her mind . . . until . . . until finally, Quentin turned to find her looking at him and into him, with sharpshooter precision. It pierced him, and he flinched. Then she smiled triumphantly and turned away.

~ ~ ~

EPILOGUE

One Year Later

November 26, 2019

El Gourmet Burger

Downtown

NORA AND FRED sat at their usual table, eating the same breakfasts they'd eaten every Tuesday for decades. Amelia, their regular server, poured coffee without cuing; her food presentation had markedly improved after her recent cataract surgery that they'd long encouraged.

Nora asked Fred, "So, you *promise* you're coming to Carrie's Thanksgiving this time?"

"Yes," he said, hand over his heart. "Me, Vickie, the kids—all on board. Right after the second annual Thanksgiving cookout that Ella and Charlie are organizing at the lake. You're coming to that, too, right?"

"I wouldn't miss it. Alex will be joining me."

Fred grinned. "I'm happy for you, Nora. Seems like things are going well for you two."

She rapped her knuckles on the table. "Knock on Formica."

"You realize, exactly one year ago, you were facing down Quentin Ocambo in a storage locker . . ." He stopped and winced.

"Hey, I'm okay. You don't need to be so careful around me anymore."

After Amelia swung by with the bill, Nora said: "Frankly, I feel good knowing I helped to put Ocambo in prison. God, I've never known anyone—*personally,* at least—who was so narcissistic . . . destructive . . . empathy-deficient . . . just plain *awful.* Rigging soil and bribing cleanup contractors at Epitome to fake tests! What corrupt and soulless creatures."

"Still, I feel bad—"

"About your ex-board member with the great legs?"

"Course not! Samantha Greeley deserves every bit of epic legal trouble she's contending with. Her voluntary blindness was complicity, far as I'm concerned. She should be held accountable." He took a deep breath. "I meant, I feel bad about giving you trouble back then."

"I knew that. But, clearly, it's too early to joke about."

He nodded. "Well, at least some good will continue to flow from the Greeley billions."

"True. Though the reparations to people who'd been living at the stadium can't compensate for all the harm and abuse, what a world of difference they're already making. Daleen and Yusra in their garden cottage. Gianni and Red in business together. Then Luis, with his trust fund. Oh, FYI—I'll be picking up Luis and Jack on my way to the Thanksgiving cookout. You'll be amazed to see how tall Luis has grown."

"'Amazed' is my middle name these days."

Nora leaned back in the chair and stared at her old friend. "What?" he said. "I got egg on my face?"

She shook her head and tenderly held his gaze.

He put down his fork. "Okay. But I still need to say it: I apologize for the way I behaved back then."

"It was a complicated time, Fred. We each made mistakes. But, tell you what." She shoved the check toward him. "Pay this, and we're even. I just can't hear you say that ever again, okay?"

He fought back tears. After steeling himself, he said, "No way! This is almost twenty bucks!" He threw money on the table, complaining, "And for a meal that's just going to clog our arteries."

She smiled. "Speaking of—tonight, we're having Delmonico's pizza and ice cream."

"That's what Carl's serving?"

"It's what the Boudreaux sisters wanted for little Carla's first birthday. And, of course, Carl remembered: there'll be pizza for you and me—without onions, peppers, or anchovies."

"Well, sounds like a four-vessel-bypass kind of day."

"Still, it's sweet to celebrate such a joyful occasion on the one-year anniversary of that horrific day."

Fred nodded while trying to remember anything about Ella or Charlie at one year. But his memory of those early days was blank, having lived any family life at the periphery of his medical career and long-term relationship with Lydia. He said, "I'm happy for Carl, too. He's over-the-moon about that little girl. And, of course, hyper-attentive, from the *moment* of her birth! He'll remember every detail of her growing up. He'll be devastated if the Boudreauxs ever move."

Nora placed her hand on his. "Well, if everything goes according to plans, we'll soon have two *more* children in our circle of life."

"Hmm. I only know of one—Aditya and Lizbeth's."

Nora grimaced. "I may have revealed a secret."

"Ah! Then it must be Fergie and Winston! Fantastic!"

"I guess the cat's out of the bag. Yeah, they're leaving on Christmas for the honeymoon they've postponed for years. And, as Fergie said, they're going to try crazy-times-a-million to get pregnant."

"Sounds like great fun. Where are they going?"

"To China, to tour the country and visit Winston's family in Wuhan for the holidays."

~ ~ ~

ABOUT THE AUTHOR

KATE SCANNELL is a physician and author who has written extensively in lay and professional media about healthcare and medical practice. She is the author of the memoir *Death of the Good Doctor: Lessons from the Heart of the AIDS Epidemic* and the novel *Flood Stage*. Her first Doctor Nora Kelly mystery, *Immortal Wounds,* was published in 2018. She practiced medicine in the San Francisco Bay Area, where she currently lives.